KT-149-491

Also by Jessie Keane

Black Widow
Scarlet Woman
Jail Bird
The Make
Playing Dead
Nameless

NOA
4/16

DIRTY GAME

Jessie Keane is the bestselling author of *Black Widow*. *Scarlet Women*, the third in the Annie Carter trilogy, shot straight into the *Sunday Times* bestseller list. Jessie lives in Hampshire.

WITHDRAWN

B000 000 019 8824

ABERDEEN LIBRARIES

JESSIE KEANE

Dirty Game

HARPER

This novel is entirely a work of fiction.
The names, characters and incidents portrayed in it are
the work of the author's imagination. Any resemblance to
actual persons, living or dead, events or localities is
entirely coincidental.

Harper
An imprint of HarperCollins*Publishers*
77–85 Fulham Palace Road,
Hammersmith, London W6 8JB

www.harpercollins.co.uk

This paperback edition 2012
5

First published in Great Britain by
HarperCollins 2009

Copyright © Jessie Keane 2009

Jessie Keane asserts the moral right to
be identified as the author of this work

A catalogue record for this book is
available from the British Library

ISBN: 978-0-00-749178-0

Set in Sabon by Palimpsest Book Production Limited,
Falkirk, Stirlingshire

Printed and bound in Great Britain by
Clays Ltd, St Ives plc

All rights reserved. No part of this publication may be
reproduced, stored in a retrieval system, or transmitted,
in any form or by any means, electronic, mechanical,
photocopying, recording or otherwise, without the prior
permission of the publishers.

This book is sold subject to the condition that it shall not,
by way of trade or otherwise, be lent, re-sold, hired out or
otherwise circulated without the publisher's prior consent
in any form of binding or cover other than that in which it
is published and without a similar condition including this
condition being imposed on the subsequent purchaser.

MIX
Paper from
responsible sources
FSC
www.fsc.org
FSC C007454

FSC™ is a non-profit international organisation established to promote
the responsible management of the world's forests. Products carrying the
FSC label are independently certified to assure consumers that they come
from forests that are managed to meet the social, economic and
ecological needs of present and future generations,
and other controlled sources.

Find out more about HarperCollins and the environment at
www.harpercollins.co.uk/green

To my Dad, who loved a cracking good book.
Here's to you Dad. God Bless.

Acknowledgements

A small battalion of people helped me along the way, in particular Louise Marley, Trisha Ashley and Anne Bennett, all great friends and fellow writers. Thanks too to Lynne and Steve for the monitor and for being such lovely neighbours, and to Judith my agent and Wayne Brooks my lovely editor. Several books were of great help to me, notably Paul Bailey's *An English Madam* and Tony Lembrianou's *Inside the Firm*. And last but never least, thanks to Cliff, who held my hand through all the madness.

Prologue

Annie Bailey knew she was dying. She was in an ambulance, she knew that too. It was very bright. She could hear the siren, feel the motion. She had drifted in and out of consciousness several times since they had bundled her in here. She knew that someone was leaning over her, saying her name, clamping a mask to her face, telling her it was going to be all right, Annie. While someone behind him shook his head.

Yeah, she was dying all right.

She could taste blood and her face was wet with it. Couldn't seem to get her breath. Which was what you'd expect, if you'd been shot in the chest.

'You're all right, Annie, you're going to be fine,' said the medic.

Bullshit, she thought.

But she was okay with that because at least now there was no pain. They'd given her a shot of

1

something, a sharp sting in her arm and suddenly she was floaty and hazy, but still aware. Aware of too-bright lights and the man bending over her telling her lies, aware when that same man turned and looked at his companion and nodded, aware that the other one moved to the front and said: 'Every red light's a green one, Steve.'

She closed her eyes. Too bright in here. But this seemed to cause the man agitation.

'Come on, Annie, look at me. My name's Simon. Look at me, can you see me, I'm right here.'

It was too bright in here. She kept her eyes closed, despite what he said. Stubborn as a mule, as always, going her own way. Going, for sure.

So this is what it's like to die, thought Annie. Actually it wasn't too bad. No pain, anyway, not now. She gulped down a breath. It was difficult, breathing. She tasted blood again – unpleasant. But now she couldn't feel the movement of the ambulance as it roared, tyres shrieking, siren screaming, through the night streets of London. Couldn't feel anything much, really, and that was good.

She was sinking into a warm cocoon. The medic's voice was fading.

'Fuck, she's flatlining,' she heard him say.

She felt a little movement then, someone doing something at her chest where the bullet had ripped through, severing flesh, exploding bone, but there was no pain now, no pain at all, and that was good.

She thought of Max, Ruthie and her mother, but there were no regrets now, it was too late for regrets. It was too late for anything because she was too busy dying. Her mind felt detached, disengaged from what was happening here. She let it wander back, to find the place where it had all begun for her.

1

Annie Bailey lay naked in the arms of Max Carter. They were in his bed in the flat over his club, the Palermo Lounge, and she could hear the sound of the star turn coming through the ceiling, a new rising star called Billy Fury. A good singer, but such silly names they had. That Heinz for example. What a joke! Dyed blond hair and a name taken straight from a tin of baked beans.

Max had left the small bedside light on while they had sex. He said that she'd been driving him mad and he wasn't going to have her in the dark, when instead he could see her and enjoy her all the more.

She lay there, ecstatic, feeling the heat of his big hard body and stroking her fingers over the crisp damp curls on his chest. His right hand was flung over his waist. He had strong hands, a fighter's hands. On his index finger he wore a gold ring, engraved with Egyptian cartouches on either side of a square slab of lapis lazuli.

Annie stared at his curving nose, at the smoothly tanned skin, the gleaming thickness of his black hair, the flat brows above the long dense black sweep of his lashes. His eyes were closed. She could hardly keep from laughing out loud with triumph and joy.

She'd been to bed with Max Carter!

Annie had wanted Max from the first moment she'd set eyes on him. She knew she was only twenty and he was thirty, but she'd been instantly struck by his elegance, his poise, his presence, and had quickly developed a massive crush on him. She was a girl who could smell power and wealth through a four-foot concrete wall, and Max had both.

Well, he owned the club. Three clubs, actually.

This, the Palermo Lounge, was the one his father had started out with. It was his favourite, and the one he frequented the most. But there was also the Shalimar, and the Blue Parrot. Max exuded an aura of danger and riches, and she loved that. It turned her on. And she had seen a reciprocal flicker of interest in his eyes, much as he might have tried to conceal it.

That flicker was all she needed. She had set out to get Max Carter.

She looked at him again and shivered with the excitement of it. Then there came a pang of guilt, but she quickly suppressed that. No, she was going to relish this moment. Nothing was going to stop that.

He must have felt her shiver. He opened his eyes, his head turned. God, he had such beautiful eyes! They were a bright clear blue, very deep-set and penetrating. Those eyes seemed to look straight into her soul.

'You didn't mind, did you – that I was a virgin?' asked Annie.

Max shook his head, but truthfully she had surprised him. He had thought she was a right little tart, the way she'd come on to him, a dolly bird flashing her arse in those tiny miniskirts, showing off her long slender legs in those trendy white boots. Hanging around the club on the nights she knew he'd be there and giving him the glad eye even when her sister was there taking the punters' coats and hats.

She had some front – but fuck it, she was a little beauty.

Max liked her big bouffant of long dark hair and her dark green eyes. He liked her low, husky voice. She followed the fashion of putting that horrible panstick on her mouth, making it look white, but he'd kissed all that away and now her lips were pink and she looked even more beautiful, rumpled and warm. No doubt about it, Annie was a handful.

Strictly mistress material, he thought. Unlike her older sister.

His old dad had given him just one piece of advice about women. He said: 'Son, marry a plain woman. Keep her well fucked and poorly shod, and she'll never give you a moment's trouble.'

Max knew his dad was right. Ruthie was the sort a man married, Annie was the sort he took to bed.

Max cupped one of Annie's full breasts in his hand. She shivered again, and arched her back as his mouth got to work there.

God, if Ruthie could see her now! Again she felt that tickle of guilt. Annie knew she shouldn't be here like this with Max, but the temptation had been irresistible.

All her life Annie had grown up in Ruthie's shadow. Ruthie was a good girl, home-loving and quiet, or so Mum always said. Mum favoured Ruthie, and always had. Annie had got used to that over the years, and she'd had no father to take her part when her more unruly nature had landed her in trouble.

Dad had left when the two girls were little, and Mum had worked like a slave, holding down three cleaning jobs, God knew how many catalogues and a job folding greetings cards that paid a princely four shillings and sixpence for every thousand folded. Connie never tired of ranting on about all the sacrifices she'd made to bring her two girls up decent and to keep the family home going.

There had been no money for luxuries. It was enough that they had food on the table and could just about pay the rent. Well, sometimes. There were times when Connie had to send Annie to the door when the rent man called, to say that Mum was out and would settle with him next week. No good sending good-as-gold Ruthie, who would have choked on the barefaced lie.

As part of their frugal existence, Annie had long since got used to wearing Ruthie's cast-offs. She often went to Carnaby Street to window-shop on her days off, to drool over Chelsea Girl and Biba and Quant, just to stare longingly in shop windows. But she only worked in a corner shop, she couldn't afford new stuff. It was all mend and make do.

And then their ship had come in! Ruthie got a job in the Blue Parrot and hit the jackpot. One night she caught Max's eye, with her unremarkable looks and her reserved manner. Max started escorting Ruthie about town, taking her up West and lavishing money upon her. He moved her from the Blue Parrot to the Palermo so he could keep a closer eye on her.

One unforgettable day, Max Carter – *the* Max Carter – had bought Ruthie an engagement ring. Their mum Connie had been in heaven. She said that once Max married Ruthie all their money problems would be over, Ruthie would see them all right.

But all Annie could see was the prospect of more hand-me-downs of Ruthie's. Ruthie the rich married lady would dole out cash and goods to her mother and sister, the poor relations. Resentment festered in Annie's heart. Trust Ruthie to be at the front of the queue, getting a man like Max to marry her and never having to worry again where the next meal was coming from. Annie had always fancied Max like mad. But Ruthie had hardly even noticed him. How could it be fair that Ruthie got the wedding ring, when Annie was the one who really wanted Max?

So Annie had set about getting him for herself. Just for once in her life, she would have something first, before demure, ladylike Ruthie got her claws into it.

He was *such* a man. Not a bit like his brother Jonjo, who was always out on the town and fooling around with different women.

Nothing like his other brother, too-pretty Eddie, who, it was rumoured, went out on Clapham Common in the evenings touting for young men. But if that was Eddie's bag then it was fine with her. After all, he wasn't murdering nobody, now was he?

Max, she was pleased to find, was all man. And she'd had him first, on the night before her sister was to marry him.

When many another man would be out on the

town with his mates getting blotto, Max was here bedding her. Not that Max ever seemed to drink much, and he didn't like drunks around him. Drink made people loose-mouthed, she'd heard him say, and he wouldn't have that.

'This is lovely,' Annie sighed happily.

'Yes it is.' Max raised his head and smiled down into her eyes.

'You really don't mind that I was a virgin, do you?' she asked again, nuzzling her nose playfully against his.

'No,' said Max, caressing her cheek. 'It doesn't matter a bit. Because this is a one-off.'

Annie felt the smile freeze on her face. 'What?'

'You heard me, Annie love. This shouldn't have happened, and we both know it. But now it's done, and finished.'

Annie felt panic growing inside her. She hadn't known what to expect from tonight. She didn't know whether she thought Max would carry on seeing her covertly, or call off the big wedding that Ruthie had planned for tomorrow and announce that he was going to marry her instead. She had just aimed for this one night and believed that things would sort themselves out.

Oh, she had imagined various outcomes, played with visions of her walking up the aisle in white and Max waiting for her at the altar, of falling into bed with him all laughing and happy on their honeymoon. But the last thing she'd expected was what he'd just said.

'But Max,' she started, trying to sit up, her eyes wide with shock.

Max's hand on her face was suddenly hard and hurtful. He grabbed her chin and stared into her eyes.

'No buts,' he said flatly. 'This is it. Finished and forgotten. No one's ever going to know about it. Clear?'

Annie nodded as best she could and he let her go. He patted her cheek. 'Good girl,' he said, and reached for a cigarette.

Annie lay staring at the ceiling, her face throbbing and her mind seething with resentment. So Ruthie won again. As always.

The phone rang and Max snatched it up. 'Jimmy. What kept you?'

Someone spoke. Max put his hand over the mouthpiece and looked at Annie. 'Go and get cleaned up, eh love?'

So she was dismissed. Had and then forgotten. Rage started to eat at her. Bastard! She threw back the covers and stormed from the bed, aware that he was watching her. Not that she cared. She was proud of her body. It was good, better than Ruthie's. Better than a lot of girls could hope for.

Annie went into the bathroom and slammed the door behind her. She could hear Billy Fury still singing away downstairs as she ran water into the sink to clean the blood off her thighs. She snatched up the flannel and started to wash. She could hear Max on the phone talking about some club or other. She blinked back stupid, weak tears. She never cried. *Never.*

She turned the tap on harder to drown out the sound of his voice. Max's business was best not known about.

2

The killer drove through the night and parked the car a mile away from the Tudor Club in Stoke Newington. Then the shadowy figure walked to the club and waited, cloaked in darkness. The killer was patient and could wait for hours, but this time wouldn't have to. The information was sound, the soundest you could get.

The killer felt the cold, hard weight of the .38 Smith & Wesson and was reassured. The gun was familiar, like family.

The punters were coming out now. And it was fortuitous that Tory Delaney was – as usual – towards the back of the crowd and without a minder. The killer sneered at the man's arrogance. He would pay for it.

The figure followed Tory at a discreet distance as he went to his car, a flashy-looking Rover. When

Tory had the key in the lock and there was no one about, the killer stepped out of the shadows.

'Hello, Tory.'

Tory was fast on his feet, always had been. You didn't have to paint Tory no pictures, and that made him dangerous.

Tory turned and suddenly there was a knife in his hand. He came at the interloper with the blade slashing. The killer felt the knife swish past, missing by an inch as Tory lunged, teeth bared like a madman.

The gun lifted and shot Tory three times in the chest. Tory dropped the knife and fell back over the bonnet of his car. He slid down, his face draining of blood, and landed on the tarmac.

The killer kicked the knife away from Tory's groping hand, then looked around to be certain no one was in sight. They would come soon, staff and management pouring out of the club to see what was going on. The noise would have alerted them. But there was a moment.

Just a moment.

'You,' gasped Tory, and his killer smiled.

One more shot was fired between Tory's eyebrows. Pink jelly spattered, brain and bone. Then at last Tory was still, staring sightlessly at the balmy evening sky.

No time to gloat.

The killer was already walking away, slipping

15

the gun back into its oiled bag and then into a larger polythene container – *don't want any cordite on our coat pockets, now do we?* – then moving into deeper shadows as people started to appear at the door of the club, looking around to see what the noise had been about.

The killer walked away in darkness and strode out the mile back to the car, then got in, pleased with a job well done, and placed the gun in a concealed compartment under the passenger seat, removed the thick leather gloves and drove home.

Later that same night Max Carter sat in his Surrey kitchen and cleaned and oiled his gun. While he was doing it, his kid brother Eddie came in and sat down at the kitchen table.

'Busy night?' asked Eddie.

'Fair,' said Max, carrying on with his work.

Max looked at Eddie. Eddie was queer as a fish, but he was a good kid and trustworthy. He liked to wear all those floral shirts and cords, and his mid-brown hair was over his collar, like that new group The Beatles wore theirs. Mum would have thrown a fit to see it.

But she was gone. The bleakness filled Max again at the thought of that.

Gone for ever.

'Where's Jonjo?' he asked Eddie.

Eddie made a face. 'Out with a new blonde.'

That cheered Max up a bit. Jonjo was good entertainment value, that was a fact. Jonjo and his fucking blondes. When Marilyn Monroe offed herself last year, Max almost thought that Jonjo would off himself too. Marilyn, to Jonjo, had been the ultimate.

Max couldn't see it himself. He preferred dark-eyed brunettes. And Eddie preferred pretty young blokes, but so long as he didn't frighten the horses, so what?

Eddie was looking at the gun in his brother's hand.

'You did it then,' he said flatly.

Max paused and looked at Eddie square in the eye. Max's eyes were suddenly a chilly blue, like arctic ice. 'I did nothing.'

Eddie swallowed nervously. His lips quivered. 'Holy Christ,' he muttered.

Max replaced the gun in its oiled cloth and held it out to Eddie.

'Take it out and bury it,' he told him. 'I don't want to know where.'

Eddie did as he was told. Max went into the lounge and put Mozart on the radiogram. He sat down with a brandy, feeling like a weight had been lifted from his shoulders.

3

'And where the fuck have you been?' Connie Bailey demanded of her daughter as Annie let herself in the front door of her mother's little terraced council house.

It was nearly dawn and one of Max's boys had just dropped her off at the end of the road. Annie silently cursed her mother's erratic sleeping habits. Connie was always trotting about in the night, making cups of tea and smoking fags, and that was in the quiet times. Now it was the day of the wedding, and with all the excitement Annie doubted that her mother had slept a wink.

Connie was perched on the bottom stair with a mug of tea and a cigarette. Annie looked at her with stark dislike and hoped it wasn't true that daughters turned into their mothers.

Connie was dirt-poor skinny, with a smoker's lined and yellowish skin. Her dry, dyed blonde hair was up in the sponge rollers she always wore at night, and her candlewick dressing gown, once peach-coloured, had faded to dirty beige.

Oh God, Annie thought, I could do without this. She was still smarting from the fact that Max had barely bothered to say goodbye to her. Annie wondered if he'd had Ruthie yet, but she doubted it. Ruthie was the Virgin Princess, the sort that men took home to meet their mums. Ruthie had been presented to Queenie Carter over tea at Christmas and, when she had met with Queenie's approval, the marriage had been given the go-ahead.

Annie had never even met Queenie, although she had seen her about now and again with Max and his brothers. She'd never meet the imperious old woman now. She'd croaked back in the spring, heart attack or something.

There had been a lavish funeral on a rainy April day, a huge fleet of black Daimlers gliding through the East End behind the hearse. The pink carnations on either side of Queenie's coffin had spelt out MUM. The streets had been lined with silent, respectful watchers.

All the men had removed their hats.

Some of the women had cried.

The Carter family were held in high regard around this manor, and that day was the proof.

'I stopped at Kath's,' said Annie, closing the door behind her.

'You're a bloody liar,' said Connie flatly, snorting smoke from her pinched little nose. 'I spoke to Maureen two hours ago and she said that Kath was home by eleven and she didn't have you with her. You've been up to no good.'

Annie let out an angry breath. 'I'm twenty, Mum, not ten. What I do is my business.'

'Not while you live under my roof,' snapped Connie. 'You've been out mucking around with some bloke or other.'

Annie stared at her mother. She ached to wipe that smug look off Connie's face by telling her that the *bloke* was Max Carter, who was marrying good-as-gold Ruthie today.

It would be quite a laugh, standing behind them both at the altar in her role as bridesmaid, looking at Max's broad, expensively suited shoulders and knowing that her scratch marks were still on them.

'What's going on?'

They both looked up. Ruthie was standing at the top of the stairs yawning as she shrugged into her red dressing gown. Her mousy hair was rumpled around her plain, placid face.

Ruthie wasn't bad-looking, really.

There was a serenity about her.

But she didn't have Annie's incendiary beauty, and she didn't have that flirtatious spark that made men lose their heads and sometimes their hearts. Connie always said that Ruthie was her good little girl. She also said that Annie was trouble just like her father, always had been, always would be.

Annie had been hurt by that when she was little. For a while she had tried to be good like Ruthie, to prove her mother wrong, but then Dad had left so it was clear that the good-behaviour policy had got her nowhere. Bad behaviour won her a lot more attention. All right, it was a clout around the ear or bed without supper, but it was attention nevertheless, and she had to claw a little back from perfect Ruthie now and again, or go mad.

'Nothing's going on, sweetheart,' said Connie, and Annie's lip curled because even Connie's voice was different when she spoke to Ruthie. It was soft and gentle and soothing. When Connie spoke to Annie, her voice was harsh with dislike. 'Just Annie out on the tiles, hooking her pearly about for any lad that wants it.'

Now that was unfair. Sure, she went down the pub with her mates and up West sometimes when she was flush, and she flirted and danced and teased, but she'd never come across for a man until last night, and she wanted to tell her mother that but she couldn't. Pride wouldn't let her.

'Oh Annie,' said Ruthie. 'I don't want you looking all washed-out for the big day.'

'I won't,' said Annie tightly, pushing past Connie

and running up the stairs. She paused in front of Ruthie. 'What time did you say we had to be at the hairdresser's?'

Ruthie rolled her eyes. 'Nine o'clock. I told you.'

'I forgot. I'll get washed up,' said Annie, and hurried into the bathroom.

She leaned on the sink and looked at her reflection. Her face was flushed, her dark eyes flashing with suppressed anger. She heard Ruthie go downstairs, heard their murmuring voices and knew what they were saying.

Poor Annie, Ruthie would say, she seems so lost.

Little tart, Connie would retort, if she isn't knocked up before Christmas I'll eat my hat.

Annie touched her belly thoughtfully. No, Max had been careful. An unplanned pregnancy would really put the cat among the pigeons. She thought back to how tender he had been at first, how sweet . . . and then how dismissive. Had and then forgotten, she thought. Her first time, a special time with a special man. That's what it had been to her. To him, it had been nothing.

Nothing at all.

She felt tears prick her eyes again and blinked them back, hating the momentary weakness. *Dig deep and stand alone*, she told herself. She never cried. Even when her dad had left, she hadn't cried, even though she had missed him like mad. She had idolized her dad and he had called her his little princess, but he had left her all the same, left them all, without so much as a kiss-your-ass.

Annie had withdrawn into herself with the shock of his leaving, but Ruthie had cried for days and got lots of cuddles off Connie as a consequence. Annie was made of tougher stuff, and she knew it. You could only ever rely on yourself in this world, she knew that too. Hard lessons, but she had learned them well.

So what if Connie had cuffed her more often than cuddled her? She had learned to cope with that.

She would cope with this.

4

Billy Black was excited. He stood among the gathering crowds outside the Bailey house and stared with awe at the pristine white Rolls-Royce parked at the kerb. Peach-coloured ribbons fluttered from the flying-lady mascot on the bonnet and flowers were draped over the parcel shelf behind the rear seats. Small, wide-eyed boys in short trousers ran their grubby hands over the paintwork.

The chauffeur stood there in his peaked cap and glared.

Aproned mothers with curlers in their hair and fags in their mouths snatched the boys back, but not too roughly. Everyone was in a good mood. The sun was shining, that was good too. Ruthie was a sweet girl and she deserved the sun shining upon her on this special day.

Then the front door opened.

The onlookers surged forward with smiles and cheers.

'Look out, here she comes!' rippled through the crowd, but it was the bridesmaids. It was Annie, Ruthie's sister, and Kath her cousin, done up in empire-line peach silk and awkwardly clutching bouquets.

Billy held his breath.

'Don't they look a picture?' cooed a woman beside him, but he was deaf to all that, his attention focused one hundred per cent on his beautiful Annie.

That was how he always thought of her: his beautiful Annie. He had adored her since she was eleven years old and he was sixteen, but not in a pervy way. In a pure and noble way. Her sister was all right, but Annie's beauty glowed like a beacon, eclipsing all around it. He'd never been in love until he clapped eyes on Annie Bailey across the school playground. Once he'd seen her, he'd been lost.

Not that she would ever show the slightest interest in him, he knew that. He knew he was odd-looking. He had a long, thin face and a vacant look to his eyes. He'd had rickets when he was little and so he had a limp, and a bit of a humped back. Sometimes he stammered.

Billy had always been the outsider, watching everyone else having a good time and wanting to be included in that charmed circle. He had desperately wanted to be in Max's gang when they were at school. All the others were part of Max's gang, and they had grown up still in a gang and become Teddy boys together and gained a reputation for being tough nuts to deal with.

Billy remembered Max back then, how elegant he'd been in his royal-blue, black-trimmed Teddy jacket, black drainpipes and blue brothel-creepers, while his brother Jonjo had gone for red with black trim.

Billy didn't like Jonjo.

Jonjo had a bit of a temper.

All the boys in the gang had gone on to work for Max in the rackets. Max was the leader and everyone else was doing his bidding. This had always been the case. When Max was a boy, he'd hung his white shirt out of his bedroom window, the signal for all the gang members to come running; and they had.

Billy had so wanted to be one of them, summoned by Max, valued by him, and he had been as proud as punch when one of Max's boys had approached him in The Grapes and asked if he wanted some work. He wasn't the sharpest knife in the drawer but he was dependable, everyone knew that. It was just picking up and dropping stuff around town, that was all. He didn't have to split the atom or anything. He'd jumped at the chance to be on the inside for a change, a part of the action; and he'd done his job punctiliously, pleasing Max and prompting him to trust Billy with other jobs.

Now he regularly did the milk round for Max. That was what the boys called collecting the takings from the billiard halls and arcades and parlours. Billy relished the responsibility and he was scrupulously honest.

Max appreciated that.

Billy was a bit slow but he was not a fool. The temptation was there sometimes to pinch a bit, but no one in their right mind would cross Max Carter.

Sometimes the Delaney mob pushed their luck, and Max didn't like that at all. Billy felt a tremor of unease when he thought of the Delaneys. They'd done him over many times at school, but he'd pushed in on the edges of Max's crowd and so gained a tenuous place of safety.

The Delaneys were scum, that's what Max said, a mad, red-haired family of self-serving, devious Irish tinkers who didn't belong here, and there was big trouble brewing. Tory Delaney and Max Carter had always been sworn enemies, and there had been many minor rucks between hot-tempered Jonjo and Mad Pat Delaney.

The whole thing made Billy nervous. The Delaneys were right cheeky gits and getting bolder all the time. He wondered at their nerve. Billy knew it was madness to upset Max. There were stories of people being done over by the boys, broken bottles and chains and even knives and guns coming into play.

There were even rumours about a pub landlord who'd parted company with a hand and a foot because he'd been into something nasty. Billy didn't know what the man had done and he didn't want to either. Keep your head down and do your job, that was his policy. That way you kept Max sweet, and nothing was more important than that.

Oh, but Annie was beautiful! She grinned, full of self-confidence, and waved to the crowd. Billy edged back among the throng. He didn't want her to see him. He was too bloody ugly even to be in her presence. But he loved her. Worshipped her.

She ducked into the Rolls and was gone from view. Kath followed, looking surprisingly good for a change. She was an ugly mare, but today she looked okay. Her mum Maureen stood by, beaming with pride, in a purple suit and one of those feathery little clip-on hat efforts. Annie's mum, Connie, was in yellow which didn't suit her. Her weary, washed-out, smoker's skin was emphasized by her yellow cartwheel hat.

Billy had a fine appreciation of hats. He'd seen Jack the Hat McVitie in his trilby around town, doing a bit of business and rattling the Kray clan, and Billy thought he looked quite stylish. He had quickly realized that here was a way of attaining sartorial elegance.

He chose for himself a deerstalker, which made him look intelligent like Sherlock Holmes. He teamed the hat with a raincoat and a large brown leather briefcase in which he carried the tools of his trade, his notebooks and pens. People looked at him, and he felt proud. He had achieved what he had long craved for; to be a respected member of Max Carter's gang.

He watched regretfully as the Rolls roared away. It would come back in ten minutes and collect Max's bride-to-be, but Billy wasn't going to wait around with the rest of them to catch a glimpse of Ruthie on her big day and throw confetti all over her sweet, laughing face.

He turned on his heel and walked away. He'd seen all he wanted to see.

Billy went down The Grapes because they always made him welcome there. The Grapes was on Max's manor, and all Max's boys were respected there, even himself. There was never any trouble. Two of the boys, Gary Tooley and Steven Taylor, were in, wearing their best suits and white carnations in their lapels. They were sitting just inside the door of the snug, talking in low voices.

Billy moved about quietly and he had good ears, Max always said so, and Billy heard Gary say:

'No offence, all respect to the man, but you'd have to be a bit of a cunt to do that, don't you think?'

'I'm not paid to think,' said Steven.

'Yeah, but even so. Buying a fucking mansion in the arse end of the country, what's that all about? He's an East End boy like us, why the airs and graces? He's getting out of touch.'

'Nah, he's in touch,' said Steven, shaking his head.

'No, he ain't. And he's been odd since his old mum died like she did, you have to admit that. He's starting a shitstorm war with the fucking Delaneys, and that means all our cocks are on the chopping block, see what I mean? Fair play to him, he's got to do something about it, but I dunno.'

Steven saw Billy hovering there. 'Watch your mouth,' he said, and nudged Gary. Gary looked up and went pale.

'Heyup, it's creeping Jesus,' he said with bravado. 'All right, Sherlock? How's Doctor Watson keeping, then?'

Billy smiled uncertainly at the pair and moved over to the bar to order his usual lemonade. He never drank alcohol, and that was another thing that Max valued about him.

Billy thought that the atmosphere in The Grapes felt strange today, and he drank up quickly and left as soon as he could, noticing as he did so that

Steve and Gary were already gone. It was a big day; Max's wedding. Billy hadn't been invited but then he hadn't expected to be. It was close friends and family only.

It was a day of celebration for the Carters. It would have been nice if old Queenie Carter could have lived to see it, but her heart had given out, that was the word that was going around.

Billy frowned.

There had been a robbery. There was a story circulating that someone had meant to rob the annexe where she lived at Max's posh place in the country and finish her off at the same time; a deal had been struck with someone, maybe one of the other mobs. Maybe the Delaneys. But her heart had given out before the deed could be done.

Lots of rumours, nothing definite. It worried him.

Ruthie Bailey had never felt so happy. Her life had been hard, with Dad going like he did and Connie taking to booze for the duration. And she'd always been the plain one next to Annie, the dull one, the worthy one, the one everyone approved of. Which wasn't all it was cracked up to be, even if it did win her Mum's approval while Annie caught all the drunken knocks. Ruthie had always felt boring beside Annie; predictable, staid – a homebody.

Then she'd got the push from the hairdresser's

because business was slack and it was last one in, first one out. Connie had told Max. He was always ready to help the people on his patch. Suddenly her little Ruthie was a hat-check girl in one of his swanky clubs. The job was all right, but it was Max who made it for Ruthie. From the minute he'd handed her his coat and winked at her, Ruthie had been in love with him.

She hadn't told a soul.

She watched him charming everyone, throwing parties for famous people, even mixing with members of parliament, and she silently adored him.

He came in and out of the clubs and as the weeks passed he'd say hello to her, ask her how the job was going, then he'd started to chat to her and – oh God! – then he'd asked her out on a proper date. She couldn't believe it was true. She, dull little Ruthie Bailey, was dating Max Carter.

He'd taken her to this really posh restaurant where you sat in a vast lounge before dinner and a chap in evening dress played the piano. The chairs were huge and comfy, and you drank something called an 'aperitif' while your table was prepared. The menu was all in French and there were no prices beside the dishes. Ruthie was over-awed. She was struck dumb by the opulence of it all.

And then Max asked her what she'd like, and

she panicked, she couldn't understand a word on the menu. Blushing and feeling a fool, she had to ask him to explain what the food was, and her ignorance seemed to amuse him. He looked at her fondly, and she started to relax.

There were people around them who looked rich and spoke in that haw-haw way that posh people did. The men wore dinner jackets, the ladies wore glittery dresses, fur stoles and heaps of jewellery. Ruthie drank it all in, knowing that such good fortune was unlikely to come her way again.

But it did.

Max took her out again.

And again.

Although he kissed her, he never tried to go all the way. He was always the perfect gentleman, and she liked that. She knew this was a permissive society now, with girls on the Pill and enjoying a free sex life without fear of the backstreet abortions that had been the plague of women all through the fifties. But that wasn't her. Max treated her with respect, and she loved him all the more for that.

Finally they were engaged, and now plain little Ruthie Bailey was emerging from the gleaming white Rolls-Royce into sunlight outside the church. Her Uncle Tom, Mum's brother, was giving her away. He took her arm with a smile. Annie and Kath kept hold of her long lacy train. It had rained last night, and it mustn't be allowed to trail in the mud. It was an expensive item.

But then, Max was paying. Max always paid. He knew the Baileys didn't have much, and he had plenty. There were new nets up at Connie's windows now, and she was the proud owner of a television, and even a fridge. She was made up.

Ruthie looked around her at all the smiling faces. The vicar was standing at the church door waiting for her. For her! Ruthie Bailey. Soon to be *Mrs Max Carter*.

The photographer was fussing around them now, setting up shots.

'Veil up for this one,' he said, and Annie lifted the veil off Ruthie's face, which for once was radiant with pride and happiness.

'I can't believe it,' said Ruthie to Annie, who was very quiet today. Unusually quiet.

Connie, their mother, was clucking around, trying to tell the photographer how to do his job. This was a big day for her too – her daughter, marrying into the Carter clan. People around here were going to have to start treating her with more respect after today. Connie was relishing the idea and throwing her weight about already. She knew that Max's boys always met upstairs in the house that had once been Queenie's, but Connie was going to suggest that they meet at hers instead. After all, she would be family. She would take care of them, make tea and cakes. Imagine the neighbours' faces when that happened!

Ruthie looked sympathetically at her younger sister. 'Don't worry, Annie,' she said. 'It'll be your turn before you know it.'

Annie eyed her sister with dislike. How dare the smug cow patronize her!

Annie was in a foul mood, still smarting from the fact that Max had walked past her fifteen minutes ago without even acknowledging her existence. All right, she hadn't expected hearts and flowers, but after what they'd shared last night she expected at least a show of warmth.

All the hurt of years seemed to flood up into her throat, choking her. Ruthie the favoured one, Ruthie the good girl. Ruthie the one who was making a fantastic marriage while she, Annie, stood behind her and watched the man who should have been *hers* wed himself to her holier-than-thou sister.

She'd had years of it.

All the hand-me-downs. All those seconds worn first by Ruthie; things that were too long, too loose, threadbare, washed out and worn out. Second-best. Everything Annie had ever had was second-best. Ruthie came first.

But not this time.

'Maybe I've already had my turn,' Annie said, her eyes hard and angry.

Ruthie's smile faltered. She stared at Annie. 'What do you mean?'

'Oh – nothing.'

'Yes you do. What are you talking about?'

The photographer had gone into the church to set up his tripod for the aisle shot. Connie was fussing around Kath's peach draperies. Uncle Tom was taking a furtive nip of brandy from a hip flask. The vicar was talking to Gary Tooley, a close associate of Max's, who was one of the ushers. For the moment, the two sisters stood alone.

'Nothing. It's nothing,' said Annie. Then her eyes looked straight into Ruthie's and her mouth curved into a vicious smile. 'I've had your hand-me-downs all my life, Ruthie. But today, guess what? You're getting one of mine.'

'Come on, Ruthie. Let's get your veil down, oh, don't she look a picture, Tom?' Connie was there again, pulling the veil down over Ruthie's shocked and stricken eyes.

'Beautiful,' said Uncle Tom obligingly, his eyes lingering covertly on the far more eye-catching Annie.

Ruthie saw the look. She swallowed, reeling, sickened, as the full meaning of Annie's words sank in. She tried to compose herself again as she stepped up to the church's grand entrance.

'My little girl, getting married,' gloated Connie.

Kath and Annie stepped in behind Ruthie and

the vicar, and then the Wedding March sounded loud and clear from inside the church.

Annie followed her sister up the aisle to join Max at the altar. Her throat was closed and she was choking with hatred and misery. She saw Max there looking impossibly handsome and his brother Jonjo as best man standing by his side. She saw the expression in Max's eyes as he looked back and saw Ruthie.

He'd never looked at her like that.

The bastard.

But at least she'd had her revenge for the way he'd so casually dismissed her. Ruthie knew. There was no going back from that.

Ruthie *knew*.

5

They sat outside in the car and looked at the shop. They were Max's boys, and they were following orders. One of his most trusted lieutenants had told them to do the shop late on the Saturday afternoon when the information was that there would be upward of three thousand quid in the till.

They knew that they were on the Delaney patch. They knew the shop-owner was paying protection to the Delaneys, and this had caused them some concern.

'Just do the fucking job, leave the thinking to those that can,' came the orders when they questioned this action.

There were four of them, all of them handy but still worried. If the Carters were looking to take a pop at the Delaney manor, there was going to be seven kinds of shit flying about, and they weren't happy.

Some things were set in stone. The Richardsons and the Frasers had the South, the Regans the West, the Nashes had The Angel, the Delaneys held Battersea – and a small pocket in Limehouse down by the docks, often disputed over – the Krays had Bethnal Green and the Carters had Bow. You never argued with that. But the boys were loyal, and there was a bonus in it for them. When they had asked what their cut was to be, the answer had come swiftly back from Jonjo Carter.

'Take the fucking lot. Piss it all up against a wall if you want to, just take it.'

Which was very unusual. The Carters were notoriously keen on taking their pound of flesh. The boys took this to mean that this job was intended as an insult to the Delaneys, a message to say, look you cunts, we can take you any time you like, no worries.

They were worried all right. There had been rumours that Tory Delaney was out of circulation, maybe ill, maybe God knew what.

But orders were orders, and Max Carter was the guvnor. He knew what he was doing, and he didn't like people questioning his judgement.

'Right then, here we go,' said the driver when the last of the punters departed at five to five, then one of Max's boys pulled on his mask and gloves and ran into the shop.

The owner was there, mopping up after the day's

trading. He froze like a deer in headlights, which was good. The till was one of those big heavy efforts, but Max's boy was tasty and could lift it easily, he'd already taken care to look it over.

He leaned over and grabbed the thing.

Or he tried to.

'Shit!'

It was screwed down.

The shop owner started gabbling away in a foreign language. Christ knows what he was saying. Fuck you, probably. The man started slapping at Max's boy with the wet mop. It was a bit funny but Max's boy was getting steamed up.

Two of the others had seen there was a problem and came running in to help, while the driver stayed put. The mop attack and the slopping of water all over the place and the shouting was getting worse and worse. Then the shop-owner chucked the remains of the bucket of water over the lot of them and suddenly they were skidding and sliding all over the fucking place. Then he reached for the phone.

One of the boys yanked the cord out of the wall and gave him a cautionary slap.

Another went back out to the car and grabbed a pickaxe from the boot. With it he demolished the counter and then they had it away with the till, no problem.

They took the till, with bits of broken counter

clinging to it, outside and got it into the car. They piled back in and the driver gunned away. They pulled off their masks and gloves and roared with laughter in the aftermath of the excitement. They were drenched to the skin.

'Jesus, it was like being slapped in the face with a cod,' said one, trying to dry himself on a rag from the dashboard. 'Good job Jonjo wasn't there, he'd have wrung his fucking neck.'

Two of them were in the back with the till.

They opened it.

Plenty of notes.

They sat back, smiling.

'That's what I call a good day's work,' said one.

'Yeah,' agreed his companion.

6

Ruthie was very quiet, thought Max.

He knew she was never one to gabble on, but this was quiet even by her standards. Because there was heavy business going on they had to forgo a foreign honeymoon, but he knew she would be impressed with his Surrey place and he took her straight there after the reception, his Jag rattling with tin cans until he stopped round the corner and took them off.

During the rest of the drive she was silent. Then they got home to Surrey and she was still too quiet. Maybe she was just overawed.

She was mistress of this grand manor house now, she would live among the fancy furnishings and crystal chandeliers and would step on to deep-pile carpets when she emerged from her bath or from the big bed they would share tonight.

There were grounds instead of gardens, huge

stretches of green to do as they liked with. There were garages and outbuildings. There was an *annexe*, for Christ's sake. It was a far cry from the East End, a very long way away from what she was used to.

That was it, he thought. She was probably just overcome with it all. Max could see that she was tired, and suggested they go straight up. It was after two in the morning. It had been an exhausting day for them both.

He opened a bottle of the best champagne that had been laid out ready by the bed. His housekeeper Miss Arnott had turned back the sheets, stoked up the fire, made everything comfortable for the newlyweds. His mum would have done it had she been here and, as always when he thought of Queenie, he felt the wrench of grief at her loss and the gut-deep anger at those who had taken her from him.

He poured the bubbly while Ruthie hovered uncertainly by the bed. She looked almost pretty today in her going-away suit of soft cream wool. Her hair, always her best feature, was swept up in an elegant chignon, throwing the clean lines of her face into sharper focus.

'You look lovely today,' he said, pouring the champagne into expensive crystal flutes and holding one out to her.

Poor kid, she looked more lost than lovely. But

there were three things that never failed with women. Talk to them gently, tell them they look good even if they didn't, please them sexually.

Ruthie came around the bed and took the glass and drank from it.

'Hungry?' he asked. 'I'll get something sent up.'

She shook her head and gulped down more champagne.

'Steady with that,' said Max with a smile. 'It goes to your head.'

Ruthie drained the glass. She still felt numb after what Annie had said.

Annie and Max.

She'd been so happy to be marrying him, she'd loved him so much, worshipped him almost. She'd felt that he was too good for her from day one. But somehow he'd convinced her that it would all work out okay. That she was what he wanted.

But now she knew the truth.

Annie and Max.

How long had that been going on? And – oh God – would it still go on now that Max was married to her?

How could she stand that?

She felt anger thaw the numbness until she flushed with heat. They'd made a fool of her. All the time she'd been misty-eyed with love, they'd been at it, screwing like animals. Like dogs in the street.

Max took the glass from her and placed it on a side table. All the furniture in here looked costly to Ruthie's eyes. The whole place was full of lovely antique pieces, things she had never even been close to before. Connie's furniture was charmless Utility stuff from the war and a few modern bits that had come off the back of a lorry, no questions asked.

This was a whole new world, a world that she had felt so excited to be entering. But now it was all ruined, and she hated Max and Annie for doing this to her, for killing her dream.

'I'll get ready for bed,' she said coldly.

Then she looked around. He'd brought her small suitcase upstairs with them and she was so tired, she just wanted to change into her nightdress and go to sleep. But Max was here. He was here, and things were expected of her. But she couldn't undress in front of him.

She just *couldn't*.

Max saw her sudden confusion and took pity on her.

'You get yourself settled in,' he said, swigging champagne then putting the flute aside. 'I'll be back in a tick.'

He went into the adjoining bathroom and relieved himself, then shucked off his suit and washed, shaved and splashed on cologne. He felt excited at what was to come, every part of him seemed to pulsate with anticipation.

His wedding night.

Christ, married at last.

Well, it had to happen. He wanted to pass all this on to someone, and Jonjo was still the crazy bachelor, showing every sign of staying a fucking playboy for the rest of his natural, while Eddie was a bum-bandit and unlikely ever to father a kid. Some fucker had to carry on the Carter family line, to build the family back up into the force it should be, and it was going to have to be him.

He put on his dressing gown and went back out to the bedroom. Ruthie was sitting up in bed looking like she was about to be shot. Her hands were gripping the bedcovers so tightly the knuckles were white.

Her nightie was one of those cotton floral things, nothing seductive but somehow sweet and showing her purity, he thought. He knew he'd made a good choice in Ruthie. She would do very nicely. He was pleased.

He faced the bed and took off the dressing gown. He saw her eyes widen as she clocked the size of his erection, but he didn't hesitate, he got into bed and cuddled right up to her.

She was cold to his touch.

Poor kid, he thought. She'd never had it before and probably had never even felt the urge for it, this was bound to be a shock.

'It's all right,' he said softly, hugging her. 'We'll take this slowly, okay?'

46

Ruthie was trembling with rage and disappointment. Max Carter, the man of her dreams, was naked in bed with her, his hands working their way under her nightie, and all she could see was her treacherous sister's face.

'Lie back,' he said, kissing her neck and touching her between the legs. A spasm of pleasure shot through her as he touched the little button there, but she was unresponsive and so upset that she just couldn't let go.

Bitterness welled up in her, smothering all prospect of enjoyment, but Max was shoving the nightie up under her armpits and cupping her small breasts in his hands. Ruthie knew they weren't as lush or as pert and big as Annie's, and she imagined him doing this to Annie, and she knew that Annie would be up for it, far more so than she was.

Max moved between her legs, panting now, and she felt that big stiff thing nudging her sex open.

'No,' she said, pushing at his chest, furious, gasping with pent-up rage.

'Come on sweetie,' cooed Max, pushing at her.

'I know about you,' spat Ruthie.

'We'll talk afterwards,' said Max, nudging harder. She was as tight as a duck's arse, he thought. Tight and dry.

'About you and Annie!'

He burst through her hymen and thrust in deep.

Ruthie screamed. Max froze, not believing what he'd just heard, but he was in now and too excited to stop. He thrust quickly, ten, twenty times, while Ruthie groaned and shoved helplessly against him, then he came. He rolled off her. Ruthie curled up into a foetal ball, aware only of the pain between her legs and the bitter hurt in her chest. She started to sob.

Max lay there and looked up at the ceiling in a daze.

Shit, that little bitch Annie.

Her and her fat gob, she'd ruined this. He'd told her to keep it buttoned, but she couldn't resist rubbing Ruthie's nose in it. The fucking little cow. He touched Ruthie's shuddering back, but she twitched away from him.

After a while he got up, put on his dressing gown, and went to the adjoining bedroom. He got into the cold bed and lay there cursing Annie Bailey and swearing to himself that she would pay for not keeping her trap shut.

7

Kieron Delaney stood shivering at the side of his brother Tory's grave. Summer had given up for the day and was drenching the funeral party in cold rain. The weather suited their business here. His mum and dad were standing like statues beside him.

He stole a glance at them.

His mother was devastated, her white curls and floods of tears hidden by a thick black veil. His father seemed to be swaying on his feet, as if he would fall at any moment. Kieron was appalled to see how much weight his father Davey had lost. Suddenly, big strapping Davey Delaney, founder of the family firm, looked his age. Kieron saw his older brother Pat clutch at their dad's arm to steady him.

'Ashes to ashes, dust to dust,' intoned the priest, dropping dirt on to the coffin in the hole.

He held the box out to Redmond, who took a handful and slung it in. Then Pat. Then Orla, who was tearless and composed. Then Kieron. Then their mum and dad.

Kieron tuned out the rest of it. He thought of Tory Delaney, his big brother, carrying him on his shoulders when he'd been tiny. He remembered the soft feel of Tory's curly golden hair beneath his little fingers, remembered the booming Irish laugh of this man who was now nothing more than a corpse being buried in the dirt.

They'd drifted far apart over the years. Kieron was the youngest of Davey and Molly Delaney's five children, and he had benefited from the family firm's wealth without ever having to get involved in it.

He'd stuck his head in the sand and refused to acknowledge the sort of dodgy business his siblings were engaged in. He'd gone to art college and then had a year travelling. Ignorance was bliss. But in his guts he'd known that his dad had been into all sorts in his time, including a spell in Strangeways, and that Tory, Pat and Redmond had built the firm up from that base into what it was today.

He knew damned well his brothers were racketeers, thugs, criminals; he knew they ran girls and were into the 'heavy game', their term for armed robbery.

Live by the sword, die by the sword, he thought.

'I wonder you bothered to show up,' said Pat when it was over and they had moved away from the grave.

Kieron looked at Pat. There had always been a sting of animosity between them. Kieron thought Pat a stupid bully, and Pat thought Kieron a fairy. The two were never going to happily co-exist, so Kieron had been glad to get away from home and see the back of his thuggish older brother. But it was clear to see that nothing had changed between them despite time and distance.

A few years back, Kieron would have flown at Pat in a rage. Today, he merely smiled.

'I'm here, aren't I?'

'Brought your sketch pad, did you?' Pat sneered.

'Padraig!' said Molly sharply, coming up to them and touching Kieron's arm.

'It isn't a crime to have a talent,' said Kieron.

'It's a gift from God,' said Molly, patting his arm. She looked back towards the grave where Davey her husband was still standing, supported by Redmond. 'This is going to kill your father,' she predicted with a tremble in her voice.

'No it isn't, Mum,' said Orla, hurrying over and embracing her mother. 'Dad's a tough nut.'

A year away had given Kieron a new perspective. His sister Orla was a lovely young woman now, no more the freckly girl. Her red hair was long and sleek, and her green eyes were gorgeous.

She was tall and slender, like Redmond her twin, and the black of mourning flattered her pale skin.

'Tory was a tough nut too,' said Molly. 'And now look.'

The priest was striding back towards the vestry for his tea and biscuits. The crowds were dispersing and there were many sad faces.

Things would change now.

If Tory was no more, then who would take over the manor? The Carters were chipping away at them day by day. It would be down to Redmond, the eldest, to take over the firm, but for now no one could face that prospect. Everyone on the manor had respected Tory Delaney and they were all sick at heart to see him gone. The streets had been lined with bare bowed heads when the cortège drove through to go to the church. No one would be celebrating on the manor tonight.

Davey and Redmond joined the rest of the family.

'I want to know who did this,' said Redmond. Unlike big golden Tory, Redmond's hair suited his name. It was red like his mother's had once been, long ago. He had green eyes and pale lashes. He did not appear a man of action, but he looked sleek and elegant in his black coat and leather gloves.

Redmond hadn't got into boxing like Tory and Pat, like their dad before them. Accountancy was his game, adding up figures and doing deals, and he was good at it, Pat had to admit that. Pat looked at his effete older brother and wondered if Redmond could ever hope to fill Tory's shoes.

And then Pat wondered, not for the first time, if he could do the job better. Jaysus, he knew full well that he could.

'We'll find out who did it,' said Pat.

The police seemed clueless about the shooting, or at least took pains to appear so. It was how the Bill always reacted to gang business. All the boys knew that the police's attitude to a feud in the East End was, fair enough, so one of them's dead, so what? Cut down the numbers a bit, that's a good thing.

And there were plenty of coppers in the pay of the other major gangs, everyone knew that. Sometimes a blind eye was turned because the payment had been right. A fortnight on the Costas, a cash sum, all helped to obscure the vision of the boys in blue. That was just the way it was. You couldn't rely on the police to do your work for you.

All this week the papers had been full of the news of this alleged 'gangland killing'.

The public were enthralled.

The police didn't give a fuck.

'Let's get home,' said Molly from behind her veil. 'I'm sick of this day. Kieron, you can show me all these paintings you've been doing and tell me all about your travels. Cheer me up a bit.'

Kieron nodded. Padraig looked at him daggers, but Orla was smiling at him. His big sis had often saved him from a beating from the pugnacious Pat. Kieron looked at Redmond, but those strange green eyes gave nothing away at all. Not grief. Not elation. If Tory had been hot-headed, Redmond was unfailingly controlled.

No, cold was more the word, thought Kieron, suppressing a shudder. Cold as fucking ice. That was Redmond.

8

The minute Annie got home from work, she knew something was wrong. Connie was sitting at the kitchen table alone, chain-smoking, an ashtray brimming with stubs in front of her. When Annie came into the kitchen Connie jumped to her feet and gave her youngest daughter a heavy slap around the face.

'What the hell was that for?' asked Annie, holding a hand to her stinging cheek and watching her mother as if she might go for the carving knife next. Annie's eyes were watering with pain.

Connie waved her fag in Annie's face, ash spilling down her tightly belted trench coat. Fucking English weather, she was tired and drenched through and now this.

'You know what it's for, you little slag,' she yelled.

Annie was about to open her mouth to speak

when she saw a suitcase at the foot of the stairs through the open hall door.

'What's going on?' she asked, her heart racing.

'What's going on?' sneered Connie. 'What's going on? Christ, you've got some front, I'll say that for you.'

'I don't know what you're talking about,' said Annie, beginning to shake with the shock of her mother's attack.

'Oh you don't?' Connie took a deep drag, sucked the nicotine right back into her lungs. Christ, if Connie Bailey lasted until fifty Annie would be amazed. She was used to her mother's bad temper, and it was even worse since golden-girl Ruthie had got married and flown the nest. It wouldn't be too long before Connie got herself invited to stay at Max's posh place in Surrey. Annie knew her mother, she knew that this would be Connie's master plan. She'd take Queenie's place at Max's table, and lord it over all she surveyed. As for Annie, she would have to piss off and fend for herself. If she had Ruthie near at hand, Connie would certainly not want Annie.

'Then why is it I've had poor Ruthie in tears to me on the telephone, telling me all about you, you dirty little whore, and her new husband?'

Annie recoiled as if Connie had struck her again. Her words were a total shock. Annie had never imagined that Ruthie would be so stupid as to tell anyone that she knew Max and Annie had been together. She felt her belly start to crawl with dread.

'Oh that,' she said, deliberately casual. 'We had a little fling, that was all. And Ruthie found out. But it was nothing. Just a fling.'

'A fling? Ruthie's in tatters down there, you selfish little tart,' roared Connie, her face inches from Annie's. Annie shut her eyes. Connie's breath was foul from all the fags, and flecks of saliva spattered Annie's face with the force of her mother's shrieking.

'What the hell were you thinking of?' demanded Connie. 'We're talking about your sister's intended. You should have had the decency to leave him alone, not go spreading your legs for him at the first opportunity.'

Annie opened her eyes. Something snapped inside her head. 'I saw him first,' she said flatly. 'He should have married me, not her.'

Connie threw back her raddled head and howled with croaky smokers' laughter. 'You?' she mocked. 'He didn't have to marry you to get what he wanted, did he, you bloody little fool. Trust me, no bloke would want to put a wedding band on your finger. You've got whore written all over you. Not like Ruthie. Ruthie's a good girl.'

'Yeah,' flung back Annie, stung. 'I bet the wedding night was a barrel of laughs. She's as frigid as a fucking nun and we both know it. That won't keep a man like Max happy for long, trust *me*.'

Connie flung her fag down on to the scratched lino and stamped it out with a gesture of finality.

'I want you out of here right now,' she said.

'What?'

'OUT!' yelled Connie. 'O. U. T. Out. Out that bloody door. Your stuff's all packed, pick up your bag and clear off. I've had enough of your tarting about. And doing this to your own sister? It's the final fucking straw, and I've had enough.'

Annie started to speak, but Connie grabbed her with surprising force and pushed her out into the hall. Connie flung open the front door while Annie stood there in a state of shock. Connie snatched up the suitcase and flung it out on to the pavement. She grabbed Annie's arm and hustled her out after it. Annie found herself out on the pavement in the drizzling rain. People were passing, and they looked curious but carried on by.

'What the fuck are you doing?' she yelled.

Net curtains were starting to twitch. A couple of doors opened and female heads peered avidly around doorframes.

'Chucking you out, you worthless tart,' said Connie. 'And good riddance.'

The door slammed shut.

Annie stood there, wondering what had hit her.

'Annie?' The low male voice broke into her tumbling thoughts. Where would she go? What would she do? She looked around to find a hunched man in a deerstalker hat standing there staring at her with limpid brown eyes. He wore a mac and held a large, brown leather briefcase. It was Billy. He was a bit slow in the head, but he was one of Max's boys. She knew him of old. He was always wandering around the manor with that vacant look on his face, poor bastard.

'Hello Billy,' she said absently.

A car went by, nearly hitting the suitcase which was lying in the road. The horn blared. She went and retrieved it and put it on the pavement. She glared at their next-door neighbour, who was still peering out nervously. 'Seen enough?' she demanded loudly, and the door closed. A curtain twitched again across the street. 'Nosy old bitches,' shouted Annie, and the curtain fell.

She snatched up the case and started walking. She didn't know where she was going or what she was going to do about a roof over her head. She'd think of something – she'd have to. She was deeply irritated to see that Billy had fallen into step beside her. Why didn't he just bugger off? This was just what she needed, an idiot for company when she was on her uppers.

'Has she chucked you out?' asked Billy.

'No, I'm off on my holidays. Of course she's chucked me out. What else did you think when you saw this suitcase flying past your ear?'

'What will you do?' he asked. Billy was impervious to mockery and deaf to insults. He'd suffered them all his life. He was happy for the moment because he was at last talking to the beautiful Annie, the girl of his dreams, and she was talking back to him.

'Who knows?' Annie shrugged, but deep down she was worried. She wondered who else Ruthie had told about her and Max. This could turn out to be a difficult situation if she'd blabbed it about too much.

It was starting to rain more heavily. People were diving for cover, ducking into shop doorways, heading for home. Home! She didn't have a home now. She looked up and down the road and saw a big black car drawing nearer. Her heart seemed to stand still in her chest. The car drew level with them. Annie and Billy stopped walking. The back window wound down and Max looked out with cold blue eyes.

'Fuck off, Billy, there's a good lad,' he said.

Billy glanced between Max and Annie. He hesitated, but knew better than to disobey. He scuttled away up the rain-misted street and was soon lost to view. There wasn't a soul about now. Annie's hair was hanging around her shoulders in rat-tails, her mascara was running in the rain. She was shivering.

The car door opened. 'Get in,' said Max.

* * *

'Take a walk, Tony.'

The driver got out and walked off, flicking his collar up and hunching his shoulders, into the rain. The windscreen wipers were still going. Ker *thunk*. Ker *thunk*. Ker *thunk*. Annie felt the sound inside her head. She felt as if she were going mad. Max just sat there, cool as you like. He was always cool. Usually, she liked that about him; but she didn't like it now. It smelled of leather in here, and petrol, and expensive cologne. She felt as if she was going to throw up. Yet despite her fear she felt that old treacherous tug of attraction. Max had an aura of intense male sexuality. Even when he was looking at her as if he despised her, still she felt its pull.

'Some men hit women,' said Max.

Annie's head flicked round. She stared at him. He looked right back at her, dispassionately, like she was a bug wriggling on a pin.

'My old man,' Max went on, 'was going to hit my mum once. Came home from the pub all tanked up and full of himself, she had a go, gave it some verbal, and then he thought *he'd* have a go. Funny how you remember these things.'

Something was required of her. Annie worked some spittle into her dry mouth and swallowed before she could speak.

'What happened?' she asked, trying to make it sound casual.

'I broke his arm,' said Max. 'In two places. Men who beat up women are scum. They're not men at all.'

Annie nodded. It was too soon to feel relieved, but still, she did. She knew Max had a strict code of honour. A man on equal terms, fair game. Women or children, forget it. So she was safe enough. And yet, she doubted it. He was seriously pissed off with her, that much was plain.

'Why did you do it, Annie?' Max asked.

Annie shook her head. It was all a jumble. All those years of being second-best with Ruthie forever the favourite. All those small slights and hurts that had somehow burrowed beneath her skin until they formed one huge uncomfortable *boil*, that somehow had to be lanced. When she had whispered in Ruthie's ear on her wedding day there had been one blissful moment of utter release. At last, she had her revenge. But then there had been the numb hurt on Ruthie's face, Ruthie who had always been kind to her, even when she was far from deserving it.

'I don't know,' she said hopelessly. It was all a mess, muddied by rivalry and bitter black hatred and deep despairing love.

Max suddenly grabbed her chin and dragged her face close to his.

'What do you mean, "I don't know"?' he snarled. 'You wreck your sister's happiness, you piss me off, and you say "I don't know"? What the fuck's all that about, Annie? What the bloody hell did you go and do that for?'

'I'm sorry,' said Annie.

'You're sorry? You don't know the meaning of the fucking word yet, girl.'

Yet. Too soon to be relieved, then. Far too soon. Her jaw was aching in his grip, but she kept still.

'I told you it was a one-off. I told you to keep it buttoned. What did you think, that I was having a laugh or something? That I didn't mean it? Do you think I say things I don't mean, Annie Bailey? For fuck's sake, say something.'

'I've got no excuse,' said Annie, closing her eyes with the pain. 'She got on my nerves, all right? She was so smug and self-satisfied.'

'Well you must be pleased now. She's in fucking bits.'

Yeah, I should be pleased, thought Annie. *But somehow I'm not.* There were all these confusing images in her mind. Ruthie at ten, giving Annie a lick of her ice cream when she'd dropped her own on the mucky pavement. Ruthie picking her up and dusting her down when she fell over and scraped her knee. Ruthie defending her when she committed the indefensible and was down for a hiding from Mum. Ruthie, Ruthie, Ruthie. She hated her and loved her in equal measures. After the relief of hurting her had come the remorse. A sick, soul-eating remorse that had been gnawing at her ever since.

'I'm sorry,' muttered Annie. 'All right?'

'No, it ain't all right.' Max released her with a derisory flick that sent her reeling back against the car door. The expression on his face was one of complete disgust. 'What a selfish little tart you are,' he said.

Annie rubbed her jaw. 'Yeah, that's right,' she said bitterly. 'That's me.'

'Go on, bugger off.'

Annie stared at him.

'*Bugger off!*' yelled Max. 'And keep the fuck out of my way in future, or you'll be sorry.'

Annie hardly knew she had opened the door, but she tumbled out on to the pavement. Tony, the driver, was there in an instant, plonking her suitcase down at her side as she scrambled to her feet. He stepped into the driver's seat, and the car pulled away. Annie was left there, the rain beating down on her head. With nowhere else to turn, she started walking up the road towards Limehouse, towards her only possible place of refuge.

9

'She told me you'd be coming,' said Aunt Celia when she opened the door and found Annie there, wet, bedraggled, and clutching a suitcase.

Annie was irritated to be so obvious. But where else could she have gone? Connie would have lost no time in spreading the word about her tryst with Max, and all the relations would side with little angel Ruthie against her; they always had. Annie's best friend was Kath, her cousin, but she was on Mum's side of the family, and her mother would kick up bloody hell if she knew Annie had been in touch and got a good response. Bailey family bonds were strong. Max's influence was even stronger.

But Connie detested her husband's sister, Celia. Annie didn't know why. She said 'that family' were all the same; wasters and thieves. Annie hadn't seen Celia for years. She hadn't even been sure that she still lived in the same place. Celia and Connie had had a major falling-out when Dad left and all contact had been lost. But here she was, still in the same large Edwardian semi. Still pretty – although slightly faded. Still with that same wry smile on her face, still wearing her neat two-piece suits, still with a fag in her hand. The fag was still stuck in an ivory holder, too.

'Tarty bloody piece,' Connie had always said of Celia with a sneer. 'Poncing around all affected with that thing in her mouth, thinks she's the fucking Empress of India.'

But Annie had always liked her chic aunt.

'I had nowhere else to go,' said Annie.

'She's fucking mad at you,' said Celia.

'I did a stupid thing.'

'We all do stupid things, Annie. She said I wasn't to take you in under any circumstances.'

'Oh.' Annie's shoulders dropped. Her feet were killing her, she was worn out; now Celia was going to turn her away.

'She didn't tell me why, though.' Celia opened the door wider. 'Come on in, then, and spill the beans. Put the wood in the hole after you.'

'I slept with Max Carter,' said Annie as they sat at the kitchen table. Celia's dark, glittering eyes lit up.

'You never did,' she said breathlessly.

'The night before the wedding.' Annie sipped her tea. Nice and warm. The kitchen was cosy. She'd been frozen to the bone out there in the rain. This was lovely.

Celia let out a plume of smoke. 'Never!'

'And I told Ruth I'd done it. On her wedding day.'

Her aunt clicked her tongue in disbelief. 'Fucking hell. What did you want to go and do that for?'

'I told you it was stupid.'

'You must have had a reason.'

'Nothing that matters.' Annie looked at Celia in anguish. 'I loved him before Ruthie did. She gets everything! And I saw him first.'

Celia stubbed out her cigarette. 'This ain't the bloody playground, Annie. You really in love with him?'

'Can I have a fag, Auntie?' Annie had never smoked in her life, but now seemed like a good time to start.

'No you bloody can't. It's a disgusting habit, don't ever start doing stuff like that. And don't call me Auntie, it makes me feel a bloody hundred. Call me Celia, you're old enough. Drink your tea. Were you careful, Annie?'

Annie felt herself colouring up. She nodded.

'Well thank God for that.' Celia started tapping on the tabletop with her long, red-painted nails. Tart's nails, Connie would call them. Annie thought they looked incredibly elegant. Her mother's were stained yellow from nicotine, broken, ridged. Hideous. Celia was the same age as Connie, but she had looked after herself, that was obvious. Her dark hair was teased into a stylish bouffant. Her figure was still trim. Her tailored suit was a flattering powder-blue wool. It looked expensive. Annie remembered what else Connie had said about Celia, and wondered if it could be true.

'So Connie knows all about it because Ruthie told her?' asked Celia.

Annie nodded.

'And what about Max – does he know what you've done?'

She nodded again.

'Blood and sand,' breathed Celia, and lit another cigarette from the packet of Player's with an air of urgency. She stuck it in the holder, took a deep draw and regarded her niece with disfavour. 'Have you spoken to him?'

'Yeah, I did.' It hurt Annie afresh to think of the words they'd exchanged in the back of his car.

'Did you tell him you were coming here?'

'No,' said Annie.

'Keep it that way. I don't want to upset the Carters. What did he say to you?'

'To get out of his sight and stay out,' said Annie bleakly.

'Well just make sure you do. It's good that he

doesn't know you're here, although how long we can keep it that way is anyone's guess. Connie needn't know, either, in case you were thinking of letting your mother know where you've got to.'

'I wasn't,' said Annie bluntly. 'She doesn't care about me. Do you mean I can stay?'

'Of course you bloody can. But here's the house rules, Annie. You don't go poking around outside your room. You can use the lavvy and this kitchen, but I don't want you wandering about in the other rooms, got that?'

Annie nodded. She looked around the kitchen. It was clean and neat, nothing fancy. She put her cup down and bit her lip.

'Whatever you're thinking, you might as well say it,' said Celia, tapping ash on to a saucer. 'Tell the truth and shame the devil.'

'No, it's okay,' said Annie. She didn't want Celia getting the hump and changing her mind about letting her stay.

'Come on,' prompted Celia. 'Out with it.'

'You won't like it.'

Celia looked her niece square in the eye. 'I'm not going to change my mind.'

'Mum said you ran a massage parlour,' blurted Annie. 'And that you were all pally with the Delaneys.'

Celia looked momentarily startled. Then she threw back her head and roared with laughter.

'Is it true?' asked Annie.

Celia's laughter subsided. She took another drag. 'What do you think, Annie?' she asked, watching the younger woman keenly.

Annie looked at Celia's neat turnout and made-up face, at her shrewd button-bright eyes.

'I think she's probably right,' said Annie.

'And *I* think we're going to get on fine,' said Celia, standing up and stubbing out her fag. 'Come on up, doll-face, let's get you settled in.'

10

Jonjo Carter was getting seriously annoyed. Not that this was anything new – anyone who knew Jonjo also knew that he had a short fuse. He was on his way out to the Shalimar. Nothing like having your own club to impress your latest lady, and this one was *sweet*. Blonde and cute with a rosebud mouth and big black-lashed blue eyes. A little scoop-necked white top and tight leopard skin trousers showing an ass you could stand a pint on. All bubbly and chatty, the sort he went for big-time. He'd picked her up when she was working in one of the new clip joints not far from the Starlight Club on the Richardson manor; there was never any trouble between the Richardsons and the Carters, they had a mutual respect and were always pleased to welcome each other.

Julie – or was it Julia? – was a hostess there, and she never tired of rattling off at the mouth about her working life, which was a drawback but with an ass like that, was he bothered?

'The johns like me,' she prattled on to him when they were in bed together and had just concluded a pleasurable session. He'd worn a French letter, of course. If he had his way he'd wear three, tart like this. Women always wanted to get you tied down with a baby, either that or they'd give you a dose of something nasty. Like the Boy Scouts, Jonjo was always Prepared.

'They're such mugs,' she went on. 'They buy me drinks all night and think I'm going to come across for them. Not that I ever would, Jonjo sweetheart, I've only got eyes for you,' she added quickly when his brows drew together.

Jonjo was handsome, but not so handsome as Max. Jonjo was bulkier and she guessed he'd go to seed as he aged. His dark hair was curly, his eyes were dark too. He had a bullish look to him. But he was a Carter, and she was pleased and proud to be seen with him.

'What else do they do?' Jonjo grunted, not that he gave a shit or wanted to know, but he never did like the idea of dirty old men drooling over his current girl. What was his was his, no argument.

Julie or Julia shrugged and her breasts – not her best feature, he thought, too small for his taste really – jiggled nicely.

'I arrange to meet them up the road,' she giggled. 'Not that I ever do.'

Which was a lie, Jonjo suspected. If a good-looking punter gave her the eye and spent enough, he reckoned she'd come across in the blink of an eye. Women were no good. They loved whoever they were with, he knew that. Hadn't Ma told him so often enough? And she was right. The conversation was starting to irritate. He rolled over on her and she squealed with delight.

'You talk too much,' he said, and kissed her into silence.

So things were good. She fucked like a weasel and she fucked only him. Well, that was the case since he'd been going out with her, he knew that because he'd had his contacts watching her to make sure. Everything was nice and neat.

So a drink in The Grapes to do a bit of business on the way to the Shalimar had not seemed too big a deal. Julie, or possibly Julia, who gave a shit, was pleased to be on his arm as they strolled up to the bar. Eric, the landlord, started grovelling around, fetching her a Babycham and Jonjo a pint of his usual, waving away Jonjo's offer of payment like he always did. Eric paid protection to the Carters, and respect was due.

'Go and put something nice on the jukebox,' said Jonjo, handing her some change and giving her ass (wow, that ass) an encouraging pat when he saw Kyle Fox, the man he had the meet with, come up to the bar alongside him. The place was quiet tonight, it was early. Just a couple of punters down the other end of the bar.

'Put on some Orbison or some Frank Ifield,' he told her.

Julie – he had decided he was going to call her Julie, what the hell – pouted at being dismissed but did as she was told, teetering off on her high heels, drink in hand.

'Hiya Kyle,' said Jonjo and offered his hand. 'Let me get you a drink.'

Kyle Fox was a weedy-looking type of man, thin hair, bad teeth, a look of malnourishment about him and the pale complexion of the indoor-worker. Which was about right for a forger, really. The hand that shook Jonjo's was limp and damp. Being polite, Jonjo didn't wipe his hand afterwards. A tasty-looking bloke in a dark coat had come in with Kyle and was now sitting by the door, watching.

'Hello Mr Carter,' said Kyle, and swallowed nervously. 'Half a shandy, please.'

Christ, what sort of man drinks halves? wondered Jonjo. 'My brother hears you have some plates. We'd like to make an offer for them.'

'I've had several offers already,' said Kyle, starting to sweat. 'They're good quality, you'll get the best possible print runs from them.'

'Just tenners?'

'Fivers too.'

'How much then, Kyle?'

Kyle shrugged, trying to look indifferent, sorry bastard.

'Make me an offer,' he said.

Jonjo took a pull at his pint. In the mirrors behind the bar he could see Julie over at the jukebox, looking down the list of records. The men at the other end of the bar were drinking Guinness. They looked like dockers, they weren't regulars. Big men built like brick shithouses, and talking with marked Irish accents. Probably Delaney men, he thought. Fuckers. They had some front, coming in here.

'I dunno.' Jonjo pretended he was thinking. He'd had a word with Max and they already knew how much they were prepared to pay. 'Five grand?'

'I've had offers of six.'

Jonjo smiled. 'Six grand then.'

'That just meets the offer I've already got on the table.'

'So it does. That's the offer, Kyle, and it comes with a promise.'

'What's that?' Kyle's eyes flicked sideways to where his backup sat. Some backup, thought Jonjo. I could slit Foxy here open like a pear before that twat got halfway across the floor.

'We do the deal at six grand and you don't get any trouble.'

Eric was keeping well out of the way polishing glasses. He didn't want to accidentally overhear anything. The jukebox suddenly erupted into life and Kyle jumped. Ned Miller started singing. Jonjo hated it and felt annoyed. Orbison was the business, now that was class. That Australian chap Ifield was okay, too. He saw one of the Irishmen at the end of the bar turn and say something to Julie. She smiled.

'Six grand,' he reiterated to Kyle. 'And nothing happens.'

'What do you mean?' asked Kyle. Nervous sweat was rolling down his face now. He stank of fear.

Jonjo shrugged. 'Well, let's say for instance you don't fall under a bus, you don't get your legs accidentally broke, you don't unexpectedly wake up one morning fucking dead, do you see what I mean, Kyle?' Jonjo's voice had lowered and now it was a growl. Kyle's Adam's apple was bobbing up and down like a marble on a string. 'It could be very inconvenient, that, don't you think?'

Kyle's fingers were clutching the bar top so hard they were white.

'So what do you say, Kyle? Six and we shake on it?'

'Six,' said Kyle. He'd anticipated a better offer. Up to ten, he'd thought. But fuck upsetting this geezer. This one had crazy eyes. Kyle had seen eyes like that when he was inside. Killer's eyes. You didn't push your luck with a man with eyes like

76

that. 'Six then.' He held out a shaking hand.

Jonjo shook it. 'I'll arrange for collection and payment tomorrow.' He smiled. 'We know where you live, don't we.'

'Yeah.' Kyle gave a horrible grimace of a smile.

'We'll give you a bell, Kyle. Drink up. It's been nice doing business.'

He left Kyle and went down the other end of the bar. One of the Irish was putting a coin in the juke and saying to Julie: 'Go on, pick out another.' And she was giggling and sipping the drink *he'd* bought her and making cow eyes at the fucker.

She turned as Jonjo came up, and the Irish bloke gave him the once over.

'You're talking to my woman,' said Jonjo.

'What's it to you?' asked the Irish.

Jonjo snatched a glass off the bar just as the Irish started to throw a right-hander. The red mist descended and he let him have it in the face with the glass. Blood spurted and Julie screamed. The Irishman's eye was hanging out on his cheek and he was yelling blue murder. His pal came at Jonjo and Eric came round the bar with the ice pick, but Jonjo didn't need any help. He dropped the glass and decked the pal then grabbed him by the throat and squeezed. The Irish turned red and then blue. Eric was pounding at Jonjo's back without effect. The landlord bent down and looked urgently into Jonjo's eyes.

'That's enough, Mr Carter,' he gasped. 'Come on, that's enough now. Don't kill the bastard, not in my pub, that's enough.'

And Jonjo heard him at last. He came to with both Irishmen on the floor, one with his face in tatters and one unconscious. He got to his feet and ran a hand through his hair, tidied his coat. There was a speck of blood on the lapel and he looked at it with distaste. He looked around for Kyle and his minder, but they were gone. Julie was still howling her stupid head off.

'You get off, Mr Carter. I'll sort this out,' said Eric.

'Thanks, Eric. We'll pay for any damage.' Jonjo grabbed Julie's arm and marched her out the door. She still had the Babycham in her hand, and Ned Miller was still warbling on. Fucking women, thought Jonjo. They always caused trouble.

11

Ruthie sent Dave, her minder, to fetch Kath, her cousin, down to the big Surrey house on Miss Arnott's day off. It was just a month since the wedding and she should have been on cloud nine but she was bitter to the bone, knowing how completely she had been betrayed. She was miserable and she was bored too, to tell the truth.

Max had said to her, redecorate, do whatever you like, but she hadn't the heart.

He'd had clothes sent down from posh West End boutiques for her to try, saying that he liked this one, and that one, but never the one that Ruthie liked herself in best, so that one was always sent back.

Max didn't come home very often. Most nights he slept at Queenie's old place in the East End, or was out working or having a meet with the boys upstairs at Queenie's, so he phoned her and told her he'd be back tomorrow, or the day after. Sometimes a whole week went by without her seeing him. Down here there was only Miss Arnott the prune-faced housekeeper and Dave who was on the door. Her minder, she supposed. Built like a tank, he was. He never said a word.

Kath's reaction to Ruthie's new home did cheer her up a bit, briefly. Kath came in the front door and stopped dead in the centre of the huge hall with her mouth hanging open in amazement.

'Bloody *hell*, Ruthie,' she gasped, then laughed. 'I've never seen anything like it. Only in pictures. Those stately homes, you know? It's a fucking stately home.'

Ruthie looked around her and knew that what Kath said was true. The place *was* beautiful. She took Kath's coat and led her all over it, enjoying playing lady of the manor for a brief time while Kath marvelled over the lovely furnishings, the thick velvet drapes, the expensive flock wallpaper, the carpet which was so deep you sank into it, the huge soft beds.

'Jesus wept!' Kath was bouncing up and down on one of the beds, laughing like a delighted child. '*How* many bedrooms did you say, Ruthie?'

'Seven,' said Ruthie.

The feelings of emptiness, of coldness, washed over her again.

And nothing happening in any of them, she thought.

'Come on, let's go downstairs and have a drink,' she said.

Kath watched her cousin covertly as they tramped down the huge staircase and went into the drawing room.

A fucking drawing room! thought Kath. There was a roaring log fire, big couches on either side of it. A massive gilt mirror above the mantel. Drapes and carpets and . . . God, it was a fabulous place. Kath was pea-green with envy.

At least, she was until she looked at Ruthie's face.

Because this wasn't the Ruthie she knew of old.

This was a pale, drawn stranger.

Kath thought that Ruthie didn't look well. She had dark shadows under her eyes, and she'd lost weight. She was wearing an olive-green dress and jacket with a lovely silky sheen to it. Her hair was pulled back into one of those classic French chignon things. She was nicely made-up. Ruthie looked elegant, and skinny, and . . . well, *rich*. Which of course she was. But she didn't look well. She didn't even look happy. There was a sort of bleakness about her and once she'd been so warm, so full of laughter.

'It's so lovely to see you, Kath,' said Ruthie as they stood warming themselves before the fire.

Kath saw that there were tears in her eyes.

'Ruthie, Ruthie.' Kath rushed forward and hugged her. Ruthie felt frail, as if she might snap in two if you hugged her too hard. Christ, she even *smelled* different now. Kath inhaled a sweet expensive perfume when she pulled Ruthie into her arms. Whatever scent she was wearing, it wasn't cheap and cheerful four seven fucking eleven. It was exotic. It matched her look.

Ruthie pulled herself free, wiping away a tear. Kath saw that her nails were bitten down to the quick.

'Come on, let's have a drink,' said Ruthie. She went straight to the drinks cabinet and poured out what looked like a large sherry for them both. She brought the brimming glasses over and plonked herself down on the couch, kicking off her high-heeled shoes and tucking her birdlike legs up under her.

Kath had expected a cup of tea, not bloody sherry in the middle of the day. Still, she took a sip just to be sociable. She didn't like alcohol much and she was appalled to see that Ruthie knocked half of hers back straight away.

'So,' Kath said briskly, 'what's it like, being Mrs Max Carter?'

Ruthie pulled a face. 'It's okay,' she said, and dipped into the sherry again.

'He's ever so good-looking,' said Kath. 'You

always sort of fancied him, didn't you? When we were thirteen or fourteen you used to stop over with me at night. Remember? We used to lie in the dark and talk about Max Carter and Jonjo and the rest of the boys, and wonder what it would be like to be married. To be in charge of our own household.'

Ruthie nodded, her heart like lead in her chest. She wasn't in charge of this household. It was in charge of her. Or Miss Arnott was. She thought back to those carefree teenage years, of all the dreams they'd had, her and Kath; how exciting and full of promise the future had seemed.

'Yeah, I remember.' She emptied her glass and went to fill it again.

'We used to wonder what it would be like to actually *do* it,' laughed Kath, trying to lighten the atmosphere.

Ruthie seemed preoccupied. She was sitting down again, taking quick sips of the sherry. *Fuck, she's really putting it away*, thought Kath.

'It's not so great,' said Ruthie.

'*What?*' Kath spluttered. 'With Max Carter? You kidding?'

'It's like being poked with a stick, if you want the truth,' said Ruthie, and emptied her glass again. She stared moodily into the fire. Max and her hadn't done 'it' since the night of the wedding.

'Right,' said Kath, her smile fading. She could

see there was something horribly wrong here. 'Has your mum been down yet?'

Ruthie shrugged. 'A couple of times.'

'She must be made up.'

'She is.' Ruthie thought about her mother, poncing around down here like she owned the place. Visiting her daughter, *Mrs* Max Carter. She enjoyed chucking her weight about with snooty Miss Arnott, lapped up being chauffeur-driven by Dave.

Silence fell.

'What about Annie?' asked Kath a bit desperately, then wondered if she wouldn't have been better to keep her fat mouth shut on that subject.

She knew there'd been some sort of a falling-out with Ruthie and Connie and Annie, but even Kath's mum Maureen didn't know what had gone on. Connie wouldn't tell her. All they knew was that Annie had moved out. No one was saying where to.

'I haven't seen Annie,' said Ruthie, frowning.

She couldn't even bear to think about the sister who'd betrayed her. She could hardly bear to think about Max, her husband. Yet already she'd been obliged to lie for him. The police had called one evening asking desultory questions about the death of gang leader Tory Delaney, but she'd been adamant that on that night, the night before their wedding, Max had been with her.

Wasn't that a bit unusual? asked the police. Wasn't that considered unlucky?

That was the groom seeing the bride on the *morning* of the wedding, Ruthie had told them, with Max's arm around her shoulders, the happy couple, so much in love they couldn't even wait for the wedding night.

What a laugh.

What a *lie*.

But everyone on the Carter patch would swear it to be true.

'Come on, let's get something to eat,' she said, and managed to get through another hour of forced chatter until Kath said she really had to be going.

'Not already?' Ruthie was suddenly anxious for her to stay.

'I'm dating Jimmy Bond,' said Kath proudly. 'He's taking me to the Shalimar tonight.'

'He's one of Max's boys, isn't he?'

'Yeah, and he's gorgeous.' Kath looked at her cousin awkwardly. 'Sorry and all that, Ruthie. I'll come down again.'

But as they hugged goodbye, Ruthie knew that Kath felt awkward here, out of place, and that she wouldn't come back anytime soon.

So here she was, alone again with the big empty house. The ticking of the clock was the only sound in the whole place. The awful soul-churning anger and the God-awful loneliness gripped her by the throat again, nearly choking her. She swigged back another drink and then took the glasses into the kitchen and washed them. Didn't want Miss Arnott thinking she was hitting the bottle during the day and having the nosy old biddy pass on the glad news to Max, now did she?

As she stood at the sink, her eyes were caught by the keys hanging beside the back door. She'd looked at them many times – keys to unknown doors, unlocking secrets. She was fascinated by them. She knew what some of them were for, but there were a couple she didn't. Emboldened by the drink, she grabbed the whole bunch and went out of the back door and across the courtyard to the annexe. It was locked, as usual. She tried a couple of the keys and one fitted. She pushed the door open, glancing behind her to check that she was unobserved.

Of course she was.

She felt a little woozy, sherry on an empty stomach was never a good idea. She knew she should cut back, but at the moment the booze was all she had. But did she really want to end up like her mother? Just look at Mum, the poor raddled old cow, that's what the drink did to you. See and learn, see and learn, Ruthie.

Giggling to herself, she stepped into the hall. It was so small, compared with the big house. And cosy. A real little home, with nice floral carpets on the floor and up the stairs. She wandered into the silent place, feeling like an intruder. She opened a door and found a proper lounge, nothing like that big barn of a room in the main house, where she had to sit on her own day after day, night after night. This lounge had a fireplace and a sofa and lots of ornaments, pictures of Max and Eddie and Jonjo as babes in arms, kids at the seaside, teenagers wearing boxing gloves, hard-eyed men lounging against big black cars. Over the fireplace was a larger portrait. Ruthie froze.

It was Queenie Carter. Queenie with her imperious expression, her hard little mouth, her sharp blue eyes, her white hair billowing out around her face like a cloud. Queenie seemed to stare back at her and ask what the fuck Ruthie was doing, wandering around inside her home without permission. Ruthie left, closing the door firmly behind her. Her heart was racing and she felt light-headed, almost sick. She knew she shouldn't be in here, Max had said she could go anywhere but not into the annexe, and now she could see why.

This was not an annexe. This was a shrine to Queenie Carter.

'What's going on?' said a voice behind her.

She turned. Max was there, he'd found her. But no, it was okay. She blinked and clutched a hand to her hammering chest. It was only the gardener.

She'd forgotten this was his day to come and do the lawns, trim the shrubs.

'Oh, it's you, Mrs Carter,' said the gardener. 'I wondered what was going on. Sorry to make you jump like that. I haven't seen anyone in the annexe since Mrs Carter died. Mr Carter's mother, I mean.'

'I know who you mean,' said Ruthie, shoving past him and relocking the door. Suddenly she felt stone-cold sober. 'She died, I didn't. I'm still alive.'

But as she walked back to the main house, she wondered if that was really true.

12

'Don't I know you?' asked Aretha, leaning her rangy black frame against Annie's open door.

Annie was sprawled out on the bed flicking through a magazine. She wasn't in the best of moods. She didn't like being at Celia's. All that bumping and grinding in the night, people coming and going at all hours. This morning, glad to get out of the place, she'd turned in for work as usual at the corner shop. Monday morning. Ruthie had been Mrs Max Carter for a month but for Annie it was just more of the same old shit.

But this Monday, things were different. Bert Tobey, the owner, looked uncomfortable as she started to shrug off her coat.

'Better keep that on, Annie love,' he said, his eyes avoiding hers. 'Sorry, but your job's gone.'

Annie stood there, half in and half out of her coat, and stared at him. 'What do you mean, gone?'

'We don't need extra staff any more,' Bert said. His big good-natured face looked unhappy. 'Vi and me can manage on our own, we've decided. Sorry, but there it is.'

'But I need this job,' said Annie. 'You're happy with my work, aren't you?'

'I've had no complaints on that score,' said Bert carefully.

'Well then.'

'Well nothing.' Suddenly his eyes blazed with irritation. 'I've told you, the job's gone. You're all paid up until last Saturday, so we're square. Now piss off.'

Annie recoiled. Bert had never spoken to her like that before. Through the beaded curtain that led to the stock room she could see Vi, his wife, listening to what was going on. And then she understood and rage engulfed her.

'Who are you telling to piss off, you old bastard?' demanded Annie.

She knew what was going on. She knew damned well that Bert paid for protection. She'd seen Billy in here, collecting. Blushing when she spoke to him, the stupid git.

'This is Max Carter, isn't it,' she said in bitter realization.

'Look, I told you nicely, I don't want to see you here again. Clear off,' said Bert, and stormed off into the stock room.

So that was that. Annie left the shop and started walking back to Celia's. Now her job was gone and she'd be lucky to get another one, she knew that. Certainly not on Max's manor or in the areas controlled by most of the other gangs, gangs who were friendly with Max and would be only too pleased to do him a favour by making sure she stayed out in the cold. The bastard!

For the first time in her life she was on the Delaney patch. She'd lived all her life on Carter territory, seeing Max and Jonjo passing by in their big black cars, seeing them treated like royalty, people bowing and scraping. Consequently she'd grown up with the firm notion that the Delaneys were mad, dirty, red-haired Irish tinkers. The Delaneys were the enemy. But now it seemed that the Delaney manor was the only place she could breathe around here. Talk about a turnaround. But she'd brought all this on herself. She'd been a silly cow. She knew it.

And now here she was, dossing down in her disreputable aunt's knocking shop, on dirty Delaney soil, with a brass wanting girly chats. She was not in the mood.

'I said – don't I know you?' said Aretha, her dark brown eyes challenging.

'I doubt it,' said Annie, and got back to her mag.

'Only you look kind of familiar.'

'Yeah?'

'Yeah.'

This was bad news. If this tart recognized her from somewhere as Ruthie Carter's sister, then the shit would hit the fan and she would possibly have to move on. And where to? She hadn't a clue. She was already jobless. She didn't want to be homeless again. She comforted herself with the fact that the Carters and the Delaneys were at loggerheads. This was Delaney turf. But still she didn't feel safe.

Annie took a look at the girl. Aretha was beautiful, tall, muscular in the way that black women often were, no spare padding at all. A big powder puff of black curls, big earrings. A tiny pink top pulled tight across small breasts. A black belted PVC miniskirt. Thigh-high black boots. How could anyone look that good and be a brass? Or a *masseuse*, Annie corrected herself. The girls here gave massages to a surprisingly diverse range of men. She'd spotted dockers and navvies coming and going, but she'd also seen one or two well-known actors, an MP, and a high-ranking police officer. All here to be ministered to by Celia's three *masseuses* and one *masseur*, who by the way also gave blow jobs, hand jobs and a good shag at an additional fee, thank you, your honour.

'She really your Aunt Celia?' asked Aretha.

'She really is.'

'Some aunt.'

Annie shrugged.

'You a working girl too?'

Annie slapped her magazine shut. 'No,' she said, and got up and shut the door in Aretha's face.

Aretha knocked on the door.

Annie flung it open. 'Okay, what?'

'Don't go shuttin' the door in my face, baby doll. Or you'll be sorry.'

'I want some privacy. Is that a crime?'

'Ain't no need to go puttin' on airs just because you're related to Madam down there, always sippin' her tea with her little finger stuck out and paintin' her nails and smoking that friggin' fancy cigarette thing and tellin' us to be sure to get 'em to wash their winkles before we get started on any little extras.'

'You got something against Celia? Take it up with Celia,' said Annie.

'I got no beef with her. But she makin' a good chunk o' money out of us eager beavers.'

'Oh really,' said Annie.

'Yeah, really. So how come you not gettin' a little of the action? Plenty of money to be made, I tell you.'

'I'm not a brass,' said Annie.

'Nothin' wrong with bein' a brass,' said Aretha. 'You get to charge for it instead of givin' it away for free, that's all.'

'That's very interesting. Thanks for the information,' said Annie, and shut the door again.

Or she would have, if Aretha hadn't stuck a large boot in the gap.

'I'm *sure* I know you.' Aretha gave her the once-over. 'You're a looker all right. Sometimes a client like a little man sandwich, know what I mean?'

'No,' said Annie, which was true.

'Hell, you naïve.' Aretha was tickled by this. She grinned hugely. 'Man in the middle, girl either side, got that? You and me, we could be good in a threesome. You so pale, I so dark, they'd love it. Top dollar.'

'Fuck off,' said Annie, and kicked Aretha's boot out of her doorway. She slammed the door shut and leaned against it. She heard Aretha stroll off along the landing to her own room. She was roaring with laughter.

'Cheap *bitch*,' muttered Annie, and threw herself back on to the bed. God, she was fed up. And she wouldn't admit it to a living soul, but she missed having Ruthie to talk to.

13

Orla Delaney bent down and laid a fresh bouquet of blood-red roses on her brother Tory's grave. Dead brown leaves whirled in the cold wind. Months now since he'd been gone. Kieron stood back and watched as his sister replaced the old, dead blooms with the new ones. She was a lovely girl, he thought. Her red hair shone like flames in the sunlight. Her skin was alabaster-pale, like the marble of Tory's headstone. Her hands were long and moved with elegant precision. He'd drawn and painted her often as they grew up, much to her annoyance. Orla never wanted to be still. Time enough for that in the coffin, she said.

All of a fidget, that was Orla, thought Kieron. She had the nervy energy of a thoroughbred race-horse. He knew she didn't sleep well. Dreams, she'd told him more than once. Disturbing dreams. But she hadn't elaborated on that. Actually she didn't need to. Kieron understood, better than Orla could ever suspect.

'Hard to believe he's gone,' he said.

'Very hard,' she agreed.

'I've often thought it must be nice to have a twin. I envy you and Redmond that closeness.'

Orla turned and stared at him.

'I've always felt a bit of an outsider,' shrugged Kieron.

'You're too sensitive.'

'Goes with the artistic temperament, I'm told.'

'You're not an outsider.'

'Sure I am.' He smiled at her as she stood up, and took the rubbish bag from her to dispose of later. 'I don't have anything to do with the firm, for one thing.'

'You've never been here long enough to do that,' said Orla as they left the graveside. Petey, her minder, joined them at a discreet distance as they moved back to the car.

'It feels bloody odd, having heavies tagging along at every turn,' said Kieron, glancing back at the big man.

'It's necessary,' said Orla.

Their brother Pat was waiting for them in the car.

'You could at least have come to the grave,' said Orla coldly as they got in.

'No point,' said Pat. 'Dead's dead, there's nothing there but a pile of bones.'

'Even so. As a mark of respect. Redmond would appreciate it.'

'Feck Redmond,' said Pat, and Petey got in and drove them away.

'I'll tell him you said that,' said Orla.

'Do. And feck you too, Orla Delaney.'

'Hey!' objected Kieron.

There was silence as the car wove its way through the London traffic.

'I'm not kowtowing to a precious shite like Redmond, much as he enjoys all the world kissing his arse,' said Pat finally.

'He's the head of the family now,' said Orla.

'Our father's still alive, unless you've forgotten,' snapped Pat, glaring out of the window at the rows of terraced houses and the shops with their brightly lit windows.

'Dad isn't involved any more, you know that,' said Orla after a pause.

'Clubs and fecking parlours,' grumbled Pat. 'There are other trades, you know. Trades that pay a damned sight better.'

'We're not having that old conversation again, are we Pat?' asked Orla tiredly.

'You know it's true.'

Orla did know it. Drugs were the new thing, there was an endless market for pills and smokes. But the firm was doing all right. Why fix what wasn't broke? Pat was like a bloody stuck record, she thought, going on and on when they'd already decided no. When they got to Brompton Road she tapped Petey on the shoulder

'Let us out here, Petey, there's a love,' she said. 'Pat'll take the car, you come with me. You too, Kieron.'

'Yeah, you bugger off the pair of you,' said Pat, as Petey pulled in to the kerb and his brother and sister hopped out. 'I can take a hint.'

Pat replaced Petey in the driving seat.

'You're a sour bastard sometimes, Pat,' said Orla. 'I don't think you can take a hint at all. And you'd be wise to.'

Pat made a face and didn't reply. They stood on the pavement and watched him speed away, burning rubber.

'He doesn't improve with age,' said Kieron.

'He's all hot air,' said Orla, making for the huge building and dark green canopied doors of Harrods.

Inside it was a treasure trove into which Orla always loved to dip. Kieron wandered along with her, indulgent, exclaiming over this and that, having a nice time with her. Then Orla fetched up short at seeing a familiar face.

'Hello Celia,' said Orla.

Celia straightened up. Annie, standing alongside her, saw her aunt's face change. Suddenly Celia looked cautious and deferential.

'Hello, Miss Delaney,' said Celia. 'How very nice to see you.'

Orla inclined her head. It was a regal gesture. Annie stared at her. One of the famous Delaneys. And such red hair!

'I don't think you'll have met my brother Kieron?' said Orla politely. 'He's been away, he's a painter.'

Celia nodded and shook Kieron's hand.

Annie knew that if you were a Delaney you could be whatever the fuck you wanted to be. Everyone knew that. So he wanted to call himself a painter? Delaney contacts would ensure exhibitions and plentiful sales. Who, after all, was likely to turn the man away? Annie looked at him with jaded eyes. The gangs ran these streets and she'd already had a brush with the Carters, she didn't want to get into conversation with another lot.

'This is Annie,' said Celia, not elaborating further.

Annie shook Kieron's hand. Actually he was good-looking. Blond floppy hair and a long thoughtful face, brown eyes that seemed on the point of laughter. His hands were long, but strong. His grip was dry.

'Hello,' she said.

'Hello.' Kieron was staring at Annie and thinking how gorgeous she was. That long dark hair, those depthless dark green eyes, that delicious figure. His mouth was dry with sudden excitement. 'Have you ever had your portrait painted?'

Annie laughed.

Celia nudged her sharply.

Annie stopped laughing. 'Oh. Sorry. Are you being serious?'

'Deadly,' said Kieron, then, thinking that this might worry her, he added: 'Very serious.'

'No. I'm not into all that. Standing on pedestals and stuff.' Annie wrinkled her nose.

'Ah, you're like me,' said Orla. 'You like to keep on the move.'

'I'd pay the going rate,' said Kieron.

Annie's interest was perked. She had no job. Celia was being kind and letting her stay for nothing, putting aside all Annie's protestations, saying that she was family and to say no more about it. But she felt bad, like she was sponging off her. Some money coming in would be very welcome.

'What is the going rate?' asked Annie awkwardly.

'Five pounds.'

'Oh.' Well, it was something. 'Well that would be okay, a fiver for the whole thing.'

'No. That's five pounds an hour,' Kieron corrected her.

'An *hour*?' Annie echoed in disbelief. 'That's a bloody fortune. Sorry,' she added to Orla, blushing because she had sworn in front of the sainted Delaneys.

'It's all right,' said Orla. 'Celia has our number. Perhaps you'll give Kieron a phone call soon?'

'I will,' said Annie, although she felt unsure.

'If you want to,' said Kieron, looking a warning at Orla. 'If you don't, it doesn't matter.'

'Well . . . maybe in a little while,' she stalled.

'Sure,' said Kieron. 'Whenever. Just call, if you want.'

'Are you sure he's one of the Delaneys?' Annie asked Celia as they stood and watched Orla and Kieron walk away across the store. 'He doesn't act like one.'

'No, that's true,' said Celia. 'But don't upset him, Annie love. The Delaneys look after us. Don't ever forget that. Tread carefully.'

14

Celia had succeeded in cheering Annie up. They were drenched in a dozen different perfumes and clutching bags full of clothes and shoes, all paid for by Celia. They were exhausted but happy.

'Pay me back when you start earning, if it bothers you,' Celia had said when Annie protested that she couldn't pay Celia back yet. 'But if an aunt can't buy her niece a thing or two, it's a pretty poor do.'

When they got back home Annie did a double-take when she saw Billy sitting at the kitchen table. This was Delaney turf, after all.

'Billy! What you doing round here?' she blurted out.

'Oh, so you know Billy as well?' asked Celia.

'Of course I know Billy. Everyone on the Carter patch knows him.'

'No one takes any notice of Billy coming here,'

said Celia. She smiled at him. 'And he comes here every week for tea and biccies, don't you, pet?'

Annie put down her bags feeling suddenly anxious. The poor loon would find himself filleted like a kipper if he wasn't careful, wandering about down here.

'What about the Delaneys?' she asked.

'They don't bother Billy,' said Celia, her gaze pointed as she looked at Annie. 'I cleared it with Redmond Delaney, and none of his boys are going to argue with him. I lived next door to Billy's mum years ago, he nearly grew up in my house and he's been visiting ever since. We're old pals – ain't that right, Billy?'

Billy nodded shyly. He had coloured up at sight of Annie.

But Annie was still worried. Would Billy tell Max where she was? She didn't know what went on in that funny brain of his. She knew Max had been good to him, and he was probably loyal to Max before all else, which could put her at risk.

'Put the kettle on, Dolly, will you?' Celia said, collapsing into a chair and kicking off her heels. Groaning with relief, she rubbed at her feet. 'God, that's bliss. We must have walked fucking miles.'

Dolly was one of Celia's girls. She was a small, curvy and ill-tempered blonde who now slapped the kettle on the stove and slammed the doors open to get the tea caddy and the cups.

'Four cups, Doll,' said Celia, seeing that Dolly had only got out three. 'Billy's stopping for tea, and Annie's parched, and you'll join us, won't you?'

Billy, his bulging briefcase perched on his lap, his raincoat buttoned to the neck, was scribbling in his notebook with a black Biro. He often did this. Annie had peeked once or twice, interested to see what he was writing. But all she ever saw was a dense, dark scrawl across the paper, meaning nothing. The poor sod wasn't right in the head.

Dolly put four brimming mugs of tea on the kitchen table.

'Biscuits?' asked Celia, and the biscuit barrel was slapped down in front of her. 'Thanks, Doll,' said Celia, pulling out her cigarette holder and lighting up. 'Everything been quiet here?' she asked as she took her first luxurious pull.

'Dead as a morgue,' sniffed Dolly. 'Aretha's got a client in, but me and Ellie and Darren are at a loose end.'

They could hear Ellie's Dansette playing Andy Williams through the ceiling. Darren would be in there with her, having a girly chat. Annie thought Darren was sweet. She never thought she'd take to a shirt-lifter, but Darren was more like a girl than most girls she knew. And some of the male clients – particularly those who'd had a rough time with Nanny and learned bad habits at expensive

104

boarding schools – preferred a pretty boy to a girl any day of the week, so he did good business.

'It'll pick up this evening,' said Celia confidently. 'Have a biscuit, Billy,' she said.

'I'm going on up,' said Dolly, and took her tea upstairs.

'So how are you, Billy love?' asked Celia.

'I'm v-very well,' said Billy, and fell silent again.

Talk about witty banter, thought Annie. Poor bastard. Maybe he wouldn't tell Max she was here. She thought – she hoped – that Billy liked her enough to keep quiet. And maybe Max didn't care about her whereabouts any more. The thought was somehow not as cheering as it should have been. It might have been a quick fuck to Max, but she'd had real feelings for him. She still did, she realized miserably. The rotten handsome sod.

After a while, just trying to have a normal conversation with Billy, Annie felt tired. She admired Celia for her ability to wring a sentence or two out of him, but she hadn't the knack or the patience.

'I'm off up to get washed up, Celia,' she said, and made her escape.

She took the remains of her tea and her bags upstairs. Up on the landing she could hear Ellie's Dansette playing Cliff Richard. Ellie and Darren were carolling away, horribly out of tune. Annie felt herself smiling. Overlying Cliff and Ellie and Darren and the Shadows was the sound of groans and the headboard hitting the wall in Aretha's room. Annie dumped everything on her bed, kicked off her white PVC boots and was about to shut the door when Dolly appeared looking pleased with herself.

'I know you,' said Dolly. 'Aretha thought she'd seen you somewhere, and she was right. And you know that loony Billy, don't you, and he's on the Carter payroll. You're Ruthie Carter's sister. Which makes you Max Carter's sister-in-law.'

'So what if I am?' shrugged Annie.

'You fell out with her and your mother,' said Dolly.

'So?'

'Word was you'd stepped on Ruth's toes, if you get my meaning.' Dolly was smirking.

Whatever she'd said or done, there was no way she wanted to be standing here discussing it with this cheap little tart.

'That's my business,' said Annie. 'Not yours.'

'No need to get all uppity with me,' grinned Dolly. She was enjoying this. Annie had been queening it around here, Madam's niece, too posh to pull punters. 'Word is you fucked her bridegroom the night before the wedding.'

'Whatever the "word" is,' said Annie, 'I've got nothing to say about it.'

'Oh go on,' crowed Dolly. 'I could do with a laugh.'

'Fuck off,' said Annie.

'That isn't very nice, now is it? I'm only taking an interest.'

'Who asked you to?'

Dolly's smug smile dropped from her face. She came and stood directly in front of Annie. Annie was close enough to see enlarged pores clogged with too much make-up, and black roots in Dolly's blonde frizzy hair. She smelt Dolly's smoker's breath and grimaced. Jesus! She pitied the punters. Imagine having to kiss a tart like this – and pay for the privilege!

'I could tell you things I've heard,' said Dolly.

'Such as?' asked Annie.

'Word is your sister's not well.'

Annie felt a tug of anxiety but she was careful to keep her face blank. 'Says who?'

'Says everyone. You know, you ought to be nicer to me,' said Dolly. 'I could get word to Ruth that you're living in a knocking shop, how would that go down? You wouldn't be so fancy then, would you, with your sister thinking you were making your living flat on your back.'

Annie slapped that fat, smirking mouth. Dolly stood a moment transfixed with shock and then she launched herself at Annie, knocking her back on to the bed, clawing at her hair. Annie hit her again, harder, and Dolly started screeching and trying to get her nails hooked into Annie's face.

Annie grabbed her wrists and pushed her back. Dolly was small and flabby – Annie was taller and stronger, and mad enough to bite this slapper's head off and beat her with the soggy end. But all at once Darren and Ellie were pulling Dolly off her. Dolly was still shrieking and spitting. Between them they dragged Dolly back out on to the landing.

'You'll be sorry you did that,' screamed Dolly.

'What the hell's going on out here?' asked Aretha, joining the gathering on the landing wearing a very small white towel.

'They were fighting,' said Darren, who looked shocked and excited at the same time.

'Well pack it in,' hissed Aretha. 'I've got a solid-gold punter in there and he's getting nervous. He thought the sodding Old Bill were out here raiding the place.'

Darren tossed his blond head and took a step back. Through the half-open door he could see a man tied to the bed, face-down. There was a whip on the floor. The man's naked buttocks were striped with pink.

'Nice arse,' commented Darren, who was a fine judge of such things.

'Get your thieving eyes off it,' advised Aretha, stalking back to her room. 'Keep it down, okay?'

'Come on love, shake hands and make up,' said Ellie, a plump little brunette with a sweet face. She gave Dolly an encouraging smile.

Dolly took aim and spat neatly at Annie's feet.

'That's a no, then?' asked Darren.

'You'll be fucking *sorry*,' promised Dolly, and went off to her room, slamming the door behind her.

'Come in and listen to Cliff with us,' said Ellie to Annie. 'She's always getting her knickers in a twist, she'll calm down.'

'No, I've had enough excitement for one day,' said Annie. She went back into her room, closed the door and fell on to the bed.

What the hell, she thought. Max didn't care where she was. So long as she kept out of his way things would be fine, she told herself. She wondered if it was true that Ruthie was ill, or was that little tart Dolly just enjoying winding her up? She didn't like to think of Ruthie being ill. Maybe Ruthie was pregnant. That thought cut into her like a knife. *Ruthie, pregnant with Max's child?* Too restless and unhappy to settle, Annie went downstairs and got the Delaneys' phone number from Celia.

15

Eddie Carter often wondered about the night he'd buried the gun for Max. His gut feeling was that Max had shot Tory Delaney dead, but something about the way Max had denied it niggled at him. He knew the police had been round asking questions, but Ruthie had provided an alibi, as any good wife would. It was best not to speculate. Tory was dead and that was an end to it.

Or was it? Because there was still Redmond and Pat Delaney.

Best not to think about that, either.

Eddie was enjoying his life, going round the clubs and pubs with his friends tonight, calling in on the Shalimar and The Grapes and finishing up at the Palermo Lounge. Max and Jonjo were in, the place was buzzing. They had their heavies with them, standing a discreet distance away. Eddie didn't want a minder and had refused one more than once, even when Max tried to insist. He hated the idea of someone sneering at his sexual tastes, and he knew a lot of Max's macho hard men did. Then one of the boys whispered that there was the most *exquisite* boy in a house not too far away, Eddie would *adore* him, why didn't they go on over and visit?

'Really?' Eddie was intrigued but unsure.

His taste for pretty boys had got him into trouble a couple of times. He knew that Max disapproved. Jonjo despised Eddie for the fact that he liked to bed men instead of women, he knew that too. But Eddie did feel the urge, he was drunk but not incapable, so why not?

'Is he blond?' Eddie asked, his words only a little slurred. Max would disapprove of that, too. Drunks annoyed his sainted older brother. Drunks and loose women and men who liked shagging pretty boys . . . the list just went on and on. Eddie laughed at the thought of it. And there he was, the great Max Carter, sleeping in a separate room from his wife, a fact that must never ever be revealed to the wider world. Eddie liked Ruthie. The poor cow. Ruthie fussed over him like an older sister, and he liked that. He'd never had a sister, only a domineering mother who had frightened the arse off him most of the time, cuffing him around the ear or whopping his backside for stepping out of line.

Ruthie was different, gentler. She never nagged, never screamed like a tart in the street or hit people. He and Ruthie enjoyed their long chats and shopping trips. Despite the fact that he could see how unhappy she was, she never bad-mouthed Max to him or to anyone else. He liked that about her, too. Loyalty to the family was imperative. His mum had drummed that into them when they were growing up, and it had stuck. The Carters fought the world; never each other.

'Yeah,' said Deaf Derek, queer as a yellow duster with his earrings glinting in the light of the big revolving mirrored ball in the centre of the club. It winked like fairy dust over the dancers on the small dance floor, highlighted the boys in the four-piece band. It was late in the evening, everyone was feeling mellow and grabbing a last excuse to waltz up tight with their ladies. Jonjo was up on the floor hugging a curvaceous blonde in a bear grip. Max sat at his table alone, watching the dancers.

'Is he slim?' Eddie watched his own weight religiously, and dressed to flatter his elegant frame. His idea of a living nightmare was to find himself closeted with a fat, ugly old queen. Deaf Derek was sweating in the heat of the club. He wore a hearing aid, he'd been born deaf in one ear.

112

'Slim. And young. He's *gorgeous*,' Derek told Eddie.

'Well,' said Eddie, 'why not?'

A taxi took them to an address in Limehouse. Eddie stumbled into the house with Deaf Derek, only vaguely seeing the clean, cosy, red-flocked hallway, a clock on the wall shaped like a guitar, a wooden plaque showing a bull and bullfighter, red cape whirling. They climbed the stairs, Derek first, Eddie giggling because Derek stumbled and nearly fell.

'You're pissed,' laughed Eddie, but Derek was up ahead and a bit mutton so he didn't respond. Up on the landing they were met by a pretty young man. Yes, he was slim. Almost skinny. But a lovely face, a shiny mop of blond hair, friendly blue eyes, nicely turned out.

'How much for the night?' asked Deaf Derek brusquely.

'For you?' The guy looked Derek up and down and sniffed. 'You couldn't afford me, darling.'

'Not for me. For my mate Eddie.' He pulled Eddie forward and suddenly Eddie wished he hadn't agreed to this. He was wishing he'd just gone back to Queenie's old place and crashed. He felt tired. And having to pay for it yet again felt demeaning. But the boy was smiling at him. And he *was* pretty.

113

'To you,' said the boy, smiling seductively into Eddie's dazzled eyes, 'twenty.'

'*Twenty?*' Deaf Derek echoed. 'This ain't fucking Mayfair, girly.'

'Okay,' said Eddie. 'What's your name?'

'Darren,' said the boy.

'Really?'

'No, really it's Horace,' said Darren with a laugh. 'But I've been Darren since I was sixteen and left home.'

Eddie turned to say that Derek could go now, but Derek was already halfway down the stairs. He was alone on the landing with a male tart.

'Come on in,' said Darren, and they went into his room. It was neat and clean as a new pin, which was what Eddie would have expected. There was a small sink in the corner. 'Wash your dick, there's a love. Towel's on the rail.'

Again Eddie felt that stab of mortified disgust at his own behaviour, but he was already excited. He was closeted with a beautiful queen and he couldn't wait to get down to business. He went to the sink, pulled down his trousers and pants, and washed his genitals carefully. He dried himself on the towel, and when he turned around Darren was on the bed, naked.

Eddie felt a crushing disappointment. He'd wanted to talk, to get to know Darren a bit before they got down to it. This felt so cold, so businesslike.

He hated being a queer. He didn't have to hide it away like some people did because he was a Carter, and no one poked fun at a Carter. But he missed the easy closeness that men and women could enjoy. You went out, saw a woman you fancied, took her home to meet Mum, and lived happily ever after – in theory anyway. But Eddie always had to struggle to get past the 'are they or are they not queer?' question, sometimes offending people without meaning to, and it slowed things down, ruined the mood.

Sometimes he found it was easier being alone than going to the bother of finding a partner who wanted the same things out of life. Which was why he often resorted to paying for sex. Because it was a transaction – a bit of business, and that was all. Soulless, yes; but at least no hassle. He looked down, dismayed to feel his hard-on dissolving.

'Don't worry about that, deary,' said Darren casually. He patted the bed. 'Come and lie down here with me, I'll give you a bit of a rub down and he'll soon be in the mood.'

God, he'd noticed. How embarrassing. Rigid with self-consciousness, Eddie stripped off his clothes and clutched the towel in front of himself as he went to the bed. He laid down.

'That's it,' said Darren with breezy profession-alism. 'Face down now. I'll do you a nice back rub with some lavender and baby oil.'

It was a long time since he'd been touched. Under Darren's skilful hands Eddie relaxed. He hadn't realized quite how tense he'd been, but Darren had the hands of an angel. Eddie closed his eyes and drifted away, and the first he knew something was wrong was when there were heavy footsteps on the stairs and the sound of the door crashing back on its hinges.

He heard Darren say: 'Who the hell are you?' and then there was the sound of a blow being struck and Darren screamed. Eddie tried to scramble up, but a heavy hand caught his arm and twisted it up behind his back. He felt his shoulder pop out of its socket and shrieked with pain.

'Just stay right where you are, fairy,' snarled a voice in his ear, 'or I'll break your other cunting arm, got that?'

Eddie felt cold pointed steel touch his anus. 'I heard you like it up the arse, shit-stabber,' said the voice over Darren's sobs. Then there was agony. An agony so severe that Eddie couldn't even cry out. The knife went in deep, then was jerked brutally out. Hot liquid gushed over Eddie's thighs. Blood. His blood. Sickness and horror welled in his throat. Oh Jesus please stop, he thought, but he couldn't say it, his words were stuck at his lips.

'Say hello to Max for me,' said the voice by his ear, and then the knifeman was thundering back down the stairs and out.

116

He felt himself slipping away. He knew he was losing a lot of blood and tried to ask Darren for help. Then he heard a voice. Female and concerned.

Alerted by Darren's scream, Annie had run out of her room to see what the hell was going on.

'Darren, what's been . . . oh Jesus,' said Annie. She saw Darren naked and clutching his bleeding face, crouched on the floor. And on the bed . . . someone covered in blood. Drenched in it.

'Get Celia,' moaned Darren.

'She's out,' said Annie, feeling suddenly sick and giddy. She took a deep breath, steadied herself. She grabbed a towel. 'Darren, get up here. Come on. Press this to the wound, hard as you can. I'll phone for an ambulance.'

'It's Eddie Carter, Max Carter's brother,' wailed Darren.

'What?' Annie stared in disbelief.

'He's one of the Carters.' Darren crawled over to the bed and pressed the towel to Eddie's bleeding anus.

'Stay there with him,' said Annie. 'And get some trousers on, Darren, for Christ's sake.'

Heart thundering, she went downstairs to the phone in the hall. She called for an ambulance. Then she thought about Eddie's family. Max. Jonjo. *Ruthie*. She ought to let them know. Bracing herself, she phoned her mother's number and was relieved to find Connie in.

'What the fuck do you want?' asked Connie.

'Don't put the phone down,' said Annie quickly. 'It's an emergency. Eddie's been hurt at Celia's place. I've called for an ambulance. You'll have to tell Ruthie and Max.'

Annie put the phone down and tottered into the kitchen. She pulled out a chair and flopped at the table, head in hands. She was shaking with shock. When the front door opened she jumped, ready to run. Someone had walked right in here and hurt Eddie Carter badly. They might come back and do for the rest of them. Maybe whoever it was hated whores. Maybe they would mistake her for a whore and cut her about like that poor bastard upstairs.

She watched the kitchen door open, not daring to even breathe, waiting for God knew what horror to come and envelop her.

But it was Celia.

Annie's breath escaped in a rush. 'Oh God,' she gasped.

'What's happening, Annie?' asked Celia, staring at Annie's ashen face. 'You look like shit.'

Annie told her.

Celia sat down. 'Did anyone see who did it?'

'No. Nobody.'

'Who knows about this?'

'I phoned for an ambulance. And I phoned Mum, so that she could let Max know.'

118

All the life went out of Celia's eyes. She looked blankly down at her manicured hands.

'You let Max Carter know that his brother came to harm while he was in my house?' she echoed quietly.

'Celia, I had to.'

Celia nodded. 'I'm a dead woman,' she said.

16

When Annie pitched up at her mother's door a week later, Connie tried to shut it in her face, but Annie was quick and shoved her foot in the gap. She pushed hard, forcing her mother out of the way, and strode in.

'You're not welcome here,' snarled Connie.

Annie was looking around her with distaste. She hadn't been back to this place in months. The room stank of booze and cabbage and urine, there was dust everywhere and the carpets were stained. It was the middle of the day and Connie was still in her dressing gown. It was obvious that without Ruthie's sobering influence, Connie was sinking further into her dependency on booze.

Annie looked at her mother. Her eyes were puffy, her skin yellower than ever. There was a fag in her hand, as usual, and a vodka bottle not far away, if Annie was any judge.

'Don't worry, I wasn't expecting you to roll out the red carpet,' said Annie. 'I just want to know what's going on, that's all.'

'What do you mean?' Connie took a deep drag, squinting her pale eyes against the smoke.

'You've been putting the phone down every time I've called. So now I'm asking you straight. How's Eddie?'

'Eddie Carter's none of your fucking business.'

'No, you're wrong. Celia is worried sick, that makes it my business.'

'Talk about like taking to like,' Connie sneered. 'She's a tart and so are you.'

Annie gritted her teeth. 'Just tell me about Eddie, you rotten old cow!'

In her worst nightmares Annie often revisited that awful night. Eddie bleeding like a stuck pig, Darren hysterical, Celia catatonic with shock.

But a calmness had settled over her and somehow she had taken charge. Called the ambulance, got them organized. But the minute she'd phoned Connie, other things had started to happen. Before the ambulance arrived, Gary and Steve, two of Max's boys, had come and taken Eddie away, bundled him into the back of a car. She would never forget Eddie's white, tortured face. The ambulance men had arrived six minutes later and so Darren took advantage of the facilities.

'They told us two casualties,' said the men, eyeing the bloodied empty bed with suspicion.

'My mate legged it,' said Darren, holding a towel to his battered face. 'We had a fight, it was nothing.'

'Come on then,' said one of the men. 'Let's get you seen to.'

'What the fuck did you have to go and tell Connie for?' Celia asked when they'd gone. She still sat at the kitchen table, her hands shaking, her face blank.

'They had to know. They're his family.'

'He was targeted in my house.'

'Darren said there was another man with him. Man with a deaf aid.'

'One of his own?'

'Seems so.'

'I hope for his sake he's a long way away by now,' said Celia. 'That's what I should do. Just take off.'

'You've done nothing wrong.'

'It happened in my house.'

'Don't keep saying that!'

'Not saying it won't make it go away. I'm responsible. Me. No one else. Just me.'

After that night things had gone ominously quiet and Celia had seemed to shrink into herself, become smaller somehow.

So here she was, Annie thought bitterly. Back

at her dear old mum's. Who was being a bitch – as usual.

'Coming round here pretending you give a shit,' she was yelling. 'Who do you think you're kidding?'

And maybe that was justified. Annie knew she should have called before, seen how her mother was getting on. She knew she should have contacted Ruthie long before now, too, and begged her forgiveness – grovelled if necessary – but every time she felt the impulse to get in touch the guilt kicked in and she just couldn't face it.

'Is he okay, that's all I'm asking.'

'Oh, he's okay. Half dead, but doing just fine. She must let some scum in there, for a thing like that to happen. But what am I saying? Of course she does, the cheap whore. She let *you* in.'

Annie raised her hand to hit her mother as hard as she could. She wanted to wipe that pathetic, malicious smile off that drunken, shrivelled face. But she held back.

'Go on – hit me. Is that what that whore teaches you in that place?'

Annie swallowed her anger and ignored Connie's taunts.

'Is he recovered?' She let her arm drop.

'He's *dying,* you silly cow,' spat Connie.

'What?'

'I've got nothing more to say to you.' She

grabbed Annie's arm and started bundling her back out the door.

'And Ruthie?'

Annie had to ask the question, much as she really didn't want to. She was on the step trying to take in what Connie had said about Eddie. If it was true – and why would Connie lie? – Max must be devastated. And when she thought of Max, she thought also of Ruthie. Ruthie must be in the thick of it all, the poor cow.

But Connie didn't answer.

The door slammed shut. Annie heard the bolt go across.

'What about Ruthie?' she asked the closed door. She kicked it once, hard. 'What about poor bloody Ruthie?' she repeated hopelessly.

She shouldn't have come. She'd wrecked everything, why couldn't she just accept that and leave it alone? Hating herself, she turned and walked away.

When she got back to Celia's Kieron was there, sitting at the kitchen table talking to Ellie. He looked up as she came in, his eyes laughing.

'You forgot, didn't you,' he said to Annie.

Annie stood dumbstruck. 'What?'

Ellie got up and left the room, smiling at Annie in passing and mouthing: *'He's gorgeous.'*

'You said you were going to sit for me today,

at my place. Eleven o'clock. I phoned when you didn't show up, but Ellie said you'd gone out. I thought I'd come over and wait.'

'Oh.' God, how had she forgotten? Her mind was whirling. And Celia had always stressed that she should keep the Delaneys sweet. What a fool she was. 'I'm sorry. I completely forgot.'

'Not very flattering,' said Kieron.

'Sorry,' Annie said again.

Kieron looked at her as she sat down. He said: 'I'm not like the rest of them, you know.'

'The rest of who?'

'The Delaneys. I'm not part of that world.'

'Oh.'

'So there's no need to be walking on eggshells trying not to upset me. I won't take offence. There'll be no nasty comebacks. Just say if you've changed your mind about the sitting.'

'I haven't.'

'Well, good.'

'I've just got a lot on my mind, that's all.'

'I'll try to help with that,' smiled Kieron. 'You can talk while you sit.'

'Talk to a Delaney about Carter trouble? I don't think so,' said Annie.

'I told you. I'm not into all that. I'm like a priest, I hear confessions. And the confessional is confidential.'

Annie found herself looking at him properly for

the first time. Ellie was right, he was easy on the eye – and so friendly. He stood up. He was tall and gangly, with big bony hands. His jacket was tweed with leather elbow patches. There was a long, unravelling, purple scarf around his neck.

'You're staring,' he said.

'Sorry.' Annie stood up, flushing.

'You think you like the cut of me, do you?'

Annie had to smile too now. 'I'll let you know.'

'Fair enough.'

'When I'm ready.'

'I was jealous of my sister, Ruthie,' Annie said as she sat in Kieron's flat. It was way up in the top of a house in Shepherd's Bush, with cold north light streaming through big windows. It was piled high with canvases and stank of paint and linseed and turps. There was a bed and a little kitchenette in one corner, and a Bobby Darin LP was playing on the turntable on the floor. There was a one-bar electric fire at Annie's feet. It was a workplace rather than a home, but it was kept well.

'Keep the fuck still, won't you?' said Kieron lightly, busy sketching away. 'Why? Is she prettier than you?' He stood back from the canvas and looked her over. 'That's hard to believe, at the risk of getting you a big head.'

'She's not prettier than me,' said Annie.

'What then?'

Annie shrugged. 'Dad left. I was a daddy's girl. Mum loved Ruthie, not me. I reminded her of Dad.'

'Ah, that must be the handsome side of the family.' Kieron was back at the sketching.

'Are all your family as stunning as your sister Orla?'

'Redmond is, they're twins after all. But we're not talking about my family, remember.'

'Sorry.'

'It's okay. Keep still, you.'

'For how long, exactly?' Annie was squirming on the stool. She couldn't feel her lower half at all any more, she'd been on this damned stool for an hour. She was cold, despite being wrapped up in cardigan and skirt. 'And we're talking about the Carters, let me remind you. My sister's one of them now.'

'And happy to be so, I would imagine. Living the high life and enjoying it.'

'I've heard different.'

'She's unhappy?'

'I don't know. Mum won't talk to me. She thinks I'm the world's worst whore because I set out to get my sister's man.'

'You can see she'd be peeved.'

'I was jealous! How many times do I have to say it, I was wild with jealousy. Years and years of it. She had everything I wanted, just the thought of him

127

and her together made me want to rip her eyes out. I was going mental with it, I had to do something.'

'Well you did that – and now I guess you're sorry?'

Annie pulled a face. 'It's too late for that. Mum won't listen. I can't get in touch with Ruthie, she's buried down in the country somewhere so I don't know what's happening with her.'

'You're in a mess.'

'You can say that again.'

'Your mother threw you out, that's the story? No, *don't* move that arm.'

Annie nodded and got the arm back into position. 'So I went to Celia's. I had nowhere else. Lost my job as well.'

Kieron paused. 'The Carters have influence.'

'You'd know all about that, being a Delaney.'

'Off limits. So that's why you agreed to sit for me? You needed the cash?'

'Why else?'

'I was thinking you loved my Irish blarney.'

Annie laughed. 'You've got plenty of that.'

'Although Orla did warn me against you.'

'What for?'

'She thought you were trouble. Didn't like your connections.'

'I don't bloody have any. They've all buggered off.'

'Ah, you poor thing. Would you consider taking your clothes off next time you sit for me?'

'Fuck off.'

'Oh, go on.'

Annie's eyes opened wide at his audacity. She had to laugh. 'Are you taking the piss or what?'

'The pay's better.'

'I don't care.' Annie paused. 'How much better?'

'Double.'

'Never.'

'It's true, I'm telling you. So will you?'

'No.' But she was smiling. Kieron was easy to talk to, she liked that about him. But she had the feeling she could have been a bowl of fruit or a landscape or any damned thing, he was looking at her as an object, not as a woman. Which she felt sort of relieved about, and annoyed about at the same time. Granted, he was trying to get her clothes off, but not with any lustful intention. Which was a bit bloody insulting in a way. She was used to men slavering over her, and his approach threw her off balance.

'I didn't expect this,' she said.

'What?' He was busy, absorbed.

'That you're a real artist. That you really *do* it.' Kieron paused.

'I thought you were just playing at all this,' said Annie. 'You're a Delaney, for God's sake. Delaneys don't usually arse about painting pictures, do they? They . . .' Annie hesitated.

'Yeah, what do "they" do?' asked Kieron.

'They run their manor,' said Annie. 'People respect them.'

'And fear them.'

'That goes with the turf.'

Annie hesitated again. She thought of the Delaneys, and how they had bided their time, lulled the Carters into a false sense of security after Tory was knocked off, then suddenly gone for Eddie. These were dangerous people, cunning and cold.

Kieron paused. 'Come on then, spit it out.'

'Will they protect Celia? She's afraid the Carters are going to get her.'

'I told you, I don't discuss the family.'

'You could put in a word. If you wanted to.'

'No, Annie.' Kieron drew back from the drawing. 'I told you, I don't get involved.'

Annie looked at him. 'Do you sell your work?'

'What?' Now it was Kieron's turn to be off balance.

'You heard me. You sell it, don't you?'

'Of course I sell it.'

'In London galleries?'

'Yes.'

'Ah.'

'What do you mean, "ah"?'

'Doesn't the fact that you're a member of the Delaney family work in your favour when it comes to getting gallery-owners to display your stuff?'

Kieron stared at her.

'Or am I wrong? Do those gallery-owners kiss

the Delaneys' arseholes rather than risk the consequences?'

'You're a cheeky little mare, ain't ya?' said Kieron.

Annie shrugged. 'All I'm saying is, you're a
Delaney when it suits you.'

Kieron threw aside his nub of charcoal. 'Go on,
get out. Get out before I kick your audacious arse
down those stairs.'

'The truth hurts, doesn't it?'

'Out!'

Something flared in his eyes, something Annie
hadn't seen before. She frowned as she left.

He'd noticed her now, all right. And she wasn't
sure how she felt about that. But as she hit the
street she was smiling again.

When she got back to Celia's place, she found
Darren, Aretha, Ellie and Dolly sitting around the
kitchen table sunk in gloom.

'What?' she asked, feeling high because she'd
managed to get one over on a Delaney without
getting herself killed in the process.

Darren looked up at her. He still had two fabulous shiners from where Eddie's attacker had punched
him in the nose. He didn't look good at all.

'Celia's gone,' he said.

Annie sat down. 'What?'

'She went overnight,' said Aretha. 'All her clothes
are gone, and her suitcase, she's scarpered.'

'Did she say anything before she left?' asked Annie. This didn't seem feasible. This place would be lost without Celia.

'She left this for you,' said Ellie. She gave Dolly a scathing look. 'Dolly was going to rip it up.'

'Grass,' spat Dolly.

'Open the thing, we've been dying to know what she says,' said Aretha.

'I was going to steam it open,' confessed Darren.

'What stopped you?' asked Annie.

'Ellie said she'd tell.'

Annie nodded. Ellie would always tell. Dolly would always be stroppy, and Darren would always be sweetly reasonable. As for Aretha . . . Annie thought she wanted watching. Aretha was the expert on supplying the needs of their kinkier clients, there was a dark side to her temperament. All these things she had learned. She tore open the envelope and unfolded the letter inside. It said:

Annie love,
    I'm going away for a bit, I can't say where. Take over here, sorry I can't say for how long. You know the ropes, and if you get stuck Darren will help, he's a good boy.
    Love
    Celia.

Annie read it twice, the breath catching in her throat, a thousand thoughts running through her head. Celia, gone. Celia who had taken her in and given her a home when the rest of the world had spat at her. It didn't seem real somehow. And she didn't want to even think about this place without her, it would be empty, soulless.

She passed the letter to Darren. He read it, and passed it to Aretha. She passed it to Ellie, then Dolly, who looked ready to explode.

'I'm not taking fucking orders off you,' she told Annie.

Annie felt bereft. She'd become so close to Celia, and her presence was going to be sorely missed. But she couldn't blame her for putting some distance between herself and the Carters. Eddie sounded really bad, and what if the worst – God forbid – happened? Celia would be up shit creek, no doubt about it. Celia had done the wise thing. But Annie was going to miss her like a limb.

Annie took a deep, calming breath. All right, so Celia was gone and God knew for how long. But she owed her everything, and it was up to her to make sure that Celia could return to a going concern, not a washout.

'You don't have to take orders from me,' said Annie.

Dolly looked at her. 'I should bloody-well think not,' she huffed.

'You can fuck off out of here right now, if you want to.'

Dolly's rosebud mouth fell open. Darren, Aretha and Ellie sat rigid with shock.

'You *what*?'

Dolly stood up, knocking her chair over with a clatter.

'Are you deaf as well as stupid?' asked Annie, giving her a hard stare. 'Celia's put me in charge and I'm going to do the right thing by her. If that means losing your services, fair enough. Bugger off then. If you want to stay, you can put the kettle on and fucking-well button it, okay?'

Ellie would always squeal. Annie knew it. So she wasn't surprised when Pat Delaney called in person a few days later. Ellie was the Delaneys' inside source, she knew it. She handed him the usual wad, and he pocketed it thoughtfully.

'I hear there's been trouble,' he said, making himself comfortable at the table.

Annie nodded coolly. As powerfully as she had taken to Kieron on first sight, his older brother Pat repulsed her. He had a big leery face and was busy looking her over, but he was a Delaney. Although she didn't want to, she had to give him some respect. Of course the Delaneys were supposed to make sure there was no trouble, although you wouldn't know it judging by what had happened to Eddie and Darren.

134

'There has,' she agreed, sitting down opposite so he'd take his eyes off her legs for a minute. Darren and Ellie and Dolly were upstairs; Aretha was out. I'm in charge here now, she thought, and tried to remember it.

'A client was attacked here,' said Annie.

'That's a shame,' said Pat, obviously not meaning it.

'Yeah, it is,' agreed Annie. 'He was an important one.'

'I heard that shirt-lifter Carter got slit,' said Pat with a grin.

'Celia didn't want any trouble with the Carters. Neither do I, and she left me in charge.'

'And you are . . . ?'

'I'm Annie Bailey, Celia's niece.' Annie pushed Celia's letter across the table to him. Her heart was thumping and her mouth was dry, but she kept up the cool front.

Pat read the note then looked up. 'You think you can run this place?' he asked, and his eyes said he found this funny.

'I know I can. I've learned the ropes from Celia.'

'I could put a manager in,' said Pat.

'Celia didn't want that. She wanted me to take over.'

Pat eyed the girl carefully. Annie was a real beauty. And he was in a position of power here.

'And you want to do that?' he asked.

135

'Yes.' She didn't *want* to. But she owed Celia big-time. Okay, she hadn't seen herself running a knocking shop, but if that's what she had to do, then fuck it, she'd do it.

'Well, I don't know if you'll be suitable,' said Pat with a smile. 'So shut the door and come and give me a nice blow job, and I'll consider it.'

Annie's heart nearly stopped in her chest. She'd been afraid of this. But she kept her voice steady and her gaze direct. 'I'm not a working girl, Mr Delaney. Like my Aunt Celia I run the show, I don't perform in it.'

They locked eyes.

'Ellie or Dolly would be pleased to oblige. On the house, of course.'

Pat smiled and stood up. 'No thanks, girly. I wouldn't touch any of the scuzzy old whores in this cathouse. We'll leave it at that for now. But if you fuck up, watch out.'

'Understood,' said Annie, feeling nauseous as he passed her chair and left the room. She didn't relax until she heard the front door close behind him. Then she slumped on to the table, head in hands.

17

'How is he?' asked Max from the shadows as Ruthie came out of Eddie's room, pulling the door gently closed behind her.

Ruthie put a hand to her chest. 'Not good,' she said. Funny how her husband always made her jump. They should be easy with each other, like any other married couple, but they tiptoed around one another like strangers. Eight months they'd been married, and they barely knew each other.

Max stepped forward so that she could see his face.

'The nurse is just changing the dressings,' she told him.

'He's had the best care,' said Max.

'I don't know. I think he should be in hospital.' Ruthie looked at Max. She knew Max had pet doctors, the very best, who owed him or were afraid of him. So Eddie had received the best possible care.

But his condition didn't seem to be improving. His wounds hadn't healed. The nurse and now the doctors were looking nervous and talking about possible blood poisoning. The knife could have been dirty, but then Eddie had been stabbed in the dirtiest possible place. Faecal matter could have added to the risk of infection, that was what the doctors had told them, looking at her with nervous eyes. She'd shaken their hands, wet with fear of what would happen if they failed to get Eddie Carter well again.

'He's staying here, at home,' said Max.

'Max . . .'

'I don't want to hear any more about it.'

'He's unconscious. Feverish.'

'That'll pass. He's a tough little bastard.'

'I hope so.'

'For fuck's sake, go and pour us both a brandy, will you?' Max was irritated with her. She'd lost what little looks she'd had. She was skinny, her hipbones stuck out and her tits were gone. Her hair looked like straw. Her face was thin, like she'd been sucking bloody lemons. Her clothes had cost him a fortune, but she looked like shit in them. On the rare – almost non-existent – occasions that he attempted to fuck her, she reacted like he was a filthy rapist fresh from the sewers. There was no sign of a kid on the way. And now she was nagging him about Eddie, trying to get him to send him to some fucking clinical hell-hole to die.

'You ought to go in and see him in a minute,' said Ruthie.

'I will, when she's finished in there.' In fact, he hated going into his brother's sickroom now. The stench in there was horrible – the smell of mortal sickness. But he had a duty to Eddie. He had to go through it, because Eddie was going through it. Jonjo was no fucking use. If anyone was sick, Jonjo was nowhere to be seen. He just kept ranting about getting the bastard who'd done Eddie, and he'd given Deaf Derek the pasting of his life for taking Eddie to the parlour where it had happened. All of which was no use anyway. Ruthie was right. Eddie was in a very bad way.

They went downstairs to the drawing room and drank brandy. Max hadn't the heart for Mozart at the moment. Only the *Requiem* would be appropriate anyway.

'Gordon said he saw you in the annexe last week,' said Max, sitting down heavily on the sofa.

Ruthie started guiltily. 'I just had a look in,' she said, hugging herself in front of the fire.

'Don't.'

'What do you mean, "don't"? I had a look inside. It's a lovely little place, I could decorate it out and make some use of it.'

'Decorate this house,' said Max flatly, downing the brandy. 'Leave that one alone.'

'What, leave it as a shrine to the sainted

139

Queenie?' Ruthie snapped, smarting from his rebuke.

'For fuck's sake!' Max lobbed his glass at the fireplace. It shattered loudly, and spatters of brandy made the fire crackle and roar. 'Don't give me bloody earache, Ruthie, don't you think I've got enough to be going on with? My brother's upstairs at death's door, and you want to cunting-well redecorate?'

Ruthie went pale. 'I'm just saying.'

'Well *don't* fucking-well say.' Max jumped to his feet and grabbed her arms and shook her. Her brandy glass dropped with a splatter on to the carpeted floor. 'Leave the fucking annexe alone. Keep out of there. Make yourself busy. Other women do. Why not you?'

'Maybe because other women are happy with their husbands,' flung Ruthie.

'Jesus, not this again.'

'Maybe because their husbands don't *fuck* their bride's *sister* on the night before their *wedding*,' shrieked Ruthie.

'Um.' The nurse tapped awkwardly on the half-open door. She had coloured up on walking into the middle of a row. She radiated agitation. 'I'm sorry to disturb you, Mr and Mrs Carter. I think we should have the doctor over, quickly.'

Max was halfway up the stairs before she had even finished speaking. He burst into Eddie's room and ran over to the bed. Eddie was tossing about on the pillows. His face was flushed, he was wet through with sweat. His eyes were open and he saw Max there. God, thought Max with revulsion – the stink in here.

'Max,' croaked Eddie.

'I don't think he should be speaking too much,' said the nurse, wringing her hands. 'He's very weak.'

'Phone the doctor, Ruthie,' said Max, dismissing her. Ruthie left the room. 'Give us a moment,' said Max to the nurse.

'I don't think I should . . .'

'Fuck off out of it,' said Max fiercely.

The nurse went.

'I've been thinking about things, Max,' said Eddie.

'What things?' asked Max, holding Eddie's hand in both of his.

'I think the Delaneys done me because of Tory Delaney dying like he did,' said Eddie.

'No, Eddie. That's not true.'

'Yes it is. It's poetic bloody justice.'

Max stared at the wreckage of his brother, his hair slick with grease and sweat, his skin erupting. The weight falling off him. The stench.

'That night I buried the gun for you . . . did you do it? Did you shoot Tory Delaney? Everyone thinks you did.'

Max took a breath. 'No,' he said.

'You're lying.'

'I'm not lying, you berk. Why would I lie to you?'

'You let me think you shot Tory Delaney, because of Mum,' panted Eddie.

'Maybe I did. But as God's my witness, on Mum's grave, I didn't shoot Tory Delaney.'

'Then who the fuck did?'

'He had a lot of enemies.'

'Yeah, mostly you.'

'I didn't do it, Eddie. I'll tell you what I did, shall I?'

'I know you fired the gun. I took it out and smelled it. It had been fired.'

'You remember there was a break-in in the annexe, and Mum was there and her heart gave out with the fright of it.'

'I'll never forget it.'

'Well I found the ones who did it. They were two nobodies from the sticks, the Bowes brothers. They'd been paid by the Delaneys.'

'They confessed?'

'Yes, Bruv. Before they died.' Max's eyes blazed with the memory. 'I traced their uncle who ran the pub where they drank. My boy down at Smithfield made the uncle talk, and he fingered his nephews. Not that he had many fucking fingers left at the end of it. So the night Tory Delaney died, the night before I married Ruthie, I was busy. I was conducting a bit of business with the Bowes scum.'

'You shot them?' gasped Eddie.

Max nodded.

Eddie gave a weird little laugh. 'Then ... oh fuck me, this is almost funny ... I'm dying for nothing.'

'You're not dying,' said Max. 'Put that right out of your head.'

'Sure.' Eddie gave a faint smile and lay back. Max stared at Eddie's face and felt the tightness in his throat, the ache in his belly. He'd never cried in his life, but seeing Eddie like this really hurt him. If this was the Delaneys, he'd rip their fucking heads off one by one.

Then suddenly pus was coming out of Eddie, out of every orifice it seemed. Pouring from his nose, ears, mouth, even – Jesus – from his eyes. Max sprang off the bed with a cry of disgust and roared for the nurse to come. She did, and shooed him away. Ruthie stood in the doorway biting her knuckle to stop herself from screaming at the sight before her. Eddie was convulsing, it seemed to go on for hours but it was seconds, just seconds. Then he was still. The nurse was pounding at his chest, but it was too late for that, Max knew it was too late for anything.

Eddie was dead.

18

'I've decided to open up the front room,' said Annie to the girls and Darren as they sat with her around the kitchen table. She'd been at Celia's place for nearly nine months now, and it was starting to feel like home, like *her* place.

'Celia never used that room,' said Dolly, tapping fag ash into an ashtray and taking another deep drag. 'She kept it for best.'

Trust Dolly to put forward reasons why not. 'I know that,' said Annie. 'But I've had an idea. I'm going to do it up and throw monthly parties in there.'

'Parties?' Darren looked blank. His shiners were almost gone now, Annie saw. He was back to his good-looking self, ready to work again.

'Parties for the discerning clientele,' said Annie. She'd been awake half the night thinking this through. 'We'll charge a fee on the door. A steep one, to keep out the riff-raff and the youngsters, they're always trouble. We've got plenty of established clients, we don't even need to advertise, they'll pass it on word of mouth.'

'You'd have to watch the parking outside,' said Ellie, pouring more tea and diving into the biscuit tin again. 'Celia always worried about that. She was very careful not to upset the neighbours.'

'We'll tell our clients to park around the surrounding streets. They usually do anyway when they come here, they don't want to draw attention to themselves any more than we do. Go easy on those biscuits, Ellie, you're getting an arse on you.'

Ellie blushed and put the biscuit back.

'I don't see why we can't just carry on as before,' said Dolly, smirking at Ellie. 'It worked for Celia, why go changing things around?'

'When Celia comes back . . .' began Annie.

'You mean *if*, girl,' said Aretha.

'*When* Celia comes back she's going to find this place humming along like a fucking Rolls-Royce.' Annie looked around at her little gang of workers. 'We still offer the massages and the personal services, should our clients require them.'

Dolly smirked at Darren now. 'Bad luck, Darren, you've got to keep putting postcards in the post-office window. That ugly bloke in there fancies you something rotten.'

'In his *dreams*,' sniffed Darren.

'Just don't bend down to pick up your paper,' said Dolly.

'Last time he asked me to go into the back room with him,' said Darren with a shudder. 'Said he needed a hand lifting some heavy boxes.'

'Whatever he was thinking of lifting, I don't think it was boxes, honey,' said Aretha with a big grin.

'Aretha will put the ads in, she'll be safe enough,' said Annie. 'I've reworded them a bit. How's this? French polishing carried out with discretion and skill. And the phone number. And this one with the flute lessons, we'll put one of those in too.'

The assembled company looked at the cards and nodded begrudging approval. Everyone on the street knew that French polishing indicated chargeable sexual favours, and that flute lessons were blowjobs.

'We'll have themed parties,' said Annie. 'Lay on booze and food, music on the radiogram, it'll be good. Any questions?'

She waited for the protests to come. Who are you to give orders? What makes you think you can just take charge here? But, much to her surprise, nobody said a word. She couldn't quite believe it.

And what if she'd got it wrong? What if the party idea was no good?

They'd laugh their bollocks off at her and she knew it.

The phone was ringing in the hallway. 'Okay then, that's all for now,' she said, and went out into the hall.

Annie watched them go upstairs and then snatched up the phone. 'Hello?'

'Tell me you'd consider a nude sitting. Just one,' said Kieron.

'No.'

'Heartless cow. I've an exhibition in two months and it needs a centrepiece, and that centrepiece has to be you in all your glory, how about it?'

'No.'

'I told you, the money's good.'

'I don't need the money, Kieron, I've got another job.'

'Then do it as a favour to a pal. Come *on*, Annie. It'll be the ruin of the exhibition without it. Am I to tell Redmond or Pat that you aren't co-operating with my requests, is that it?'

Annie's good-natured smile vanished. 'That isn't funny, Kieron.'

'Sorry. Forgive me, but you're talking to a desperate man. Come on. You'll be safe. I've no desire to jump on your lovely bones.'

Why not? Annie wondered, feeling affronted. She knew he was speaking the truth. He wouldn't abuse the situation. She wondered if she'd mind if he did. She hadn't even thought about sex since that one night with Max. Ah, not true, she'd thought about sex with Max over and over again.

'I'd be embarrassed,' said Annie.

'Think of me like a doctor. I'm not eyeing you up, I'm painting you, for fuck's sake. Ah, come on. Didn't I show you the other day that you can trust me?'

Annie wasn't so sure about that. He'd looked really riled up when she'd left the studio last time. But maybe he'd only been playing with her.

'Kieron, I'm really busy. Maybe Pat's told you I'm looking after Celia's place for her?'

'I don't talk to Pat if I can help it,' said Kieron. 'You sure you know what you're doing?'

There was real concern in his voice. When had anyone last shown concern for her? Annie tried to remember. Ruthie had. A stab of pain wrenched at her gut as she thought of Ruthie, always leaping to her defence. God, she'd been such a bitch to her, what had the poor cow done to deserve her for a sister? She hadn't deserved Ruthie's kindness. And she could do without Kieron's. But he was a friend. And she thought she could trust him. After all, he was totally indifferent to her charms.

'I'll do it as a favour to you,' she sighed.

'What a great girl you are.'

'Spare me the Irish bit. I want triple wages, not double.'

'A great girl and a hard one,' groaned Kieron. 'You can afford it. You're a Delaney.'

'Deal then. Come on Wednesday and we'll make a start.'

Annie said goodbye and put the phone down. It rang again. She picked up. 'Hello?'

'Eddie Carter's dead,' said a scratchy female voice.

'Mum?' Annie clutched the phone harder.

'I thought you ought to know.'

Connie sounded sober for once. Then she began to cough, which sounded vile and seemed to get worse as the seconds slowly passed by. Annie felt cold inside. She still had the horrors when she thought about that night. The day after it had been like cleaning out an abattoir. The mattress had been too bloodstained to save and they'd had to burn the whole thing. Everyone had pitched in, scrubbing and polishing, to get Darren's room straight again. Celia had bought a new mattress. Life had gone on. But not for Eddie.

'Why would I want to know?' asked Annie, swallowing hard.

'Max said it happened at Celia's place. Not that I'm surprised. That tart mixes with all sorts. Is it true she's vanished?'

'She's on a break,' said Annie, feeling more loyalty to her aunt than to her own bloody mother. Her head was spinning, a million things were buzzing around her brain.

149

'My arse. She's legged it, hasn't she? There's going to be trouble over this.'

'When's the funeral?'

'Friday at twelve. They're burying him next to Queenie.'

Annie put the phone down. Her mother was still talking but there was nothing else she wanted to hear. Max's brother dead. Killed here, in this house. For once in her drink-sodden life, Connie was right. There was going to be trouble.

Annie called Darren back down to the kitchen.

'Eddie's Carter's dead,' she said when she'd shut the door and was sure they wouldn't be overheard.

Darren went white. He sat down quickly at the kitchen table. Annie sat too and waited for him to gather himself.

'Did you see who did it, Darren?'

'Would I say if I did?' asked Darren.

'It won't go any further.'

They exchanged a long look. Finally Darren shook his head. 'I wish I had. No, I don't. What am I saying? If I'd seen the bastard's face he'd have done me too.' He ran his hands through his hair, leaving it stuck up on end. 'No, I didn't see anything. He was wearing a bowler – he had a scarf tied round his face. He was heavy-set, tallish. But more than that I couldn't say. He just smashed me right on the nose and then carved up that poor little git while I was half out of it on the floor. You know the rest. Honest, Annie, that's all I know. I thought I was a goner. It was horrible.'

Annie patted his hand. She didn't know what to say.

'Will the police come?' asked Darren anxiously.

'Don't be daft,' said Annie. 'No outsiders know he was attacked here, and Max Carter will keep it quiet at his end. He'll have one of his tame doctors make out the death certificate, say Eddie died of natural causes, pay off any coppers if they get a sniff of anything iffy from the ambulance men, and that'll be that.'

'So we're in the clear?'

Annie shrugged. 'I don't see why not. It was bugger-all to do with us, I just wish Celia could have realized that before she did her moonlight flit.'

'Have you thought that maybe Celia didn't go of her own free will?' asked Darren.

'Meaning?'

'You know what I mean, Annie. Don't come the innocent with me. They could have sat her down at this table and forced her to write that note, then taken her off and done God knows what to her.'

'You mean the Carter mob?' said Annie.

'Who the fuck else would I mean? Come on, admit it. It's crossed my mind and I bet it's crossed yours.'

He was right. But every time the suspicion of wrongdoing had entered her head, Annie had ruthlessly pushed it out again. She had to go on believing that Celia was somewhere sunning herself, safe and well.

'Look, Darren,' said Annie impatiently. 'Fuck all this speculation. What good does it do us? We've got a place to run and it's business as usual. We're not going to have any more trouble, I'm going to get someone on the door from now on. No more open house.'

There was a lot to get straight, and Annie was glad of the distraction. She threw the front parlour windows wide to get rid of the musty smell in there. Then she got everyone to help her clear up. The furnishings were okay, old but of good quality. There was a big table to put the food and drinks on, and in the radiogram she discovered a stash of Connie Francis and Ruby Murray LPs. She started priming their regulars with the news that there would be a monthly party on offer. She had already made up her mind that any excess food from the parties would be distributed among the neighbours, to keep them onside. Then Billy turned up unannounced at the kitchen table one day, scaring her half to death. She made a mental note to ring Redmond Delaney without delay and get some muscle sent over for the door like she'd told Darren she would.

'Hello, Billy love,' she said, after she'd recovered herself. Fuck, why did he have to creep about like he did? Couldn't he ring an effing bell or something?

'Hello Annie,' said Billy. His long face lit up at the sight of her. He sat there clutching his briefcase on his lap, his deerstalker pulled down over his eyes. Poor bastard, she thought. The word was that the cord had got wrapped around his neck when he was born and he'd been starved of oxygen. He couldn't help being as he was, now could he?

So, despite the fact he'd given her a fright, she made him a cup of tea and plied him with biscuits. Celia had always made him welcome, and Annie was filling Celia's shoes. She didn't have Celia's happy knack of chattering about nothing, however, so she soon made her excuses and was pleased to see him go. She got straight on the phone to Redmond. It was a call she'd been trying to avoid making, but Billy had done her a favour by making her see it was something she had to do.

'Mr Delaney,' she said respectfully. 'I hope you're well?'

Annie had heard Celia making calls like this, she knew the drill.

'I'm very well,' said Redmond. Cool as ice was Redmond. You wouldn't find him in the parlours taking advantage of the facilities. Annie wondered if he ever did it at all. He'd probably put on rubber gloves first.

Annie proceeded to tell him about the monthly parties and that things had become a little more rough than usual lately, could he spare a man for the door?

'Permanently?' asked Redmond. She could hear that sharp brain of his ticking over, weighing up how much this would cost.

'If possible,' said Annie.

'Are you going to pay him out of your funds?' asked Redmond.

Bugger. That hadn't been at all what she'd had in mind.

'I thought you might help me out with that,' she said smoothly. 'There was a very unpleasant incident here not long ago. We pay already to make sure things like that don't happen.'

There was a silence. Perhaps she'd overstepped the mark, thought Annie. But what the hell, it was bloody true.

'Sometimes,' said Redmond, 'unpleasant incidents are difficult to prevent.'

Annie swallowed. Talking to Redmond, even at a distance, was like staring into the eyes of a cobra. You felt hypnotized.

'I need your help here,' said Annie. If he had a better nature, then she was going to try to appeal to it. 'My Aunt Celia was always straight with you, wasn't she? Paid up fair and square? Never gave you any trouble?'

'That's true,' allowed Redmond.

'I can't afford to pay for a man on the door. You can. The takings will be well up from the monthly parties.'

'You hope.'

'They will.'

'So you want us to stand the expense of the extra man.'

'Yes, I do.'

Silence again. 'No, take his wages out of the party profits. This isn't a charitable institution.'

'Mr Delaney.'

'Yes, Miss Bailey?'

'Seriously, I don't want any more trouble here. You let us down before. Badly.'

This time the silence was deafening. Oh fuck, thought Annie.

'I've got a man who'll be good for the door,' said Redmond at last. 'I'll send him over. But you pay his wages, Miss Bailey, not me.'

Well, thought Annie, you couldn't win them all. She quickly dialled Kieron's number.

'Yep?'

'Can I cry off Monday?' asked Annie.

'No, you fucking well cannot. Why?'

'They're buying Eddie Carter on Friday.'

'I thought you'd fallen out with your family? Didn't get in touch any more?'

'I just don't think I'll be in the mood on Monday, that's all.'

'Ah, come on. I'll cheer you up.'

I doubt it, thought Annie. 'Kieron, I'll ring you next week. Let you know.'

Annie put the phone down while he was still protesting. A chill had settled over her with the news of Eddie's death. She was Celia's representative, standing in Celia's shoes, and it had happened here in their normally peaceful little parlour. If Celia was here she would have sent a wreath at the very least, and she would have put in an appearance at the funeral to pay her respects. Annie knew she had to do exactly the same, although she dreaded it.

She wandered through to the front room and looked at the newly stocked drinks cabinet. She wished she could throw back a stiffener, but drink disgusted her and she hardly ever touched it. It reminded her of her mother. Fuck, she didn't even smoke.

Dig deep, she thought. She'd told herself that all her life. When her Dad had left, when her mother was out of it and choking on vomit and she'd had to clear her throat out and turn her on her side after a bad drunken binge. Dig deep. When she'd had to face Max in a rage over what she'd

156

Jessie Keane

done to Ruthie. Dig deep and stand alone. She'd lived by that rule all her life, and it gave her strength now. She fetched Brasso and rags from the kitchen and gave the ornaments on the front-room fireplace a polish. The first party was to be in two weeks. No time for slacking.

19

Jonjo was worried about Max. They were having a meet with all the boys at Queenie's old place, as usual. They were upstairs in the unused back bedroom, all of them crammed in around the big table. As usual. But there was a difference these days. There was no Queenie coming up the stairs with trays of tea and cakes, laughing with the boys and sending her regards to their mothers. The place was stone-cold and their voices echoed through its empty rooms.

No wonder Max had pissed off to the stockbroker belt to live, thought Jonjo. Jonjo knew that Max slept here sometimes when he'd had a heavy day, but Jonjo wouldn't stay a night here if you paid him in gold bits. He had a flat across town where he took all his birds. Fuck this place. They had been in the process of selling it when Queenie died. At that point Max had taken it off the market. He refused to discuss getting rid of the old mausoleum now. It gave Jonjo the creeps to come here. He kept expecting his mum to appear at the door.

They were all here. Him and Max. Jimmy Bond and Gary Tooley and Steven Taylor. Several other staunch men, all trusted lieutenants. Deaf Derek was down the bottom there, looking sullen since Jonjo had to give him a slapping over the Eddie business. Derek should have looked after Eddie better, thought Jonjo, watching the little bastard with distaste. If it hadn't been for Max's intervention, the little fucker would have had a lot more than a slap. Jackie Tulliver was there too, smoking his bloody horrible cigars. All the boys were neatly dressed and wearing black armbands. It was nice that they were showing respect, but Jonjo would have expected no less of them at a time like this.

But Max. Max was as always immaculately turned out, in a black Savile Row suit, white shirt and black tie. His black vicuna coat, lined with purple silk, was laid over the back of his chair. Max's eyes looked blank. Granted, Max had taken the brunt of Eddie's death, he'd been on the spot when it happened. Jonjo felt bad about that, but he'd been carrying on with business while Max stayed down there in Surrey. Someone had to mind the fucking shop, didn't they?

And Jonjo knew he'd been doing good. The parlours were all running smoothly, the clubs were fine, all the halls and shops and arcades who paid protection to the Carters were behaving themselves and paying up promptly. There had been no insurrections, no lack of respect that would have had to be instantly cracked down on; no trouble at all. Well, some. The Maltese were always acting heavy and needing a sharp slap, but so what? Same old shit, easily dealt with.

The dummy fiver and tenner plates he'd bought off Kyle Fox in The Grapes had been sold on to one of the Manchester mobs at a good profit. There were lots of new opportunities opening up in the West End and all the gangs were eager to get their slice of the action. The Barolli family from America had come over recently and there'd been a satisfactory meet. Constantine Barolli's mob now paid the Carter firm three thousand sovs a quarter to keep any rough elements out of their Knightsbridge businesses.

Rough elements like the Delaneys, for instance.

The American mob had been very courteous to Max and Jonjo. The brothers had wined and dined Constantine Barolli and his family, and the Barollis had in turn introduced Max and Jonjo to George Raft and Judy Garland. Big stars. They were mixing with the best these days. Eddie had loved meeting all the stars, he'd been in his element. It pained Jonjo badly to know that Eddie wouldn't get to do any of that any more.

Jonjo watched his older brother sitting there, blank-faced. Eddie's death had hit Max like a fucking pick handle. Max seemed to have lost his hunger for the business, maybe even for life itself. Jonjo hated to see him this way. He'd tried to brace the poor sod up, but no go.

Now Jonjo knew he had to say something. He wasn't the type to mess-ass about. Better to spit it out, say what he felt.

'We should do something about what happened to Eddie,' he said, broaching the subject that everyone else in the room was afraid to bring up. There was a murmur of assent from most of the other boys. Silence, of course, from Deaf Derek. Jonjo shook out one of his Player's, lit up and kicked back in his chair to look at Max.

'If we don't, it'll be seen as weakness,' he said.

Max was silent. He was staring at his clasped hands on the tabletop as if he might find answers there.

'Torch the place where it happened,' suggested Gary.

'Do a few of their shop-owners,' said Steven.

Jimmy Bond, Max's most trusted lieutenant, said nothing.

Everyone in the room knew that 'they' were the Delaneys. Every one of them believed that this had been Delaney work. Even Max.

'Well fucking say something,' said Jonjo angrily.

Abruptly Max stood up. He put his coat on and looked around at them all.

'There's nothing to say,' he said quietly. 'Not until after we've laid Eddie to rest, then we'll see. Until then, shut it the lot of you.'

'What about the heist, Max?' asked Jimmy.

Max paused. Over the past few weeks they had been discussing a planned heist on a department store that paid protection to the Delaneys; they'd been going to hit it in January, after the Christmas rush and the January sales, but all this shit had hit the fan over Eddie and now it looked like it was going to have to be next year instead.

'It'll keep,' said Max.

And he left the room. They all listened, gob-smacked, as he went down the stairs and out the front door. There was an uneasy silence. Then Deaf Derek once again lived up to his reputation of being a prat.

'Word on the street is that Mr Carter's losing it,' he said.

Stupid fucker, thought the others, although each of them had entertained the same thought over the past few months. Jonjo moved fast, launching himself down the table at Derek. In an instant Jonjo had the squirming idiot pinned to the wall and was banging his stupid head against it.

'*What* did you say, you ponce?' roared Jonjo.

'Nothing!' bleated Derek. 'I didn't say nothing, Jonjo.'

Jonjo gave his head another knock and then

nutted him. Derek sank dazed to the floor, where Jonjo put the boot in.

'Watch your mouth, you cunt,' said Jonjo, brick-red and bulging-eyed with rage. Then he was following Max out the door and down the stairs. The others sat there shaking their heads and looking at each other. Only Derek would be thick enough to disrespect Max in front of his brother Jonjo.

'Tosser,' said Steven, as he passed Derek by.

Gary and Jimmy and the others followed too. Derek sat hugging his guts. All he'd said was the truth. He knew it. And so did they.

20

Like most, Annie Bailey hated funerals. It was bad enough when a person was old and frail, death wasn't so hard then. A bit of a mercy, really. But when it was the death of a young man, and a death so bloody and vicious, then you started to say to yourself: if there's a God, why did he let something like this happen?

When she got up on Friday morning and took a bath and styled her hair, she thought of Eddie. Eddie as she had last seen him, bloody and broken on the bed in Darren's room. As she dressed she tried to get a grip. Think of happier times, she told herself.

She thought of dancing with Eddie at Max's and Ruthie's wedding. It was no good. She remembered not Eddie's tipsy laughter but the tight misery gripping her throat and chest on that day. Max ignoring her. Ruthie, who should have been so happy, looking distraught and confused. When she'd got home that night, it had been a mercy to lock herself up in her room, alone. Even then there had been no real relief. All she could think about was Max and Ruthie in bed together. All she could feel in her bruised, aching heart was *it should have been me.*

She put on her neat black suit with the cream piping and gold buttons. It was a Chanel rip-off, elegant and understated, one of Celia's selections.

'A Madam may have to mix with whores but she doesn't have to look like one,' Celia had always told her. 'The right clothes give a woman authority.'

Annie looked in the mirror and knew that Celia was correct. She put on the black pillbox hat she'd bought specially, and black stockings, black court shoes. Her dark hair she tucked up in a neat chignon. She picked up her bag and went downstairs. Darren was making tea and toast.

'Want some?' he asked as she came into the kitchen.

Annie shook her head. 'I'd throw it straight back up.'

Darren looked her up and down. 'You look great. I'll come with you if you want, you know that.'

'No, I'm best on my own,' said Annie.

Christ, that would really put the cat among the pigeons. Darren, the male prossie Eddie had been attacked with, turning up at a Carter funeral.

'Are you sure you should go?' asked Darren.

'Celia would go,' said Annie flatly, and was relieved to hear the taxi tooting away outside. She didn't want time enough to talk herself out of this. It wouldn't take much to make her bottle it altogether. But she owed it to Celia to at least show up and pay her respects. *Dig deep and stand alone*, she told herself.

'Take over, Darren,' said Annie, and left.

The streets all around the cemetery were thronged with people turning out to show respect to the Carters. Annie paid the taxi driver, told him to come back in an hour, and decided to walk the rest of the way. She caught snatches of the conversation of other mourners.

'See, 'flu can be nasty. Carry you off in a minute.'

'Our Gillian had it last winter, she was fucked. Too weak to lift a finger.'

'And he was so young.'

'Yeah, but never strong.'

'Just goes to show.'

So that was the story. Eddie Carter had died of complications brought on by influenza. She went into the church. It was already nearly full, and she was pleased about that. She tucked herself away at the back, glad to be lost among the crowds.

Annie thought that organ music was the most depressing thing in the world. All around her people were talking in whispers, scared to appear disrespectful by raising their voices in a place of worship. She looked up at the stained-glass window. Angels were clustered around Christ on the cross. Candles glimmered on the altar. It was pretty and serene in here. When she thought of how Eddie had died, it pained her to look at any of it.

There was a rustle of louder whispering now. The hearse had arrived. The music changed, swelling with Saul's *Dead March*. There was movement and lowered voices from the porch, then the coffin came, beautifully draped in white lilies, borne aloft by six men. She saw Jonjo Carter and Gary Tooley, Jimmy Bond and Steven Taylor, Jackie Tulliver – and Max.

Annie felt her heart kick violently in her chest. She hadn't seen him since he'd chucked her out of his car. Christ, such a lot had happened since then! She'd changed. She could see that he'd changed, too. He'd lost weight. His face was sharper, his dark skin almost pale. Every pulse in her body seemed to have speeded up. She quickly looked away from him, it hurt too much.

All her stupid unvoiced hopes for this day had proved worthless. She had almost convinced herself that his power over her would be gone, that she would look at him and not feel what she had always felt. She didn't know what this was – love or lust? More like a fucking obsession. Whatever it was, she had to get rid of it.

Then the six grim-faced men were moving slowly on up the aisle. They stopped in front of the altar and placed the coffin carefully on the dais. The music stopped. The vicar told everyone to be seated. Annie sat numb throughout the readings then stood up to mouth the words of hymns. She lost track of time, it was like a waking nightmare, but at last the coffin was coming back down for the interment. This time she didn't look at Max. But she saw Ruthie and Mum following on behind the coffin.

Mum looked fucking awful, but then she always did. Black drained her, made her look scrawnier and pastier than ever. But Ruthie was a shock. She was so skinny now, and her expensive dress hung on her like a rag. Where had Annie's plump, warm-featured sister gone? Ruthie looked like a mannequin, painfully thin and cold.

It was better outside in the air, even if the wind cut like a knife near the grave. Queenie's headstone was huge and elaborate, a tribute from Max and Jonjo and Eddie. Now Eddie was joining her, to lie beside her for eternity. The many mourners, Annie among them, stood back and let the close family cluster around the grave. The vicar was saying the ancient, soothing words. Ruthie was crying and dabbing at her eyes. Connie put her arm around her and Annie felt her guts clench in sympathy. Jonjo was a big, bulky presence, standing with head bowed beside a rigidly upright Max.

Annie allowed herself to look at him again. One look, one last guilty moment of pleasure before she stopped this silliness once and for all. She stared at his face. The hooked nose, the dark hair being tossed by the wind, the steely blue eyes that raised and now looked – oh God – straight into hers. Annie's breath caught with the shock of it. Their eyes locked for a long time, then Max looked down at the grave again.

'It's a fucking shame,' someone was saying behind her. 'Not that long since the old lady went, and now the boy.'

Then it was over. Thank God, thought Annie. She rushed out of the cemetery gates to the waiting taxi. She didn't look at Max Carter again. She didn't dare.

21

Redmond Delaney sent over an ex-boxer called Chris Brown for the job on the door. He was an ugly bald man, six-and-a-half feet tall and eighteen meaty stones of muscle, with a battered nose and misshapen ears. Chris had a gentle, respectful way with women and a hard but polite way with men. He dressed immaculately. Annie took to him at once, but was appalled to realize how much he expected to make out of her. She hammered him down to the lowest possible basic, adding that there would be perks to the job.

'Tips on the door, food and drink, a bed if you should need it, and the use of the facilities.'

'The facilities?'

'The girls. Or Darren. Work out any charges with them.'

'No freebies?' Chris smiled.

'This is a place of work, not a dating agency,'

170

said Annie firmly. 'And the golden rule here is discretion. We get on okay with our neighbours, because they don't know our business. I don't want them to, either. Keep inside, don't make yourself obvious out in the street. Break that rule and you're out. And Mr Delaney will be told why.'

'Mr Delaney said you were tough,' said Chris, unruffled. 'I respect that, Miss Bailey.'

'Good. Then we'll get along fine.'

With Chris installed from late afternoons to early morning, she felt safer. Poorer too, but still – everything came at a price in this world. He was handy as well. He reviewed their security, telling her she needed better locks front and back, security chains, a peephole on the front door, locks on all the windows and a firmer line on house personnel. She needed to monitor more closely who was in and who was out. He hit on the idea of a book on the hall table. When someone, staff or punter, left, they were signed out. When they came back, they were signed in. That way, Annie insured against any nasty surprises. And keys must be more carefully guarded.

'See to it,' said Annie. More fucking expense, but she knew he was right. 'But remember . . .'

'Be discreet. Got it,' said Chris, squeezing into his Zodiac and roaring off to the hardware store.

Kieron was still being a pest. A week after the funeral, he phoned and at last she agreed to sit for him again – and this time in the nude. She wasn't happy about it. Her mind was in turmoil. The pressures of Eddie's death, seeing Max and Ruthie, preparing for the first of the parties and not knowing whether it would pay or not, wondering where the hell Celia was and if she was okay – it was all getting to her.

And now – *this*.

'I'm not sure about any of this,' said Annie when she got to his flat at Shepherd's Bush and stood there in the paint-spattered room with the smell of turps and linseed oil nearly choking her.

Kieron was busy putting a prepped new canvas on the easel, not taking any real notice of her. As usual. *What was the matter with the bastard?* she wondered in sudden fury. He'd pushed a tatty, red velvet chaise to the centre of the room, ready for her to recline upon. Probably heaving with nits and all sorts by the look of it, she thought angrily. For God's sake, did she really need this?

'There's a robe on the door, get changed in that little room through there,' he said, not even glancing at her, tossing boxes aside as he hunted for fresh charcoal.

The 'little room' turned out to be a broom cupboard. She barked her shins on a metal bucket and knocked over mops and brushes when she tried to turn round.

'Fuck it!' she muttered.

'Okay in there?' he trilled.

'Oh sure. Marvellous,' said Annie.

She got stripped off and put on the grubby, red silk robe, then went back out and looked at him expectantly. He didn't even look up. This time he was cleaning brushes. Fuck! she thought and took off the robe and threw herself down on to the dirty chaise. Dust plumed up and she started to cough.

'When did you last clean in here?' she asked him.

'I clean up,' said Kieron defensively, adjusting the easel. 'That sink over there gleams like pools of piss in the moonlight.'

Annie realized that, like all men, Kieron had select-ive vision when it came to dust. They cleaned one bit of the room intensively and ignored the rest.

'Look.' Annie was getting irritable. 'I hope this isn't going to take long.'

'Sure, you can't hurry the creative process,' said Kieron, straightening up. 'Right, I'm ready.'

Kieron looked at the woman on the red chaise for the first time and nearly dropped his charcoal. Christ alive, but she was a beauty. Her skin was luminously pale, her hair long and dark, her eyes as deeply green as tourmalines.

'Right,' he said, staring.

'Let's get on with it,' said Annie. 'How do you want me?'

'Right.' Kieron swallowed hard. 'On your front then, if you will. Look back at me over that shoulder. Like that, yes. Put that arm down a bit. That left leg up slightly.'

Think of her as a bowl of fruit, he thought to himself. *Or a landscape*. Kieron started to sketch Annie's curvaceous outline on to the canvas. His hand shook slightly.

'How come you don't have a minder?' asked Annie while he drew.

'I can't be doing with all that,' said Kieron. There was a stunning woman lying in her pelt in front of him. Bowl of fruit. Bowl of *fruit*.

'Yes, but you're a Delaney. And there's a lot of trouble going on at the moment. Wouldn't you feel safer with a minder?'

'Ah, but you're forgetting that I don't get involved with the family business side of things.'

'That's a naïve attitude,' said Annie. 'You may not be "involved", but you can't help being a member of the family. I mean, your parents care for you. They wouldn't want any harm to come to you. And people might not pick and choose. They might just see a Delaney, "involved" or not.'

By people Kieron knew she meant the Carters. He paused and smiled.

'Ah, but you're forgetting I have another family connection,' he said.

'Oh? Which one is that?'

'You. *You* are my insurance.'

'What?' Annie thought that sniffing turps had obviously affected his brain.

'You're Max Carter's sister-in-law.'

Annie snorted. 'Kieron, you fool, I've told you the story. I've no influence with the Carters.'

'They could have burned your aunt's place to the ground after that business with their brother,' he pointed out.

'But they didn't.' Although it had crossed her mind. It had obviously crossed Celia's, too. Celia had been so panicked by it all that she had fled.

'Ah, but they could have. You and your gang of workers could have been dust and ashes.'

'Shut up, Kieron.' Annie was uncomfortable with this line of conversation. She didn't like being on some invisible line between the two gangs, but somehow this was where she had ended up. It was an unnerving place to be. All she could do was keep her head down, do her job, and hope for the best.

'And I wonder *why* they didn't,' considered Kieron, busy with the charcoal. 'Not because you were there, I suppose?'

'Kieron, you're dreaming,' sighed Annie.

'Am I though?' Kieron grinned. 'You see, what I'm thinking is that you will plead for me.'

'*What?*'

'If I ever get into trouble, if on one dark moonlit

night I get grabbed and people want to do unpleasant things to my poor sweet innocent young body, you'll be there putting in the glad word with your brother-in-law – won't you, Annie Bailey? You'll come to my rescue.'

'What, and stick my own stupid head above the parapet to be shot at?' She had to smile back. What a nutcase he was.

Kieron looked at her. 'Word is that Max Carter might be persuaded by you.'

'By me?' Annie turned her head away from his gaze. 'Forget it, Kieron,' she said glumly. 'Max isn't interested in me.'

But that look, she thought.

Something electric, something almost visceral in its power, had passed between Max Carter and her on the day of Eddie's funeral. Something she couldn't bear to think about.

22

Max got the shock of his life when Ruthie said she wanted to go back to her mother's. He was so used to her being apathetic and accepting, but this was the worm turning in a big way, and it startled him.

'What the fuck for?' he asked.

He sat on one of the big couches in the drawing room at his Surrey place. She sat on the other one, her legs pulled up beneath her. They were miles apart, in every way. She'd got thinner still. And she'd done something to her hair, it was no longer mouse but almost blonde. He didn't like it. Only brunettes had ever done anything in the bedroom department for him. Not that there was a fucking thing happening in their bedroom anyway, he thought bitterly.

'She's not very well,' said Ruthie with a shrug, her eyes not meeting his. She took a sip of her brandy.

'She's pissed as a fart most of the time, if that's what you mean,' said Max.

God, he despised drunks. He watched Ruth drinking the brandy, relishing it almost like a lover's kiss, and wondered if she was going the same way. He'd done a few discreet checks around the place when it seemed the drinks cabinet was emptying too fast. He'd looked at the empties, sounded out the housekeeper and got Ruthie's minder to mark a few bottles.

If Ruthie was a drunk, she was a smart one. He knew she'd spotted the marks and kept the bottles topped up with water so that her real consumption was masked. But he smelt it on her breath sometimes, when he got close enough, which was bloody rare. Sometimes she concealed the alcohol tang with mints. She wasn't a fool. But she couldn't hide her bleary eyes or the way she staggered sometimes when she stood up. He looked at her, his wife, his Ruthie, and felt more miserable than he'd ever felt before.

'I just think I should spend some time with her, that's all,' said Ruthie mulishly. 'She isn't coping very well on her own. Of course, if she could come and stay here with me, I wouldn't have to go, would I?'

'She isn't moving into the annexe,' said Max.

'But Max . . .'

Christ, not this again! Ruthie was always

banging on and on about the same old thing. Max stood up. He was bored to the fucking back teeth. You could only say sorry so often before you started to feel that sorry ought to be accepted. He had apologized for what had happened with Annie, over and over again. But Ruthie was unforgiving. She used his guilt over the incident to beat him with whenever they argued. And they *always* argued. Fuck her, he thought. He'd had enough.

'Look, do whatever you want,' he said, 'but leave that fucking annexe alone, you got that?'

Not waiting for her to reply – he didn't need any more bloody earache – he left the room.

He tore across the hallway, grabbed his coat, then shot out the front door and into the car.

Even if his wife was in the process of leaving him, even if Eddie was dead, life had to go on. Max knew it. He was too tough to just give up and lie down. But he had too much other shit going on right now to go ahead with the job he'd been planning.

That was why he called the boys together that night in the office of the Blue Parrot and told them that the heist was definitely put back for next year. They didn't like it, but fuck them, they'd do as they were told. He gave them their orders and told them to bugger off. Jonjo didn't attend, he was out somewhere with another blonde. Max knew he'd have to weather that particular storm later on, Jonjo was keen to get the job done and he was going to be upset at the delay. But fuck him, too. Max sat alone late into the night in the office above the club, listening to Johnnie Ray seeping up through the floorboards.

The Prince of Wails, they called him. Johnnie went all through his repertoire and ended with 'Cry'. You had to hand it to the man, he could sell a tune. Better than these new boys, The Beatles or Billy J. Kramer and the Dakotas or Freddy and his Dreamers. Max preferred the songs from his twenties, the good balladeers like Sinatra, like Ray and Darin, those you simply could not beat.

The music was so emotive. When he listened to Johnnie Ray pouring his heart out in song he thought of Annie Bailey standing in the graveyard when they'd planted poor little Eddie.

She'd looked more beautiful than ever. Polished, somehow. Grown up. No longer the dolly bird, but a woman in a chic suit, her dark hair neatly groomed. She'd looked almost odd among the rough crowds. She'd shone out like a beacon. Their eyes had met. There had been a spark of the old magic there. In the depths of tragedy, he'd felt a treacherous sexual arousal. Useless. His wife's sister.

What a fucking disaster his life was turning out to be.

23

The phone was ringing as Annie shot past it on the stairs. Chris, sitting like a well-fed Buddha just inside the door reading the *Daily Sketch*, reached out but she shook her head and snatched it up. It was Friday. Party day. She had decided that her parties would be held at lunchtimes, when all the other women in the road would be busy in their kitchens – too busy to take an interest in what was going on here. She was wound up fit to burst.

'Good morning, Miss Bailey,' said Redmond Delaney.

'Ah, Mr Delaney,' said Annie, hopping from one foot to the other in her impatience to get on. 'Good morning.'

'I hope you are well?'

'Very well. Thank you. And you?'

'I'm fine.'

Annie was getting used to the weekly calls now.

She didn't nearly shit herself with fear any more when she heard that cool Irish lilt on the end of the phone. Redmond was just keeping an eye on his business interests, that was all. It was nothing personal. It was sort of reassuring, really.

'Is everything ready for the party?' asked Redmond.

Darren and Aretha thundered down the stairs. Aretha went into the front room, but Darren paused. *Who is it?* he mouthed.

Redmond Delaney, she mouthed back.

Oh, mouthed Darren. He threw Chris a flirty smile and followed after Aretha.

'Just about,' said Annie.

'Well, good luck with it.'

'Thank you, Mr Delaney.'

'I'll be in touch,' said Redmond, and put the phone down.

Annie did the same.

'Chris, what does Mr Delaney look like?' she asked thoughtfully. 'I've met his sister Orla. Is he like her?'

Chris laid his paper across his knees. 'Identical,' he said.

Annie had a think about that. A tall, red-haired, green-eyed man. Cool as could be. No small talk about him. Nothing like Kieron with all his blarney. Nothing like Pat either, Pat was a disgusting and frightening bruiser. Funny how one family could contain so many disparate elements.

'What about the mum and dad?'

'Molly and Dave?' Chris took up his *Sketch* again. 'Retired.'

No more information was forthcoming, so Annie decided to go up and get changed. Today she was the hostess, neat in a black shift, pearls and black-patent-leather pumps, nothing tarty. Nothing to suggest she was a player instead of an observer. Hopefully all their regulars would be here to have fun and spend money both on the door and upstairs in the bedrooms. Drinks on the house. Food on the house. It had to work, she thought. Or she was going to end up looking a right berk.

As she came downstairs the phone was ringing again. She waved Chris away and picked up.

'Annie darling, will you sit for me tomorrow morning?' asked Kieron.

'No, Kieron, I can't.' There would be clearing-up to be done. She anticipated a lot of mighty hangovers among the staff too.

'Afternoon?' wheedled Kieron.

'Is this the last time?' groaned Annie.

'Last one, I promise.'

She'd sat for him for the nude portrait three times now, lying there in the altogether feeling horribly self-conscious. She hated it. But if this really was the last time, she supposed she could bear it. And the pay was good. If the party idea bombed and no one showed up, she was going to need every penny. Dolly came clumping down the stairs in her dressing gown. Annie put a hand over the phone.

'Dolly, will you sort yourself out?' she asked, shooing her back up. 'It's nearly eleven, get clean, tidy and dressed.'

Dolly pulled a face. 'Oh for fuck's safe, what is it with you? There's plenty of time yet,' she said.

'Dolly, what did I tell you? What did I say?' asked Annie.

Dolly sighed. 'You said . . .'

'I said it's my way or the fucking highway,' said Annie. 'Go and get ready.'

Dolly looked pissed off but she did as she was told. Annie was pleased at how Dolly was coming along, on the whole. Poor Dolly. Celia had been too easy on her, she needed a firmer hand, but Annie could appreciate why Celia had been so lenient. Celia had explained to Annie about Dolly's background. Annie got the horrors every time she thought of how Dolly had been dragged up.

Poor cow, a backstreet abortion with an enema syringe and half a packet of Daz was enough to turn any woman sour. And to know that the dead child that came away was your father's . . . it was nothing less than a nightmare. Celia had told her all about it.

Celia. God, she'd been so busy she'd hardly had a second to think about her, but she thought about her now, wondered where she was, wondered if she was okay. She'd been watching the post since Celia went, hoping for a letter, for even a fucking postcard, anything would be good. But there was nothing – no news, no contact. She thought of asking Redmond Delaney if he had a clue where her aunt had got to, but she knew she couldn't do that. Her conversations with Redmond were always business, never personal. It was an unwritten rule.

Annie sighed and said to Kieron: 'Tomorrow afternoon. Two o'clock until three, Kieron, I can't spare more. See you.'

Ol' Blue Eyes was booming out from the front room.

'Not so *loud*,' shouted Annie. Jesus! The neighbours!

'Sorry,' yelled Aretha and Darren as she joined them. She quickly tweaked down the volume and looked around the room. It looked good. She popped open a bottle of bubbly.

'I've been putting the word round to my regulars,' Darren was saying. He was looking very dapper in purple cords and a matching flowered shirt.

'Mine too. God, hope we don't get any more of those Golden Rainers showin' up at the door,' said Aretha. 'I don't mind kinky, but a girl has to have her limits.'

Annie handed them each a glass. Living at Celia's place had quickly proved to her what an innocent she was. Now she knew that Golden Rainers were men who liked to be pissed on. The diversity of their clients' sexual tastes was a constant source of amazement to her, but she was fast becoming unshockable.

'To us,' said Annie as Ellie and Dolly joined them. Everyone was done up to the nines; they all looked good, and they knew it. They raised their glasses. 'And to the success of our parties.'

They clinked their glasses together as the doorbell rang. Annie tweaked up Frank and deftly removed the covers from the food. The ambience was good, with candles on the mantelpiece and soft side lights, and lovely comfy seats. She looked around and nodded with satisfaction.

'First client,' she said, as she heard Chris opening the door. There was a pause. Chris was taking the client's coat and accepting payment. They drank and pasted smiles on their faces as the first punter came into the front room.

'Hello,' said Annie brightly, extending a hand to the gentleman, one of Ellie's older regulars, and putting on her best posh voice. All right, she knew it wasn't her. She had her roots and was never going to deny them. But this was business. The punters would expect a lady, and if that was what they wanted, that's what they'd get. 'How *lovely* to see you again. Come and sit down.'

The party was on.

Annie sat at the kitchen table next morning and reviewed the situation. She was not as unshockable as she'd thought. The party had gone with a swing, but it wasn't a tea, dinner or bloody wine-and-cheese party with one of those new-fangled fondue sets at the centre of the table for dipping. It was a *sex* party, and the twenty-four gentlemen (she had anticipated twelve, tops) who had shown up had expected some pretty lively entertainment to be on offer.

Dolly had soon proved her worth. Dolly could take on three men without even drawing breath. And Aretha had quickly provided a large proportion of their public-school gents with what they craved, which was to be tied up, handcuffed, blindfolded and soundly thrashed while she wore a selection of open-crotch panties and cut-out bras. Darren had set to and serviced the gentlemen who craved male rather than female attentions, and Ellie with her gentle wheedling ways was a favourite with the older gents who might take just a little longer over their fun.

Throughout all this Annie had kept a straight face and dispensed drinks and food to keep the revellers nourished while they played. Chris, equally po-faced, had kept a discreet eye out for people getting too drunk or abusive, but everyone behaved themselves. Chris, Annie realized, was a wonderful visual deterrent to bad behaviour.

By four in the afternoon it was over. The place looked like a bomb had struck. All the workers were hung over and battle-weary. But then they had to set to and get it all cleaned up ready for the evening's trade.

Now the dust had settled and Annie was counting out the proceeds on the kitchen table. She was coming to the conclusion that Celia had been a fool. She'd been sitting on a fucking gold-mine and hadn't exploited the fact. Annie realized that she needed three or four more girls for the parties, and she needed a skilled barman too, how the hell was she to know what went into a Gin Sling? But these were minor problems, she thought as she counted out the loot. In all her time at Celia's place, Annie had never seen money flooding in like this.

There was a knock at the back door. Annie jumped. She could see a shadowy figure out there through the frosted glass. A hat, the bulk of a man. Chris had heard it too. He came hurrying purposefully through from the hall.

'It's okay, Chris, it's only Billy,' Annie realized, scooping up fivers and tenners and quickly shoving them in the dresser drawer.

Jessie Keane

Chris let Billy in. Billy preferred the company of women, and he was uneasy around macho men like Chris. He looked nervously at the man-mountain.

'Chris, this is Billy, a friend of ours – Billy, meet Chris, our new doorman,' said Annie.

'Hello Billy,' said Chris. He looked annoyed. Annie knew that he had spent a lot of time over sharpening up security; it shouldn't have been possible to even reach the back door. And he'd told Annie that she needed something solid there, not a door with glazing, but she liked the light it let into the kitchen. 'How did you get round the back there?'

Billy looked awkward. 'I climbed over the fence,' he said.

Annie could see Chris making a mental note that involved higher fences and barbed wire. She suspected her nice frosted-glass door was soon to be bound for the tip. Billy had always used the back door, and in his mind that was the only door to use. Annie understood that, but Chris didn't.

'Use the front door in future, okay?'

Billy nodded and blushed.

'Come and sit down and have a cup of tea with me,' said Annie, putting the kettle on while Chris went back to his business. 'How are you, Billy?'

'I'm very well. Are you well, Miss Bailey?'

Although Billy thought of her as 'his beautiful

Annie', he would never dream of addressing her by her first name. His mum had brought him up to respect ladies and to treat them properly. He sat down at the kitchen table, his briefcase on his lap. He removed his deerstalker. You didn't keep your hat on when there was a lady present.

'I'm fine. Keeping busy, you know. Biscuit?'

'Thank you.' Billy paused. He wasn't sure whether he should say it, maybe Max wouldn't like everyone knowing his business. But Annie wasn't *everyone*, Annie was a Bailey, and family was important. His mum had always hammered that home to him. 'I came to tell you that Mrs Carter is back living with Mrs Bailey.'

Annie dropped the biscuit tin. She turned and stared at Billy. 'Ruthie's moved back in with Mum?' she said.

'I thought you would want to know.' Billy looked at her anxiously. 'I didn't want to upset you.'

Annie snatched up the tin. 'You haven't upset me, Billy,' she said. Flaming hell, did that mean that Ruthie and Max were over? Was this a permanent split?

Billy was afraid that he had upset Annie. Suddenly she looked distracted. He hoped not. He loved coming here and seeing her, they were so kind to him here. It had always been a nice warm place, a bit of a haven for him, even when Madam Celia had been here. When she had gone, Billy

Jessie Keane

feared he would no longer be welcome, but his beautiful Annie seemed to have taken over where Celia left off.

Actually he wasn't too clear about what they did here. He knew they paid protection to the Delaneys, just as places like this on Max's patch paid protection to the Carters. That was just the way things were. But as to what they got up to, upstairs in their bedrooms, Billy wasn't too sure about that. He had a feeling that they did dirty things. The same sort of things Mum had warned him about, the things that would make him go blind, she said – things that he sometimes did himself, much to his shame, but only ever alone in the privacy of his room.

And now here she was, chatting to him like she was interested in what he had to say! He was in heaven. When she'd upset Max – he didn't know how but she had – he'd been afraid she would move right away, that he would lose her for ever. But here she was, talking to him. And then the phone rang, and Chris poked his head round the kitchen door.

'It's Kieron, Miss Bailey,' said Chris.

'Oh no,' said Annie. 'I'm late. I know I'm late. I'm coming, tell him.'

'She's coming,' said Chris into the phone.

Annie ran out into the hall. 'Kieron, I'll be about half an hour,' she said.

A pause. Billy listened.

'Look, Kieron, you know I was reluctant to do this in the first place.'

Billy's attention sharpened. Was this 'Kieron' making Annie do something she didn't want to? His mind churned. Not something like they did in the bedrooms upstairs?

'I said from the start, didn't I, that I didn't want to be lying there in my birthday suit for all to see? I don't like it.'

Billy felt himself blush uncomfortably at what she was saying. What was this man doing to her, that she had to be naked? He thought he knew. His mum had told him about the birds and the bees and how only dirty people did things like that. His jaw clenched in anger. This wasn't right, this man forcing Annie to do things against her will.

'Okay, Kieron, half an hour,' Annie said, and walked back into the kitchen only to find that Billy was gone. He'd only drunk half his tea. The back door was standing open and the rain was coming in. She closed it, paused for a moment to think again about what Billy had told her, then quickly got back to counting out yesterday's takings. She had to scoot. It might only be Kieron, but you didn't keep a Delaney waiting.

24

At four o'clock on a Sunday morning an arsonist slipped a rag soaked with lighter fuel through the letterbox of the Galway Club. Then the arsonist did the same at the Liberty. The clubs were both owned by the Delaneys. By five o'clock the fire brigade were in attendance, hosing both places down. By six, dawn was breaking and the twin jewels in the crown of the Delaney empire were nothing more than smouldering wrecks, black and gutted, open to the early morning rain. By seven, Orla and Redmond and Pat Delaney were outside the Galway looking at the wreckage. At seven-thirty, Kieron showed up, bleary-eyed and incredulous as he saw what had happened.

'Fucking *Carters*,' Pat roared, and hit the blackened wall.

The police were there, standing some distance away. They knew the score. This was a gangland reprisal. They had already taken details from Redmond, but every one of the Delaneys knew that the Bill would take the paperwork back down the station and promptly lose it. They had enough work on their hands policing law-abiding citizens, they wouldn't trouble themselves over mob fights.

'You think it was them?' Kieron asked, open-mouthed with shock.

'Give the boy a coconut,' sneered Pat.

'Because of what happened to Eddie Carter?'

Pat said nothing but kicked the wall.

Kieron looked at Redmond and Orla, both standing there like statues, saying nothing. He hadn't ever allowed himself to think about what had happened to Eddie Carter. But at the back of his mind was a suspicion that his family had been involved. They might not have done the deed, but he suspected they had been behind it.

Pat was violent and a natural-born liar, and Kieron knew it. Pat had always been a loose cannon. But hadn't Pat also been keen to get the family involved in the lucrative drugs trade? He'd talked about it to Orla in front of Kieron and, although Redmond had said no, Kieron knew that Pat chafed under his brother's rule. They all knew that Pat wanted to be boss after Tory got himself killed. Maybe Pat had done some independent work and stirred up a hornet's nest. Maybe this wasn't the Carters at all. Maybe Pat had started getting interested in dealing and had stepped on someone's toes.

Maybe, maybe, maybe. Kieron stared at the wreckage of the Galway, Tory's favourite of their two clubs, named for their Irish homeland. All gone now. As usual he found that he had to cut dead all thoughts of his family business. He had never been a part of it. They were involved in dangerous games. It was a nightmare to him, and that was why he had stayed away so long, travelling the world, forgetting where the wherewithal that allowed him to do so had come from. From crime. From gambling dens and prossies and casinos and dodgy deals and intimidation. He'd shied away from it. Enjoyed the privileges it bought, yes, but turned his head away from the facts of his family's livelihood.

Now it was staring him in the face. At least they were honest about it all; whereas he was just a fucking hypocrite. He was glad Mum and Dad were back in the old country and didn't have to see this.

His exhibition was starting tonight in Toby Taylor's Jermyn Street gallery. Toby was a crime junkie. He nearly had an orgasm just talking to the Delaneys. He got high on the danger of it, tried to dress like Redmond, treated Orla like a queen. When Kieron Delaney asked about an exhibition, he'd turned him down flat. Fuck it, Toby said, he had Hockney lined up, he was having talks with Lucian Freud, he'd exhibited Warhol just last year, he was *hot*. Who needed a fucking no-hope novice? But then Kieron had given in and told Toby he was one of *the* Delaneys. He'd uttered the magic word. Toby was all over him now like hives.

Kieron had been at the gallery all weekend, working on getting the positions of the canvases just right and checking that the lighting did them justice. The nude of Annie was smack in the centre of the thing, visible the instant the punters walked through the door, raised up above all the other works, stairs ascending to either side of it. He'd sweated hard over the exhibition, had gone to bed in a state of high excitement and happy exhaustion.

Now this. A reminder.

What was it Annie had said? That the gallery-owners wouldn't say no to him, because he was a Delaney. She was right, and he knew it. It soured his achievement more than a little, to know people so feared his family. So did he have this exhibition because he was a great artist – or because Toby Taylor didn't want his gallery to burn to the ground one night, or to find himself lacking a pair of kneecaps?

He knew the answer to that. All too well.

'I'm going home,' he said, turning away sick at heart.

Maybe he should stay and comfort Orla, but he knew from years of experience that she and Redmond were a pair, entirely co-dependent. As for Pat, big stupid bully that he was, banging on walls and snorting with rage, what a joke. Kieron didn't even recognize Pat as his brother any more. He didn't miss Tory. Tory had been a bastard. The *worst* kind of bastard. He wished Mum and Dad could be here. Ah, but they were old now, too old to stomach all this shit. Better for them to be where they were. The game was changing. The game was getting too dangerous.

25

'Oh Christ, not you again. I've been wondering when you'd show up to gloat.'

What a welcome. Annie stood on the doorstep and wished she was somewhere, anywhere, else.

She looked at her mother through the fug that was seeping out of the half-open front door. God, what a pesthole this whole place was. Funny how when she'd been living around here she'd never noticed the litter in the streets or the dog mess on the pavements, or how scraped and battered Connie's front door was, or how Connie never cleaned her front step or got the window sills painted, or how the new nets Connie had splashed out on for Ruthie's wedding were now coffee-coloured and caked rigid with dirt.

'I haven't shown up to gloat, Mum,' said Annie flatly. 'I've shown up to see Ruthie.'

Or at least this had been her intention when

she'd got up and dressed this morning. Her stomach had been churning with nerves ever since. It had been so long since she'd seen her sister. She'd had that brief glimpse at Eddie's funeral, but that hadn't helped; Ruthie had been as changed and as remote as a total stranger.

'She don't want to see you. I don't know how you've got the nerve to ask.'

Annie held on to her temper. When she looked at Connie she felt a sort of sad contempt. Connie was as scruffy as this shit-tip of a rented house. God knows how she kept up the payments. Annie didn't even want to think about that. Maybe Ruthie pitched in to help? Annie didn't suppose Connie was up to working any more. Her mother was more to be pitied than hated.

'Why don't we let her decide that?' said Annie. 'Is she in?'

'Yes, she's in,' said Ruthie, stepping into the doorway beside Connie.

Annie looked at her sister and was suddenly struck dumb. No, this wasn't the Ruthie she had known all her young life. This was a cool, sophisticated woman with pain-filled eyes. Pain that *she* had caused. Annie swallowed and licked her dry lips.

'Hello, Ruthie,' she said.

'Hello Annie. Well, aren't you coming in?'

'You don't have to see her if you don't want

to,' said Connie, looking at Annie with open dislike.

'What good would that do?' asked Ruthie. 'Let her in, for God's sake, Mum.'

They went through to the kitchen. There were plates piled high in the sink and on the draining board. The lino was scuffed and sticky underfoot. The stove looked as if it hadn't been cleaned for a month. Annie sat down at the kitchen table, looking carefully at the chair before she did so. Ruthie sat too, and smiled grimly as she saw Annie's mouth thin with disgust at their surroundings. Jesus, thought Annie, she lived in a flipping knocking shop but she would never stomach this sort of mess around her! Surely, even if Connie was too drunk or bone-idle to clear up, Ruthie could shift herself and do it?

But this wasn't the Ruthie of old. She had to keep reminding herself of that. This Ruthie didn't do housework. This Ruthie had sleekly dressed hair and polished nails. This Ruthie wore a smart two-piece suit not dissimilar to the one Annie wore. Fuck it, they looked like two flamingos perched on a muck-heap in here! The thought was amusing, but Annie didn't share it. Ruthie wouldn't see the joke. Ruthie's face – so much thinner than it used to be – was set in grim lines. She didn't look like she'd laughed in a long, long time. *And that's my fault*, thought Annie. She felt shrivelled inside with the guilt of it.

'Don't think you're getting a fucking cup of tea,' snorted Connie, hovering threateningly over Annie, scattering venom and fag ash and drink fumes. 'What did you think I'd do, roll out the bloody red carpet for a cheap little whore like you?'

'*Mum*,' said Ruthie loudly.

'Well, she's got a fucking nerve, showing up here. Hasn't she done enough damage?'

'Just give us a few minutes, will you Mum?' asked Ruthie coolly.

Connie withdrew, leaving the kitchen door open into the hallway. Ruthie got up and shut it. She sat back down and looked at Annie.

'So,' she said. 'What is it you've come for, Annie?'

'I've come to see how you are.'

Ruthie looked at her blankly. 'You've come to see how I am,' she echoed. Then she laughed. 'I'll tell you how I am, shall I Annie? I'm surviving. That's all.'

'Ruthie, I'm sorry.'

Ruthie nodded. 'You should be.'

'I wish you were happy, Ruthie. I really do.'

'Well I'm not.' Ruthie's eyes were hard. 'Let me tell you about my life, Annie. I spend a lot of time sitting alone in that mausoleum in Surrey now that poor little Eddie's gone. If I go out to get my hair done or to go shopping I have to take my minder with me. The stockbrokers' wives with their little

201

Pony Club kids and their twinsets and pearls don't like my accent or my dodgy connections and they shun me. I don't see my husband very often, he's a busy man, but when I do we're at each other's throats. Mum's in bits on her own but Max won't let her come and stay with us because she might mess up Queenie's rugs or leave drink stains on the tables. So I came back to the Smoke. I go out to the shops here, but still I've got to take my minder with me. The shopkeepers all serve me first, before all the other women. I go straight to the front of the queue, even if I don't want to. I have to apologize for that, but the other women say, oh don't worry, we're not in a rush. But they stare at me and they hate me and they envy me. They're afraid of me. Or rather they're afraid of Max. That's my life, Annie. That's my life.'

Suddenly there were tears in Ruthie's eyes. Instinctively Annie put out a comforting hand, but Ruthie snatched hers away.

'Don't you *dare* pity me,' she said.

'I don't,' lied Annie.

'I'd rather be me than you,' sniffed Ruthie, her expression one of disgust. 'Running a massage parlour! For God's sake, whatever possessed you to get sucked into all that?'

'Mum threw me out,' Annie reminded her. 'Where the hell else could I have gone? And Celia always liked me.'

'And now she's left you in charge?'

'Yes.'

'You ought to be careful,' said Ruthie. 'You'll get all sorts banging on your door.'

Don't I know it, thought Annie. But the parlour had been her lifeline. She was busy expanding it. Fuck it, she was *proud* of the work she'd done there. It had been running at a quarter of its full capacity under Celia. Under Annie's rule, it was thriving.

'I'm always careful,' said Annie. 'So . . . are you and Max still together, Ruthie?'

Ruthie looked at her sister scornfully. 'Yes, we're still together. Contrary to rumour. I'm going back at the weekend, we're going to spend it together. Don't think you're going to step into my shoes, Annie Bailey. I'm still wearing them.'

'I don't,' said Annie, colouring.

'No?' Ruthie gave a derisive snort. 'He always wanted you, really. But he won't ditch me for you, Annie. Max doesn't dump his commitments. He isn't Jonjo. He takes his responsibilities seriously.'

'I don't want him to,' said Annie, standing up sharply.

'Sure you don't,' scoffed Ruthie.

'I don't!' God, was she trying to convince Ruthie or herself? Flustered, Annie snatched up her bag. Her cheeks felt hot. She looked at Ruthie. 'I just wanted to see you,' she said.

'What for? To see the damage you've done?' snapped Ruthie.

'We were so close before,' said Annie.

'Before? You mean, before you fucked my bridegroom?'

It wasn't like Ruthie to swear. But then this was a different Ruthie – hardened and sharpened by life, by all that had happened to her. Annie stared at her and could see nothing of the Ruthie she had known and loved. Nothing at all.

'I'm sorry,' she said.

'Yeah,' said Ruthie. 'Of course you are.'

26

'I think he's had enough,' said Annie, passing through the hallway and pausing to look at what Aretha was up to.

More and more Annie was becoming blasé about the sex parties. Men were a strange lot, straight sex seemed to be the last thing on their mind. One client had begged her to let him redecorate the kitchen – while stark naked of course – while Aretha whipped the crap out of him and told him to do it better. Annie had declined his request. The kitchen was off-limits to clients. Men! What a bloody strange bunch they were. In her limited experience, women were so much easier to please. Most women wanted a nice warm one-to-one cuddle – blokes wanted much more diverse pleasures.

'Why? He's a very naughty boy,' purred Aretha.

This was becoming a practised part of their little act. Aretha was the slave mistress, the beater and abuser dressed in a leather basque and holding the whip, Annie was the prudishly clad, sweet voice of discipline and reason who said enough was enough. It was good cop/bad cop, really. Which was ironic, when you considered that the bloke who was strung up from the stairwell was a chief inspector.

'Who's a naughty boy then?' asked Aretha, biting pineapple and cheese from a cocktail stick and then giving the copper a playful stab in the buttocks with the point. He shrieked with ecstasy and writhed about.

Frankly, Annie had seen prettier sights than this middle-aged man, his fat arse slick with baby oil, hung up there like a sodding Christmas ham. It tickled her that Chris was still sitting by the front door, his face impassive. He could have been a eunuch standing guard in a harem for all the interest he showed in the proceedings.

'Another ten minutes.' Annie looked at the alarm clock set up on the hall table. It would ring at three o'clock in the afternoon, announcing to their visitors that it was time to get gone. She was always relieved at this point, however much she became accustomed to what happened here. Dolly was upstairs with two punters, Ellie was drinking sherry with one of their dear old fellows in the front room. Darren had a judge upstairs, doing God knew what. Connie Francis was belting out her latest on the radiogram, Annie loved that song.

She was tired now, tired of smiling and being Madam. Their new barman, Brian, was boxing up the empties, putting the dirty glasses to one side. All the food had been cleared today. It had been a busy party, and very profitable. No trouble, either. All in all, a good day's work.

Annie went through to the kitchen and put the kettle on. She kicked off her courts and sighed with pleasure. You couldn't beat a cup of tea and a sit-down at the kitchen table with all your mates to talk over the day together. She looked around her happily, then frowned at the new kitchen door.

Not frosted glass now. She didn't like it, but this one was solid wood, with a peephole and a Yale lock. At the kitchen window, which looked out over a tiny square of garden, there was now an iron grid. There was also a discreet strip of barbed wire on the fence at the bottom of the garden and the side of the house, and a solid securely locked side gate had replaced the pretty, white painted, wrought-iron one that used to be there.

None of this pleased Annie. She felt like she was living in fucking Stalag 13, and the wooden door blocked out a lot of light from the kitchen. Everyone was admitted from the front of the house now. No surprises, nasty or otherwise. She picked up Chris's paper from the table and browsed through it, stopping dead when she came across a piece about two nightclubs being burned to the ground. Arson was suspected. The clubs were owned by the 'influential' Delaney family, it said. Enquiries were ongoing.

Annie sat down at the table. Yeah, sure, she thought. The Bill were sure to enquire closely about what happened to gangland clubs, weren't they. She hugged herself and shivered. She'd been feeling down since going over to Mum's to see Ruthie. She didn't know what she'd expected. Maybe a tearful, happy reunion? Perhaps for Ruthie to hug her and say, there, there, it's all forgotten. To be forgiven for the unforgivable? What a fucking laugh. She'd told herself to buck up and get a grip. She'd done the deed, and these were the consequences. Still, she'd been undeniably low ever since. And now this!

Did the fires have anything to do with Eddie Carter falling off the twig? She couldn't forget her own involvement, or Darren's. Or the way Celia had bottled it and taken off, who the hell knew where. She looked again at the solid door and the metal grille over the window. No surprises, nasty or otherwise. Perhaps it was best to be on the safe side after all.

Redmond Delaney's call came at four o'clock that afternoon. Everything was cleared and ready for the evening's trade, Annie had luxuriated in a hot, deep bath, she'd got over the jitters. Wrapped in her thick towelling dressing gown, she came downstairs from her room at Chris' call and picked up the phone.

'Mr Delaney,' she said as Chris shook out his paper and took his usual seat in the corner by the front door. 'Are you keeping well?'

'Very well, Miss Bailey,' said Redmond. 'And you?'

'I'm good, Mr Delaney. Thank you.'

'And how is business?' he asked.

'Thriving,' said Annie. She considered mentioning the fires, but thought better of it. Her relationship with Redmond was strictly formal. She knew that any hint of familiarity would be met with a sharp rebuff.

'The barman is satisfactory?'

'Brian's perfect, Mr Delaney.' And I'm paying *his* wages out of my profits, thought Annie. But she couldn't complain. The profits were bloody good. 'I shall need more girls for the next party.'

'I'll put the word round,' said Redmond.

'Only nice girls,' said Annie. 'Presentable and clean and experienced.'

'Exactly so,' said Redmond.

'Maybe six?'

'Six it shall be,' said Redmond. 'Goodbye, Miss Bailey.'

'Goodbye, Mr Delaney,' said Annie, and started to put the phone down.

209

'Oh, Miss Bailey?' said Redmond.

'Yes, Mr Delaney?'

'I hope I shall see you at Kieron's exhibition on Saturday night?'

Annie nearly dropped the phone. 'Well . . . yes,' she said in surprise.

She hadn't planned to go, but she supposed she ought to put in an appearance, if only to give Kieron a bit of a boost. She was amazed that Redmond had mentioned it. This was surely crossing the line into informality. That wasn't like him.

'I look forward to it,' said Redmond, and the line went dead.

'Blimey,' said Annie.

'Problem?' asked Chris.

'No, not at all. Just Redmond Delaney being nice to me.'

Chris smiled and returned his attention to his paper. Annie put a call through to Kieron.

'Listen, am I invited to this shindig on Saturday? This exhibition thingy?' she asked.

'Of course you are, if you want to come. I didn't think you would.'

'Why not?'

'Because you've been such a reluctant sitter!' barked Kieron. 'Jaysus, you've acted right the way through as if I was trying to sell you into white slavery instead of painting your ruddy picture. I thought you'd hate to see the thing hung on a wall.'

'Sorry,' said Annie.

'Apology accepted. Come as my guest, I'll pick you up at eight, will that do you?'

'Hadn't you planned to take anyone else?'

'No, I hadn't. I'm a working artist, I haven't time to be chasing girls all around the town, you'll be doing me a favour. How about it then?'

'Okay,' said Annie. 'Saturday at eight.'

After she'd put the phone down she realized that she hadn't talked to Kieron about the fires, either. Ah, it was just as well. What would she say about it anyway? She didn't want to go treading on dangerous ground. She didn't want to know more than she knew already.

211

27

Toby Taylor was bricking it with excitement. He had never seen so many faces in one room at the same time. The Delaney twins had come to the opening, and the Regans were in with all their heavy friends. The Foremans of Battersea had already bought up several of Kieron Delaney's paintings out of respect to their Delaney colleagues. The Nash family were in too, and some of the real hard, heavy boys from New York, the Barolli lot. And the Kray twins. Fucking good job Eddie and Charlie Richardson had been nicked, because they had been mixing it with the Krays, which wasn't wise.

'Christ,' said Toby, mincing around the gallery with his long-term boyfriend Paolo. Vivaldi's *Four Seasons* was emanating discreetly from the expensive sound system. 'You can smell the testosterone in the air, can't you sweetie?'

Paolo nodded. He didn't share his older lover's taste for danger. These people looked like they could cut up rough in an instant. He didn't like it. Toby was a silly old queen, prancing around arse-licking to these people. Paolo thought that Toby was a joke with his spare tyre straining to get out of his pink floral shirt and his stupid toupee slipping sideways on his billiard ball of a head. Toby was sweating with excitement as the crowds grew thicker. The noise level rose with each bottle of Moët that was opened.

'Darling, sweetie,' said Toby as they stumbled across Kieron and Annie. 'Mwah, mwah.' Toby air-kissed either side of Annie's head. 'Don't you look absolutely *stunning*, what a wicked dress. Have you seen it? Have you seen it?'

It was very hard to miss, thought Annie. She'd been gob-smacked when she'd walked through the double doors at the front of the gallery and been instantly confronted by the painting of herself in the nude. It was placed at the centre of the landing above the big, double, open-tread staircase, cunningly lit and impossible to overlook. It made all Kieron's other work, the beautiful African landscapes and the finely detailed wild-life studies, fade into insignificance. *Everyone* had seen it.

'I've seen it,' said Annie.

'And aren't you *thrilled* with it?' demanded Toby, clutching clammily at her hand with his beringed and pudgy digits.

'It's very impressive,' said Annie.

'She hates it,' said Kieron with a laugh.

'I don't hate it,' said Annie. 'I just feel a bit, well, *exposed*.'

'But this is Art,' said Paolo in his charming Italian-accented English. 'It is an honour to be the subject of such an artist.'

'You won't convince her,' said Kieron. He chucked Annie under the chin. 'Cheer up, Annie. I'll go and get us another drink.'

Toby and Paolo took themselves off to mingle with Ronnie and Reggie. Annie went and looked at a painting of a snarling tiger. Anything rather than look at the painting that was capturing everyone else's attention.

'Gorgeous, isn't she,' she heard.

'Fantastic tits.'

Oh Jesus!

Annie moved further out of earshot. She was glad she'd chosen her discreet black dress and pearls to wear this evening. Like camouflage, it enabled her to move a bit more freely among the patrons and their wives and girlfriends. Not many of the women praised her tits, she noticed. They tended to admire the brush strokes and the texture of the paint rather than the jugs on the sitter.

'There you are.' Kieron was back with two brimming champagne flutes. 'What are you doing, hiding away over here? Why not get behind that cheese plant there and have done with it?'

Annie gave him a whack in the stomach. She wished they'd put something more lively on the sound system. Some Stones or Beatles, she liked them. All these violins wailing away depressed her.

'Ow,' complained Kieron.

'How would you feel, to have a roomful of people admiring your bits?' asked Annie, glancing around. There was a very polished and strikingly good-looking, silver-haired man in his late thirties across the room, looking at her. He was with two teenage boys, one dark, one fair, and a very hand-some middle-aged woman who looked faintly Italian.

'I'd feel flattered and proud,' said Kieron. 'I would probably give them my elephant impression as an encore.'

Annie slapped his stomach again, but she had to smile.

'Who's that?' she asked, curious, indicating the silver-haired man.

Kieron's gaze followed hers.

'Constantine Barolli. American mob, New York. They call him the silver fox. Loads of business inter-ests in the West End, it was Redmond's idea to invite him and his family tonight. Redmond's trying to woo him but Barolli seems to prefer doing busi-ness with the Carters. Those are his sons, I think.

There's a daughter too, a stunner, I wanted her to sit for me but her father wouldn't allow it.'

Annie looked back and her eye caught Barolli's again. She shivered.

Someone just walked over my grave, she thought.

Toby went hurrying past trailing his chiffon scarf and a worried-looking Paolo. Something about Toby's manner made Annie look more closely. Toby was a mob tart and at his happiest among bad lads, but now he looked genuinely alarmed.

'Kieron, I wonder if I could have a word with you about this fine job you've done over here,' said one of the Delaney's male hangers-on.

Kieron wandered off and Annie found Orla Delaney standing in front of her beside – Jesus! – a man who looked so like her it was incredible. His thick Titian hair was swept back off his pale face and his eyes were luminously green as they looked into hers. He was dressed in black, his turnout immaculate. He was very handsome and had a cool, unfazed demeanour. Orla was in black too, and against her long red hair it looked truly chic.

'Hello, Miss Bailey, do you remember me?' asked Orla, holding out a hand.

'Of course I do,' said Annie. Once seen, never forgotten – that was Orla Delaney. Celia had been here then. Annie had been gauche and over-whelmed. Now things were different. She shook Orla's hand coolly.

'This is my brother Redmond – Redmond, this is Miss Annie Bailey.'

'How nice to meet you at last, Miss Bailey,' said Redmond, shaking her hand too. His hand was cool and dry, his touch light. Just like Orla's. Annie found herself remembering what Kieron had said about the twins – that they were a pair, entirely independent from everyone except each other.

'Mr Delaney,' smiled Annie.

'We've only spoken over the phone,' Redmond explained to Orla. 'Miss Bailey has taken over Celia Bailey's business interests. Celia is her aunt.'

'Really?' Orla did her best to look interested. 'And how is business, Miss Bailey?'

'Good,' said Annie. 'Better than ever.'

A sort of hush was spreading around the room. It was coming from the doorway, where Toby and Paolo were fussing around some new arrivals. Annie looked and her mouth dropped open. It was Max Carter, with two heavies. There was a move-ment near Orla and Redmond as their minders drew in closer. Toby was glancing nervously back at Redmond and Orla, while Paolo was taking Max's coat. Redmond and Orla exchanged a look.

'Jaysus, what's he doing here?' asked Kieron, rejoining them.

Redmond paused. He looked across at Max, then at Toby. He nodded. Toby relaxed a bit. Then Redmond said: 'Mr Carter is very welcome.'

'Thank God Pat couldn't be bothered to turn up,' said Orla.

'*Very* welcome,' said Redmond. 'This is Kieron's night, and we want no trouble.'

And he walked off to where Max was standing, Orla and two heavies trailing behind him. Kieron edged up to Annie.

'That's Max Carter?' he said.

Annie nodded.

'That's the one you had the fling with.'

Annie gave him a look.

'Only asking,' said Kieron, and went off to get them something to eat.

Annie followed, anxious not to be anywhere near Max. She didn't trust herself. And where was Ruthie? If Max was coming to the gallery, couldn't he have given the poor cow a night out on the town? But then she knew the answer to that question. Max was here to make a big show of doing whatever he wanted, and fuck the Delaneys. If they wanted trouble, he'd provide it. That was the message.

They raided the buffet table, but Annie's appetite was gone and she gave most of her blinis with caviar and devils on horseback to Kieron, who wolfed them back. The evening wore on, everyone behaved themselves and Annie wished to God she was home in Celia's kitchen drinking tea and gossiping with Darren and the girls. Her feet hurt in her new high heels, and her head ached with tension. All she could think was *Max is here*.

Then the inevitable happened. Kieron nipped off to the bathroom and suddenly Max was standing in front of her.

'How's things, Annie?' he said. His minders were standing two paces behind him, looking at her with suspicion.

'Max,' she said, feeling almost dizzy because he was standing here, so close to her. 'I called in to see Ruthie at Mum's the other day,' she blurted out.

'Did you.' Max nodded.

Jesus, he was so gorgeous, she thought. That strong profile, the dark skin . . . his hair, so thick, so black. His eyes, blue as blue, bored into hers. She felt she could drown in those eyes.

'She's looking well,' said Annie.

'She's too skinny.'

'That's the fashion.'

'Yeah, it is.'

'It was a terrible thing about Eddie,' she said.

What the hell was he saying to her, wondered Kieron, watching them from a distance. He'd come out of the loo and was winding his way back to Annie's side when he'd stopped and looked ahead for the first time. The ready smile faded from his face. They were talking intensely, looking at each other so closely. He'd seen that kind of look before. Fuck it, Annie Bailey had never looked at him like that. And now he could clearly see why. She was still in love with this Max Carter, this fucking mobster. It would be obvious to a blind man, he thought, and felt a tightening in his guts that he hadn't experienced before. He had to think about it for a while before he recognized the sensation as jealousy.

28

If this was what love did to you, thought Annie irritably a few days later as she sat at her dressing table, then you could stuff it. She stared at her face in the mirror, looking for answers and finding none. Was this love? Or just lust? She didn't know. She'd only felt like this once before, she knew that much. And look at the trouble it had caused. It had been him that time and it was him again. It was *always* him. The bastard.

'Annie girl, you look like shit,' she told herself. She snatched up a hairbrush and tried to sort out the haystack which seemed to have landed on top of her head.

Bugger this, she thought, wrenching the brush through, punishing herself with the pain. But her insides were fizzing like she'd eaten a packet of Love Hearts. She was waking up at all hours of the night since the exhibition, lying there in the dark alone,

221

thinking of him. Of how good he looked, and – oh yes – of how his skin had felt against hers on that one night, that unforgettable night. The heat of him, the hardness, his hands that were so strong they were almost hurtful as they held her.

She had started biting her nails, something she hadn't done since Dad left home. She was off her grub too, and that wasn't like her. She'd be as thin as Ruthie soon, and then where the hell would she be?

She was considering taking up smoking fags, if only to relieve the tension. Out of the question to have a drink. She'd sipped some champagne at the exhibition, but she hadn't really enjoyed the taste. For her, drink was forever linked to her mother and memories of an endlessly miserable childhood. Connie lying on the sofa crying in self-pity, sodden with booze and bellowing orders, Annie or Ruthie having to go to the door to see the rent man, the baker, the milkman, and tell them Mum was out, to call back later, scared of what the tradesmen would say but scared of her even more. They were even frightened to go to school, because they never knew what they would come home to. Would they find her dead on the lounge floor, having choked on her own vomit? Or find an ambulance outside with Connie about to be whisked off to hospital?

Annie shuddered. Enough of all this. She put the brush down. At least her hair was straight now. She touched up her make-up, checked her black dress was clean, her pearls straight, her shoes gleaming. Showtime, she thought, and stood up and went downstairs to play hostess at yet another party.

Funny how used to all this she was getting. She was no longer shocked by naked arses, exposed breasts or rampant hard-ons. She oversaw it all with the calm discretion of a ringmaster. A leather-clad Aretha passed her at the top of the stairs, leading a blindfolded man dressed only in Y-fronts by a chain around his neck.

'One step more,' Aretha lied, because there were two steps and the man went sprawling on to the landing carpet. 'Stupid clumsy boy!' Aretha snapped, yanking the chain. The man groaned enjoyably and crawled along the landing into Aretha's room. Annie paused at the top of the stairs, shaking her head as she watched. There was music and laughter drifting out from the front room. She looked down into the hallway. Chris was there in his usual spot, and there was a bulky, sandy-haired man bending over him, whispering. Chris nodded, and something changed hands between them. Annie got a shock when the man turned and she saw that it was Pat Delaney. What the fuck was *he* doing here?

'Hello, Mr Delaney,' she said when she reached the downstairs hall. 'How are you?'

'Oh, I'm *spiffing*,' said Pat nastily.

223

Annie's smile tightened. 'Enjoying the party?' she asked.

'I told you once before, I wouldn't touch any of these tarts with someone else's, let alone my own,' said Pat with a sneer.

Then why are you here, you arsehole? she thought. She looked at Chris, but he was looking shifty. Not like Chris.

'Of course, if *you* were to offer me a shag, I might reconsider,' said Pat, wrapping his arm crushingly around Annie's shoulders.

Annie nailed her smile in place and gently but firmly detached herself. God, he was disgusting. Was he drunk? She couldn't smell booze on his breath, which was sour and unpleasant but not alcohol-induced. His eyes looked weird, his pupils were huge.

Chris was looking concerned and Annie could understand why. He didn't want to get into a ruck protecting Annie from one of the Delaneys; it was a clear conflict of interests.

'I told you, Mr Delaney,' said Annie. 'I'm a manager, not a worker.'

'Ah, all women are whores at heart,' said Pat. He winked at Chris. 'I'll catch you later, Chrissie boy,' he said, and lurched out the door.

There was a tense pause. Then Annie said: 'What's he on, Chris?'

Chris shrugged and his eyes slid away from hers.

'I won't have any rubbish in this house,' said Annie, but Chris did not respond. Annie went on into the front room, where Ellie and Darren were hard at work. She fixed her smile back on. Brian handed her the usual orange juice, but her mind was still on Pat Delaney, wondering what the fuck he really wanted.

29

Kieron phoned the following week. Now the exhibition was over, she'd expected not to hear from him again. After all, he'd been adamant that their relationship was strictly business. He was the artist, she was the model, and now their work was done.

'So how are you, Annie girl?' he asked.

Annie thought his voice sounded odd. Sort of different.

'I'm fine and dandy. And you?'

'Ah, fine.'

Silence.

'The exhibition went well, didn't it?' said Annie.

'Oh yes. I was pleased.'

'Did you sell much?'

'Every damned thing in the place.'

'Including the nude?' Annie wasn't going to ask, but the words sort of popped out.

'Yeah, including the nude.' A long pause. 'Actually,

Max Carter bought it. There was a bit of a bidding war going on between him and some other chap. Toby's been on cloud nine with it all. Put the price right up, so we did well.'

'Good.' Annie's heart was thumping sickly in her chest. Fuck it, she couldn't think about that. Not yet. 'I'm pleased for you,' she said.

'Was he bothering you?'

'Pardon?'

'At the exhibition,' said Kieron. 'Only I saw the two of you talking, and you seemed a bit awkward. Was he hassling you, Annie? Was that it?'

'No, he wasn't hassling me,' said Annie.

'Only I know there was something between the two of you at one time, you told me about it, you remember?'

God, why didn't he just shut up?

'I remember. But that was then and this is now, Kieron. That was a mistake. One best not repeated.'

'Won't it be?'

'What?' Annie stared at the phone. Chris was looking at her over the top of his paper. Jesus, she was blushing. She could feel herself getting hot.

'Repeated,' said Kieron.

'No.' She couldn't go there again. God, no. Never. Poor bloody Ruthie, hadn't she suffered enough? What would it do to her if all that started up again? Hadn't it hurt her enough the first time?

'Only I'm worried about you,' said Kieron.

'Well don't be,' snapped Annie. 'I'm a big girl, Kieron. I'm not a bloody kid.'

'Listen, it's none of my business,' said Kieron.

'Too fucking right it isn't.'

'Whoa! Don't bite my ruddy head off, I'm just concerned.'

'Kieron, who asked you?' said Annie, and slammed the phone down.

'Trouble?' asked Chris.

'No. No trouble.' *And even if I had trouble, would I discuss it with you?* Annie wondered. Since the last party when she had seen Pat and Chris in a huddle she had really started to worry about what was going down here. Was Chris selling drugs to her clients? Suppose the shit hit the fan one day and they had a raid. All right, it was unlikely. The Delaneys had plenty of tame coppers around here. But what if the unlikely happened? And what if they found drugs on the premises that *she* was in charge of?

It was a shame. She had taken to Chris straight away, but this had soured her feelings about him. She'd been aware for a long time that she had to be careful what she said to Ellie because it would go straight back to the Delaneys. Now she had to watch Chris too.

To cheer herself up she went up West and cleared out the shops. It helped, but only a little. Her mind was in a mess and it didn't help to come back and find a long black car and a driver outside her place. Her heart rate picked up to a gallop. It was him. It was Max.

But it wasn't. She went past Chris into the kitchen and found Ruthie sitting at the kitchen table.

'Fuck, you gave me a turn,' said Annie, dropping her bags and clutching at her chest.

'Sorry,' said Ruthie coolly. 'The man on the door said you should be back soon, so I thought I'd wait.'

Annie nodded. Christ, she felt bewildered. Her brain seemed to be in a fog. She took a hold of herself and put on her smile.

'Tea?' she offered brightly.

'No, give me something stronger,' ordered Ruthie.

Annie looked at her sister. It wasn't like Ruthie to boss people about. And it was two in the afternoon, and she wanted a drink? Ruthie might be beautifully turned out, but she looked even skinnier than when Annie had last seen her at Mum's. She might not be eating, but she was obviously drinking.

'Bit early, don't you think?'

'No, I don't think,' said Ruthie. 'Get me a sherry or something.'

Annie bit her lip and got down a bottle of Amontillado from the store cupboard. She put out a schooner and filled it. Ruthie, to her dismay, threw half of it back in an instant. Annie's heart seemed to freeze in her chest. This is my doing, she thought, I did this to my own sister.

'So, is this a social call?' asked Annie as she busied herself putting on the kettle.

'I got fed up at Mum's,' said Ruthie, polishing off the rest of the glass while Annie watched out of the corner of her eye, appalled. 'Kath's away on holiday, I thought it was time I came and paid my dear little sister a visit.'

Christ, she was already drunk. Her words were slurred. Ruthie held up her empty glass and tapped it.

'No, you've had enough,' said Annie firmly.

Ruthie grabbed Annie's arm with surprising strength. 'I'm Mrs Max Carter,' she shouted. 'I'll decide when I've had enough.'

Chris's head came round the hall door. 'Everything okay?' he asked.

'Everything's fine,' said Ruthie with a giggle.

'Yeah, it's okay Chris,' said Annie, wrenching her arm free. 'Thanks. Make sure we're not disturbed, will you?'

Chris looked at them both and then withdrew, closing the door softly behind him.

She sat down opposite Ruthie and looked at her.

'You want to kill yourself?' Annie asked. 'Haven't

you seen enough of what drink does to somebody? Haven't we both had years of it to know better?'

Ruthie shrugged and reached for the bottle. Annie grabbed her wrist. Ruthie winced. Annie was fitter and stronger than this wreck her sister had become.

'Ruthie,' she said, letting go. 'Whatever life's thrown at you, don't let it grind you down like this. Don't chuck it all away.'

Ruthie threw back her head and laughed. 'Jesus, advice on life from the husband-stealer!'

'All right, Ruthie. Listen. If you can't get over it, if you hate him so much, why go on with it? Get a divorce.'

'Oh no.' Ruthie shook her head. It waggled like a rag on a stick. 'What, and leave the way clear for little Annie? I don't think so.'

'You're only hurting yourself, Ruthie. What good is that?'

'I don't care,' said Ruthie, sloshing more sherry into her glass. 'I don't care about anything any more. I'm going back home tomorrow, back to Surrey. It's nice in the country. If you ignore the peasants.'

Ruthie roared with laughter, as if she had just said something extremely funny.

Annie looked at her sister, nonplussed. She had never thought of Ruthie as weak, but now she clearly saw that she was.

'I thought of having a baby,' said Ruthie. 'But you have to have *sex* to get babies. We don't even sleep in the same *bed* any more.'

This was more than Annie wanted to know. So their sex life was over. She should feel sad for her sister. Fuck it, she *did* feel sad for Ruthie, desperately sad. But a small, treacherous part of her was relieved.

'You're a young woman,' said Annie, hating herself for how she felt.

'Yeah, so I am.' Ruthie nodded vigorously as she slurped back another belt. She swallowed and then looked Annie dead in the eye. 'And you know what? I don't care whether I live or not.'

'Ruthie!'

'It's the truth. I don't care any more. About anything. Because you've ruined my life.'

Now Annie felt real anger take hold.

'For fuck's sake, Ruthie!' she burst out. 'I'm sorry as hell, I've said it over and over again, how many more times do I have to say it? I won't let you keep punishing me like this, it has to *stop*.'

And then Ruthie just sat there and sobbed.

30

'Good afternoon, Miss Bailey. I hope you're well?'

Thank God for Redmond Delaney and a sense of normality, thought Annie. Ever since the exhibition she had felt that she was losing her mind. Seeing Max had rattled her, seeing Ruthie so upset had rattled her even more. It was hard for her to keep on track, to keep everything running as it should, but somehow she was managing.

Dig deep and stand alone, she thought. She had to carry on doing that however hard it might be.

She had started making elaborate plans, frantically occupying her thoughts with business, trying to cope with her emotional disorder through diversion. When she heard that deep cool, Irish voice on the phone, it steadied her somehow. And now she had a face to put to the voice. Handsome, chilly Redmond Delaney. Twin to Orla and brother to sweet and scatty Kieron – not to mention that disgusting lout Pat.

'I'm very well, Mr Delaney. And you?'

'Perfectly fine, thank you. How is business?'

'I'm going to expand,' said Annie.

'Indeed?'

'The parties are going so well I'm going to have them three times a month. We can't cope with the demand and we don't want too many punters in here at any one time.'

'That's good news, Miss Bailey.'

'Also, I've been thinking.'

'Yes?'

'Quite a few of our clients are prosperous professionals, Mr Delaney. They need a place to go that's close to the City – to Whitehall.'

'I see.'

'So in addition to this business, I'm also planning to rent an apartment – a nice one – perhaps in Mayfair?'

'That will be expensive.'

'Not if you chip in half the rent.'

There was a short silence before he came back: 'We'll need to renegotiate my cut.'

'That goes without saying,' said Annie, who had already thought all this through.

'By the very nature of the business, the rentals may have to be short-term. If you are not in our area other interests may come into play. Neighbours may have more influence. You will have to be cautious. And extremely discreet.'

'Yes, I do realize that.'

'Find a suitable property and we'll talk again, Miss Bailey.'

'Thank you, Mr Delaney.'

'Was there anything else?'

Annie glanced over at Chris, sitting there like Buddha in the corner. Not the time or the place to tell Redmond about her suspicions regarding Pat, she thought. Maybe Redmond knew, anyway. Maybe Redmond didn't care.

'No, there's nothing else.'

'Goodbye then.'

Ruthie was right, Annie thought. She was sitting on a powder keg. One dropped spark, and pow! A feeling of fatalism was coming over her. Sooner or later it was all going to erupt around her. But for now, she was alive. She was in charge. She was Madam Annie. The minute she put the phone down she shouted up the stairs for Ellie. A dark head appeared over the banister.

'Get smartly dressed, Ellie,' said Annie. Ellie knew that 'smart' meant 'nothing tarty'. Ellie could look like a novice nun when she set her mind to it. Her 'novice nun' was in fact very popular with some of the clients, nearly as popular as her 'schoolgirl'.

Annie had every confidence in her ability to appear demure. 'We're going up West to do some business.'

'Jesus H Christ in a sidecar,' said Ellie two and a half hours later. Annie gave her a sharp nudge. 'Sorry,' she muttered. 'But look at it, Annie. Just fucking-well *look* at this place.'

Annie was looking. She was looking and she was wondering what it would be like to actually live here. It was a high-ceilinged, bright and incredibly big apartment set in a gorgeous block on the corner of Oxford Street and Park Street. Buck House was just up the road. So was the Ritz, just a step away in Piccadilly. The Houses of Parliament were close by too. It was a perfect place in a perfect location. There was a private balcony and even porterage.

'Someone to carry your stuff up for you,' said Annie when Ellie gave her a questioning look.

There was a lift. There were two beautiful bathrooms. The apartment was furnished in luxurious gold and pale blue tones, offset by a warm, muted cream. It was the most exquisite, the most truly luscious place Annie had ever seen. It damn near brought tears to her eyes, it was so lovely.

'So ladies – what do you think?' asked the estate agent, emerging from one of the bathrooms and beaming from ear to ear.

Christ, even the estate agents in this area looked

prosperous, thought Annie. He had a healthy tan and lustrously styled hair. His suit looked like Savile Row, elegantly pinstriped and teamed with white shirt, gold cufflinks and discreet silk tie. You could have made your face up in the reflection off his shoes, she thought. The bastard looked *rich*. Fortunately, so did she. Or rather *Anne* Bailey did. Anne. Like the Princess, she had told him and smiled charmingly when she shook his hand. And so did her little sister for the day, whom she introduced with a flourish as Elisa.

This was the third flat they had viewed. The first had taken her breath away, and she had been inclined to go for that one – but it was slightly further out than she really wanted, although it boasted stunning views over Green Park. Then the next. Dazzling, alluring. But a little dark with a lot of wood panelling. But this one. This was *it*.

'We'll take it,' she said.

They went back to his office and Annie wrote out a cheque for six months' rent in advance. A staggering amount. But she'd been busy saving a large wodge of her considerable profits. She could, for the first time ever, afford to follow a whim.

Chris drove them back to Limehouse stopping on the way, at Annie's instruction, so that she could make a call from a phone box.

'It's urgent,' she said. 'Something I forgot.'

She phoned through to Redmond Delaney and

kept her back turned to Chris and Ellie, who were both waiting in the car. She told him that Pat Delaney had shown up at her last party, that he appeared to be on something and that he had passed something to Chris.

Redmond took it all in silently.

The pips went. Annie shovelled in more change.

'I'll look into it,' said Redmond.

'I'd rather he didn't know I told you,' said Annie.

'Of course.'

'I got the flat,' said Annie.

'Good work, Miss Bailey. Get the details to me as soon as you can.'

'Of course,' said Annie, and rang off.

She was moving on up. Everything was going to be all right. But she felt jittery. She got back in the car, clutching the flat details to her. She sat there staring out at the traffic and reviewing her recent past with blank amazement. Funny how Billy hadn't called in for a while. She almost missed the poor loon, he'd become a familiar face to her. But she supposed he was intimidated, being confronted by Chris every time he called. It wasn't something she could help. Chris was necessary now. Protection. Security. She lay back against the leather upholstery as Ellie prattled away excitedly beside her and thought what it would be like to just take off to that beautiful Mayfair flat on her own, to live there as Miss Anne Bailey, happy and prosperous. To forget Celia's place and the danger and the excitement of running it. *Sure*, she thought. And live on what? Peanuts?

The big black car was outside the house again when they got home, the driver sitting stolidly behind the wheel, waiting.

Ruthie! thought Annie, anxiety and anger gripping her. She tore through the hall and flung open the door to the front parlour.

'Look, Ruthie, if you've come here for another bloody row . . .'

But it wasn't Ruthie waiting to see her.

It was Max.

Every time she saw Max Carter she was hit by the sheer physical impact of him. Of course whoever had let him in had shown him into the front room, not the kitchen. You didn't show Max into a kitchen.

Annie stood frozen in the doorway for a moment.

Chris came up close and hissed: 'You want me to phone Redmond?' in her ear.

Annie shook her head. 'I'll deal with this. See that nobody disturbs us, will you?'

She went into the front room and closed the door behind her and leaned against it, breathless, heart hammering crazily in her chest.

'Sorry. I thought you were Ruthie,' said Annie. Her mouth was dry.

'She's been here then?' said Max.

'Yeah,' said Annie coolly. 'Can't seem to make up her mind whether your marriage is dead or alive, but she was here. You mean you didn't know she called?'

'I don't own her.'

'Sorry, I thought you did.'

Max nodded. Slowly he came over to where she stood, placed one large hand on the door beside her head, and leaned in.

'You've got a fucking nerve, Annie Bailey, talking to me like that,' he said.

'Ruthie might be afraid of you,' said Annie. 'I'm not.'

'No?' Max was half-smiling as he came in closer still. He knew the effect he had on her.

Annie gulped. 'No,' she said.

'You've changed, Annie. Look at you. You're all grown up now,' he said, his eyes moving over her.

Annie nodded. 'I had to grow up fast, Max. I got kicked out by my mother, remember? If I hadn't been able to come here I'd have been walking the streets.'

'Is this what you wanted out of life, running a knocking shop?'

Annie shrugged, trying to be cool, but her heart was racing and now – *oh shit!* – her nipples were hard. The flat details in her hand were crumpled

240

and damp, forgotten. She wished he'd back off. But she knew he wouldn't.

'It's a living,' she said.

'Word is you're making a good job of it,' said Max.

'I like to think so.'

'You shouldn't be here,' he said.

'Why?' Annie was stung by this. What fucking business was it of his where she was or what she did? He'd made his feelings plain enough when he'd kicked her out of his car into the pouring rain; she'd never forget that, or forgive it. 'Is something going to happen? Is the place going to burn down around my ears, is that it?'

She saw anger in his eyes and then he smiled. 'You may not be afraid of me, Annie Bailey, but I think you're afraid of yourself.'

'I don't know what you mean,' said Annie, but she did.

'So I'm asking the question,' said Max.

'What?' Annie's voice was barely more than a whisper. She could feel Max's breath on her face, feel the heat coming off his body.

'How much?'

'What?'

'How much do you want?' Max's eyes were sharp now, predatory. 'You know I want you. Always have, always will. So if it makes you feel better we'll keep this strictly business. How much?'

For fuck's sake! The cheek of him, to treat her like a tart! Annie shook her head violently. She wanted to hit him.

'God, you're a bastard,' she said. 'And let's get this straight. Even if I was selling it – which I'm not – *you* couldn't afford me.'

'Yes I could,' said Max. 'I could have you for free, and you fucking-well know it.'

Now she did hit him. Or she tried to. He caught her arm on the upswing and pinned it back against the door. Then he kissed her and she was lost. She couldn't help it. The heat of his body, the smell of his cologne, the slickness of his tongue as it entered her mouth, everything overwhelmed her.

Ruthie, she thought.

But it was no good. She was gone, the touch and feel and smell of him was something she had dreamed of every night for too long. Then he was lifting her, carrying her over to the couch, lowering her on to it, pushing up her dress.

'No,' she managed to say. 'No, I don't want this.'

But Max wasn't listening. His mouth covered hers again and she was powerless to resist. He was shoving aside the flimsy pants she wore, then she felt him undoing his trousers. *We mustn't do this*, she thought, but the wetness was flooding her.

Then suddenly he was inside her, huge and pumping and just as she remembered. She cried out and he covered her mouth with his hand and had her quickly and silently. Annie lay there, pinioned, trapped, loving it. Then he stiffened and groaned as his seed spilled into her, God, no protection, nothing, there could be a baby, anything could happen, she was in terror and in rapture, she loved it, couldn't get enough of it, God she must be a whore, what else was she, this was her sister's husband, Ruthie's husband . . .

It was over. He was finished, but instead of withdrawing he stayed there, kissing her, nuzzling his nose into her neck, crushing her with his strength, hurting her a little but she still loved it.

'I want this,' he murmured against her skin. 'I want you. I've been going fucking mad ever since I saw you again, dreaming about you.'

At the gallery, she thought. And at poor Eddie's funeral. It was Eddie's death that had really brought them back together. She remembered that hot, lingering look they'd exchanged as Max stood at Eddie's graveside.

'But Ruthie,' she groaned, nearer to tears than she had ever been before.

'She lives her life, I live mine,' he said roughly. 'Whatever you and I do, it'll make no difference to her.'

If Annie tried hard enough she could almost make herself believe that it was true.

'What's this?' He was taking the scrap of

mangled paper out of her hand, pulling away from her a little, adjusting his trousers. Annie straightened too, feeling sore and achy. She wasn't used to bearing a man's weight. Her hands were shaking. She felt hot, ready for more. She wanted him to touch her again, be inside her again. No wonder she felt at home in a whorehouse – she was a whore.

'We're expanding the business,' she said, trying to steady herself as Max spread out the details and looked at the photo of the apartment's interior.

'We?' He looked at her.

'The Delaneys will chip in.' There, she'd said it.

He was silent. Then he said: 'It looks good.'

'It's beautiful,' said Annie. 'Walking around it, I felt like I was in another world.'

'Come here,' said Max, and kissed her again, his hands deftly stroking her until he had to cover her mouth again to stifle a scream. 'Good?' he murmured, covering her mouth with his own again and pushing her back, going on to his knees and freeing himself quickly and pulling her legs apart, sliding her arse down the sofa until they were joined again, he was plunging inside her again, riding her.

This is crazy, thought Annie. But she was dazed. Unable to resist. Loving it.

'We shouldn't do this,' she whispered hopelessly.

'We have to,' groaned Max.

And it was true. They had to, the feeling was too strong, too long denied.

I'm lost, she thought. And when he had finished and was gone, she stood there in the empty room and clutched her head in her hands and screamed with the sheer frustration of wanting him so badly – because she knew she couldn't have him.

Her nerves were in shreds. She found a pack of Player's and a lighter in the sideboard and smoked her first-ever cigarette. Christ, she had to do something. She sat down on the sofa, her knickers wet and her hair like a fright wig, and wondered what had hit her.

'I'll call you soon,' he'd said.

Maybe he wouldn't. She knew enough of the world to realize that this was probably a kiss-off. He'd got what he wanted after all. Annie started to choke on the cigarette. She stubbed it out and dropped her head into her hands.

'Fuck it,' she muttered. It was *good* that he was probably not going to come near her again. He was her sister's husband. All right, so the marriage was in ruins, but wasn't that her fault too? Everything was her fault. Wasn't that what her mother had always told her? Connie might be a lush, but Annie thought now that she had probably got that exactly right.

Christ, she couldn't believe what a pushover she'd been. One kiss and she'd crumbled into dust.

And now look at her. She didn't know whether she felt punched or bored. Her head was all over the place. One moment she was excited, the next devastated, the next so full of guilt over Ruthie that she thought it would choke her.

'*Fuck* it,' she muttered again, more savagely.

There was a knock at the door. Annie pushed back her hair with a shaking hand and tried to get a grip of herself.

'Come in,' she called out.

Darren put his head round the door. 'You okay in here?' he asked.

'I'm fine. Thanks.'

'He's gone then,' said Darren.

'Yeah. Did you show him in?'

'Sorry. He's not the sort you can turn away, is he?'

'No,' said Annie bleakly.

'Ellie said it went well with the flats,' said Darren.

'Oh. Yeah. It did.' Annie felt that the flat business had happened about twenty years ago. Long before Max had hit her like a fucking force ten gale.

'Only we'll have to get the room cleaned up in a bit,' said Darren.

'Right. Sorry,' said Annie, standing up. Her legs felt like pipe cleaners. Max's seed was running down her inner thighs. She felt dizzy. *Bewitched, Bothered and Bewildered,* she thought with a shred of humour. Like the song.

246

'It's okay,' said Darren, watching her closely. 'That's one gorgeous man,' he said.

'That's one very dangerous man,' corrected Annie, going upstairs to get cleaned up. 'Okay, Darren, let's get this show on the road. Get the room straight.'

She didn't even notice that she'd dropped the flat details in there. Suddenly all her grand schemes didn't seem very important at all. She wondered when he would call. *If* he would call. But then, she mustn't answer the call if he did. Oh shit, she was in trouble, right up to her neck.

31

Max phoned next day. Chris took the call and handed her the receiver. Chris's face was blank, not showing the disapproval she was sure he must be feeling. He was a Delaney man to his bones. The Carters were the enemy.

'Hello?' Be cool, she thought. Show him you can take it or leave it. But her hands were clammy and her face felt hot the instant she heard his voice.

'I'm taking you out this afternoon,' he said.

'Oh, are you?'

'Yes, I am.'

'I might not be free,' said Annie.

'You will be.'

'I'm pretty busy.'

'Two o'clock. I'll send the car.'

And he put the phone down. Annie stared at the receiver for a moment and then replaced it on the cradle. Her heart was hammering. She was wet between the legs. I'm going mad, she thought. I've just made a date to meet my sister's husband.

Without a word to Chris she went through to the kitchen where the troops were enjoying their elevenses. Dolly put a mug of tea in front of her and took Chris's through to him.

'Thanks,' she said, aware that they were all watching her. Darren must have told them about Max calling yesterday. They could see she was in a state of disarray. But no one said a thing about it, and she was grateful for that.

'I thought I'd seen it all, but the punters always come up with a new one,' Aretha was saying to Ellie and Darren. 'You know that stockbroker chap, that Coogan?'

'One of your best regulars,' nodded Ellie, eyeing the biscuits. Annie had straightened her out with the biscuit habit, and she was svelte now, but she still hankered after the bloody things.

'I took him upstairs and was going to strap him into the Punishment Chair as usual,'said Aretha.

The Punishment Chair had been yet another lucrative idea of Annie's. It was set up in Aretha's room to accommodate their more masochistic clients. It was an ordinary kitchen chair adapted with black paint, leather thongs and chains and straps. It was a big hit with certain gentlemen.

'He likes that,' said Darren.

Dolly came back and sat down. 'Men are weird,'

she chipped in. 'What's so great about having a woman beat the crap out of you?'

Aretha shrugged. 'Anyway, there we were all ready to get down to business when he wanders off and starts looking in my wardrobe and fingering my gear. Then he says he's always wanted to try on women's clothes. Well honey, I says to him, if that's what Massa wants, then that is what Massa is gonna *get*.'

'We aim to please,' said Darren.

'Indeed we do,' agreed Aretha. 'We was havin' us a real good time after that. He tryin' on my best threads and gettin' pretty excited about the whole thing. You know he usually has a little trouble in the excitement department.'

They all nodded. The Right Hon. Philip Coogan needed a lot of stimulus to get it up.

'But with my threads on?' Aretha rolled her eyes. 'Man, that boy was *away*. We on the bed, on the floor, on the chair, every damn where you care to mention. He just a natural born trannie, never admitted it to a living soul before.'

That was the secret of sexual success, Annie knew. Find out what works for you, and go with it. Like Max worked for her, maybe. But should she really go there when her sister's happiness was involved? But then – weren't Ruthie and Max damn near living separate lives? Wasn't the marriage as good as over even before it had started?

And if *that* was the case, what difference would it make?

Annie drank her tea and listened with half an ear as Aretha, Ellie, Dolly and Darren chatted in the warm and cosy kitchen. First Celia's, and now it felt like hers. Her place, filled with her friends. They soothed her, just by being there. And she knew she was going to see Max again. But only to tell him it was all over, that she had weakened once but that it was a one-off and not to be repeated. She thought of Ruthie's face, ashen with hurt on her wedding day, and knew it was the right decision.

She didn't know what she had expected from him, but she hadn't expected this. Max's driver was there at two o'clock and he'd taken her back to the apartment in Park Street that she had visited with Ellie just yesterday. The doorman let her in and told her that Mr Carter was waiting for her up in the penthouse. She took the lift up to the top floor and stepped out straight into Max's arms. Before she could say a word he kissed her deeply. She gave in to it and kissed him back. It would be for the last time, after all.

'Come on,' he said against her mouth. 'Something to show you.'

'I've already seen it,' said Annie in bewilderment as Max walked with her into the beautiful apartment. 'I'm expanding the business to accommodate the Whitehall lot. I've rented this for six months.'

'No you haven't.'

Annie turned to him. 'Yes, I *have*.'

Max shook his head. 'You've been beaten to the bid, Annie love.'

'Meaning what?' demanded Annie.

'Meaning I made an offer to your estate agent for a year's rental and he told me what you'd offered and I upped it. He nearly snatched my hand off. When you get back to the house you'll find he's called to tell you the deal's fallen through.'

'But I wrote the cheque. Signed the contract.'

'So he said. He took a bit of persuading.'

'And tore up my contract.'

'Correct.'

'You really are a bastard,' snapped Annie. 'Why did you do that? I was so pleased with this place, I really love it. And why bring me back here? To rub my bloody face in it, I suppose.'

Max had opened the French doors on to the balcony and was gazing out at the view. He turned and came back to her and took her in his arms.

'Don't touch me,' said Annie, furious. 'I hate you.'

'You hate the man who just got this flat for you to live in, fully furnished and with *porterage*? You hate the man who's liberating you from that knocking shop in Limehouse? The man who's putting a car and a driver at your disposal, paying the fucking rent on this place, buying you anything you want?'

Annie's jaw dropped. For a moment she couldn't speak at all, she was too shocked.

'*What?*' she said at last.

Max grasped her arms and stared intently into her eyes from inches away.

'I already said it yesterday, Annie Bailey. Weren't you listening? I want you. You're mine.'

Annie pulled herself free of him. 'I'm not anybody's,' she said hotly.

'Wrong. You're *mine*,' said Max.

'No.'

'You'd let anyone walk in off the street and fuck you?' he demanded.

'No! You know I wouldn't do that.'

'Only me.'

Annie swallowed. It was true. She knew it, he knew it. But this! She couldn't take it in. It was too much. And what about all her fine intentions to cut this dead?

'You want me to be your mistress,' she said numbly.

'Yes,' he said, putting out an arm and indicating the apartment's luscious interior. 'I want you right here, with me.'

'You want me on tap, whenever you feel the urge.'

'That's right. My mistress will want for nothing, Annie. Nothing at all.'

'You've got a fucking nerve,' she stammered. And now was the perfect time to tell him to piss off, she knew it. Again the tormenting sight of Ruthie's face rose in her mind.

'You already knew that. And you like it.'

'No I fucking don't.' The cheek of him, storming back into her life and now trying to run it.

'Come and see the bedroom.'

'I saw it yesterday.'

'Let me put that another way,' said Max, bending and lifting her up into his arms. Annie shrieked in surprise. 'Come and see the cunting bedroom, and shut your yap, okay?'

'Bastard,' said Annie.

'Bitch,' said Max, and walked through and dumped her on the bed, following her down on to it and stopping all further objections with his mouth on hers.

Annie looked up and there, above the bed, was Kieron's nude of her.

'Good God,' she said in shock.

'Like it?' asked Max, his eyes following hers.

'It's . . . okay.' Max kissed her again. 'I still hate you for this,' muttered Annie when he let her up for air.

But not as much as I hate myself.

'Hate away,' said Max, and started stripping off her clothes.

*   *   *

'I married the wrong sister,' said Max later as they lay naked and entwined in each other's arms.

Annie was almost asleep, she felt so relaxed. The sun was going down and the light in the apartment was dim. Annie thought she must have died and gone to heaven. How long had she dreamed of being like this with Max? Too long. But what he'd just said jolted her back to reality. He was her sister's husband. She might fool herself that she was happy about this, but she knew it was still a mess of her own making.

'Don't say that,' pleaded Annie, turning over, turning away from the truth.

Max cuddled into her back, lying with her so that they were like spoons in a drawer. It was so nice. So *right*.

'Sorry,' he said, and kissed her neck. 'It's how I feel. It was you I wanted, but you were headstrong and I thought I didn't want that in a wife. Ruthie's more docile, softer. You're a powerful woman, Annie. Like my dear old mum, come to think of it. I made the choice, and I chose wrong.'

Annie screwed her eyes shut, disappearing into the dream again – her and Max, here together. Yet there was Ruthie, too, looking sad, betrayed, accusing.

She snapped her eyes open. 'You could change it. Get divorced.'

'No I can't.'

His tone was so sharp that Annie turned her head to stare at him in surprise. 'Why?'

'*Why?*' He drew away from her. 'I would have thought that was pretty fucking obvious. I can't be seen to screw up. Filing for divorce would be seen in my business as a weakness, a failure to keep my house in order.'

Annie's face clouded. 'So this way you get the best of both worlds,' she said. 'You get the respectability of having a wife, and all your mates think you're a great big man because you've got a mistress set up in a fancy apartment.'

'It's the way it works,' said Max.

'What if I say no?'

'You've already said yes. Four times.'

Annie thumped his chest and coloured up. He knew exactly how to please her during sex, they both knew that. 'You know what I mean.'

'How the fuck can you blush when you've been running a cathouse?' Max was smoothing his hands down over her back, making her shiver. But there was something she had to say and she was going to say it.

'That isn't going to change,' said Annie.

It was Max's turn to look surprised. 'You're having a laugh.'

'No, I'm not. Celia wanted me to sort it and I'm going to carry on doing that.'

Celia. She hadn't thought about her in a while,

with her coiffed hair and her bright brown eyes and her ridiculous ivory ciggie holder, giving herself funny little airs and graces. She loved Celia for her kindness and her warmth. Missed her too. Annie frowned.

'Max,' she said.

'Mm?' He was looking thunderous at what she'd just said.

'Did you hurt Celia?'

Max stiffened. 'Why do you ask that?'

'Because she went so suddenly,' said Annie. She took a breath. 'Soon after Eddie ... you know. She was frightened because it happened in her house and you knew about it.'

'I didn't hurt her,' said Max.

Annie breathed again. 'Good.'

'And I don't want you living there any more.'

Annie stared at him. 'We can't all get what we want, Max,' she said.

Max drew closer to her. They were staring eye to eye.

'Some of us can,' said Max. 'Some of us always do.'

'Not this time.'

'I don't want you doing it. End of.'

'I'm going to do it. End of.'

'No you're fucking not.'

'Yes I am.'

'For your own safety.'

'Not to save you embarrassment among your mates?' Annie arched a brow.

'All right, both. It can't go on, Annie. See sense.'

Annie gave it some thought. 'Max, it's something I have to do,' she said at last.

'No,' said Max. 'It isn't. Put a manager in.'

Annie gave it some more thought. A manager – now why hadn't she thought of that? She reviewed her troops. Ellie was in the Delaneys' pocket. A nice enough girl, but an arse-licker, as Celia had called her more than once in the course of conversation. Too eager to please and not to be trusted too far. Aretha was too bent in the head to be relied upon. Which left Dolly and Darren. Dolly! What a case. Always kicking against Annie's authority. She got on Annie's bloody nerves, and that was a fact. Annie knew Darren would do a good job; she often left him in charge now when she had to nip out.

'I'll think about it,' said Annie.

'Make sure you do.'

Annie looked around at the bedroom, suddenly feeling as happy as a child at Christmas. 'Christ, how do they get the dust down off these ceilings? They're a mile high.'

'Not your problem,' said Max. 'I've arranged for a cleaner.'

'You've arranged everything,' said Annie, linking her arms around his neck and kissing him. 'It's perfect.'

'Not mad any more?' asked Max, kissing her right back.

'I'll think about that too,' she said. But Ruthie was still there in her brain, looking sad, looking betrayed.

259

32

After the Friday lunchtime party Annie sent Chris out for a fag break and phoned Redmond Delaney. It was something she'd been trying to avoid, but now she had to do it. She was about to announce her changes to her workers, and it was only polite to break the news to him first.

'Miss Bailey. Always a pleasure,' he said smoothly. 'How can I help?'

'I've changed my plans,' said Annie.

'Oh?'

'I'm moving out of here and putting a manager in charge.'

Redmond was silent. Then he said: 'Who?'

Annie told him.

'You're sure that's wise?'

'Positive.'

'And you will be moving where?'

This was the bit Annie had dreaded.

'The apartment I viewed last week, I'm moving in there.'

'Are you planning to oversee the business there and have the Limehouse concern managed for you?'

'No,' said Annie, bracing herself. 'I'm going to live there, not conduct business.'

'That's an expensive undertaking.'

God, this was harder than she'd thought.

'I'll have help.'

'Whose?'

Fuck it, she thought. 'That's my private business,' she said.

'Yes, of course,' said Redmond. 'As you wish.'

'Sorry if this puts you out,' said Annie.

'It doesn't. Was there anything else, Miss Bailey?'

'No.'

There was a pause.

'Keep in touch,' he said, and rang off.

Annie put the phone down feeling uneasy. Of course the Delaneys would soon find out what was going on, but her relationship – *if you could call it that*, she thought – with Max was not negotiable or for the public domain. If Ruthie should ever get to hear about it, it wouldn't be because Annie had blabbed it about the town. She knew she had just made her position even more unstable, but it couldn't be helped.

Annie gave everyone time to get cleaned and

cleared up, paid off the extra girls and bade them goodbye, then summoned the troops into the kitchen for tea and biscuits and a chat. She told them that she was moving out but would remain in control. She explained that the apartment she and Ellie had been to view was where she would be living, and she would not be running it as a parlour after all.

'How can you be in control if you're not even fucking-well here?' asked Dolly.

'I'll put in a manager,' said Annie.

'Over my bloody dead body,' said Dolly.

'We don't want some stranger comin' in here an' givin' it large to us,' warned Aretha. 'An' come on girl. How you goin' afford a place like that? Ellie told us the details. It out of your league.'

'My business is my business,' said Annie bluntly.

'Not when it affects us,' said Dolly. 'Aretha's right. We don't want some creep ordering us around.'

'You won't have some creep ordering you around. What do you think, Darren?'

Darren shrugged, but he looked unhappy. 'You're the boss,' he said.

'Ellie? You're not saying much.'

'You seem to have made your mind up,' said Ellie, weakening and reaching for the custard creams.

'I have.'

'Well I for one am *not* happy,' scowled Dolly.

'Same here,' said Aretha.

Annie drank her tea and let them stew for a minute or two. Then she said: 'I'm not going to bring in a manager. I am going to *create* a manager.'

'Create?' Aretha laughed. 'What, you goin' make like that record, take a hundred pounds of clay and make a man, like Craig Douglas sang about? Dream on, honey.'

'I'm going to create a manager from within,' said Annie. God, they were dense. She was having to spell it out word for word.

'You mean one of us?' asked Darren.

'At last,' said Annie sarcastically.

They all exchanged looks. Annie could see she'd grabbed their attention now.

'I'm not taking orders off that great lummox Chris,' said Dolly.

'Nor me,' said Aretha.

'Aretha,' said Annie. 'Dolly. Take your tea into the front room, will you? I want a quiet word with Ellie and Darren.'

'I'm not joking,' warned Dolly, shoving her chair back and storming off to the front room with a scowling Aretha.

'Ellie,' said Annie, when the front room door slammed shut. 'You're a good worker. You have a lovely way with our older gentlemen. I value your work very highly.'

Ellie looked pleased and preened herself, throwing Darren a triumphant look.

'I hope you can carry on working for me. Go and try to calm Dolly down, will you? Send Aretha back in.'

Ellie looked bewildered but obediently left the room. Darren looked curiously at Annie, but her face was blank. Aretha strode back into the kitchen, pulled up a chair and sat huffily down.

'Okay, what?' she demanded.

'You're a great worker, Aretha. I really want you to stay on here and be happy with the arrangements,' said Annie.

Aretha grunted. 'Well, that depends on what you goin' to do,' she said.

'Nothing you'd be unhappy with. Go back into the front room and have a chat with Ellie, will you? I really want to keep you both if I can. Send Dolly through.'

Darren poured himself and Annie another cup of tea, then sat and gnawed a hangnail. 'This is doing my nerves in,' he told her.

'Just keep calm,' said Annie.

'I'm afraid you're going to say something horrible.'

'Like what?'

'Like, "Darren, Chris is going to be your new boss." Or "Darren, I want you to take over here."'

'Wouldn't you like that?'

'God, I don't know. I hadn't thought about it.'

Dolly came in slamming the door into the hall shut behind her. Dolly was a terrific door-slammer, but it cut no ice with Annie.

'I'm not happy with any of this,' Dolly fumed.

Annie nodded, she knew all about Dolly's resistance to change of any sort. When you'd been humped around like an unwanted package all your natural and pushed about and abused by your own father, it would make you that way. It didn't take a shrink to see that.

'I've been talking to Darren about him being in charge,' said Annie.

'I told you, I'm not taking orders from anyone. Particularly not an arse bandit.'

'Charming,' said Darren.

'Well that's what you are,' said Dolly. 'You shove shit uphill, isn't that right? It's all tears and queers in your room on a Saturday night.'

'Enough,' said Annie sharply. Dolly getting panicky she could understand, but there was no call to take it out on Darren.

'Well,' pouted Dolly.

'Well nothing. Be nice.'

'It's just that . . .'

'I know how you like things steady,' said Annie. 'I know how much you appreciate what Celia did for you, taking you in here off the streets like she did, giving you a settled home. I know how much you value this place. That's why I want you to manage it.'

Darren's jaw dropped. So did Dolly's.

Annie sat there and smiled at them both.

'Good idea?' she said, and grabbed a biscuit. 'Darren, you'll be number two, you'll stand in for Dolly whenever she's not here and back her up when she is, would you like that?'

Darren's natural position was number two. Annie knew it, and so did he. Darren nodded, relieved.

'Dolly, you'll be managing. That means no more entertaining clients and it means looking like a lady and not kicking off and swearing like a navvie at the first sign of trouble. Could you do that?'

To Annie's surprise, Dolly's eyes suddenly filled with tears.

'No more shagging?' she said faintly.

'Not unless you really want to.'

'Christ, no.' Dolly's laugh was shaky. 'Fuck it, I don't understand this.'

'You're tough, Dolly. I like that. Think you can take charge?'

Dolly wiped away a tear, but she was grinning. 'You just fucking watch me,' she said.

'Call the others in, Darren,' said Annie. 'And bring a bottle of champagne. This calls for a celebration.'

33

Ruthie Carter phoned her mother at eleven a.m. every day. Not that she really wanted to. Her mother disgusted her and yet Ruthie still loved her. The daily phone call had become a habit and now it was a job for life. If Ruthie didn't phone, Connie became waspish and cruel, accusing her of not caring, of not loving her mother, of being a bad daughter. None of which could truthfully be said of Ruthie, but when the drink was on her – and when wasn't it? – Connie could come out with all sorts.

Ruthie had started calling her every day because she was worried about her. Feeling worried was a prominent feature in Ruthie's life. She worried about her failing marriage. She worried about how much she drank these days, she worried about Connie, who ought to be with her instead of living alone in London. Connie didn't work any more. She couldn't, truth be told. Most days she was too rat-arsed to crawl out of bed, let alone do a day's labour.

When Ruthie sat and thought about it she could trace this gnawing, constant anxiety back to when Dad left. It had been like the lunatics taking charge of the nuthouse on that day. Connie couldn't run a piss-up in a brewery, and that was a fact. Running a household alone had turned out to be beyond her. When Dad went, everything started to crumble away; it was still crumbling. And now Connie wasn't answering her phone and Ruthie felt her anxiety spiralling out of control.

She couldn't phone Max. He must never be bothered with domestic stuff, and her mother came in that category. She knew very well what Max thought of Connie. There'd be merry hell to pay if she troubled him because Connie was drunk again. Instead, she phoned her cousin Kath who was now married to Jimmy Bond, one of Max's boys. Kath's mother, Maureen, lived just three doors along from Connie.

'Mum's not answering her phone, Kath love. Could you get your mum to pop round and check on her?'

'Of course I could,' said Kath. 'You're all right, are you, Ruthie?'

'Oh, I'm fine,' said Ruthie.

'I'll phone Mum,' said Kath, and rang off.

Ruthie sat there, alone in the big Surrey house.

The silence was oppressive. After a minute she got up from the couch and poured herself a Scotch.

Maureen took Kath's call and without hesitation went and knocked at Connie's door. After a while of waiting in the rain, with her brand-new perm going frizzy, she swore and took out her spare key and let herself in. She and Connie had had the keys to each other's doors since the Blitz, it was no big deal. But Gawd, what a mess the place was in.

Curling her lip in disgust she went through to the lounge and there, as expected, was Connie spark out on the sofa. She was a mess. The cardigan she had on over her food-stained dress had two buttons missing. Connie's gut was swollen, Jesus, she almost looked like she was up the duff. As if. Who in his right mind would lay a finger on Connie Bailey without fumigating her first? Connie had never been house-proud or tidy about her person, but she had now sunk to a new low. There was a trickle of drool running out of her half-open mouth.

'Fucking hell,' muttered Maureen, wrinkling her nose at the smell in there. Impatiently she shook Connie's shoulder. 'Connie! Come on girl, rise and shine.'

She shook her again. Connie's head waggled from side to side and Maureen saw the blood in the drool. 'Jesus,' she said, her stomach clenching in alarm. She shook Connie once more. She couldn't rouse her.

'Come on Connie,' said Maureen nervously. 'Don't arse around.'

But Connie was dead to the world. There were empty vodka bottles all over the front room, on the floor and on the coffee table. Fag ash everywhere too. The place was a tip. Maureen placed a tentative hand to Connie's neck. Oh thank Christ. She wasn't dead, anyway.

Maureen looked at Connie's sunken cheeks and yellowish colour and thought she'd seen betterlooking corpses than this. She'd laid out her own mother and she'd looked as if she might sit up and start chatting away at any moment. Poor old Mum had looked a fucking sight better dead than Connie did alive, and that was a fact. Maureen went back out to the hall and unravelled the piece of paper with Ruthie's number on it. She phoned her first, and then she called the ambulance.

34

Annie was in Harrods poring over one of the make-up counters when someone grabbed her in a bear hug from behind. She turned and found that her new minder Donny, a Mancunian and as tough as they come, had Kieron Delaney in a headlock. Kieron's face was turning puce. Annie touched Donny's steely arm quickly.

'It's okay, I know him,' she said.

Donny let Kieron go. Kieron clutched at his throat and took a deep breath.

'Fucking *hell*,' he gasped.

'Give us a bit of space, will you?' Annie told Donny, feeling irritated.

She'd never had a minder before, never wanted one, never needed one. Now Max insisted. She was Max Carter's woman, she had to have protection day and night. She didn't like it. Donny doubled as her driver. She had a car at her disposal,

271

but she couldn't drive, so Donny drove her wherever she wanted to go. Today, she wanted to go shopping and she was already in the heart of Knightsbridge so she wanted to go on foot. Donny had insisted on coming along, and now this. Kieron was getting his breath back. Annie was getting ever more irritated.

'Sorry,' she said to Kieron.

'It's okay,' he said, his colour back to normal. He glared at Donny, who gazed impassively back at him from a few yards away.

'Since when have you had a minder?' asked Kieron.

Annie shrugged. She didn't want to go there.

'You're looking good,' said Kieron, regaining his composure. 'You know, this is sort of romantic, barring the near-death by strangulation.'

'Pardon?'

'This is where we first met. You remember? You with your Aunt Celia, me with Orla.' He looked around. 'She's here somewhere, spending like a man with no arms, God bless her. How are you, Annie? Long time no see.'

'I'm fine,' said Annie. 'And you?'

'Yeah, fine. Busy, you know. Planning another exhibition. Landscapes this time, though. No nudes.'

'Thank God for that.'

'Ah, you enjoyed getting into your pelt for me, don't deny it,' he twinkled.

'I hated every minute of it,' said Annie truthfully.

'It was a great exhibition.'

'Did you sell the lot?'

'Everything! Even the stuff I thought I'd have to hang on my own walls.'

Annie laughed. Kieron thought how beautiful she was, exquisitely groomed and seeming almost to glow. But it was a lost opportunity. He had heard from Redmond that she had some sort of serious romantic involvement now. When pressed, Redmond had said that he'd heard Annie was involved with her sister's husband. Sure, hadn't Kieron always suspected that particular fire was still smouldering away? So she was with Max Carter now. He'd missed his chance with her. His taste for playing the light-hearted joker had backfired on him. He was mad as hell about it, if you wanted the truth.

'I heard,' he said carefully, 'that you have a boyfriend now.'

'That could be the case,' said Annie reluctantly.

'I also heard that it's Max Carter.'

Annie shrugged.

'I heard he's keeping you, actually,' said Kieron, growing annoyed at her evasiveness.

'I have an apartment on Park Street,' said Annie.

'Right, right.' Kieron felt furious now. He had expected better from her somehow. He knew how much she loved her sister. How the fuck could she do a thing like this to the poor cow? 'And how many banks did he have to rob to pay for that?' he asked her.

Annie's smile faded. She turned on her heel and started to walk away. Kieron grabbed her arm. Donny was there in a flash and grabbed his.

'Fuck it,' said Kieron, wincing. 'Sorry. I shouldn't have said that. Don't just walk off, I'm sorry.'

'It's okay, Donny,' said Annie, and once again Donny dropped him like an obedient attack hound.

'Jeez, that hurt,' said Kieron, rubbing his arm.

'No more than you deserved,' said Annie, as Donny moved away again.

'I'm just surprised, that's all. Fuck it, I'm more than that. I'm appalled.'

'I love him, Kieron.'

'He's married to your sister,' said Kieron.

'The marriage is dead.'

'Oh, come on! They all say that, don't they? My wife doesn't understand me, we don't sleep together any more, we have separate rooms, poor little me, won't you let me jump your bones?'

'Donny,' said Annie, 'hit him. Hit him *hard*.'

Donny lumbered over. Kieron backed off. The customers milled around them, getting worried about all the aggro.

'No, stop.' Annie shook her head. 'I didn't mean that. Sorry, Donny.'

Donny subsided.

'Yeah, you great tame gorilla, give us some space here,' said Kieron, braver now that Annie had given Donny the hard word.

'You've got no right to comment on my personal life,' said Annie.

'I know, I know.'

'Don't ever do that again.'

'I won't. I was just . . .' Kieron hesitated. He didn't know what he'd been intending to say. That he'd been disappointed in her? Or jealous as fuck of Max bloody Carter?

'You were just concerned for me, I know,' said Annie.

Or that, thought Kieron, maybe he'd been intending to say that. Whatever, it was too late now. She was committed elsewhere. Still, it galled him, niggled at him like a rash he had to scratch.

'Hello?'

It was Orla, gliding over, her green eyes bright with curiosity as she looked between Kieron and Annie. She smiled and held out a hand. Annie clocked the minder, ten paces behind her. She saw Donny clocking him too.

'Annie Bailey! It's good to see you again,' said Orla.

Annie shook Orla's warm, dry hand in greeting.

'I saw Kieron's portrait of you, it's wonderful.'

'That's down to the talent of the artist,' said Annie.

'And the beauty of the sitter, I'm sure,' said Orla graciously. 'Are you well, Annie?'

Annie was starkly reminded of Redmond when Orla said that. Cool, polite Redmond. They were startlingly alike. She rather missed Redmond's weekly phone calls. She hoped Dolly was nice to him when he phoned and minded her language a bit.

'I'm very well. And you?'

'Ah, fine. We ought to be getting along, Kieron, if you're ready?'

'Yeah, sure.' Kieron took one last lingering look at Annie. 'Goodbye then Annie. It was nice to see you, if slightly painful.'

He grinned at her and she grinned back. His arm ached, just a bit. His heart ached too, quite a lot. But maybe he was still in with a chance.

35

All in all, Annie was pleased at how smoothly the switch had gone. She had moved into the apartment, Dolly had taken over in Limehouse. Dolly had panicked a bit at first, phoning her all the time with questions the daft bint already knew the answers to.

Annie took her up West shopping for some suitable clothes. Nothing Dolly currently owned fitted the bill. Miniskirts short enough to show her rent book, long tarty PVC boots, low-necked tops, all that had to go. Dolly didn't like it.

'We all have to do things we don't like in life, Dolly love,' said Annie. *For instance, I have to have a minder*, she thought, as Donny trailed behind them like a bad smell.

Annie ushered Dolly into posh Knightsbridge boutiques where the salesgirls looked at her like she was something they'd have to scrape off their shoes. No doubt about it, they had a point – Dolly looked like a tart. But when Annie showed them the money it was a different story. Suddenly they were all eager to please, they started acting like they were going to adopt Dolly and take her home.

'Christ,' she said as she wrestled, sweating, into yet another dress in the changing room. 'All this fuss over a fucking frock.'

'It's not just a fucking frock,' said Annie, pulling the costly thing straight and zipping Dolly up. She grabbed her shoulders from behind her and told her to look in the mirror. The oatmeal shift dress was tasteful, discreet, and it flattered Dolly's blonde looks. 'What do you think? You like?'

Dolly screwed up her face. 'I dunno.'

'Well I do. And what I say goes. So we'll take this one, and the navy, and the pale blue. We'll get your hair sorted too.'

'There's nothing wrong with my fucking hair,' said Dolly.

'It needs cutting.'

Dolly grabbed her flowing curly blonde locks in alarm. 'You're not cutting my fucking hair off. No way.'

'A short cut will flatter your small features,' said Annie decisively. She peered at Dolly's face in the mirror. 'Now you've packed up the fags your skin's improving. And you've lovely eyes.'

Dolly stiffened. 'You're not a closet lezzer, are you?'

'Don't be daft. I've always thought you could be a very attractive woman, but you're hiding behind all that sheepdog hair and half a ton of cheap make-up.'

'Christ, this is a nightmare,' said Dolly, but she trailed around for the rest of the day with Annie, moaning and groaning and throwing out curses like confetti. At the end of it, Annie was pleased to see that Dolly looked halfway decent. Job done.

Annie was pleased to get back to the apartment. The chap on the door in his neat red uniform nodded politely to her as she entered. God, it was nice, coming back here. It was nice to be treated right, like a real lady. It was nice to leave that fucking po-faced Donny at the door too. She took the lift up and tossed her keys into the little dish on the hall table. Max's keys were already in there. She kicked off her courts and coat, and wandered through into the drawing room. Max was sprawled out on the couch and she joined him there, curling into him.

'Want a drink?' he asked.

'No, just a cuddle.' Annie sighed. 'I'm knackered. I've been out all day with Dolly. That Donny gives me the right hump, always watching me like he does.'

'That's what he's paid to do.' Max kissed the top of her head.

'I don't think I'll ever get used to it.'

'You'll have to.'

'Jesus, you're a hard taskmaster, Max Carter,' said Annie, but she was smiling as she lifted her lips to his.

'He comes in handy though, doesn't he?' Max asked against her mouth. 'He said one of the Delaneys was bothering you the other day in Harrods.'

Annie drew back in surprise. 'No one was *bothering* me,' she said. 'That was Kieron. The painter? He just came up and hugged me. We're friends, Max. It's a bit off when a friend can't come over and say hello.'

Max smoothed down her dark hair. 'Do you believe that old fanny? That men and women can just be "friends"?' he asked seriously.

'Of course I do.' Annie was frowning at him. 'Don't you think they can?'

Max laughed. 'Not where I come from. D'you reckon any of my boys would just be "friends" with a woman? The only reason any of the men I know are nice to a woman is to get her on her back.' Max frowned. 'That fucker's getting far too familiar with you, if you ask me.'

Annie knew he had a point about his macho 'boys'. Niceness was a weakness as far as they were concerned. Look at them the wrong way and they'd knock your head off. They wouldn't understand a man like Kieron at all. They were hard men; Kieron was an artist.

'He's a different sort of man,' said Annie.

Now it was Max's turn to frown. 'How d'you mean, different? He's got two legs and a cock, just like the rest of us.'

'He isn't like that.'

'Darlin', we're all like that. So you're telling me you were laid out in his studio stark naked and he never tried it on?'

'Of course he didn't.'

'There was absolutely *nothing* between you?'

'No!' For God's sake, she didn't realize any of this had even entered Max's head. He couldn't really think that she and Kieron . . . could he?

'But you like him. And he's got a charming way about him, I hear. If he can charm the birds out of the trees, why wouldn't he charm the knickers off you?'

'I like him. That's it. I like him, but I *love* you.'

Max looked at her closely. Then he shrugged. He was supposed to say he loved her back, but he didn't. Annie felt a bit disappointed, but she knew that a man like Max would never wear his heart on his sleeve.

'I've never developed Jonjo's knack of taking women lightly,' said Max, slipping his hands around her neck, lifting her chin with his thumbs. His mouth came down and he kissed her, hard, bruising her lips against her teeth.

'I know,' she said when he drew back.

281

'Fidelity's very important to me.'

But you're cheating on your wife, she thought. But she knew what he meant – her fidelity to him. Her total faithfulness. Anything less would disgust him and cause him loss of face among the boys, she knew that. Anything less would be unacceptable. Perhaps punishable. But she didn't want to think about that. She had no reason to stray, she was in love with this man, she always had been. If he couldn't trust her, that was his problem.

Maybe Kieron's too, Annie wondered. But she brushed the thought aside.

Dolly phoned again a few days later.

'Fuck me, not again. What is it this time?' asked Annie, exasperated.

'Your sister pitched up this morning looking for you. Said it was urgent, that you were to phone her on this number.' Dolly reeled it off. Annie grabbed a pen and wrote it down. It wasn't her mum's number, it must be the Surrey house.

'Oh. Okay. Thanks. Dolly?'

'What?'

'You didn't give her this number, I hope?'

'You told me not to give it out to anyone.'

'And you didn't.'

'Of course I fucking didn't.'

'Wind your neck in, I'm only asking. I'll give her a call. Thanks, Dolly.'

Ruthie must have been sitting right by the phone. She picked up immediately.

'It's me,' said Annie.

'Not before time. It's like trying to reach the Queen.'

'Well I'm here now,' said Annie. 'What's up?'

There had to be something going off. She had no illusions that Ruthie would have phoned her for a girly chat. This had to be some sort of emergency.

'It's Mum,' said Ruthie.

'What about her?'

'She's not well.'

'What, she's drunk again?'

'No, it's more serious than that. I phone her every day but a couple of days ago she didn't answer. I asked Maureen to go round, and she found her in a ruddy coma.'

'What do you mean, a coma? Is it the drink?'

'Yeah, it's the drink. They drained a load of fluid off her, they said her liver's shot. Cirrhosis.' Ruthie's voice cracked. 'I tried to get hold of Max, but he's off doing business and I couldn't speak to him.'

Annie gulped. She hadn't seen Max for a couple of days either. Again, the guilt took hold of her guts and screwed them into a tight knot. She took a breath to calm herself.

'Is there anything they can do?' she asked.

'They say no.'

'God, this is awful.' It had been a long time coming. Annie had been expecting this call for years, and now the time had come. Finally, Connie's love affair with the bottle was going to kill her stone-dead. The funny thing was, she felt almost relieved. At last, it would be over. All the torment, all the hate and love, would be gone.

'Oh come on. You can't pretend you're broken hearted.'

'It's upsetting,' said Annie. She didn't want to fight with Ruthie.

'*Upsetting?*' Ruthie spat down the phone. 'I'll tell you what's upsetting. That I couldn't get hold of you to tell you your own mother's on her way out. That I had to phone you to let you know, because you never go and even see her.'

'She wouldn't want to see me,' said Annie sharply. 'She made that very clear.'

'Oh don't give me all that, Annie. The truth is you're very happy with your own life, so what do you care about hers?'

'Of course I care.'

'No you don't. You don't give a monkey's, we both know that. You were always a daddy's girl, you never had any time for Mum.'

'That isn't true.'

'Yes it bloody-well is.'

'I don't want to fight with you,' said Annie tiredly.

'Oh, of course you don't. You're all ladylike now, I forgot. But you're a whore, that's all you are. Kath told me all about your privileged life as Max's kept *slag*.'

Fuck it, she knew. Ruthie knew. Annie sat back on the couch, at a loss.

'Yeah, I know all about it,' said Ruthie. 'You bloody *tart*! Max and me were going to try again, too.'

'Oh for God's sake Ruthie,' snapped Annie. 'Both you and I know that's wishful thinking on your part.'

'He'll never marry you,' spat Ruthie.

'I know,' said Annie. 'Don't you think I don't know that better than you? He won't divorce you. He can't.'

'So that's spoiled your plans, hasn't it?'

'I don't have any plans, Ruthie. All I know is I love him and he loves me.'

'Love?' roared Ruthie. 'You're his *tart*! He don't know the meaning of the word love and he certainly don't love you.'

God, that hurt. But Annie knew she deserved it. Both barrels, straight through the heart. Ruthie had really hit the target.

'Where's Mum at the moment?' she asked.

'Yeah, you don't want to hear the truth, do you? The truth hurts. She's in hospital. They don't think she'll last the night. She's not coming out of this one.'

285

Annie put the phone down. She wished Max was here, but he was on business and she knew not to disturb him, even if Ruthie didn't. She could handle this.

Dig deep and stand alone, she thought. She'd lived by that credo all her life, but for once she wished that he could be here to support her. When, of course, he should have been with Ruthie, supporting his wife. Not his *tart*. Grimly she went to get ready for hospital visiting. Her mother was dying, but she didn't feel a thing.

Connie looked like a corpse already. That was all Annie could think as she stood by her mother's hospital bed. There were tubes going in and out of her skinny, yellow little body. She wore a hospital gown. She looked fucking awful. But Ruthie was Mrs Max Carter and Carter money had provided the best for her, so she had a private room. Ruthie had managed to get in touch with Max at last and although he hadn't visited – and wouldn't, Annie was sure of that – he had sent flowers, a huge bouquet of mixed pinks and creams. Not red and white, thought Annie. You never sent red and white – it meant blood and bandages. And yellow meant forsaken, didn't it?

Annie tried to look anywhere else but at her mother's face. Connie didn't have a tooth left in her head and she had her dentures out, giving her wrinkled cheeks a sunken look. Her hair was like wisps of dried straw. Annie looked at Ruthie instead. No comfort there. Ruthie was sitting there holding Connie's gnarled hand. Look at the mother and you'll see the daughter in thirty years' time, that's what they said. Annie looked at Ruthie, and saw Connie sitting there as clear as day. Weak women left to their own devices and failing to stand alone. One drunk following in the footsteps of another.

What a way to end up, thought Annie. Connie had struggled to get by all her life. Annie knew that she had never got over Dad leaving like he did. Her one triumph had been Ruthie's wedding to Max. But even that hadn't worked out for her. Max despised drunks and wouldn't have them near him, in-laws or not. Without Ruthie close at hand to monitor her intake, Connie had sunk fast. Now all that remained was for her to give up her last breath and leave this world for good.

'This is my fault,' said Ruthie. 'I should never have left her.'

Annie drew up a metal chair and sat down.

'What were you going to do, Ruthie? Spend all your life propping her up? Never have a life of your own?'

'God, you're a hard cow,' said Ruthie, glaring.

'I told you, I'm not going to argue with you.'

'I bloody hate you, Annie Bailey.'

'I know,' said Annie. 'You hate me because I get what I want out of life and you're too soft to try.'

Shit, why had she said that? She had promised herself on the way over here that she wouldn't get into any rucks with Ruthie. It was pointless. And here they were again, trading insults.

'Fuck, I'm sick of this,' she said, and stood up.

'Don't go,' said Ruthie in panic. 'Don't leave me alone with her.'

Annie froze.

'Stay with me this once,' said Ruthie, her voice shaking. She put a hand up to her disordered hair. Her hand was shaking too.

Of course it is, thought Annie. Ruthie had been here for hours and she probably left home in a panic and forgot to pack a bottle. She had the DTs because she hadn't had a drink. Fuck it, talk about history repeating itself.

'I can't cope with this on my own,' said Ruthie, tears in her eyes.

Annie slowly sat back down. 'No more arguments,' she said.

Ruthie shook her head frantically. 'No. No more arguments, I promise.'

'Or I walk,' said Annie, feeling sick at heart.

So they sat there together, in silence, and waited for Connie to die.

*　　*　　*

288

At half past eleven that night, Annie said good-
night to Donny and quietly let herself into the
Park Street apartment. Max's keys were in the
dish; he was back. She switched on a table lamp,
then went to the open bedroom door and looked
in. Max had fallen asleep with the bedside light
still burning. His chest rose and fell smoothly
with the rhythm of his breathing. Annie softly
crossed the room and turned off the light. Then
she went back into the sitting room and sat
down, knowing that she couldn't get into bed
with him tonight, not after spending time with
Ruthie, not after watching their mother quietly
fade away.

She sank her head into her hands. Jesus, what
a day. She stank of disinfectant, she realized.
Disinfectant and death. Her mother had slipped
so quietly into that final sleep, the nurse checking
her pulse, shaking her head, then walking away
to let them say their goodbyes.

She had been more choked by it all than she
had expected. Ruthie had sobbed and wailed incon-
solably, but Annie had been unable to cry, although
she had felt waves of misery engulf her. All she
had been able to do was hold Ruthie tight, stroke
her arms and kiss her hair.

It was a measure of Ruthie's distress that she
had allowed this. And to Annie it had been
painfully poignant, reminding her how long it had

been since she had enjoyed this close contact with the sister she still – despite everything – loved so much.

So no, there was no way she could sleep with Max tonight.

Although she loved him.

Adored him.

She lay back against the couch and thought about Max. God knows it was easier than thinking about poor bloody Ruthie. Max who so enthralled her, who shared her life here in this apartment. This felt like reality, what they shared here, not the harsh, threatening outside world. They were at it like rabbits most of the time, they had christened every part of this place – this couch, the floor, the bath, everywhere. The sexual pull between them was so strong, so overpowering. Everything there was to do, they had done it together. Nothing was off-limits. And they were close. *Really* close.

But still he was Ruthie's husband and he should have been with Ruthie, she knew that, comforting her, waiting in her bed. Not in Annie's.

'How'd it go?' asked Max from the bedroom doorway.

Annie glanced around, startled. He was running a hand through his dark hair, pulling on his robe, yawning. So bloody casual.

She felt anger rise. 'Oh fine. My mother, and

incidentally your wife's mother too, died about an hour ago.'

Max came and sat down beside her. 'I'm sorry.'

'What for?' Annie looked daggers at him. 'For not being there for Ruthie? For my loss? What?'

'Both,' said Max. 'I know how bad I felt when my mum died.'

That wasn't at all the same. Annie knew that Max had idolized Queenie and mourned her passing with genuine grief. Ruthie had been horribly cut up to lose Connie, but for Annie it was different. Of course she was sad at her mother's death, but most of all she was glad that Connie's suffering was over.

Annie took a breath, shut her eyes. 'Sorry,' she said, opening them and looking at him. 'I just feel so bad about Ruthie. At least she had Mum before. Now what's she got, the poor little cow? I'm worried about her.'

Max nodded. 'I'm selling the Surrey place. That's why I've been busy these past few days,' he said.

Annie stared at him in surprise. 'Why?'

'Ruthie hates the fucking place. *I* hate the fucking place too. I think it's jinxed. Everything bad that's happened, it's happened there. Mum going like she did. And poor bloody Eddie. I'll be glad to see the back of it.'

'But what about Ruthie? Where will she go?'

Every time she saw her sister, it seemed to get

worse. The guilt, the worry, the anxiety. It was eating at her more and more. The thoughts she'd had in the hospital about Connie declining after their dad left kept niggling away at her. Now she saw a parallel with Ruthie and Max. If Max abandoned Ruthie, what would become of her? Would she have the strength to carry on? Oh, they would still be married, Max would never contemplate divorce. But they would live completely separate lives. Shit, they already did.

'Ruthie can move into Mum's old place in Bow.'

Annie thought about that. She knew this was a huge concession on Max's part. Queenie's place was sacrosanct. To live in it was, to him, an honour. She just hoped Ruthie saw it the same way.

'Don't give up on her, Max,' said Annie tiredly. 'I really am worried about her.'

'What, you mean the drinking?'

'Oh. You know about that.'

'Bloody sure I know about that. You'd be amazed what I know, Annie. It pays to keep your ear to the ground.'

Now what did *that* mean? Watch out, I've got my eye on you?

'She needs a bit of support,' said Annie.

'Like her mother?' asked Max. 'Sweetheart, you could have propped Connie Bailey up with iron staves and she would still have keeled over.'

'I know. But as a favour to me, Max? Be nice to Ruthie.'

They locked eyes.

'I'll be nice,' said Max. 'I promise.'

36

Another fucking funeral, thought Annie. She ought to feel sadder. This was her mother being planted in the ground. Sooner or later she might begin to feel some sort of real loss instead of relief – but she doubted it.

'Thanks for coming with me, Dolly love,' she said to the woman sitting beside her in the back of the black Jaguar Mk X. Donny was up front as usual, sitting silently behind the wheel. Max was, of course, with Ruthie. Some of Connie's friends would be here, although times had been hard for Connie and friends had been few. But all Max's boys and their families would turn out. This was Max Carter's mother-in-law, after all. One of the family and to be shown the appropriate level of respect. Jonjo was there, so were Jimmy and Kath and her mother, Maureen.

Annie sat and watched them all walk past and

disappear into the church with the funeral cortège. The coffin was draped in pink flowers. Pink had been Connie's favourite colour. It was Ruthie's, too. She'd seen Ruthie, arm in arm with Max, following behind the coffin. That was where Annie should be too, but that would be pushing it too far. She'd already decided she would wait until everyone else was inside the church, then follow on and just sit quietly at the back.

'It was good of you to keep me company,' she said to Dolly.

'That's okay.' Dolly pulled a face. 'I know what it's like when you don't get on with your mum and dad. You hate them but you love them too, ain't that right? I cried buckets when my old dad died, the rotten bastard. You feel guilty because you hate them, and you hate yourself because you love them.'

Annie looked at Dolly with a new warmth. Dolly was respectably dressed today in a neat navy dress and matching coat. Her hair was styled in an urchin cut and the colour had been toned down – less brass, more honey. Dolly looked a treat, and Annie was proud of her. She'd backed a winner in Dolly, she was sure. Whatever Dolly had previously lacked in polish, she more than made up for in spirit.

'We ought to go in,' said Annie, not wanting to.

'It'll be okay,' said Dolly. 'These things are never

as bad as you think they're going to be. People behave themselves at funerals. Max Carter won't have anyone kicking off, trust me.'

'Yeah, you're right,' said Annie. She took a breath. 'Right, let's go.'

They got out of the car. It was a bright, sunny day, which seemed wrong somehow. At Eddie's funeral there had been spatters of rain and an icy wind, which had suited the occasion better.

'Let's get this over with,' said Annie with distaste, then she spotted the woman standing out by the lych gate. She felt a twinge of annoyance. She wanted everyone inside before she went in. What was the hold up? Then she froze. She grabbed Dolly's arm and stared intently. 'Hey, Doll. Don't that look like Celia out by the gate?'

Dolly turned, and looked. The woman had a black veil over her face, but there was something about her dress and demeanour that shouted *Celia*.

'Yeah, it is. I think it's Celia.' Dolly started waving. 'Hey, Celia,' she shouted.

Fuck it, thought Annie as the woman turned and hurried away. Trust Dolly to open her yap and scare her off.

'Come on,' she said, and hurried after the woman. She heard Donny lumbering out of the car and slamming the door, the heavy tread of his size twelves on the gravel behind her as she legged it towards the lych gate. She wasn't ever supposed to rush off without Donny, she knew that. But fuck it, this was *Celia*. Well, she hoped it was.

When they reached the gate the woman was already some distance away, walking fast towards a waiting taxi.

'Fuck, she's getting away,' said Annie, and kicked off her courts and ran. The woman had the back door of the taxi open and was climbing inside when Annie barrelled into her and grabbed her and held on tight.

'Hey!' said the taxi driver. 'You gettin' in, or you havin' a friggin' dance?'

Dolly came hobbling up clutching Annie's shoes. Donny arrived right on her heels, panting.

'Jesus, I didn't realize we were havin' a fuckin' tea party here,' said the taxi driver.

'Hold on,' said Annie. 'Celia?'

The woman got back out of the taxi.

'*Now* what the fuck?' roared the taxi driver. 'Make your bloody mind up love, in or fucking out?'

Donny leaned into the front passenger window. The taxi driver leaned away from him.

'Shut yer mouth, my friend, or I'll shut it for you,' Donny said gently.

The taxi driver held up both hands. 'Hey, no offence, pal. I'm just the driver.'

'Then drive,' Donny suggested, and the taxi driver gunned the engine and roared away.

'I already paid for that cab,' came Celia's voice from behind the veil. 'Let me go, Annie. I shouldn't have bloody come here.'

Annie didn't give a shit. She pushed back Celia's veil.

'Fuck me,' said Dolly breathlessly. 'Celia!'

Celia looked miffed, but well all the same. Annie hadn't known what to expect when she'd shoved the veil out of the way. Scars or something maybe. She didn't know. But now she felt almost limp with relief. The button-bright brown eyes were the same, and the carefully made-up face. It was Celia. She looked a little older, more care-worn, like she'd had it hard. But she was okay.

'For God's sake, Celia, where have you been?' demanded Annie. 'What the hell were you thinking of running off like that and leaving nothing but a fucking note? We were thinking all sorts, we were bloody frantic with worry over you.'

'I'm sorry,' mumbled Celia, eyes downcast.

'*Sorry?* Is that all you've got to say? We were pulling our ruddy hair out and you say *sorry?*' Annie grabbed Celia's shoulders. 'What's been going on, Celia? Why'd you go like that?'

Celia just shook her head.

Annie looked at her aunt. Maybe she was being too hard on her. She must have had her reasons. She let go of her shoulders and reached for her hand. Celia stepped back, almost cringed away from her.

'No, let me go . . .' she started to say.

Annie looked down. The ivory fag holder was missing. The ivory fag holder in the right hand. Annie stared and suddenly felt faint.

'Jesus,' she said.

Celia had no right hand.

'Don't tell him you saw me here,' said Celia. Her voice trembled.

'Celia.' Annie was staring at the space where Celia's right hand should have been. She felt sick, dizzy. 'Celia.' It seemed to be all she could say. She couldn't take in the horror of it.

Dolly was standing there dumbstruck, white as a sheet, her hand covering her mouth as if she was about to spew her guts up, her eyes locked on the stump of Celia's right wrist.

'Celia . . .' Annie swallowed convulsively and somehow managed to get a sensible word out. 'What happened . . . ?'

'Promise me you won't tell him,' pleaded Celia.

Annie shook her head, staring. You turned up for your mother's funeral and found your long-lost aunt here minus her right hand. She couldn't take it in.

Donny was giving Celia the hard eye. Celia caught him staring and her expression transformed into one of total dread. She knew one of Max's boys when she saw one.

Annie got the message. She turned and said, 'Donny, fuck off will you? Go and wait for me by the lych gate.'

Donny hesitated. His eyes flicked to the cringing Celia once again.

'Did you hear me?' Annie snapped. 'And listen up. You never saw a thing, Donny. Not a fucking thing. Okay? Or I tell Max you made a pass at me. Don't think I won't, I'm telling you I will. Do you believe me?'

Donny said nothing. He nodded.

'He'd have your arse on a spit if I said the word,' said Annie. 'So keep it buttoned – or else.'

Donny stalked off and stood by the gate with a face like thunder.

'Christ, that told him,' said Dolly with a trembling voice.

Annie looked at Dolly. Her colour was coming back now, but she still looked shaken. Annie knew what she was thinking. Who did this? And if they could do such a hideous thing to Celia, where did that leave any of Celia's girls – and Celia's niece?

'You won't tell him you saw me, will you?' asked Celia. 'I shouldn't have come here. I know that. But she was my sister-in-law, the poor bitch, it was the least I could do. I didn't think anyone would see me if I kept my distance. You won't tell him, will you?'

'I won't tell him,' said Annie. They both knew

300

they were talking about Max. 'Is he responsible for this?' She nodded at Celia's right arm.

'He didn't do it,' said Celia.

'Of course he didn't. Max don't have to do his own dirty work, unless he really wants to.'

'They made me write the note at the kitchen table.'

'Max's boys,' said Annie. *Oh God no*, she thought. *Please no*.

'Of course she means Max's bloody boys,' said Dolly. 'Who the hell else would she mean? I *knew* there was something bloody fishy going on.'

'Then they blindfolded me. I thought I was a goner, straight up.'

'Then what?' asked Annie. She felt more than sick now – disgusted. Disbelieving.

'They took me somewhere. A meat market.' Connie drew a shuddering breath. 'There was a bloke there . . . he cut off my hand.'

'Jesus,' said Dolly.

'You won't tell him you saw me, will you?'

Fuck it, would Celia never stop saying that? 'I won't tell him.'

'You're all right, Celia,' said Dolly, patting her shoulder. 'We won't breathe a word.'

'He told me to keep away. I shouldn't be here.'

'You're safe,' said Annie. 'Safe as houses.' Not even she believed that.

'Do you know what he said when he did it? The chap who cut off my hand?'

Annie and Dolly shook their heads. Dolly looked as if she was about to be sick again now. Annie felt as if someone had hit her with a brick. She was stunned by what had happened to Celia, staggered by the implications of this act of brutality.

'He said it was a little message,' Celia sobbed. 'From Max Carter.'

37

By three o'clock on the day they buried her mother, Annie had moved all of her stuff and herself out of the Park Street apartment and back into the Limehouse place.

She left a note on the hall table of the apartment and her keys with an unhappy Donny.

'Remember. You saw nothing.'

Donny nodded.

There was nothing else she could do. She didn't want to even look at Max, far less crawl into bed with the bastard. All she could think about was Celia's panic-stricken face as she hailed another taxi and vanished out of their lives once again.

Celia had been too spooked to conduct a conversation. Annie asked if her dad ever got in touch with Celia, trying to keep her there for a moment or two longer. But Celia said a flat no. The last she'd heard of Annie's dad, he was a milkman in

Manitoba. He had his own life, and she was bloody lucky to still have hers, so she had to go. She wished them good luck. She didn't even comment on how different Dolly looked, she was too eager to get away, back to safety. Annie could understand that. She watched her beloved aunt shoot away in the taxi and just knew that she'd never see her again. Because of Max.

'What will you do?' Dolly asked Annie.

But Annie could only shake her head. She felt too devastated to speak.

'Listen,' said Dolly. 'You don't have to stay with him. You know that. Your room's still standing empty. You could come and stay with us. If you want to.'

And so that was what she did. In a state of stunned disbelief she walked out of the apartment and out of Max's life. Donny dropped her back at Limehouse. He still looked unhappy. But then, so did she.

'I'll have to tell him where I took you,' said Donny.

'I know.'

'He's going to be seriously pissed off.'

'I know that too.'

'When you see him, tell him it had nothing to do with me, will you?'

Annie's eyes met Donny's in the driver's mirror. He looked fearful. Everyone around Max looked fearful sooner or later, she was coming to realize that.

'I won't see him,' she said.

'Oh yeah?' Donny's laugh was hollow. 'Trust me – you'll see him.'

Max came to find her next morning. Chris let him into the front parlour and shouted for Annie. *Sweet Jesus, how was she supposed to cope with this?* Annie wondered. She composed herself with an effort and came downstairs.

She felt a mess. She hadn't slept. Darren and Ellie and Aretha had spent all last evening tiptoeing around her, not asking the questions they were dying to. It was obvious that Dolly had told them to button it. Annie was grateful for that. She had gone to bed early, wanting to be alone, and lay awake for most of the night, thinking about Max. Thinking of Celia too, screaming with fear and agony as they hacked her hand off in cold blood, just because Eddie Carter died on her premises. Thinking of the times she had shared with Max in the apartment, falling into bed together laughing and then becoming serious as they made love.

She was unable to reconcile the two images – the wonderful lover and the heartless bastard who had mutilated her aunt. Now he was here. She went into the front room and closed the door behind her and looked at him. It hurt to look at him, like a thousand stab wounds.

Max looked right back at her. Then he said: 'No one walks out on me.'

Annie swallowed. 'I just did.'

Max threw a scrap of paper on to the floor.

'And what the fuck does this mean?' he asked with venom. '"I'm sorry but it's over"! What sort of fucking note is that?'

'What sort of fucking note do you want, Max?' she shot back.

Max lifted a finger. 'I don't want any lip, Annie. I want an answer, that's all.'

'I've told you. It's over.' Fuck, he looked furious. Annie thought of Celia's hand, dropping on to a sawdust-covered floor like a piece of dead meat. She tried to keep her voice steady, but her heart seemed to be lodged in her throat.

'It's over,' she said again.

Max was silent for a long time. Then he walked across to where she stood and leaned in close.

'Is this about Kieron fucking Delaney?' he asked.

Annie stared in surprise. 'What?'

Max grabbed her chin. 'Is it?'

'No it fucking isn't!'

'What then? What's happened over the past day or so to make you change? I saw you at the apartment before your mum's funeral, you were fine. I saw you waiting outside the church in the car with

306

that blonde tart and Donny at the wheel. I didn't see you inside the church. When we came out, the car was gone and you with it. So what happened?'

Annie couldn't breathe. He was too close. She kept seeing that image. The hand, dropping away, Celia screaming with pain. She was going to faint, or vomit, she didn't know which.

She had even thought of confronting him with it, telling him about Celia and what had happened to her, saying 'Look you bastard, I know you did it.'

But she knew he would only deny it like he'd done before, and she didn't feel strong enough to argue the toss with him now. She was too tired, too sickened. This time he wasn't going to get the chance to win her round. He could rot for all she cared, he was dead to her now.

'Donny must have told you what happened,' said Annie. Oh Christ – and what if he had? What if Donny had ignored her warning and spilled the beans, told Max that Celia was there at the church?

'He said he dropped you back at the flat and that you seemed a bit upset. That you'd changed your mind about attending the funeral. You told him to go home, that you wouldn't want to go out again. What did you do, wait until the coast was clear and then nip off to see that Delaney piss-artist instead?'

'For God's sake, no!' Fuck, she couldn't let him

even start to think that Kieron was at the root of all this. She had thought all this through, she knew what she had to say now. 'Max – I saw you with Ruthie at the funeral. And I suddenly saw that what I was doing was wrong. *Wicked*. She's my sister. I can't go on betraying her.'

Which was partly true. Who the hell had she been kidding, thinking she could go on with this behind Ruthie's back? She couldn't do it any more, *wouldn't* do it any more. And then seeing that Celia had been cut for something that wasn't her fault – well, that was knowledge she could never live with, not when Max had ordered it done.

He drew in closer still.

'Like it or not, you're mine,' he said.

Annie steeled herself. 'I told you before, Max. I don't belong to anyone. Only to myself.'

He released her chin with a flick of his fingers. He was nodding. 'It's that fucker Delaney.'

'No. It's Ruthie. I can't go on doing this to Ruthie.'

Max turned away. 'Yeah. Sure.'

'It's the truth,' said Annie, heart racing. 'We were good together.'

Now Annie knew she'd been kidding herself. She looked into his eyes and saw only deception and cruelty there. Max Carter wasn't the romantic hero she'd always believed him to be. Max Carter was a vicious, low-life thug, he always had been and he always would be. He would kill any fucker who crossed him, she knew that much. So would he really draw the line at wreaking vengeance for a crime against his family?

Annie stiffened her spine.

'We might have been good together once,' she said coldly. 'But that's over. It couldn't go on. I see that now.'

Suddenly he turned back to her, grabbed her, kissed her hard.

Annie held herself rigid. He was hurting her. Punishing her. She tasted blood on her lip. She kept still, forced herself not to respond to him the way she always responded.

'You're mine,' he said again against her mouth.

'No,' said Annie.

'This is only over when I say so.'

'No.'

'We'll see.'

The following morning, the nude portrait of her that Kieron had painted was thrown on to the pavement in front of the parlour. A car roared away. Chris came out and cautiously picked up the painting. The canvas was slashed right through.

38

Annie was sitting at the kitchen table next morning when Darren walked in. She was staring at the ruined canvas, propped against the wall in tatters. Darren looked at it, then at her.

'Well, girl, he's properly pissed off with you,' he said.

Annie nodded. 'There's tea in the pot.'

Darren poured and sat down beside her. 'Been up long?'

'Hours – couldn't sleep.'

'Dolly wouldn't say what had gone on. She said we ought not to talk about it to you.'

'Dolly's right, there's nothing to say.'

'Nothing at all?'

'Look at the painting, Darren, don't you think that says everything?'

Good old Dolly. She knew how to keep quiet, thank God. She might have a mouth on her like

310

the Blackwall tunnel, but she knew when discretion was needed. Jesus, it was needed now. No one could know about Celia. Hadn't the poor cow suffered enough? God knew what Max would do to her if he found out she'd come back, Annie knew all too well what he was capable of.

Still, Annie could scarcely believe that he'd trashed the painting. Slit it wide open with a knife, by the look at it. She thought of Celia's missing hand. Of Kieron. Max seemed convinced this had something to do with Kieron.

'Oh fuck,' she moaned, and put her head in her hands.

'It'll all work out,' said Darren, patting her shoulder.

'Yeah?' Annie dropped her hands and glared at him. 'How, exactly? It's a total bloody mess, and I've got no one to blame but myself.'

'You sorry you left him?'

Annie thought of lying in bed with Max. All right, he was a man. Mum – God rest her, the poor cow – had told both her daughters over and over that men were bastards, that all they needed was a hole to stick it in and they were happy. But it had been different with Max and her. There had been passion, yes, but there had also been laughter, and Annie believed that she had got closer to Max Carter over the last month or so than anyone else had in a long while.

Maybe she had just been kidding herself, because just look – he'd done this. He was behaving like any other thwarted male, raging about the place destroying things and threatening revenge.

'I'm not sorry I left him,' said Annie dully. 'There was nothing else I could do.'

'Then you've got to pick yourself up and move your life on again,' said Darren.

That easy. Annie sat there and felt like a puppet with its strings cut.

She stood up. 'I'm going back to bed,' she said.

Darren watched her go. Christ, this wasn't the Annie Bailey he knew.

Annie had managed to sleep for an hour or so when Aretha knocked on her bedroom door. Annie lifted her head from the pillow and squinted up at her.

'Fuck, girl, you look rough,' said Aretha.

'Thanks,' said Annie.

'You got Mr Big on the phone. Wants to talk to you.'

Annie shot upright. 'Max?'

'Redmond Delaney.'

Annie hauled herself out of bed, wrapped herself in the expensive turquoise silk dressing gown Max had bought her, and crawled downstairs. Chris was there in the corner. He nodded at her and went back to his paper. Dolly and Darren and Ellie were in the kitchen, chatting. Everything was as if she'd never left.

'Hello?'

'Miss Bailey,' said Redmond's cool, calm voice. 'Are you well?'

Annie drew in a quivering breath. 'Fine.'

'I heard you'd come back,' he said.

'Yeah.'

'Are you going to stay?'

'I don't know.'

'Do you *want* to stay?'

'I don't know that either.'

'Only there could be difficulties. Miss Farrell's in charge now, she's doing well.'

Annie had to think for a moment. Who the fuck was Miss Farrell? Of course. Dolly. Dolly had settled into her job as Madam and Redmond didn't want her treading on Dolly's toes.

'I know,' she said.

'You sound very tired.'

It was simply an observation, but Annie's eyes filled with unexpected tears.

'Yeah,' she said.

'I heard about Kieron's painting,' said Redmond.

'Yeah. Sorry.'

'Not your fault. Take care.' And the line went dead.

Annie wandered through to the kitchen. Conversation stopped. Then Dolly piped up: 'What did he say?' There was an edge of unease in her voice.

'Nothing much.'

'You look like shit, Annie Bailey,' said Dolly a touch unkindly.

While she looked great. Annie thought that Dolly had never in her life looked so good. So polished, so elegant. How the tables are turned, she thought, how the mighty have fallen. Dolly looked like the cover of a magazine, and she, Annie Bailey, formerly queen of this establishment, looked – yes, Dolly was right – like shit.

'You poor thing. Sit down and have some tea and toast,' said Ellie, a little too sweetly.

Annie sat and exchanged a look with Darren. Ellie was hedging her bets. Annie was back, and she might kick Dolly out of pole position as lady boss. It might pay to suck up. Ellie could get a degree in sucking up, she was that good at it.

The painting was gone, Annie noticed. Someone had put it away, out of sight. Stuffed it in a cupboard or something. Not that she cared. They could burn the bloody thing for her. It represented another time, a time she'd rather be allowed to forget.

'He didn't say anything about this place, did he?' asked Dolly.

Annie looked at her and Dolly looked away. Annie knew what she was thinking – that Annie intended to take over the reins of command here again, and maybe Redmond was going to put Annie back in charge over Dolly's head.

'He didn't say much,' said Annie.

Dolly's eyes moved back and locked with hers for a moment.

'Fine,' she said, and stood up. She clapped her hands. 'Come on then, troops. Let's get this place tidy, the punters will be arriving soon.'

Of course, thought Annie. Friday. Party day. Ellie put her tea and toast in front of her and she was left alone at the table. She took a bite, but couldn't eat the rest. She drank some tea. Then she went out into the hall and back up the stairs. Fuck it, this was no use, she couldn't go on like this.

She took a bath, washed her hair, got dressed. There was music coming from the front room, and people were laughing and talking. Maybe this was just what she needed.

She went back downstairs. Chris was at his station. Ellie was servicing an elderly gentleman on a chair just inside the front-room door, jumping up and down on the poor chap fit to break his brittle old bones, but he seemed to be enjoying it. Two whores she didn't know were rolling about on the sofa with three men who looked like barristers or High Court judges. Probably Aretha was at work upstairs in her room, strapping another poor twisted soul into the Punishment Chair. And Darren didn't much care for an audience while he performed, so he was probably upstairs too with some outwardly respectable gentleman who preferred to take it up the arse. Dolly was doling out drinks as Brian mixed and served, and passing around canapés. She looked up when Annie entered the room and her smile tightened.

'I thought I'd come down and lend a hand,' said Annie, feeling suddenly awkward. Maybe this was not such a good idea after all. Dolly looked miffed, although she was trying to hide it.

'There's no need,' she said.

Annie dropped the pretence. 'Fuck it, Dolly. Don't be like this.'

'Like what?' asked Dolly, still smiling that horrible false smile.

'*This*. The last thing I want to do is upset you. You're the boss here now, I don't want to muscle in on your territory.'

'Oh.' Dolly had the good grace to look abashed. 'It's just . . .'

'I know. You don't want to go back to where you were. I understand that. You're safe, Dolly. Don't give it another thought. I'll go back upstairs, okay?'

'Thanks,' said Dolly, shoulders slumping with relief.

Feeling like a fool, Annie made herself scarce.

She could easily understand that Dolly didn't want to go back to shagging for a living. But what could *she* do, now that being Madam here was no longer an option? She had to do something, she couldn't afford to just sit on her arse all day.

39

'Remember your plan, Miss Bailey?' asked that chilly voice on the phone.

Annie was standing in the hall. It was Saturday morning. Chris was sitting there, watching her impassively. She felt tired and irritable. Redmond *fucking* Delaney had got her out of a nice warm bed to play mind games. Okay, it was eleven in the morning and she should have been up and dressed. She knew that. But knowing it was one thing, doing it was something else. And so she was here – again – in her dressing gown with hair like a haystack in a gale. Dolly passed by, looking with disapproval at the state of her. It was almost funny. She was turning into Dolly, and Dolly was turning into her.

'Plan?' echoed Annie.

'Expansion, Miss Bailey.'

'Oh.' Annie dragged a hand through her hair. 'That plan.'

'Why not go ahead with that?' asked Redmond.

Why not, thought Annie. Because she could hardly summon the energy to stand up, far less launch a new business? Right now she could think of a thousand reasons why not.

'I don't know,' she said.

'Only I've looked at a few places with good potential.'

'Right.'

'Perhaps I should leave it with you, let you mull it over.'

'Mm. Okay.' She put the phone down. She'd forgotten to say a polite goodbye, she realized afterwards.

'Bugger,' she muttered.

You didn't just put the phone down on Redmond Delaney. But then she was so deeply in the shit, would another few inches matter? She had dumped Max Carter. You didn't do that, either. But she had. Was she brave, or just stupid?

Stupid, she thought. Because now she was miserable as sin. She missed him far more than she would ever have thought possible. She knew he was a bastard, but she was still in love with him. And what was there for her here? She was strictly surplus to requirements. Dolly had brightened up after Annie's little peacemaking speech yesterday, but she was still edgy. The message was clear; she was here on sufferance, and the sooner she went, the better.

Annie went through to the kitchen and found Dolly there at the table with Billy. She hadn't seen him for quite a while. He'd obviously been intimidated by Chris standing on guard and by the formality of using the front door, she knew that, but now it looked like he'd overcome it. Annie could see, to her shame, that her appearance startled him. Fuck, she knew she looked a wreck. Dolly poured her some tea. Dolly looked immaculate from her hair down to her fingernails.

This can't go on, thought Annie.

'Hello Billy, how are you?' she asked, making an effort.

'I'm f-fine, thank you Miss Bailey,' he said, looking sideways at her while scribbling in his notebook.

She looked over at what he was doing. As usual, it was just scribble, blackening the page. There was nothing intelligible there, nothing that made sense at all. Maybe it made sense to Billy. Who knew? It was rather sweet, the way he still came calling even though Celia was gone. And it was good of Redmond Delaney to turn a blind eye to Billy's continued presence on his manor.

She took her tea out to the hall and dialled the Delaneys' number.

'Hello?' said Redmond.

'Mr Delaney, I'm sorry, I think we got cut off.'

'Yes.'

'What you were saying, about plans,' said Annie.

'Yes?'

'I might have a place in mind,' she said. It was probably gone by now, but if it was, so be it.

The first place she'd looked at with Ellie had been a favourite, with its fabulous views out over Green Park, but it was unfurnished and it would cost an arm and a leg to get the place done out as she'd like it; it was also a little too far out.

The second had been closer to Whitehall and was rather like a gentleman's club inside, fully furnished with lots of dark wood panelling and large comfy chairs. Even the bedrooms were sumptuously done out in reds and golds. She could picture her gentlemen there, making themselves at home.

She didn't want to think about the third apartment. The apartment where she had lived and loved with Max. She put that straight out of her head.

'I'll contact the agents and get back to you, if that's all right?' said Annie.

'Good, Miss Bailey.'

'Goodbye then.'

'Do keep in touch, Miss Bailey. I'm following your career with interest.'

Annie was surprised to find herself smiling as she put down the phone. Against all probability, she quite liked cool, collected Redmond Delaney with his soft and sophisticated Irish lilt. Like Orla, he seemed to have a polish and poise the other Delaneys lacked.

It was about time she got herself back on track.

The same estate agent she'd spoken to before met her at the Whitehall apartment. The place still looked mightily impressive. The panelling lent it a grandeur, the chandeliers cast a soft, clubby light down on the costly rugs, occasional tables and leather Chesterfields. The drapes were thick gold velvet. She liked this place. She could do business here, she felt.

'I'll take it,' she said, even though the shortest lease was six months and the price was astronomical. But that was where Redmond Delaney came in.

Back at the agent's office she wrote a cheque for a month's rental in advance. The agent shook her hand, she got a taxi back to Limehouse and straightaway put a call through to Redmond.

'I've rented a place in Upper Brook Street,' she said, and described it to him in detail.

'It sounds perfect,' said Redmond.

'You said you'd chip in with half the rental if we negotiated a cut of the profits.'

'So I did. And you remembered.'

'Will you, then?'

'Yes, of course. But I'll want input on how the business is run.'

'Understood.'

'I'll meet you there at ten tomorrow. Give me the full address and notify the agent. I look forward to seeing you again, Miss Bailey. And I'm pleased you're back.'

Which was nice, thought Annie. But Redmond wanted his pound of flesh out of this. She didn't much like the idea of him having too much of a say in how she ran the business, but she wanted his cash input so what could she do? Needs must, she thought.

Yeah, thought Annie as she ran upstairs to sort out something suitable to wear for meeting the boss of the Delaneys tomorrow. She was *back*.

At nine o'clock on Monday Redmond Delaney was shown into the front room. Annie had been up and dressed early, before the rest of the household in fact. Only Chris had been about.

'But I thought he was meeting me up West?' said Annie.

Chris shrugged and sat down in the corner.

A man of few words, Chris. Obviously Redmond had decided on a change of plan. Annie straightened her pearls in the hall mirror and went into the front room, shutting the door behind her, a smile of welcome in place.

It wasn't Redmond, it was Kieron.

'Oh,' she said blankly.

'As warm welcomes go, that leaves a little to be desired,' he smiled.

'I was expecting Redmond,' said Annie.

'And the welcome's not getting any warmer,' noted Kieron.

'Kieron, why are you here?'

Kieron's smile dropped. 'Sure, I'm beginning to wonder about that myself.'

Annie was shocked and alarmed. She had already seen something horrible happen to someone she was fond of. It wasn't an experience she wanted to repeat. It wasn't safe for Kieron to be anywhere near her, and she knew it. Somehow she was going to have to push the point home. Brutally, if necessary.

'What are you seeing Redmond about?' asked Kieron when Annie stood there in silence.

'Business.'

'Should you be getting involved in that?' asked Kieron.

Annie decided enough was enough. He had to be told, and she had best tell him right now.

'Fucking hell, Kieron,' she exploded. 'What's it to you what I get involved in? What am I, pure as the driven snow? Has it escaped your notice that I live in a whorehouse?'

Kieron looked taken aback. 'Yeah, but you're not a whore,' he stuttered.

'No, I ran this place and pretty soon I'll run another. I'm a Madam, Kieron. I'm not a school-girl. I don't need anyone's permission to conduct my business any damned way I please.'

'Okay, okay.' Kieron held up his hands, looking amazed and a bit hurt by this unexpected tirade. 'I just wanted to see you, that's all. I was told you'd split from Max Carter, I just wondered how you are.'

'You wondered how I am?' Annie's face was hard. 'I'm fucking hunky-dory, Kieron. I'm *fine*.'

Kieron was silent then. His face was a picture of hurt. Annie steeled herself. She wanted to hug him, to see him smile and laugh, but she didn't dare. For his sake.

'I thought we were friends,' he said at last.

We are, thought Annie painfully. *That's why I have to do this.*

'Oh, grow up,' she said harshly.

'You've changed,' said Kieron.

'Maybe I have. Maybe I've had to.'

'I missed you, Annie,' he said in a voice suddenly thick with emotion.

'For God's sake.' Annie turned away. She hated seeing him in pain.

'When you were with him, when you were with that fucking animal Max Carter . . .'

'Don't do this, Kieron,' said Annie, shaking her head.

'I have to. I have to get this out or it's going to fucking-well choke me to death. Annie Bailey, when I didn't have you in my life I missed you. And I started to realize . . .'

'*No,*' Annie howled.

'*Yes.* I'm going to say this because it's the absolute truth. I saw you as nothing at first. A beautiful face. A subject to paint, that's all. Then I started talking to you, getting to know what you're really like . . .'

'What I'm really like is hard as nails, Kieron,' said Annie, clutching her arms around herself because this was horrible, it hurt too much. 'I'm hard because I've had to be. I've no time for anyone unless there's something in it for me. I hated my mother and I took my sister's husband, how's *that* for sheer fucking nastiness?'

'Your mother was a drunk who put you through hell all your young life. And you were in love with the man.' Kieron grabbed her shoulder and she shook him off. 'You loved him and he took advantage of that.'

'Oh sure. Good as gold Annie corrupted by big

bad Max Carter, that's me. Come off it, Kieron. I'm a bitch of the lowest order. You've heard all about it, you ought to know it's true.'

'None of that's the real you,' said Kieron. 'You're sweet and you're funny and you care more than you ever let on. And I miss you like fuck. I don't like not having you in my life. I should have said all this before, and maybe you would never have got involved with him again.'

Annie turned and gave him a look full of scorn. 'Who do you think you are, Kieron Delaney? Do you really think you could ever measure up to Max Carter?'

Kieron flushed with temper. It was only the second time Annie had seen it happen. He grabbed her arms and shook her.

'I may not be a thug like he is, but I'm a man,' he spat out. 'I can get women. Any women I want.'

'Well bully for you,' said Annie coldly. 'Go out and find one of those women, Kieron, because *I* want a real man, not a sorry excuse for one.'

'You cow,' said Kieron, and kissed her.

Annie fought like a tiger and quickly got free.

'Chris!' she shouted.

The door was flung open and Chris stood there, alert.

'Oh don't bother,' said Kieron. 'I'm going.' He turned and gave Annie a bitter smile. 'Chris won't touch me, anyway, don't you know that? I could tie you up and rape you with a bag over your head and he wouldn't lift a finger. Because I'm a *Delaney*. But then maybe that's the sort of treatment you prefer.'

'Fuck off out of it, Kieron,' said Annie.

Chris stood aside.

Kieron went.

40

Jonjo Carter was with yet another blonde, shagging away on the big bed at his place.

'Oh come on, sweetness,' she whined, because she was tired and she wanted to get this over, and Mr Stiffy kept turning into Mr Bendy, at this fucking rate she'd be panting and gasping all night, and she was ready for a kip.

It had been a long day for Jonjo. Not a bad one, really. Cara worked in the bedding section of a department store the firm was taking an interest in. It always paid to have an insider to call on, should you need one. And it looked as if they might need one. So Jonjo had gone to look around, and had pitched up in bedding where he was naturally attracted to blonde pretty Cara. She seemed ideal. She had the face of an innocent angel and the soul of a greedy harpy. She was perfect.

Jonjo had taken her to the dogs and doled out

cash for her to bet a fortune at the track, winning some but losing more. Which had put him in a bad mood, but he'd hid it because he was trying to keep the grasping cow sweet.

They had moved on to the Shalimar, where he had drunk too much to show off to his mates and their girlfriends, and now look at the result. Cara sighed. Mr Bendy was back in the saddle again.

Jonjo rolled off her. 'Fuck it,' he said. 'Not in the mood.'

Maybe the blonde thing was getting to be a problem. He liked blondes, as a rule. He liked them dim and big-busted. Cara was all of that – fantastic tits and a brain bypass. Perfect. Maybe he ought to ring the changes, though, swear off blondes for a bit, try a brunette.

But then, look at what had happened to Max with that fucking Bailey slag. Jonjo was pleased that was all over, but Max was still fuming over the whole thing. It was making him edgy and eager for a ruck. Not a bad thing, really. There was this big heist in the offing now, and Jonjo was made up that Max was back.

So maybe not a brunette. Big thinkers, brunettes. They always seemed to have a plan and a way of squeezing your balls until they squeaked. No, the last thing he needed was pussy-whipping.

Maybe a redhead. He'd never had one of those. He thought of Orla Delaney – mad Irish bitch she might be from a long line of mad Irish bitches, but she was a corker. Apparently as frigid as fuck, though, if the rumours were to be believed. Which was a bit of a drawback.

Maybe he'd stick to blondes. Like Cara. If they used her on the heist he would have to lay out the rules. Pay her well, that went without saying. But maybe also give her a light slapping and explain to her that the police might be scary but the firm was scarier. That they must never be mentioned, that if they could pin anything on her at all and it came to doing time, then she did it and was well looked after when she came out. Inside or out, though, she kept quiet. Because inside or out, they would know and they could get to her whenever they wanted. Or to her family, of course. There was always that.

He turned back to Cara, who was pouting prettily because he hadn't come. Women. They always liked you to come. Took it as a deliberate affront if you didn't. Christ, it must be nice to be a tart. Just lie there and let it happen, no worries about getting it up, no worries at all. He was trying, but he couldn't get his mind off the job that was coming up. It was exciting. You couldn't concentrate on your oats with a job like this on your mind, unless you were made of stone. Which reminded him. He was running late.

He reached over to his trouser pocket and pulled out a few sovs. He tossed them at Cara.

'Get yourself a taxi home, there's a love,' he said, and got out of bed.

Cara sat up, indignant. 'Is that it, then?' she demanded.

And that was the other thing, they always wanted to talk after sex. If it went badly they wanted to pull it apart and find out why. If it went well – which usually thank God it did – they wanted you to stay awake for hours whispering sweet nothings in their little ears when all you wanted was to peg out for the night.

'What do you want, "God Save the Queen" or something?' asked Jonjo, covering his limp dick with his pants. 'The evening's over. I've got a meet to get to. Now shift your arse. I'll phone you, okay?' He dropped a kiss on to her rumpled hair. Keep her sweet. Maybe she'd be needed, maybe not. Hedge your bets.

'And they say romance is dead,' she grumbled, crawling out of bed and retrieving her undies from the floor.

Jonjo's mind was already over at Queenie's old place. The boys would be assembling there again, Max at the head of the table.

He hoped that sour-faced wife of Max's wouldn't be there. If there was one thing Jonjo hated it was a woman with a face like a smacked arse on her. He thought Max was far too soft with Ruthie. If she was *his* woman, Jonjo would have kicked her straight up the puss by now. His sister-in-law didn't seem able to make up her mind where she wanted to be. Sometimes she was at the old house, sometimes she was down in Surrey at the big posh place that was now on the market, talking to the estate agent and packing up all their belongings. *Jesus, what a pain in the backside she was.*

Max had confided to Jonjo that Ruthie was a bit too keen on the bottle. She was a loose cannon, Jonjo thought, rattling about the place, skinny as hell and ugly as fuck. At least Annie Bailey had a good set of knockers and a great arse on her.

Even if she was a brunette.

Ruthie Carter was at the Surrey house and, despite the lateness of the hour, she was still up, wrapping things in paper and packing them into tea chests. Max had told her not to bother about the annexe, of course. *He* would see to that. Ruthie sneered to herself and took another pull of her voddy and tonic.

Blimey, this place was a size. She'd already completed the packing up downstairs, helped by Miss Arnott; now she was working her way through the bedrooms. This particular room had been Eddie's. She didn't mind being up here in Eddie's room late at night on her own, with the Surrey night so still and dark all around her. Ruthie didn't believe in ghosts. The dead wouldn't hurt you, she was sure of that. It was the bloody living you had to watch out for.

It was a bit sad to be sifting through his things, though. Eddie had been such a snappy dresser. His clothes were designer, and immaculately clean and cared for. Now what the hell would become of them? She piled all his shirts and trousers and stuff to one side ready for disposal. Unless Max wanted to keep them, but she couldn't really see that happening. Of course he'd kept Queenie's annexe just as it was on the night she'd died, maybe he'd want to build a shrine to his dead brother, too.

She shivered.

Clutching her drink, she went over to the dressing table where Eddie's silver-backed brushes looked forlorn as if they were waiting for him to come back. Well, they'd have a bloody long wait. She pulled out the bottom drawer and yanked out the piles of vests and pants laid neatly in there, then moved on to the next large drawer up and found jumpers and a couple of waistcoats.

All that remained of a life, she thought.

God, she was low today. Lower than usual, and that was saying something. She moved on to the smaller drawers at the top and opened the left-hand drawer to reveal a stack of brown bottles, every one full of the pills they had given Eddie before he died. Pills to ease the pain. Pills to clear infection. A fat lot of use they'd been. And pills to make him sleep. Jesus, how she would love to sleep! Ruthie laughed and the sound was loud in the room. She jumped a bit and looked around, suddenly feeling nervous.

Maybe spirits did linger. Who knew? Maybe Eddie was right here with her now, showing her the way to go. She picked up one of the bottles of sleeping pills. It was full to the brim. She unscrewed the cap and shook a few into the palm of her hand. She raised her hand to her mouth. The taste on her tongue was slightly bitter, but the voddy and tonic washed it away.

41

Annie collected the keys to the Upper Brook Street apartment, and went straight over to see it again. It was perfect, she was made up. In ebullient mood she returned to Limehouse with the keys in her purse and her head full of plans.

She found Dolly alone in the kitchen with a face on her. Jim Reeves was playing on the little red radio by the sink. Dolly loved Jim, usually she sang along to his ballads and was happy. But not today. Annie asked her what was wrong.

'Oh nothing at all,' said Dolly. 'Only you setting up in business with the Delaneys and taking my sodding trade, that's all.'

You could always rely on Dolly to call a spade a shit-shovel.

Annie sat down at the table. After Dolly's reaction to her moving back in, she had been expecting something like this.

'I'm not taking your trade,' said Annie. 'I'll be operating up West.'

'Look. My gents come out from Whitehall to get here to Limehouse for a good time. They won't bother if you're right there on the bleeding doorstep.'

'Yes they will. You've got a nice client list going. Lots of regulars, and they're loyal. They'll still come.'

'No they won't.'

'They will. And you know damn well that the parties are oversubscribed. You do three parties a month, I can do one on the week you don't, how's that? You must agree there's already an overspill. I can take care of that. You can pass business to me and I'll pass business to you. It'll work.'

Dolly looked sceptical. 'Those brasses up West are going to expect to be paid the earth,' she warned. 'They know the clients have got plenty of cash.'

'We'll work something out.'

Dolly nodded. 'What's he really like then – Redmond Delaney?'

Annie thought of how it had been in the Upper Brook Street apartment when she had been there with Redmond. He'd looked the place over with his pale eyes and his calculator brain. Two minders with him, because there'd been a lot of trouble on the manor lately. The estate agent had been white and sweating while they followed him around,

337

there had been a lot of nervous laughter. Poor bastard. Annie didn't miss not having a minder. She wondered what had become of Donny, her own personal hulking shadow. He might have gone back to Manchester. Or down to Smithfield meat market like Celia, if Max wasn't happy with his answers about her leaving.

'He's scary,' said Annie. 'Cold.'

'Just like on the phone then,' said Dolly. 'You being polite to him when he rings?'

'God yes. Arse-licking like mad.'

They both knew that respect was due, and lack of it was dangerous. Look at what had happened to Celia with Max. Annie still shuddered when she thought about it. She still couldn't quite believe it. She'd never thought Max would make war on women, but he had. Who knew with boys like these where the lines were drawn? These were hard men, and you stepped carefully around them.

'If there's nothing else?' Annie asked, standing up.

'Your sister phoned while you were out.' Dolly pulled a face. 'She sounded pissed. Wanted to talk to you.'

Yeah, to heap more abuse on her head. Annie didn't need any more aggravation. It was bad enough that she felt like a cruel bitch for giving Kieron the hard word. All she needed was Ruthie spitting poison down the phone at her. Annie picked up her bag.

'I might give her a call later on,' she said. *Or I might not.* 'I'll be moving out on the Monday after next, Doll. I need to get some girls lined up, I hope you don't mind if I do that while I'm here?'

'Nah, I don't mind,' said Dolly. 'So long as you don't pinch my new girls out from under my nose. They're good girls and I want to keep them.'

'I just need their contacts,' said Annie. 'A couple of them are classy, they'll know the West End working girls.'

Dolly thought. 'Okay then,' she said.

Talk about walking on fucking eggshells, thought Annie, but she was more amused than put out by Dolly's carping.

'I just want to say thanks for this,' she said. 'For letting me stay and everything.'

'What else are friends for?' asked Dolly. She hesitated. 'I hope it goes well up West. I really do.'

The best and most trustworthy boys were in for the meet upstairs at Queenie's old place. Max and Jonjo were there, with Jimmy Bond their number-one man, and Gary Tooley and Steven Taylor – all staunch men. Deaf Derek was off somewhere getting pissed; since Eddie had come to grief, Derek had learned the hard way to give Max and Jonjo a wide berth; he was no longer welcome in their inner circle. He counted himself lucky to be still breathing.

Sitting near the head of the table with Jonjo and Max was an ex-telephone engineer and a gelly man, both recommended to Max by one of the other London firms.

'So run that past me again,' said Max.

Jonjo loved to see his brother like this, focused on business like he should be. Life was too short to get hung up on a piece of skirt. He was pleased to see that Max had finally realized this. Jonjo was excited about the job. It was a large department store on the Delaney patch, rich pickings from all accounts. With any luck it would cause the Delaneys major grief, which would be a bonus.

'There's a frame room where all the lines come into the premises and cross-connect,' said the engineer. He was lanky and bald and his eyes were active, like his brain. 'All the lines inside the building, to each department and to the alarm, come out of this point. I have to get in there.'

'Piece of piss,' said Jonjo. 'Jimmy can open any locked door, he'll be with you.'

Jimmy nodded. He had already cased the store; Jonjo's insider had pointed out a room marked Staff Only that the security guy never bothered to check on, where they could hide away before the store closed. All they had to do was wait until the appointed hour and then get inside the frame room.

'Once I'm in there, I go to the records and find the alarm's DP on the cards.'

340

'Meaning?' asked Max.

'The distribution point, the line the alarm's on.'

'Then what?'

'It's simple. I bare the wires here and here.' He did a little drawing on a notepad. 'Then I put on two crocodile clips to the bare surfaces with a diverter wire attached. The circuit's still complete but the alarm's inactive.'

Max nodded. 'That's good. We come in the back entrance. The alarm's out. Then it's over to you, Jack.'

Jack was the gelly man. He was sandy-haired with a red moustache. He had the look of an airline pilot or a submarine commander – icy cool under fire. Jesus, thought Jonjo, when you were handling gelignite you had to be bloody cool, or you were in trouble. No good getting all hot and sticky. That stuff sweated like a bastard as it was.

'No problem,' said Jack, and placed a packet of three condoms on the table. 'I use these.'

'You're having a fucking laugh,' said Steven.

'French letters or balloons,' said Jack. 'They're the best things for keeping your gelly in.'

There was a surge of laughter from around the table.

'I've heard it all now,' said Gary.

Jack went on to explain how he intended to crack the department store safe wide open, so they could pocket the thirty grand that should be inside it. Not a bad night's work, and it sounded easy enough. Made you wonder why more people weren't out on the rob, really.

The meeting broke up after midnight and, as the other boys filed out, Jimmy took Max to one side.

'Kath asked me to tell you that Ruthie's not answering the phone,' he said.

'Oh?' Max was pulling on his coat.

'Kath rings Ruthie on Monday at seven in the evening, then Ruthie rings her on Tuesday, and so on all through the week. Only Kath's been ringing and getting no answer, and Ruthie hasn't called her either.'

Fuck it. Bloody Ruthie was a liability. She was probably on the piss again, laid out on the sofa and drunk as a lord.

'I'll give Miss Arnott a call.' Then Max remembered that they'd already let Miss Arnott go. Damn. Ruthie was on her own down there apart from his boy, and he wasn't exactly the brain of Britain. If he heard the house phone ringing off the hook, he wouldn't trouble himself to wonder why.

'I thought I'd better mention it,' said Jimmy apologetically.

'Yeah. Thanks.'

With everyone else gone, Max went downstairs to the hall and phoned the Surrey place. No bloody answer. He rang Dave's number, but no answer from there either. He flung the phone back on the cradle. Fuck that raving drunk. He ought to just let her stew. But . . . there was something else he could do. He dialled again.

'Hello?' One of the Limehouse tarts had picked up.

'Put Annie on, will you?' he asked.

'Who shall I say?'

'Max.'

There was a pause.

'This is Dolly,' said the woman. 'I'm sorry, Mr Carter. Annie's told me she don't want to talk to you.'

'Put her the fuck on this phone,' said Max. 'It's about her sister.'

Yeah, revenge was sweet. Annie was so concerned about Ruthie, was she? She couldn't go on doing Max behind her sister's back? Fair enough. So let her look after her fucking sister, if they were so tight together.

'Hello?'

It was Annie. Sounded like she'd been dragged out of bed. Well, good. Fuck her.

'Ruthie's not answering her phone. Kath's been trying to reach her, and she can't. I haven't the time. You can go down and see what she's up to,' he said.

'*Me?*' Annie sounded aghast. 'It's after bloody midnight.'

'Yeah, you. Didn't you say you were concerned for your sister? Prove it. Put your money where your fucking mouth is. I'll send the car round and the key.'

'Wait! Just a bloody minute.' Annie clutched her head and tried to think. Ruthie would be passed out drunk again, that was all. Max was just playing silly buggers, winding her up deliberately. 'Okay. I'll go in the morning. Send the car at ten. All right?'

'Deal.' Max threw the phone back into the cradle. Women! They were a pain in the arse, a bloody torment. Jonjo was right. And why, when he had everything he wanted out of life – money, prestige, respect, all that shit, and he could have any woman in the world he wanted – why then did he only want *that* one, that fucking Annie Bailey?

It was a mystery.

It was beyond him.

42

At ten on the dot on Friday morning one of Max's boys pulled up outside the house. Annie had been watching from the window, waiting. She hadn't slept a wink all night. As she lay awake in bed she started to think, what if Ruthie wasn't just arsing about drinking herself into a stupor? What if she was in trouble and needed help? Maybe she should have gone down there last night, or maybe she was just panicking over nothing.

God, she wasn't looking forward to this.

Ruthie hated her, and it hurt like fuck.

At lunchtime Dolly put one of her favourites on the radiogram in the front room. Brian the barman was lining up bottles and polishing glasses, setting out the food the girls had prepared this morning. Dolly hummed and twirled along to Andy Williams. Smiling, she looked around; the whole room gleamed, the food looked good. Brian poured her a voddy and black, she liked that. Everything was going well.

She was happy. She was in control.

'Hey, babe, got one of those for me?' asked Aretha, coming in wearing black PVC thigh boots and a white plastic bikini.

Brian poured her a shot.

'Everything ready?' Aretha asked Dolly.

'Yep.'

'What crap's that you've got playing? Girl, ain't you heard of the Stones? This stuff is just *gone*, Dolly.'

'It's a classic, Aretha.'

And then the bell rang, and they were on.

It was a good party. There were a few gentlemen from the Horse Guards, nice, fit, muscular men who had been recommended by friends and family. Dolly's was the place to be for fun. Experienced men loved the diversity of the girls here. Young innocents were brought here by their fond papas to be properly introduced to the arts of love.

Ellie set to work with two of the Guards upstairs. Darren had one of his regular politicians, and Aretha was doling out severe punishment to a High Court judge. Two of the new girls were going at it like good 'uns with a couple of the older clients in the front room – the stairs were difficult for them, poor old sods – while Dolly circulated and made sure everyone was happy. Chris was on duty at the door. Brian was mixing drinks and keeping a deadpan face on him, as ordered. Annie had cleared off somewhere, Dolly didn't know where. Everything was fine – until Pat Delaney showed up.

Dolly didn't like Pat Delaney. She wondered if anyone did. He was a creep. Annie reckoned he'd been passing stuff around at a couple of the parties. She'd told Redmond about it, apparently, but Redmond hadn't brought Pat into line. If Redmond couldn't do it, they sure as fuck couldn't. You didn't cross a Delaney. It would be madness.

So she greeted him politely while he sneered at her and glared at Chris.

'It's the new Queen of Tarts,' he said with a laugh. 'Where's the old one then? Busy upstairs, is she?'

'If you mean Annie, she's out,' said Dolly.

'Shame,' said Pat. He was swaying on his feet and sweating. His eyes looked odd. He was high as a kite, Dolly realized with a sinking feeling. 'I like a high-class cunt like her.'

Suppressing an expression of disgust, Dolly guided him into the front room, throwing a look back at Chris. *Watch him*, she mouthed. Chris nodded.

'What can we get you to drink, Mr Delaney?' asked Brian.

'You a poof? You look like one,' said Pat.

Brian flushed brick red.

'Mr Delaney likes whisky,' said Dolly quickly, and Brian poured him a Bell's.

Pat reeled away with his drink and collapsed on to the sofa, nearly landing on one of the girls and a frail old gent.

'Watch it!' complained the girl.

'Fuck off out of the way, you filthy whore,' said Pat icily.

The girl took one look in Pat's eyes and scrabbled up, dragging her old gentleman with her, his trousers still at half-mast. They fell to his ankles and he clawed at them, embarrassed. Pat let out a shout of laughter.

'Everything okay?' asked Darren, coming down the stairs with his client and seeing Dolly's face as she stood in the front-room doorway.

'I don't know,' she said. And then she noticed that Chris wasn't in his seat any more.

Annie let herself into the Surrey place. There was no sign of Ruthie's minder. She looked around at the great dark barn of a hallway and the big sweep of the staircase and heard only silence.

Christ, the place was huge. She thought of Ruthie living here, all alone. She must be going out of her head.

'Ruthie!' Annie called.

There was no answer.

She went through to the drawing room; empty, the fire unlit. She wandered through the whole ground floor, checked the kitchens, calling Ruthie's name with increasing exasperation. Then she traipsed up the stairs and repeated the exercise, feeling more anxious with every step she took.

'Ruthie! Where the hell are you?'

She pushed open three bedroom doors and found only emptiness beyond. She opened the fourth, and there was Ruthie, slumped fully dressed across the bed, boxes and clothes scattered around her. The nearly empty voddy bottle and the glass were there too.

'Oh Jesus – Ruthie!'

Annie hurried to her side, her innards twisting with guilt as she saw Ruthie lying there drunk – drunk because she was miserable, and why was she miserable? Because of what *she* had done to her.

'Oh, Ruthie, no,' she moaned, snatching up Ruthie's cold hand. 'No, don't do this . . .'

And then she saw the pill bottles. Lots of them.

The clients were leaving like rats from a sinking ship. Not that Dolly blamed them. Pat Delaney was insulting everyone, laughing at their elderly gents, asking the Guards why they had to pay for it, couldn't they get a woman to look at them, or did they just shag their precious horses?

'You mouthy Irish bastard,' snarled one, and Dolly had to step in quick.

'Ah, you think you'd like a bit of me, do you, you poncy toy soldier?' mocked Pat, downing tablets as he spoke.

'Let's all calm down,' said Dolly, wondering where the fuck Chris was when you needed him. 'Let's all have a drink together and be friends, okay?'

'I'm not drinking with him,' said the Guard, shrugging into his shirt and stuffing it into his trousers. And he left.

'You're driving my clients away, Mr Delaney,' said Dolly mildly.

'Like I give a feck,' said Pat. He reeled off to the toilet and came back again. 'Another drink over here, poof-features,' he said to Brian as he fell back on to the sofa in the rapidly emptying front room.

Dolly nodded to Brian. Best to give the sod all the drink he wanted, she thought. The sooner he passed out cold, the better. Then she'd just get some of Redmond's boys to carry him out and take him home. No good waiting for Chris to put in an appearance. Chris was no fool. Rather than get into a ruck with Pat and make a vicious and powerful enemy, he was keeping out of it. Dolly couldn't blame him for that. But all the Guards were gone now. It was starting to get dark outside, and the extra girls were making going-home noises. Brian was packing up too. Soon there would be just her and Ellie and Aretha and Darren alone with Pat Delaney, and that wasn't a cheering thought.

'Come on, Ruthie. Don't arse about, you're scaring me.'

Annie was patting her sister's cheek whilst feeling the sickness rise in her own stomach. She was sweating all over, the fear squeezing her in a tight vice-like grip. Jesus, she'd slit her own wrists if the stupid cow was dead. She felt Ruthie's scrawny neck and thank God, there was a pulse. She was breathing. She was alive. Her eyes flickered open.

'Oh thank fuck for that,' gasped Annie, and hauled her sister into a sitting position.

Ruthie moaned. Her eyes rolled up in her head and she sank back.

'No, Ruthie. Come on.'

Fuck, this was bad, really bad. She'd known Ruthie was unhappy, but she had no idea she was low enough to try and finish it. Annie felt her guts twist with guilt. This was all her fault. What had she been thinking of, getting involved with Max? And poor Ruthie had been closer to Mum than she herself had ever been, she must have been feeling the loss of Connie so much more than her. Annie should have been here for her, she should have made sure she was all right.

Ah, but you felt too guilty even to look your

sister in the eye, didn't you? mocked a voice in her head. *If there was damage done, you didn't want to see it, did you?*

Which was true enough.

Annie ran down the stairs to the kitchen. She put the kettle on to boil, then she flung open cupboards and found the salt. She ran water into a glass tumbler, spooned salt into it, and raced back up the stairs. Ruthie was still lying there, her eyes open and gazing glassily at the ceiling. Annie hauled her up again. Ruthie moaned and muttered in protest.

'Come on Ruthie. Drink up,' said Annie, and held the glass to her sister's lips.

It must have tasted foul. Ruthie's face screwed up and she started to gag. Annie held her nose. Water sputtered on to the counterpane and all down the front of Ruthie's dress, but a lot went down her throat. Ruthie pushed weakly against Annie as she made her down every drop of the vile-tasting liquid.

'Oh you . . . you *bitch* . . .' gasped Ruthie, and then she started to retch.

'That's it,' said Annie. 'Let's get it up,' she said, patting Ruthie's back. Her shoulder-blades were like knives poking through her skin.

I did that to her, thought Annie.

'You *bitch*,' groaned Ruthie again, and began to heave.

Vomit splattered out over the carpet.

'That's it,' said Annie, as the smell and the mess erupted out of her.

Ruthie heaved again, and more came.

'God, I hate you, you bitch, you bloody *whore*,' whimpered Ruthie as drool hung from her lips.

Annie put a hand on Ruthie's brow. She was sweaty and white, but hopefully she'd got whatever she'd taken out of her system.

Ruthie spat and wiped a shaking hand across her mouth. She looked at Annie, focused on her for the first time. 'You utter *cow*,' she said.

Annie went back downstairs and made strong coffee. She found cloths and a bowl and filled it with sudsy water. Then she took the whole lot back upstairs.

Ruthie was perched on the edge of the bed now, looked disgustedly at the floor. Annie handed her a mug of strong black coffee.

'Drink,' she ordered.

'I bet you're bloody enjoying yourself,' accused Ruthie, wet-eyed and shaking. She clasped the mug of coffee.

'Drink it up or I'll hold your nose and pour it down you,' said Annie, getting to work on cleaning up the mess.

'Cow.'

By the time Annie had disposed of all the stuff Ruthie had sicked up, Ruthie was halfway through the coffee. Annie stood up.

'Come on now, on your feet.'

'Oh, just leave, will you? I didn't ask you to come here,' said Ruthie weakly.

'I said on your feet,' said Annie, and grabbed the mug and put it aside. She pulled Ruthie up with an arm around her waist and walked her up and down beside the bed, with Ruthie all the while pouring curses in her ear.

'Call me a whore, call me what you like, just keep walking,' said Annie.

Ruthie staggered at first. Annie had to use all her strength to hold her up. But after a few steps Ruthie seemed to regain her equilibrium, and that was when the cursing really kicked in. When Ruthie could stand alone, Annie let go and poured out more coffee and thrust it at her sister.

'I hate you, Annie Bailey,' said Ruthie.

'Hate away,' said Annie. 'Drink the bloody coffee and tell me what the fuck you were trying to do. Were you trying to kill yourself?'

'Oh you'd like that, wouldn't you,' said Ruthie. 'Me out of the way and you left with Max.'

'I told you. It's over, me and Max. Drink that fucking coffee or I mean it, I'll force it down you.'

Ruthie pulled a face but drank the coffee.

'It's over,' reiterated Annie.

'Sure it is,' mocked Ruthie. 'It'll never be over, you and him. I've seen the way he reacts to the sight of you. I saw it at poor Eddie's funeral. Oh yes, I saw you. It'll only be over when they shovel him into the ground, don't you know that?'

'Don't say that.'

'Ah, you don't like the thought of that?' Ruthie crowed. 'And you said it was over? Tell me another.'

'You know, I think you were nicer when you were spark out on the bed,' said Annie. 'You finished that coffee?'

'There.' Ruthie presented the empty mug like a triumphant child. 'Pleased now, you bossy bitch?'

Annie went to the window and opened it, letting in an icy wind to blow away the stink. She gathered up the remaining pill and vodka bottles then put the empty mug on the tray with the sodden cloths and the bowl.

'Get yourself washed and changed,' said Annie. 'I'm going to clear this lot away. I'll see you down in the drawing room. Get a move on.'

Annie was almost surprised when half an hour later Ruthie appeared in a clean dress, with her face washed and her hair neatly combed. She looked pale, but okay.

Annie sat on the couch and Ruthie sat opposite. Annie saw Ruthie's eyes go to the drinks cabinet, but she didn't get herself a drink or offer Annie one.

'Why'd you do it, Ruthie?' asked Annie urgently. '*Were* you trying to top yourself?'

Ruthie dropped her head into her hands. Suddenly

she looked haggard and ten years older than she actually was. 'I was just trying to get some sleep last night, that's all. I don't sleep well. I took some pills of Eddie's, then I wondered if I had taken enough to make me sleep so I took a few more, and I drank a bit, then I don't remember anything else until you started slapping me about this morning. I wasn't trying to top myself, I really wasn't. But I hate this place, it's so lonely. Since Eddie's gone it's got even worse. There's no one here to talk to and I'm forever in the shadow of the sainted Queenie. Max is never here. When he is, he never talks to me.'

Max hated drunks, Annie knew that. To see his own wife smashed out of her face every day would drive him up the wall. But she couldn't get over the fact that it was Max and herself who had done this to Ruthie. Would she have become a bloody drunk if Max was a better husband, and if she had been a better sister to the poor cow? Annie doubted it.

'Ruthie,' said Annie carefully, 'there must still be something between you?'

For a moment Ruthie's eyes showed only raw pain.

'Nothing,' she said. 'We don't have sex. We don't even talk.'

And I shouldn't feel happy about that, thought Annie. But she did and she hated herself for still feeling that tug of attraction to such a bastard. Now here was her chance to make amends for the hurt she had inflicted on the sister she loved, and she was determined to take it.

'Ruthie . . . I promise you it's all over. I never wanted this to happen. Let me help you, please.'

Ruthie stared at her with hostile eyes.

'What, are you going to show me your whoring tricks? Show me what you and my bloody husband have been up to?'

'No! I didn't mean that and you know it.'

'Well I don't need any help from a whore like you, Annie.'

Annie jumped to her feet and stood there glaring down at Ruthie. *'Stop calling me that!'*

'What? Whore? Why not? It's what you are, after all.' Ruthie stood up too and stood nose to nose with her sister. *'Whore!'*

Annie slapped her hard across the face.

Ruthie reeled back and fell on to the couch, clutching at her cheek.

'Oh God.' Annie was instantly contrite. 'I didn't mean to do that, I'm sorry.'

'Just get out,' said Ruthie, her eyes full of tears. 'Get *out!*'

Annie's shoulders slumped. 'All right. I'll go. You know, you'll only get so many chances with me, Ruthie. I can't just go on and on apologizing for ever. It wasn't my idea to come here anyway, it was Max who sent me. He was worried because you weren't answering the phone to Kath.'

Ruthie stiffened.

'I thought you said it was over, you lying cow,' said Ruthie.

'It *is*.' Annie threw her arms wide in frustration. God, she just couldn't seem to get through to Ruthie, no matter how hard she tried.

'What, having cosy little chats about me? When did he talk to you, when you were tucked up in bed together, was that it? Just *get out of my house!*'

43

It was dark by the time Annie got back to Limehouse, and the instant she walked in she knew there was trouble. Dolly was hovering in the front-room doorway looking fraught. Chris was missing. Aretha was leaning against the stair-well with a taut expression on her face. Darren, standing beside her, was chewing a hangnail, his eyes darting to and fro. Ellie was sitting halfway up the stairs.

The place was quiet. No music, no clink of glasses. No *clients*. Except Pat Delaney, Annie noted through the open doorway, sitting in the front room alone and clearly drunk. He raised his glass to her.

'Trouble?' she asked Dolly.

'Not yet.'

'What, has he been on the uppers again?'

'Yeah. Bold as brass. He's been popping Dexedrine tablets like Smarties.'

'Where's Chris?'

'Somewhere well away from here,' said Dolly unhappily. 'He's no fool. He don't want to get into a fight with Pat. One of the clients nearly floored the bastard, but I stepped in.'

'Given him plenty to drink?'

'Yeah. He must have a lead-lined belly to take all that whisky and still be conscious.'

They looked gloomily in at Pat, who was still swigging it back. He raised his glass to them again. Both Annie and Dolly pasted smiles on their faces, which dropped the instant they turned away.

'He's a horrible, fat, Irish turd,' said Darren with a shudder.

'Just keep pouring the drink down him,' advised Annie. 'I'm off upstairs to clean up, okay?'

They nodded. Annie stepped past Ellie and at last reached the sanctuary of her room. She felt drained. Seeing Ruthie again had done nothing for her self-esteem. Too much had happened, too much time had gone by for her to even begin to set things straight again. She had to just keep away from Max. That was a start. And she had to keep trying with Ruthie. No matter how many knock-backs she got, she just had to keep slogging away; whether she would admit it or not, Ruthie needed her. And Annie still loved her. She was her blood, her kin. She meant the world to her.

Nice to be Catholic like the Delaneys, thought Annie. Nice to go to a priest and be absolved from sin. To confess, do penance, to have the whole thing over and done. Protestants – even lapsed ones like her and her family – didn't have that luxury.

She kicked off her shoes with a sigh and unzipped her dress, then froze. There were shouts and heavy footfalls on the stairs. She hardly had time to turn before the door banged wide open. The picture behind the door fell from the wall and the glass shattered. Pat Delaney was there, a bull-like presence in the doorway, swaying and leering.

'So here we are, Annie Bailey!' he said jovially, although his eyes glittered with malice. 'Not very polite, is it, to come in and not say a proper hello to a Delaney boy.'

Annie held her dress together and looked at him. 'Hello, Mr Delaney,' she said. 'Now please leave my room.'

'Eeewww! Hoity-toity, aren't we, Annie Bailey?' Pat mocked. 'Not so stuck up around the Carter boys now, are you?'

Annie saw Dolly, Darren and Aretha pile up into the doorway, their faces anxious. Ellie appeared too, half-hiding behind Darren.

'I asked you to leave, Mr Delaney,' said Annie.

Her heart was beating out a sickening tattoo. 'Let's all go downstairs and have a drink, yes?'

'No,' said Pat, lurching forward. Annie stepped sharply back. Fuck Chris, clearing off like that – looking after number one, the selfish bastard.

Dolly stepped up behind Pat. 'I think Annie's right,' she said firmly. 'We'll all go downstairs together and have some fun, how about it, Mr Delaney?'

She placed a hand on Pat's arm. Pat shook it off, spun around and slapped her hard across the face. She flew backward, knocking into Darren, who caught her with a shout of dismay and put her back on her feet. Dolly touched a shaking hand to her mouth and it came away bloody.

'Get away from me, you filthy tart,' said Pat. 'I'm not interested in your scuzzy arse, it's this one I want to have a go at. Max Carter's own personal whore. And good at it too, I'm told.'

'Hey, you don't come in here treatin' people like that,' said Aretha as she cradled Dolly.

Pat put his face up close to hers. 'You want to do something about it, girl? You tired of having limbs or something? You want to end up like the other one, without anything to scratch your black arse with?'

Annie blinked. Surely he wasn't talking about *Celia*? But there wasn't time for thinking. He was

362

coming at her again, ignoring the others crowding into the doorway. Dolly winced and spat out a tooth.

'Come here to Daddy, darlin',' he oozed. 'Let's see what makes you so special.'

'Get out,' said Annie, backing away. She'd had enough.

'You won't be saying that when I'm in,' laughed Pat.

To her horror he started fiddling with his fly. He lunged at her, grabbing the front of her dress and pulling hard. It came away, ripping loudly in the stunned silence. Annie staggered and fell to her knees, then Pat was clawing at her, bruising her arms, snatching at her breasts. Then Darren jumped on to his back, and Pat reeled sideways under the weight.

'Go on, Darren,' yelled Aretha.

Pat fell against the wall, dislodging more pictures. Annie was aware that she was kneeling in debris, blood on the floor, she'd cut her knee. She felt deathly cold and her head was humming. She was afraid she might faint. Christ knew what would happen then.

But Darren was out of his depth. Pat rammed back against the wall, trapping him with his greater weight against the solid surface. Darren screamed and fell away whilst Pat turned on him as he lay on the floor, a foot raised ready to kick. Suddenly

Aretha piled in and caught Pat a double-fisted blow on the chin.

He staggered, then straightened. His face registered dumb surprise. Then he swung at her. She dodged, and fell over Annie. Dolly came charging in then, and hit him over the head with a bit of shattered picture frame she'd plucked from the floor. He went down like a sack of shit. Then he crawled up again.

'Oh fuck,' gasped Dolly.

Blood was running down over his face where he had been cut by the sharp edge of the frame. They all watched in horror as he grinned around at them. Annie could remember Max telling her about men who got drunk and drugged and then into fights. You could hit them with a house brick, he said, and they'd just keep coming. They couldn't feel a thing. They were dangerous because they could feel no pain.

Jesus, she thought. *We're in big trouble here.*

There was no going back from this. They had attacked Pat Delaney. He would neither forgive nor forget it. He would make them pay in blood.

Suddenly he charged at Dolly. Darren came up again and so did Aretha. Ellie was backed up against the banister on the landing, screaming the bloody place down. Aretha jumped on him, her hands locked around his throat. Darren started hammering at his massive head with his fists. Pat was still moving. He collided with Dolly and she went down under his weight with a screech of pain. Annie hauled herself up on to the bed and staggered to her feet. She locked eyes with Ellie, who looked frantic. Then Annie grabbed a sliver of glass from the floor and plunged it into Pat Delaney's back.

He let out a howl, more animal than human. Annie thought that she would never forget that sound. She tried to yank the shard out again. Her hands were slippery with blood, whether hers or Pat's she didn't know. She felt numb. Dolly scrambled out from under his bulk and incredibly he came up again, rounding on them with the glass still in him, roaring out his rage and hate.

Annie looked at him. There was murder in his vile, pig-like eyes. He was going to kill them. She knew it. First her, then the others. He lurched towards her and she scuttled back, hobbling. Her leg was wet from the knee down.

'Bastard stinking whore!' Pat's arms pin-wheeled as he fought to keep his balance. He was losing blood from several places, yet he was still going. Annie rolled back across the bed to get away, and she saw Ellie dash into the room holding the cuffs from the Punishment Chair. Aretha grabbed them and got one on to Pat's wrist before he twisted on the bed and punched her away. She fell stunned to the floor.

Dolly and Darren leapt on to him on the bed. The cuff was dangling, if they could get it fastened at least his arms would be pinned. Dolly almost had it, but he knocked her away.

Annie piled back into the fray. They were all panting and grunting with exertion, like dogs on a bear. She poured all the hatred she felt for this foul bastard into one huge roundhouse punch to the jaw. Pat's head snapped back. Annie saw that his shirt was soaked with blood. She hit him again. At last, she got the other cuff closed. She was sobbing and could smell her own sour sweat. He had reduced her to the level of an animal, fighting for survival.

'Rope,' gasped Dolly. 'Ellie, fetch it!'

Ellie was gone again. All four of them were on Pat, trying to hold him where he was. He was too strong. He was throwing them off, one by one. Darren went flying, then Aretha. Dolly was clawing grimly at Pat's ankles while Annie sat on his chest, her hands locked around his throat. He was going puce with lack of air, but he was still struggling and cursing.

Ellie was back. Dolly grabbed the rope and started trying to get it around Pat's ankles, but he was kicking and lunging too much. She couldn't do it. Pat threw Annie off and got back to his feet. Annie was slumped on the floor, Dolly in a tangle with the rope. Darren and Aretha were exhausted.

Ellie was clutching at the doorframe and still screaming at the top of her lungs.

We're dead, thought Annie. *This is it. We're dead.*

Pat Delaney lurched towards her. He no longer looked even human. Blood was pouring down over his head, more blood oozed from his chest. He was making gurgling sounds and was cuffed but even so it was no good. It wasn't enough. Annie looked up at him, he seemed to fill her entire world. She waited for death. The others were finished. Done for. No fight left. Pat came closer and leaned down towards her. She shrank back against the side of the bed, nowhere left to go, nothing left to do.

Then there was a movement behind him and a screaming Ellie jumped on to his back. Annie saw the kitchen knife in her small hand, saw it come arcing round. It opened up Pat's throat from ear to ear. Blood sprayed, soaking Annie, sluicing over the bed.

Pat collapsed, taking Ellie with him. The hot metallic stench of blood filled the room. Annie felt herself starting to gag on the smell. He rolled. Ellie jumped aside, throwing the knife down with a cry of disgust. Pat lay on his back, gurgling. Then more blood came out of his mouth and his eyes went blank; they stared up at the ceiling and saw nothing.

There was a sudden, shocking silence.

They had killed Pat Delaney.

And now the Delaneys would kill them.

Annie's eyes caught Dolly's. She saw the panic she felt reflected there. Dolly knew the score. You didn't fuck with a member of the family firm you paid your dues to and then walk away from it. Pat might not have finished them, but his family would.

For a long while nobody moved. They were too exhausted from the fight, too fearful of what was to come. Ellie was sobbing gently. She crawled away from Pat's body, and one of the cuffed hands twitched. Ellie started to shriek. Dolly scrabbled over to her, grabbed her and held on tight.

'It's all right, he's dead,' she said, her voice muffled by her swelling mouth. 'It's just a twitch, just the life leaving the body, he's not going to hurt anyone any more.'

Ellie's shrieks softened to tears.

Annie looked over at Aretha. She was drenched with sweat, but she looked okay. Darren had pulled himself up into a chair and was sitting with his head in his hands. Annie's eyes drifted on and met Dolly's again.

'We're finished,' said Dolly.

Annie didn't say a word.

*   *   *

'We'll have to get out of here,' said Annie.

Dolly looked around at the wrecked room in growing panic. Her face was a picture of fear and sickness. This place had become her castle, her stronghold against the outside world. To leave it would be unbearable. She shook her head.

'I'm not leaving here,' she said.

'We have to, Doll,' said Annie. 'The Delaneys are going to want our blood for this.'

'I'm not leaving,' repeated Dolly.

'Dolly.' Annie's voice was desperate now. 'We have no choice.'

'Yes we do. We could get rid of the body.'

Annie snapped at this. 'For fuck's sake, Dolly, see sense. We couldn't even lift him. He's too bloody big for us to move. You know it, I know it.'

Dolly moved her eyes to the Irishman lying at her feet.

'Jesus, it stinks in here,' moaned Aretha.

She stood up and tottered off to the bathroom. They heard her retching. Annie had thought Aretha was tough, but this scene of carnage was too much even for her.

'What are we going to do?' moaned Darren. 'Chris could come back at any minute. He won't stand for this. He'll tell Redmond Delaney. We'll be fucked.'

'Ellie,' said Annie.

Ellie turned a tearstained face to her.

'You're going to have to keep Chris busy. Get yourself cleaned up. Go and wait for him in the hall, and when he comes back take him into the front room. Close the door. He likes you, he'll take the bait. Make sure he does.'

'I can't,' whined Ellie. She knew what was expected of her. If Chris wanted sex, she had to provide it. But after all this, she felt too shattered to take on anyone.

'Just do as you're bloody-well told, will you!' shouted Annie. 'Get going. *Hurry*.'

Ellie got to her feet like a weary old woman and staggered from the room. Dolly looked at Annie.

'There is something else we can do,' she said. 'We don't have to leave.'

'*Dolly!*' Annie said in exasperation. 'See reason. We can't stay here. We can't move him. We've got to go.'

'*No,*' said Dolly. 'It's obvious. I know what we should do.' She was babbling now, the idea in her mind putting a mad light into her eyes. 'Who would help us get rid of a Delaney? A fucking Carter! Max Carter's still hung up on you, Annie. Everyone says so. You could phone him. He'd help you.'

'No. I can't.'

'You have to. He'll know what to do. He'll send the boys round and they'll take care of this mess.'

370

Fuck it. The more she tried to extract herself from involvement with Max, the more she seemed to get sucked in. She felt like she was struggling in quicksand, sinking deeper by the minute. She knew what Dolly said made perfect sense. Max would help her. She knew he would help her. And this was his type of territory. He would know how to deal with this; she didn't.

Into her mind came Pat's words when he had threatened Aretha. He'd implied that he'd been responsible for what happened to Celia. So did that mean Max hadn't done it? But Celia had been told it was a present from Max.

Annie clutched at her aching head. What did it matter, anyway? They were all violent bastards, intent on maiming any poor fucker who got in their way. She was best off out of it, and maybe she had always known deep down that she would have to let Max go if she was ever to stand a chance of getting Ruthie back.

'*Annie!*' Dolly's voice was harsh, cutting into her thoughts. 'For God's sake, we're in deep shit here. Get down there and phone the man before Chris comes back. Max Carter will work it out. He'll know what to do.' She looked at Darren and at Aretha, who had come back and was standing there in the doorway, her dark skin tinted grey with nausea. 'Darren. Aretha. Get cleaned up and dressed, the pair of you. Quickly. Nothing's

Dirty Game

happened here. Pat went home when all the other clients left. There was nothing out of the ordinary. Behave normally. Say nothing. Got that?'

Darren and Aretha nodded tiredly.

'I don't want to phone him,' said Annie. Her mind was spinning. The cuts on her hands and legs were starting to hurt. She felt sick.

'Do it,' said Dolly. 'Or I'll do it for you.'

372

44

In the early hours of the following morning, Billy stood in the shadows opposite the Limehouse parlour and watched as Gary Tooley and Steven Taylor carried something wrapped in a tarpaulin out to a car. They bundled the thing inside, shut the doors quietly, and were away.

Max's boys.

Billy often liked to walk in the early hours. The streets were quiet, he blended into the darkness, became one with the night. You saw all sorts when you were out late. He walked, and walked, because he slept badly. He was on medication for his nerves, and that seemed to affect his sleep. So he walked. Often he ended up in the street in Limehouse, looking up at the house where his beautiful Annie lived.

He knew which room was hers. He'd worked it out. The one on the left at the front. He stood there sometimes and gazed up at that dark oblong, knowing that beyond it she slept. It was comforting to be nearby. His mum didn't care where he got to in the night. She had a boyfriend, he had to call the man Uncle Ted, but he wasn't his uncle really. His mum was busy with Uncle Ted during the night-times. It was better to be out, to walk, rather than lay there awake listening to them making those animal noises through the wall.

But his quiet stroll tonight had been different. Wearing his mac and deerstalker, clutching his briefcase as he always did, he knew that tonight there had been something going on. Something bad. All the lights had been blazing in the house. Then the boys had shown up and there had been nothing for a while, but he was patient. He had nothing else to do, so he waited. And an hour and a half later, the boys came out with the thing in the tarp. It looked the size and shape of a body, Billy thought. He made a note of it in his book.

It's as if Pat Delaney was never here, thought Annie as she looked around her room next day. Gary and Steve had done a thorough job of cleaning every trace of Pat's death away. It had all gone like clockwork. The angels had been on their side. Chris hadn't come back; he'd phoned through to say that his mum was ill and he was needed at home. They all knew he was just keeping the fuck out of it, but at least Ellie had been spared having to jump his bones. Gary and Steve had come in like shadows and did all that had to be done.

'We'll take the bastard for a swim,' said Gary jokily, wrapping Pat up in what was to be his shroud. 'A nice long dip, eh? We'll take him down Newhaven way, no bother.'

Annie couldn't laugh with them. The callous bastards. It was too horrible. They'd killed a man, and even if that man was a total bastard like Pat Delaney, he had been a living, breathing human being, and they had taken his life, and the guilt was overwhelming. The lowest point had been when she had to limp into the hall and phone Max to ask for his help.

'What sort of help?' he asked. He sounded cold and uncompromising.

'There's been an . . . incident,' said Annie. She eased her sore knee by taking the weight off it. It was bandaged – Darren had tended to all their cuts and bruises. Her hands were bandaged too, where the glass had sliced into them. She looked and felt a mess. And now Max was talking to her as if she was a stranger.

She reminded herself that his coldness to her was a good thing. But she couldn't get Pat's words out of her mind. What if Pat really had done Celia, and not one of Max's mob? No, it was no use thinking like that. She had to think of Ruthie now, and put her first.

'What sort of incident?' he asked.

'A bad one.'

'Meaning?'

'Max, I'm not kidding around here. Take it from me that I wouldn't be on this fucking phone asking for your help if I could avoid it.'

'If that's how you feel . . .' said Max. He was going to hang up on her.

'No!' Annie shouted. 'Please. Don't hang up.' Her voice broke with the strain of it. 'It's serious. Pat Delaney's dead.'

'Tell me,' said Max, and it all poured out.

'*What?*' Max demanded when she told him that Pat had come after her. She could hear his breathing, hard and heavy, could almost taste his anger. But she didn't need that now, not more violence, not more bloodshed. She needed his help.

'We killed him,' she finished at last.

'For fuck's sake. Isn't there a Delaney man on the door?' Now Max's voice had lost its distance. Now he spoke urgently.

'Chris, yes. He vanished when it all started looking like trouble with Pat. It's okay. He phoned through and said his mum was ill, but I think he's just keeping out of it because he could see Pat was

376

acting up and he didn't want to get involved – and I don't fucking blame him either.'

'Do nothing. I'll send someone.'

And he put the phone down on her.

'Max?'

She couldn't believe it, the bastard had just put the phone down. No goodbye, no nothing. And maybe that was it. Maybe he was just going to leave her to sweat, to stew in her own juice. Panic gripped her by the throat. *Christ, what was she going to do if that was the case?*

But, true to his word, he sent his boys. His best boys, too.

Next day she put her coat on and went out into the rain for a walk and stopped off at the phone box. She dialled his number.

'Thanks,' she said, dismayed because her voice shook.

There was so much more she wanted to say to him and it seemed she was able to say nothing. She wanted to broach the subject of Celia, and what she had thought he'd done, and what Pat Delaney had said, but she couldn't get into all that. She felt too tired, too dispirited, too confused. She wanted to talk about Ruthie, and how she had found her, and how frightened she had been when she had thought Ruthie was trying to commit suicide. But it had been just a stupid mix-up with sleeping pills. Had Ruthie died, Annie would have forever blamed herself. But she could say nothing because Ruthie would hate her even more than she did already if she started getting grief off Max. Annie felt drained of all emotion. She supposed dully that it was the shock of what had happened last night.

'Are you all right?' Max demanded. 'Gary said there'd been damage done.'

'A few cuts. Dolly lost a tooth.'

'Nothing serious?'

'Nothing serious.'

'You saw Ruthie.'

'Oh. Yeah. She's . . . okay.' She couldn't talk about it. Ruthie would despise her if she did.

'Right. You owe me for this,' said Max.

Annie stared at the phone.

'What?' she asked numbly.

'You still owe me.'

'Oh.'

'And I will call in the debt.'

'Max, it's over.'

'I told you. Only when I say so.'

And he hung up on her again.

Annie planned to move out of the Limehouse parlour early. She didn't want to stay any longer than necessary in the same room where Pat Delaney had died. She couldn't sleep down in the front room on the sofa in case Chris got wind of it and thought it odd. And Max had said she had to behave normally.

Normally. Like she would ever feel normal again, after she'd been party to murder.

The others weren't finding it easy either. All of them looked like death warmed up, their faces white and strained, and why wouldn't they? It wasn't every day you saw a Delaney die right in front of your eyes.

Of course Chris soon noticed that Annie had injured her knee and her hands. He noticed Dolly's swollen mouth and missing tooth. But they had already thought of this. They had covered all the bases.

'Tell him that Annie and Dolly had a ruck on Friday night over Annie setting up in business,' suggested Darren to Ellie.

This was inspired. All of them knew that the two women had been finding it hard to come to terms with their changed circumstances; an imaginary catfight would be perfect cover for what had really happened.

Ellie obediently told Chris; and Chris seemed to believe her. Dolly gave him a bit of a bollocking for vanishing when things hotted up with Pat, and told him that if he thought she swallowed that load of fanny about his sick mother he had better think again. But thank God, she told him, Pat had buggered off just after he himself had left the premises, so everything was fine – and this time she was not going to tell Redmond Delaney about the fact he'd legged it.

'Thanks, Dolly,' said Chris humbly.

Annie and Dolly beefed up the dirty looks and sullen silences between them, egging the pudding like mad. Annie knew it was time for her to go. She dialled around Dolly's auxiliary brasses and got some names and addresses together. She packed up her belongings within four days of Pat's death and was all ready to go when Kieron showed up with a huge bunch of flowers.

Chris let him in, of course. No way could he refuse a Delaney entry. Annie accepted that. But she didn't need this right now. She had too much on her mind, not least of which, the fact that she had killed this man's brother.

She came downstairs when Chris called her. Better to see him, she supposed, better to keep everything smooth and orderly. She went into the front room and there he was, lanky, blond, appealing, holding a bunch of flowers bigger than he was, the clown. She almost smiled to see it.

'Kieron,' she greeted him formally.

Kieron thrust the huge bouquet at her. 'For you,' he said. 'As an apology. I realize I upset you last time I called, and I'm sorry. I know I've taken my time, but I wasn't sure you'd see me. I've only just managed to pluck up the courage and now here I am.'

'You've nothing to be sorry for.'

'Yes I have. I'm not good at all the romantic stuff . . .'

'You're giving it a fair old try,' said Annie, indicating the bouquet.

'It doesn't come naturally to me,' rushed on Kieron. 'I get too involved in my work, and I don't see things until they hit me right between the eyes. You want to be just friends? Fine. We'll be friends. So, in the spirit of friendship, Annie Bailey, come along to my new exhibition with me or I'll have to go alone and I'll look a great tomfool into the bargain.'

'Kieron,' sighed Annie. 'I don't know.'

'Come on. I need cheering up. Red and Orla can't come, they're tied up with business. And we haven't seen Pat for days, I've no idea where he is, but I'm hoping the bastard won't come back.'

Try the sea, thought Annie. Bile rose in her throat at the thought. She felt strung out, having to remember to keep her story straight, scared shitless that she or one of the girls was going to say something that would cause suspicion, worried about what would happen with Ruthie and Max, and now Kieron hadn't taken the hint. Or if he had, he was covering it up very well.

Here she was again, sitting on a perilously high fence between the Delaneys and the Carters. She seemed unable to get down from it. If anything, it seemed to be getting higher. She couldn't see the ground any more. She barely knew which way was up.

'As a friend only,' warned Annie.

'You'll come?' His big goofy face lit up.

'Yes. All right. Just this once, mind.'

'Just this once,' agreed Kieron.

45

Annie was aware that this day should be a moment of triumph for her. It was the day of her first party in the new apartment. She stood in the centre of the Upper Brook Street place's oak-panelled drawing room and looked around her and saw how far she'd come. This was a million miles from the Limehouse knocking shop. Big leather Chesterfields for the clients to sit on. A crackling fire to keep them warm. Sinatra on the radiogram because Sinatra always said *class*. Champagne and twenty-year-old malt whisky. Oysters and salmon and caviar, all set out on a side table – the best things for the best people. Havana cigars in wooden boxes on the small occasional tables dotted all around the big room. The scene was set. Everything looked good.

'It's a gentleman's club with extras,' said Redmond when he'd walked around it with her just this morning. 'You must be very pleased with it.'

'I am.'

She was nervous of Redmond now, and she didn't have to ask herself why – the ghost of Pat stood between them.

Annie showed him the bedrooms. With any other man she'd be nervous of getting jumped. But not with Redmond; instinct told her this was not his style. She suspected he never had sex. Didn't want it, either. She had the same feeling whenever she saw Orla. Sad somehow – but she was relieved. The last thing she needed was another complication. She had complications enough. She had been bracing herself while they toured the apartment for any mention of Pat, and finally the moment came. Redmond said that Pat hadn't been seen since he left the party at Limehouse the Friday before last.

'Really?' said Annie, her heart galloping her in chest. 'Does he often just take off like that?'

'Occasionally. I hope he caused no trouble at the party?'

Oh Jesus, thought Annie, nearly paralysed with fear.

'He was a bit drunk.' She shrugged. 'No more than usual, though. He seemed fine when he left.'

And – thank God – Redmond said no more about it. He professed himself happy with all the arrangements she had made, and then he left.

Annie dragged her attention back to the here-and-now. Her three new girls, Mira, Jennifer and

Thelma, were sitting around chatting to their clients, just chatting as ladies would do. That was the first rule Annie had insisted upon – no shagging in the drawing room. There were three lovely luxurious bedrooms for that; in there, they could do whatever they wanted. They could have threesomes, foursomes, all-out orgies if they wanted, behind closed doors. But out here, there was to be a polite house-party atmosphere and no one with their trousers around their ankles and their pricks in their hands. There was music, and laughter, and drinking and eating; a prelude to the more serious action. Annie preferred it that way.

'William's invited me to Cliveden with a group of friends for the weekend,' said Mira, sidling up to Annie.

Mira was a statuesque blonde with a don't-touch-me air about her that could soften to oh-go-on-then in an instant, once you showed her enough money. Like the other girls and like Annie herself, Mira was dressed in a simple shift dress with court shoes and pearls. Annie insisted that her girls look like ladies even if they were highly skilled tarts.

'What you do in your own time is your own concern,' said Annie. 'But be careful.'

Mira nodded and moved away, back to the side of the middle-aged peer of the realm she was entertaining. They all knew about Christine Keeler. Pillow-talk was all very well, Annie had stressed when she gave the girls their initial pep-talk, but you had to be circumspect about cross-contamination. Like don't mix Soviets with British Cabinet Ministers. When you were moving in these high circles, it was easy to slip and fall, and it was always the woman who carried the can, not the punter.

'Sir Paul, how nice to see you. How are you?' said Annie in her best 'posh' voice to a distinguished, grey-haired gentleman, one of the Limehouse regulars, as she sat down beside him.

He told her, in detail. She nodded and smiled and laughed in all the right places. The party was going well. But still, she felt screwed up into a knot. She had felt that way ever since the night Pat Delaney died. She was nearly going mad with the weight of guilt on her shoulders. And having to talk to Redmond more often now was sheer torment, she was terrified she was going to let something slip. Her guilt felt like a beacon, signalling that she had killed his brother, struck the first blow anyway.

Max's boys had disposed of Pat Delaney, shoving him aboard a trawler leaving the Thames and then pushing him off the deck when they reached the open sea. She knew the body would never be found. Nothing would ever be pinned on her or the others. But the thought of Pat lying with the fishes, being buffeted by the tides and his flesh slowly decaying on his bones, played constantly on her mind. She had thought she was tough. Well, maybe she wasn't tough enough to commit murder.

And she no longer knew what to think about Max. Pat's words about Celia – she was *sure* he meant Celia – had left her feeling that she had walked away from Max for nothing. Left what made her happy, only to be condemned to feeling tense and miserable for the rest of her puff. She knew she should feel good today; but she couldn't.

'Annie!' It was one of the Horse Guards, a lovely chap with the physique of a god and flirtatious blue eyes. He leaned down, nodded politely to the old gentleman, and kissed her hand. 'Lovely to see you again, m'dear.'

Yeah, she'd come a long way from a dirty, rented two-up-two-down on the mean streets of the East End.

Maybe too far.

Annie went and got herself a glass of champagne. She sipped it. Ugh. Made you light-headed and the bubbles went up your nose. God, there was no danger of her ever getting a taste for booze. She gave up and poured herself an orange juice instead, and looked around again at all her happy punters and her high-class tarts. A couple making for a bedroom . . . another couple kissing . . . three on the sofa, they'd be off together soon. She was doing good business, and she ought to feel happier.

Maybe Kieron's exhibition tonight was just what she needed. Get her out, cheer her up. Stop her brooding.

Fat chance.

46

Toby Taylor's Jermyn Street gallery was heaving with crooks that Friday night, and he was thrilled. Regans, Nashes, Krays, Delaneys, Foremans – everywhere you looked, it was Crook City. Toby was the original mob whore. Mixing with criminal gangs almost gave him an orgasm.

He was mincing around the gallery, smiling and pressing the flesh, his ever-expanding belly straining against his fluorescent green floral shirt, his toupee clinging to his sweat-dampened head. His rings and neck chains flashed in the gallery's vivid lighting. Paolo, who was being swept unwillingly along in his partner's slipstream, thought Toby had all the easy charm of a rabid rat.

All around them hung Kieron's work. Landscapes: fields and dales, cliffs and turbulent seas. Some were already sold, but it wasn't going as well as his last. English pastoral always lost out to the more exciting African savannah. And the portraits and the nudes were missing this time. Everyone loved a good nude.

'Maybe he's lost his muse,' said Toby to Paolo.

Paolo cast a sullen look at his older lover. 'No he hasn't. There she is, right over there.'

Paolo drew closer to Toby. *Major* odour alert, he thought, wrinkling his pert nose in disgust. Couldn't the pervy old whore ever wash? If Toby wasn't so free with his cash, Paolo would have been *out* of there in an instant.

'They say she is running a very discreet establishment in the West End now,' whispered Paolo.

Toby gazed at Annie. 'She's very beautiful,' he said grudgingly. 'Looks like butter wouldn't melt.'

Paolo thought that if he were ever to fancy women – not that he imagined he ever could, with their strange sex odour and their sponge-soft bodies – Annie Bailey was the sort of woman he'd go for. She was not only beautiful. She had the unmistakable gloss of prosperity, too. Even he might be tempted. For a little while, anyway, if she treated him right, and spent plenty.

But Toby's attention had drifted on. 'Jesus!' he said. 'Not again.'

'So, are you enjoying yourself?' Kieron asked Annie as they stood in front of a painting showing a tranquil scene of a river and a bridge.

Annie was gazing intently at the painting. Thinking that she wished she could vanish into a scene like that, lose herself somewhere peaceful. Lose the guilt. Lose the ability to think. To imagine. To not constantly see Pat Delaney – *this man's brother* – dead at the bottom of the sea.

'Yeah, very much,' she lied.

She sipped her drink. Fruit juice again. Kieron had tried to get her into champagne, but it was a lost cause.

'Hungry?' he asked her a touch desperately. She was hard work tonight, stiff as a block of wood, distant. Unlike herself. Something must have upset her.

'No,' said Annie.

Since Pat had gone, her appetite had waned. Sometimes at night she had bad dreams. Even awake, she had flashbacks – the door to her room crashing open, Pat reeling into the room, drunk, drugged, dangerous, threatening rape and God knows what else.

She'd had a bolt fitted to her bedroom door at the new place. With that on, she could get a little sleep. Just a little. She knew it was silly, but she had been unable to sleep at all without it.

'I'm pleased Red and Orla could come,' said Kieron.

'Yeah,' said Annie.

'They weren't sure they'd be able to make it.'

'Oh.'

'Business, you know. I might have known Pat wouldn't show up, of course. Perhaps it's just as well. He can't seem to behave himself these days.'

Oh, he's behaving himself now, thought Annie.

'I'm pleased you came, too,' said Kieron determinedly.

'Sorry, Kieron, I'm a bit tired tonight,' said Annie. Poor Kieron, he looked anxious. She had to try to behave more normally. That was what Max had told her. Behave normally. How did you do that, when you had blood on your hands?

'It's okay,' said Kieron more gently. He put a friendly arm around her shoulders. 'You're here. That's all that matters.'

Annie wondered afterwards how it all kicked off.

She was aware of a commotion behind her. Then someone grabbed Kieron's arm. She was shoved sideways. She stumbled and her sore knee shot pain up her leg. Had someone passed out in the warmth of the gallery, and knocked against them?

'Oh, *not* your fucking minder again,' she heard Kieron say.

There was a moment of complete bewilderment. Then Annie saw that Max was there. He had hold of Kieron's shirt front and was shaking him and glaring into his eyes. Max's eyes were glittering. They looked murderous.

'Fucking hell,' gasped Kieron as all around them people drew back. 'You again.'

'What the fuck do you think you're doing?' Max demanded.

'Max!' said Annie.

'I knew it was you, you little bastard,' said Max. 'You want to fucking-well watch your step.'

'I'm not afraid of you,' said Kieron, going purple as Max exerted more pressure.

'No? Well you cunting-well ought to be, you tosser.'

'Ready to kill another Delaney, are ya? Well not me. I'm not scared of the likes of you!' gabbled Kieron.

Annie's head was spinning. She hadn't even seen Max come in. He must have moved like a rattlesnake. Toby ran up with Paolo and started making calm-down noises.

'Fuck off out of it,' snarled Max, and they both scuttled back.

All the other gangs were looking the other way, Annie realized with dismay. No one wanted to upset Max, or side with him against the Delaneys. Picking sides would be unwise. No one wanted to start anything.

'You're talking out of your arse,' hissed Max, glaring into Kieron's eyes. 'You think I don't know that it was that fat bastard Pat who did for our Eddie? I ain't even *started* with you Irish cunts yet.

And if I see you lay a fucking finger on her again, I'll fucking-well kill you, and that's a promise.'

'Stop it, for God's sake,' said Annie, horrified. 'Max – please.'

Max ignored her plea. 'I'm warning you,' he said to Kieron.

'Carter,' said a cool voice at her shoulder. 'Get your hands off my brother.'

It was Redmond. Annie turned and there he was with Orla and three minders. Where was Max's backup? She couldn't see anyone. He had come in here alone, she realized, and had seen Kieron with his arm around her and had jumped to the wrong conclusion.

Max gave a sneer and dropped Kieron. He sagged against the wall.

'Now just get out,' said Redmond.

'I'm going. I want a word with you,' Max said to Annie.

'You don't have to talk to him if you don't want to,' said Kieron.

Max gave Kieron a look that should have dropped him dead.

'It's okay. I'll get my coat.' Annie's legs were weak, she felt as if she'd just avoided death herself. 'Okay, Max. Let's go.'

Max drove them in his big black Jag. He parked the car near the Embankment and they walked along by the Thames. The Houses of Parliament loomed across the black, glittering river. Big Ben chimed out eleven. Annie sat down on a bench, shaking with cold and still trying to get over the night's events. After a moment Max sat down, but at the other end of the bench. There was a large space between them.

'I'm calling in the debt,' he said. 'I sorted the Pat Delaney problem for you, now it's time to pay up.'

Annie looked at him. So that was it. He wanted her to sleep with him again.

'Don't look at me like that,' said Max. 'All right. I'll admit it. You drive me crazy. Most of the time I don't know whether I want to fuck you bandy or wring your bloody neck. But all I want right now is the truth. I want to know what happened on the day of your mother's funeral. Something changed for you that day. I want to know what it was.'

Annie looked at the ground. She hated herself for feeling a twinge of disappointment.

'All right,' she said. 'I met Celia.'

'Celia? I thought she took off somewhere a long time ago.'

'She did.' Annie glanced at Max. 'She was frightened of what you'd do. Because of Eddie. One day, she was gone. There was a note, nothing else.'

'Go on.'

'She showed up at Mum's funeral.' Annie's mouth dried as she remembered that fateful day. 'She didn't mean anyone to see her there, but I was waiting outside because I didn't want to upset Ruthie. I didn't want a scene. So it was by pure accident that I saw Celia out by the gate and went to speak to her – not that she wanted to speak to me. She was trying to get away, but I stopped her.'

'And?' prompted Max when she hesitated.

Annie gulped. 'She had no right hand. A present from you, those who did it told her.'

Max paused, taking it in. Annie could almost see his mind ticking over. She didn't know, or even want to know, what was going on in his head.

'I told you once, Annie. What happened with Celia had nothing to do with me or my boys. Whoever said otherwise is trying to fit me up.'

Annie drew a breath. These were the words she wanted to hear, but it was so much easier to hate him than to love him.

'I know it wasn't you. I know it *now*, anyway. I didn't know it then. Then, I just couldn't face you. I hated the very thought of you. I had to leave. But now I know it was Pat Delaney who did it. Something he said before he died. It was him, the rotten, sick bastard. He did it to cause trouble for you, you're right.'

Max gazed out over the river. A barge passed by,

slipping silently through the water like a snake through oil.

'Then you left me for nothing,' he said. 'You lied to me and told me it was because of Ruthie.'

Annie turned her head and glared at him. 'It *is* about Ruthie. It always has been and it always will be! It was just . . .' she paused, feeling hopelessly confused. 'It was just easier to lose you if I could believe that you were the one responsible for Celia.'

'You're still in love with me.'

Annie looked directly at him. She quickly looked away. 'Do you still have the apartment?' she asked. 'Not that it matters.'

'No,' said Max. 'I hated the fucking place without you.'

Annie shook her head. 'I loved it there,' she said sadly.

'We could be there again,' said Max.

'No. No going back.' She felt as if her heart was bleeding. He was right, she was still in love with him. Totally and hopelessly in love. But it could never be.

'Why?'

Annie leapt to her feet and started to pace around in agitation.

'You fucking-well *know* why, Max,' she burst out. 'Because it's still about Ruthie. My blood. My kin. All right, I didn't tell you the full story when I told you I was leaving you because of her. I didn't tell you about Celia and I should have done. Maybe I should have trusted you more and doubted you less, but you made it hard for me.'

'So what are you saying?'

'I'm saying I did the right thing that day, for the wrong reason.'

'You're saying it's over.'

'Yes.'

'Is there another layer to this?'

'What?' Annie frowned. Now what the hell was he talking about?

'Kieron Delaney?'

Annie sighed. There had always been trouble between the two families, trouble from way back, and she knew it wasn't over yet.

'You and the sodding Delaneys. You're like a dog with a bone, Max.'

'It's *my* fucking bone.'

'There's nothing between Kieron and me.'

'He'd like there to be.'

'Oh, for fuck's sake!' Annie threw her arms wide in exasperation. She was shaking with nervous exhaustion. 'Make this easy for me, will you? I can't do this to Ruthie any more. It's making me sick. Let me go, Max.'

'I can't.'

'You have to.'

'Telling me what to do?'

'I have free will, Max. Like Kieron, I'm not afraid of you. Go back to your boys, and leave me to live my life again.'

Max stood up and came very close to her. They locked eyes.

'It's Kieron Delaney,' he said again.

'No. It's not.' Annie stared straight back at him.

'It fucking is.' Sudden rage flicked on in Max's eyes. 'I'm going to do that rotten little fucker.'

Now Annie was getting riled up too. 'What, like you did his brother Tory?'

'For Christ's sake, Annie, you can't get on your high horse, now can you? Or have you forgotten what happened to Pat?' spat Max.

Annie went pale. He was right, she was no better than he was.

Max was furious now, coming in close to her and glaring into her eyes.

'Listen,' he growled. 'I didn't touch Tory Delaney, but right now I could wipe every Delaney there is right off the face of the earth. Why the fucking hell you feel you have to defend the bastards I just don't know. Perhaps you could explain that to me?'

'I don't have to explain anything to you, Max,' yelled Annie. 'It seems to have escaped your notice, but you don't fucking own me, okay?'

Max leaned forward, breathing hard. He was going to kiss her. Annie braced herself for it, told herself that she would be strong, she wouldn't weaken. But he hesitated, then drew back.

'If I find out you're lying over that ponce Kieron Delaney, I'll kill the bastard, Annie. You hear me? I'll kill him.'

He turned away and started walking back towards the car.

Annie stood there staring after him. Fuck it, she had *wanted* him to kiss her. He could still get to her, just like he always could.

'Home's in a different place now,' she called after him.

'I know,' Max threw back over his shoulder. 'It's in Upper Brook Street. You're running a business there.'

'Is there anything you don't know?' asked Annie, her voice sad and low.

Max stopped walking and turned back to face her. 'I don't know how to get you, Annie Bailey,' he said. 'But I tell you this – if I can't have you, no one else is going to have you either. Particularly not a fucking Delaney.'

47

Orla Delaney bent and laid a bouquet of twelve blood-red roses on her brother Tory's grave. Kieron stood to one side and watched her as she emptied the dead blooms, put in fresh water from one of the council cans, and carefully started to arrange the fresh flowers in the urn. Petey, her minder, watched them from the cemetery gates.

She was good to do it, thought Kieron. Every week, she was here.

'I do it for Mum and Dad,' she said once when he questioned her about it. 'I promised them I would.'

Still, he thought she was good to do it. Very good, under the circumstances.

It was cold today. An arctic breeze swept through the graveyard. It was autumn and soon winter would be here. Jaysus, he hated the winter. Africa had been heaven compared to this. He pushed his hands into his coat pockets, hunched his shoulders against the cold, and watched her.

'I've been thinking,' he said. 'Maybe we should report Pat missing to the police, what do you think?'

Pat hadn't been seen for over two months now. All right, Kieron hated the bastard, but the bastard was his brother and it seemed like he had dropped off the edge of the world. Whether he wanted to or not, he was starting to feel concerned.

Orla thrust the last of the blooms into the urn and straightened up. She looked him dead in the eye.

'You're having a laugh,' she said.

'No,' said Kieron. 'I'm not. It's looking odd, Pat not checking in with any of us for this length of time.'

'We don't ever deal with the police, Kieron,' said Orla. 'Jaysus, you don't know much about this family but you must know that.'

There it was again. He was Kieron the outsider. Kieron the precious little artist, while his brothers did all the real work. It annoyed him.

'So what do we do then?' he demanded. 'Just let it go?'

'Yes, you've got it. We just let it go.'

'You're joking.'

'I'm not joking, Kieron.' Orla stuffed the dead roses into a bag and handed him the watering can.

Kieron looked at the grave. The roses looked starkly red in the cold grey light. Hothouse blooms, he thought. A frost was threatened. They'd be dead overnight, too delicate to survive the elements. A bit like him, maybe. He still felt bad about how Max had made him look the other night at the exhibition. The bastard had belittled him in front of all the important London faces, and he was still seething with hatred over it.

Annie hadn't even had the decency to call him on the phone, either. That really riled him. She'd been there as his guest, and she'd just fucked off with Carter without a word. She couldn't treat him like that, and he intended to tell her so.

'Pat's a very big boy now, Kieron,' Orla pointed out. She glanced at him. 'Hey, are you listening to me?'

Kieron snapped back to the present. 'Yeah. I'm listening. And I know that. But I suppose we should at least enquire . . .'

Orla shrugged. 'We've put the word round that we're looking for him. No one's come up with anything.'

'Well, do you think anything's happened to him?'

Orla looked at Kieron. Her eyes were cold. 'We both know that's a possibility,' she said.

'Then perhaps we ought to be more worried?' said Kieron.

'Perhaps we ought.'

Kieron thought with irritation that she sounded completely dispassionate. Orla was a cold fish and he hated her lack of feeling sometimes. Redmond was the same. Both of them, cold as haddock.

Orla stood there, looking down at their brother's grave, murmuring something under her breath. She was a diamond of a girl, he knew. She did this for their parents in Ireland. She tried always to do the right thing. Molly was old now, and their father was shot away to put it mildly, didn't know what day of the week it was, by all accounts. Didn't know which way was up. A sad end to a dynamic man. Sad for those around him, anyway. Davey himself seemed perfectly happy. It was Molly who shed tears over the man who no longer even knew her. So Orla did this little service, and phoned Molly and told her so. Just a little thing, but to Molly, so important. Davey had adored Tory.

Now he couldn't even remember him.

His eldest.

His first-born.

His favourite.

Now the old man was gaga, and the son was dust and ashes. Life was strange. It was all down to Redmond now to hold the remains of the Delaney empire together. Pat might show up next week, or never be seen again. Kieron drew closer to his sister and put an arm around Orla's shoulders.

She stiffened.

He withdrew his arm. He had forgotten that she didn't really like to be touched. Hugs and kisses were out. He stood there, frozen to the marrow, while she murmured her prayers and gazed at the grave. Her red hair danced in the breeze. He tuned in to what she was saying. Prayers for the dead, no doubt. He listened, and was shocked by what he heard.

'You bastard, dead at last aren't you, and you know what? I'm glad. And if I was alone here I'd dance on your grave.'

48

Annie had made two decisions. Now she was settled into the apartment, she felt stronger and more able to start setting her life straight.

One, she was going to deter Kieron from being a fucking nuisance and hanging around her like a lovesick hound. You didn't mix it with Max Carter like Kieron had and carry on getting away with it. When Max snapped – and Annie knew he would – Kieron would be in deep shit. And she didn't want another death on her conscience.

Her second decision was that she would try even harder to build bridges with her sister. She knew it wouldn't be easy, but however long it bloody took or however tough the going got, she was determined to bring Ruthie back to her. The thing with her and Max was over. Now, surely, there could be forgiveness and reconciliation. Feeling apprehensive, she phoned Queenie's place across town and was both pleased and nervous when Ruthie picked the phone up.

'Oh. It's you,' said Ruthie when Annie announced herself.

Not a great start, but Annie pressed on. 'I thought I'd call and see how you are.'

'That's good of you,' said Ruthie with sarcasm.

'I want us to be friends again, Ruthie,' said Annie. 'I know I did a horrible thing to you. I was young and stupid and jealous of the attention you got.'

It was only one and a half years since Ruthie and Max had married, but Annie felt she had aged ten years in that short time. She had been forced to grow up fast, and she could see clearly now how bad her behaviour had been.

'Ruthie, I can't begin to say how sorry I am. But all that's over now. I've made a new start with my life, and . . .'

'And you want to wipe the slate clean,' said Ruthie.

'Yes. Exactly.'

'I want to do the same,' said Ruthie.

'Oh? Well . . . good.'

'I want to forget I ever knew you, you cheating whore. And I will.'

'Ruthie,' said Annie desperately, 'it's over with me and Max. You've got to believe that.'

'Oh, I think I do. He told me the same thing,

you see,' said Ruthie. 'So maybe between you there might be a hint of the truth in there. He's taken the Surrey house off the market. It's a bit bloody inconvenient, to be honest. I've packed up so much, now I've got to get it all out of the boxes again. But never mind. Max says I can redecorate the place, chuck the damned boxes away if I want, start all over again.'

'That's good,' said Annie cautiously.

'Yes, it is. He's taken Miss Arnott back too. We're thinking about a second honeymoon. Max wants to try again.'

Annie felt sick. To her horror she felt her eyes fill with tears. Oh sure, it was over. But if all this was true, if this wasn't just Ruthie trying to hurt her the only way she knew how, then it was hurtful. She couldn't help how she felt, even though she wished she could.

'He told me he talked to you at that Kieron Delaney's art exhibition,' went on Ruthie. 'He said you agreed between you that it was over.'

Which they had, Annie supposed. All true. But her heart felt like a lump of lead in her chest. She wondered if this was Max's way of getting his revenge. He knew that sooner or later she'd hear about this from someone if not from Ruthie herself. And he knew it would hurt her.

'Yes, that's right,' she forced herself to say.

'So the way's clear for me and Max to make a

go of our marriage,' said Ruthie. 'So I have to say thank you, Annie. Thanks to you for finally giving up trying to steal my husband. It's taken you long enough.'

'I know that what I did was unforgivable,' said Annie.

'That's right. It was,' said Ruthie, and put the phone down.

Annie put the phone back on the cradle. Well, what had she expected? A tearful reunion, Ruthie coming over for coffee and cakes?

Oh yeah, that was sure to happen, she thought.

She looked around her, at her beautiful empty apartment. She was alone and feeling the ache. She missed the cosy chats around the kitchen table with the Limehouse girls. She missed Celia. She missed Max. She missed Ruthie more than anything. Then she jumped as the phone rang. She snatched it up. It was Ruthie, phoning back, had to be.

But it wasn't. It was Kieron.

'What do you want, Kieron?' she asked him wearily.

'I just wanted to see how you are,' he said.

'I'm fine.'

'Oh. You sound . . . I don't know. Upset.'

'Just a bad day.' One of many.

'Only you went off with Max Carter at my exhibition, and I haven't seen or heard from you since. It's been some time, I've been worried.'

409

'Nothing to worry about. He just drove me home.'

'Oh.' Kieron gave a laugh. 'I was a bit put out, I'll admit. After all, you were *my* guest. It isn't quite the done thing, leaving with another man, is it?'

Fuck it, now he was chiding her for her behaviour. Stung from Ruthie giving her an ear-bashing, she had no inclination to sit there and listen to Kieron giving her another one.

'I'm not a fucking trophy, Kieron,' said Annie. 'I went with Max because you were heading for trouble with him and you were too bloody stupid to even see it.'

'Ah, catch yourself on,' said Kieron breezily. 'I can handle the likes of him.'

'Don't be fucking funny, Kieron,' exploded Annie. 'He'd bloody-well eat you and spit out the bits. Now don't be a fucking idiot. Stay away. We can't see each other any more, and that's an end to it.'

'You don't mean that.'

'Don't tell me what I mean. Listen to what I'm saying. I don't want to see you again. Fuck off.'

She slammed the phone down.

It rang again.

She picked it up.

'Annie, listen,' said Kieron.

'For God's *sake*,' Annie roared, and crashed the phone back down.

410

It rang again and this time she let it ring.

So much for making bloody decisions. Ruthie was nowhere even close to forgiving her, and Kieron didn't seem to be taking the hint. She left the phone ringing, and went to take a bath to calm herself down.

49

Billy knew everyone thought he was dim, but actually he knew a lot. He sat in the snug of The Grapes sipping on a pint of lemonade, his briefcase on his lap, his notebook on the beer-stained table. It was lunchtime and the pub was quiet. Eric was behind the bar polishing glasses. Someone had put Des O'Connor on the jukebox.

Oh yes, Billy knew *lots*.

Like, for instance, he knew Pat Delaney had died four months ago in the Limehouse massage parlour. He'd seen Gary and Steve there, two of Max's boys, doing a clean-up job and then carting the body out to the car and driving off.

You didn't have to paint Billy no pictures, even if everyone did think he was thick as two short planks coated in pig shit. Ever since that night he'd been hearing around town about how Pat Delaney hadn't been seen since. Easy to put two and two together and come up with four. Easy, even for him.

He knew about all that had been going on with Max and his beautiful Annie, too. Billy frowned and took a long pull at his drink. He was in a quandary here. He was fiercely loyal to Max, but on the subject of Annie Bailey, Billy found his loyalty tested to the limit.

He hadn't liked her doing dirty things in the Limehouse place. He knew what they did there, his mum had told him often enough about what these sorts of women got up to, what Celia Bailey was, and how doing such things with these women would affect a man. He'd go blind, or catch something that would make his knob rot and drop off.

It was one of his most vivid memories, his mum bathing him when he was a boy, her rough meaty hand grabbing hold of his todger and her saying: 'Do dirty things with dirty girls and this will drop right off, son. And you wouldn't want that, now would you?'

But what about the dirty things Mum did with his many 'uncles'? He'd wanted to say that, but he was frightened of his mum's temper. She had a terrible temper. It was best to just nod, agree, keep quiet. Billy was good at keeping quiet.

Billy had been relieved when Annie had moved out of Limehouse, but his relief had been short-lived. She had moved into that posh place with

Max. That was awful. From doing bad things with bad men, she had progressed to doing bad things with *Max*. That was even worse.

Then that had come to an end, and now she was at it again.

Doing bad things.

Bad, *bad* things.

Now she was in Upper Brook Street, a posh place filled with toffs, and he had seen those toffs, people who should have known better, people who had a position in society and ought to have known how to behave, how to set an example to others, he had *seen* them going in and out of the building, seen the girls too, fantastically beautiful girls, going in and out, laughing and joking and tossing back their lustrous manes of hair.

They didn't look like tarts – or at least not the sort of tarts he was used to seeing around Bow and Limehouse; they were a bit raddled, a bit tired. These were luminous, glowing, but somehow still tarty. They were on a par with Annie for their looks and their elegance. So that was how he knew she was at it again.

Doing bad things.

It was awkward.

'You all right here, Billy lad?' asked Eric, coming to gather up his glass. 'Want another in there?'

'No, thank you,' said Billy.

Poor bastard, thought Eric, taking Billy's empty

glass back to the bar. Daft as a brush, sitting there staring into space with his mouth open. But no one gave Billy any real aggro. Everyone knew he was on Max Carter's payroll and that Redmond Delaney had said hands off, and you didn't piss around with that lot.

Billy mulled it all over. It was a knotty problem. Which was the trouble with knowing so much, he'd found. If you knew a lot, you tended to worry over it all. So he was worried about the Pat business because he thought Annie was involved. And he was worried about her doing nasty things all over again. And he was worried about the job Max was planning, because it was big, and things might go wrong.

Oh, he had *lots* to think about. He had to work out what he thought about it all, because he had trouble getting it all straight in his head sometimes. It was the medication, it made him feel muddled. But he'd take his time and think it all through. Then, and only then, he would decide what he had to do.

50

Annie was still in bed one winter morning when she got a call from Dolly.

'I'm coming over to see you at ten. I'm bringing Ellie.'

Annie sat up, the tension in Dolly's voice triggering her instantly into a state of alert.

'What's up?' she asked.

'Not on the phone,' said Dolly, and hung up.

Annie stared at the humming receiver. Her heart was thumping. She got up, showered, dressed, fixed herself some tea and toast then stalked around the empty apartment. Another party tomorrow. She'd been thinking of ideas to perk up the business still more, jotting down notes. It was all she had to concentrate on.

Dolly arrived bang on ten, Ellie trailing pale-faced behind her. Ellie had lost weight, Annie noticed – and it didn't suit her.

'Come in,' said Annie, taking their coats. 'Tea?'

'We need something a fucking sight stronger than that,' said Dolly, sprawling out on one of the Chesterfields and looking around her in amazement. 'You've got this place well nice, Annie, you've made some changes.'

She noticed that Dolly had a piece of chewing gum stuffed into her missing tooth – the tooth that had been knocked out the night Pat Delaney died. Annie felt almost amused by this. You could take the girl out of Limehouse, but you couldn't take Limehouse out of the girl. Dolly was terrified of dentists. Any medical procedure filled her with horror. Annie was sure this was because of the abortion she had endured in her youth.

'Take a seat, Ellie,' said Annie.

Ellie didn't look right, she thought. And she was far too quiet.

Annie went and poured three brandies. She brought them back and put them on the big coffee table between the two Chesterfield sofas. Ellie grabbed hers with a shaking hand and chucked it back in one.

'Ellie's being a bit silly,' said Dolly, watching the girl.

'I'm not being silly,' said Ellie flatly.

'Yes you are,' snapped Dolly. She looked at Annie. 'She's talking about going to the Bill and confessing.'

Annie's mouth dropped open.

'Look, this has been tormenting me for months now. We killed him,' said Ellie defensively. '*I* killed him. I can't go on like this. I'm jumping at everything and anything. I can't sleep. I can't eat. Chris is suspicious.'

'Chris is getting suspicious because you're acting like a cat on hot bricks,' said Dolly. 'Chris knows nothing. If you cool it, he'll settle down.'

'But I'll still know I killed him.'

Annie took a breath. She could sympathize with Ellie's plight. The flashbacks had gone now, but for some time after that awful night she too had been like Ellie – in a right fucking state.

'Look, Ellie,' said Annie. 'We all know what happened that night and it wasn't our fault. Pat was out of control. He was going to hurt us. We had to get in first, that was all.'

'That's *all*.' Ellie laughed loudly. 'We *killed* him. We didn't just rap him over the knuckles and tell him not to be a bad boy any more. We slit his fucking *throat*.'

Dolly gave Annie a look that said: 'You see?'

'We all know what we did,' said Annie. 'We did what we had to do to survive.'

'The Delaneys suspect something,' said Ellie.

'What do you mean?' asked Annie.

'They keep saying when did I last see Pat, have I heard anything about Pat, where is Pat . . .'

'They're just fishing,' said Dolly.

'They *know*,' said Ellie.

'They know nothing,' said Annie firmly.

'I'm telling you, they know we did it,' shouted Ellie, jumping to her feet. 'What does it take to make you two see that? We have to go to the police, they'll protect us!'

Annie stood up, hauled her arm back and gave Ellie a hefty slap across the face. Ellie recoiled and nearly fell. Annie grabbed her shoulders and shook her hard.

'Listen to me, you daft little bint,' snarled Annie. 'Go to the police? Are you off your head? Do that and the police will be the least of your troubles. Do you seriously think that when you're banged up inside for murder the Delaneys won't be able to reach you? An eye for an eye, that's their motto. They've got contacts everywhere. They'll get to you even if you are behind bars. You'll be found hanging in your cell, so sad, just suicide, these lags commit suicide all the time – or you'll somehow miraculously get hold of some razor blades and slit your wrists. Tragic! Do you think anyone will care whether or not it was suicide or if someone helped you on your way?'

Ellie was crying now. The side of her face where Annie had delivered the slap was glowing red. She was staring at Annie with shocked, wounded eyes. Annie felt bad, but she had to harden her heart.

Ellie was hysterical and she was going to get them all done for at this rate. She had to be told.

'But what are we going to *do*?' Ellie wailed.

Annie's grip on Ellie's shoulders relaxed.

'What we are going to do is nothing,' she said. 'We're going to sit tight and let the whole thing die down. There was no great affection between Redmond and Pat, everyone knows that. Redmond might look around for his brother, but he won't look too hard or for too long.'

'I don't know,' moaned Ellie.

Annie's eyes met Dolly's over Ellie's head. This was worrying. They couldn't have Ellie rattling around like this, threatening all their lives.

'Sit down, Ellie,' said Annie, and Ellie thumped back on to the Chesterfield beside Dolly. Dolly put a motherly arm around the younger girl and patted her shoulder.

Annie sat down opposite. She'd made a decision. She knew what to say.

'You don't know that Dolly and I met Celia at my mum's funeral, do you Ellie?'

That got her attention. 'Celia?' Ellie stopped dabbing at her eyes with a tissue. 'Is she . . . Jesus, did you really? Is she all right?'

Dolly was silent, watching Annie. She had an idea where this was headed, and she was going to let Annie get on with it. It might even work.

'No, Ellie. She wasn't all right at all.'

'What . . . ?' Ellie glanced feverishly between Annie and Dolly. 'What do you mean? Is she okay?'

'She's fucking marvellous, Ellie,' said Annie, sipping her brandy. She felt like she needed it. 'Only she had a slight accident, you see.'

'What sort of accident?'

Annie felt sorry for Ellie, but she ploughed on. This had to be done.

'A serious one. You see, Pat Delaney cut her hand off.'

Ellie gave an audible gasp.

Annie went on. 'He blamed it on Max Carter. He as good as told me on the night we killed him that he'd done it. He did it out of spite, on a whim. *That's* what your precious Delaneys are like, Ellie. They're vicious and they're violent. And the fact that you've been passing information to them won't help you if they've got you in their sights. It didn't help Celia. She's been paying them off for years, she must have thought she was well in. Well – she wasn't.'

'I don't pass them information,' said Ellie lamely, her face a picture of shock and dismay.

'Come off it Ellie. It was one of the first things Celia told me about you. You're a Delaney girl. That's okay. But be your own girl first, Ellie. Don't throw your life away and ours with it.'

Annie paused, letting it all sink in.

'I've had bad dreams since it happened, Ellie,'

Annie went on. 'Waking dreams sometimes. Seeing it all over again. That night.'

'Me too,' said Ellie in a shaking voice.

'It's going though, Ellie. It's passing. Soon it will be gone. Yours will too. It will get better and soon it will be nothing but a memory. Until then, we're all here to help you and talk to you, day or night. Darren and Aretha, they've been good friends to you. So have Dolly and I. We're friends. We're tight together, aren't we? We're the closest any of us have got to real family. You don't betray your family, Ellie love, now do you?'

'Thanks, Annie,' said Dolly quietly when Ellie had gone off to the bathroom to sort out her ruined make-up. 'I think you've done the trick. She was giving me the willies. Climbing the walls.'

'Let's hope that's the last of it,' said Annie.

But she wasn't convinced.

51

The department store safe was ripe for the taking. Jack the gelly man had his pack of three with him. He was pleased with the way things were going, so far.

So was Jonjo. So was Max, who had the bags at the ready to stow the cash. The telephone chap was sweating up a bit and had taken his hood off. Obvious he'd never done a job before. But he was okay. They were all dressed in gloves and navy boiler suits and thick hoods, in case anyone spotted them. Jimmy had breached the frame-room door for the ex-GPO man to do his bit, and was now outside keeping his eyes peeled. Gary was parked round the corner, ready to go.

It was midnight. Everything was peaceful, just the way it should be.

The ex-engineer found the alarm line, got his tools out and started gently stripping back the wire in two places. Then he attached the two crocodile clips to the bared wires and had the diverter wire in place in a second. He turned and nodded to Max.

The alarm was inactive. They were going to steal away the thirty thousand as quiet as a mouse's fart. Jonjo went over to the manager's office and busted the door wide open. The two others were tearing around the store grabbing fur coats, blankets, rugs, all to mask the noise of the explosion.

The gelly man went over to the safe. It had a steel door built into concrete. He looked it over, then knelt down and unpacked his pack of three and his other bits and pieces. You had to keep gelignite cool and dry. Once it started to run in the heat, you were in trouble.

'I should stand back a bit,' he said.

Max, Jonjo and the telephone man moved out of the room. Jonjo went off to pick up whatever he could carry in gemstones and watches. The telephone man took his hood off and mopped his brow. Max watched what the gelly man was doing through the open door.

Jack had already snipped the ends off the condoms. Now he started to pipe the stuff all around the door, squeezing it into the gap with gentle precision. Then he turned to the lock, the safe's weakest point, and used up the last of the gelly. Then he got out a spatula and a block of kiddies' Plasticine and slowly covered the gelignite with it.

Max looked at his watch. Nearly twelve thirty.

Jack finished with the Plasticine and started setting up the detonator, a simple battery with a wire attached. All he had to do now was close the circuit and the safe would be cracked open like a crushed nut.

'We'll pack it now,' he said.

Max and the telephone man started passing in the rugs and the coats and the sheets and blankets. The gelly man packed them around the safe until it looked like an igloo.

'That's fine,' he said, and moved out of the room with the detonator, the cable unravelling between the battery and the safe.

Jonjo came back with pockets like Squirrel Nutkin. He was beaming from ear to ear, mask still off. Sloppy, thought Max, displeased.

'Everyone ready?' asked Jack.

Cool bugger, thought Max as he nodded. He could have been leading a Sunday School prayer meeting for all the concern he registered. They got down out of the way.

'Put your hoods on,' Max told Jonjo and the telephone man.

'It's too fucking hot,' said the ex-engineer while Jonjo complied.

'Put it on, you pineapple.'

The gelly man closed the circuit. The explosion was nothing more than a soft crack, but the floor shook beneath their feet. All the covers fell off the safe and the door lolled open. There was a heavy cordite smell in the air and a little smoke, but Max was pleased. No one outside the building could have heard that. Not even Jimmy, and he had ears like a bat.

'Come on,' said Jack, and started throwing all the covers back out the door of the manager's office. He then neatly packed away his stuff.

Then Max got to the open safe and saw the huge stash of cash inside. He shook out the bags and started piling it inside and handing it back to Jonjo. God bless the January sales. Where the fuck was Jonjo? This was no time to be off on the rob around the shop.

'Hey!' someone said from behind him.

Jonjo was grappling with a man near the door.

'Who the fuck are you?' Jonjo demanded.

Max looked at the telephone engineer. His mask still off. The bloke had clocked him. Not good news.

'Get off me!' The man was squirming in Jonjo's iron grip.

'Who are you, pal?' asked Jonjo again.

'I'm the manager,' the man gasped. 'I came back for some papers.'

Now the engineer pulled his hood back on.

About a lifetime too bloody late. Max was seriously annoyed. He was going to have words with Jimmy over this. What was he doing out there, having a wank? He wasn't keeping watch, that was for sure. This bastard must have come right past him.

'Fuck it,' said Jonjo.

'Take him into the storage room. Tie him up,' said Max.

'But he's seen my . . .' yelled the engineer.

Max gave him and slap and caught the front of his boiler suit.

'Shut it, you.'

The man fell silent. Christ, spare me from bloody amateurs, thought Max. God knew what this idiot had been about to say. He could have roared one of their names out loud, he was that rattled.

'He saw my face,' moaned the man.

Max gave him a little shake.

'So? I hear Scotland's nice this time of year. Take yourself off up there. Go tonight. And keep it buttoned, my friend, or I might get upset with you.'

'But what if he identifies me?'

'You've got no record. No wife. No kids. He'd have to be fucking clever to do that, wouldn't he? But take no chances. Clear off out of it.'

'My cut! What about my cut?'

'Send a postcard in three months' time to Eric

at The Grapes. I'll see you right. So long as you remember you say nothing to nobody about this. You get careless, I get upset. Remember that. I hear anything about you mouthing off, I'll find you. And you'll be sorry.'

The man nodded. Max started piling the cash into the bags. A good night's work, all in all. And on Delaney turf, too – that made it twice as sweet.

52

'So how was Cliveden this weekend?' asked Annie absently as she thumbed through one of the copies of *The Times* newspaper she bought in for the clients. Not much to see, really. The odd scandal. The odd robbery, too. A massive thirty thousand quid had gone walkabout from a department store on the Delaney manor. Ronnie and Reggie Kray had been remanded in custody, charged with demanding money with menaces. Adam Faith had cancelled concerts in Johannesburg after refusing to play to all-white audiences.

Mira, Jennifer and Thelma were in an ecstatic pre-party huddle on one of the big Chesterfields. Mira, beaming with happiness, tossing her blonde mane, looked up at Annie who was standing over them with an indulgent smile.

'I was just telling Jen and Thelma about it. It was so wonderful. We had one of the suites overlooking the Thames. The view was stunning. I met Joe Louis.'

'Who's Joe Louis?'

'The *boxer*, silly. And I was introduced to Lord and Lady Astor. And I met Harold Macmillan. And Tony Bennett the singer, he was lovely. William was very attentive. It was *fabulous*.'

Annie didn't doubt that William had been attentive. William was Sir William Farquarson. Unfortunately his wife, Lady Fenella, was horse-faced and not keen on sex. Fortunately, she was often at their country house with her dogs, which left Billy free to entertain more glamorous companions up in town whenever he chose.

'What's he like then, Sir William?' asked Thelma, who was sleek and red-haired with a haughty manner that certain men found appealing.

'In bed?' Mira wrinkled her exquisite nose. 'He likes kinky boots. Nothing else. You have to be naked. No suspenders, no bra, no pants. Just the high-heeled boots – with dress spurs.'

'What, during sex?' laughed Jennifer, an elegant toffee-brown girl with an open, approachable demeanour.

'Oh God yes,' said Mira. 'First he likes to be ridden around the bedroom on all fours, then when he gets down to it he likes you to dig the spurs into his back so that he yelps with pain.'

'Men are very strange,' sighed Jennifer. 'My

bank manager likes me to wear five bras and do a strip for him. He likes to shout out: "First bra off!" and so on, until I remove the last one. Then he tosses himself off. Pretty odd, wouldn't you say?'

'I can go one better,' said Thelma. 'One of my older clients doesn't want sex, he just wants to lick me all over. And he has to take his teeth out first or they rattle all over the place. I tell you, I was getting serious bite marks. So I told him. No teeth out, no licky. So he takes them out. Last time he was here he got so overexcited he picked up his hankie from the side table and flushed it down the toilet with his dentures wrapped inside. Good job he's widowed. How the hell would you explain *that* to your wife, I wonder?'

Annie smiled. 'Thank God men are weird, or we'd all be out of work. Come on, girls. Ten minutes to party time.'

Annie was pleased with her little operation now. It had taken a while, but with Redmond's cash input and some lively suggestions from her Limehouse colleagues she had come up with a very comprehensive programme of fun for her clients.

A seventy-five-pound charge on the door ensured that every client was entitled to as much food and drink as he liked, a floor show from the lady of his choice, a sexy film from a small selection, plenty of fine music and laughter and cigars, the day's best papers to read, and – of course – as many fucks as he felt able to accomplish. Ten or none, it didn't matter. So long as he went away happy and came back in a hurry.

It seemed to work well. She had a barman called Joshua – a Delaney man through and through – who was as smooth as silk. Joshua knew how to mix all the latest cocktails, he was non-judgemental and very discreet. He served food on silver platters to their elite clients with all the cool charm of a Savoy veteran.

No doorman, though. Annie hadn't considered that, in such a select area. She took the money at the door and Joshua stood there with her and gave every guest a welcoming glass of the best champagne. By half past midday she had ten gentlemen happily ensconced in the apartment and busy with her lovely girls. Then Kieron showed up and Annie wished she did have a doorman, after all.

'Kieron,' she said, 'what are you doing here?'

'I've come to talk to you,' said Kieron, all floppy blond hair and pleading eyes.

'It's not convenient,' said Annie. 'As you can see, this is a private party.'

'Oh sure. I can see people are paying you money to come in. Hardly a party, is it? More an orgy, really.'

God, she was getting fed up with this.

Joshua was looking nervous. He wasn't up to

any rough stuff. Joshua was gay, skinny and un-accustomed to dealing with trouble. Annie gave him a reassuring glance.

'It's okay, Josh, I'll deal with this. You carry on here, take the cash, dole out the champagne, I'll be back in two ticks.'

Annie gave Kieron an angry look and led the way into her own bedroom, the only place un-occupied at present. She closed the doors behind them.

'All right,' she said. 'You want to talk, so talk. I'm listening.'

'Don't talk to me as if I'm a naughty schoolboy,' snapped Kieron.

'Then why are you behaving like one?' Annie hissed back. 'Why won't you take in what I've told you? I'm not interested in any sort of rela-tionship with you.'

'But you are with Max Carter.'

'Look, what fucking business is that of yours? Anyway – that's over.'

'Sure it is. That's why you left my exhibition to which you came as *my* guest, with that bastard.'

'When are you going to let that drop?' Annie asked. 'I was protecting you from yourself, Kieron. Believe me, you do not want to upset Max.'

'I don't care whether I upset him or not,' said Kieron passionately. 'It's you I want.'

'Kieron, don't be fucking stupid,' sighed Annie.

'What's stupid about this?' asked Kieron, grabbing her and kissing her hard.

'For God's sake,' muttered Annie, pushing him away and wiping irritably at her mouth.

'You know you want me too,' said Kieron, storming in again and slipping his hand inside her dress to squeeze her breast.

Annie recoiled, amazed and outraged at the same time.

'For fuck's *sake*, Kieron!'

'I know I was stupid and I didn't make a play for you when I should have,' said Kieron in a rush, trying to get his hand back in there. 'But I want you, Annie. I want you now.'

He pressed himself to her frontage and Annie knew he wasn't telling a lie. To her horror she felt him reaching down between them to unzip himself. This was getting beyond a joke.

She hauled back and brought her knee up, but he had turned to the side and it didn't connect where it should. She opened her mouth to speak, but his mouth quickly covered hers again. The feel of it disgusted her. To her alarm she realized that he was stronger than she had thought. She tried to get free, managed to get one arm away. She clawed at his face.

'Bitch,' Kieron cursed her, angry scratch marks emerging on his cheek. Then his hand was on her throat and she had *really* had enough.

She brought her free arm round and punched him straight on the jaw. He reeled back, clutching his chin, his eyes registering almost comical surprise. Annie stood there glaring at him, panting, hands on hips.

'Now listen to me, you little fucker,' she hissed. 'You and me are never going to happen. Get that through your thick skull.'

'Yeah, because of that bastard Carter,' yelled Kieron.

'Keep your fucking voice down!' said Annie. She didn't want a public ruck, not with punters in.

'Oh, you don't want to hear the truth? Because it is, isn't it. It's only that fucking Max Carter standing in our way.' Kieron straightened, wincing. There was blood at the side of his mouth where she'd struck him. 'It's me you really want, but you're afraid of what he'd do if you gave in to it.'

'You're deluded, Kieron,' said Annie coldly. She went to the door and opened it. 'Just get the hell out of here, will you?'

Josh came over instantly. 'Is everything all right, Annie?'

He glanced anxiously between the two of them, seeing Annie's agitation and the blood streaming down Kieron's chin.

'Ah, you can tell your lapdog I'm off,' sneered Kieron with an angry look at her and a sneer for Josh.

'Piss off, Kieron,' said Annie tiredly. She was sick of the sight of him now.

'You really okay?' asked Josh when Kieron had pushed past him and gone, slamming the door behind him.

'Fine,' said Annie, feeling suddenly shaky. 'Take over for a little while, will you Josh?'

Annie went back into her bedroom, closing the door behind her. Trembling, she sat down on the bed and put her head in her hands and knew that the bad blood between the Carters and the Delaneys was far from over. And here she was again – stuck unwillingly between the two. Stuck exactly where she didn't want to be.

53

Ruthie Carter had been at home in Surrey all week and she was fed up to the back teeth. All she had down here for company was the minder on the door, who had just a single brain cell rattling around in his head getting rather lonely – Dave couldn't be relied on even to string a sentence together.

And as for Miss Arnott, that old cow was forever giving Ruthie dirty looks and thinking what a common little thing she was. Oh, she knew what Miss Arnott thought of her all too well. There was naff-all to do in this place, and the silence out here in the country was deadly.

Ruthie longed for London, for the noise of traffic and voices, for the close proximity of other people going about their daily lives. But she had agreed with Max that they would do this. They had sat down together and he had been straight with her.

He knew he had made mistakes. But they could still save this, they could still make it work. That's what he said. But she had to stop the drinking, get herself busy, bringing this place to life. Ruthie had actually started to think there was some hope.

But that had been two weeks ago. Since that one night – when they hadn't slept together – Max had barely shown his face in this arsehole of a rural nowhere. He'd been busy up in town. She had phoned him at Queenie's old house. He had said not now, Ruthie, he was up to his ears in stuff, he'd be down at the weekend.

And here we are, she thought. The weekend. Her great bonus in the long haul that was being married to Max Carter. He showed up at eleven on Saturday night. Half the weekend gone, anyway. She was steaming, and Max hardly had a foot through the door when she let rip.

'You said we'd spend the weekend together,' said Ruthie, following him across the hall as he dumped his overnight bag and shrugged off his coat.

'And I'm here,' he said.

'But you don't want to be,' yelled Ruthie.

Max glanced around. 'Is Miss Arnott here?'

'No, she's off for the weekend. You don't have to worry that I'll show you up in front of your posh housekeeper, shouting about like a fishwife. I told her she could take some time off. I *thought* we'd be here together. I thought we'd need some privacy.'

'And Dave?'

'He's asleep, so far as I know. Who the hell cares?'

Dave had a flat over the garage. Miss Arnott disdained Dave, too. Margie, the cleaner, had been in his flat and got an attack of the vapours. It was lined floor to ceiling with photos of nude women. Margie complained to Miss Arnott, Miss Arnott complained to Ruthie. But whatever Dave did within his own four walls was fine with her.

She knew she should have protested more, to gain Brownie points with Miss Arnott, to convince her that Ruthie was a *lady*. But Ruthie couldn't be arsed. Miss Arnott knew what she was, all right. She knew that Max was 'in business' and she knew that Ruthie had married above herself. Ruthie wasn't going to flog her guts out trying to convince the sour-faced old bag otherwise.

'Nice welcome,' said Max.

'You don't deserve a nice welcome,' shouted Ruthie. 'I had dinner all planned, and where the fuck were you? Up in town with *her*, were you?'

'If by her you mean Annie, no, I wasn't,' said Max.

He turned his back on her and went through to the drawing room. He poured himself a brandy, and sat down.

Ruthie came and stood over him. 'I don't believe you,' she spat.

Max raised his glass to her. 'Suit yourself,' he said, and took a drink. He put his glass aside and stood up to put on some music, but Ruthie came close and glared up at him, standing in his way.

'You said you'd give her up. It was part of the deal.'

'Along with you laying off the bottle,' said Max cruelly. 'I remember. I kept my half of the deal, Ruthie. Did you keep yours?'

Ruthie's glance slipped away from his hard gaze. She'd had the odd glass or two. Miss Arnott had probably snitched to Max about it, the snooty cow.

'No, don't answer that,' said Max after a beat. 'We both know you'd be lying.'

'We're both good liars, Max. I think you're still seeing her.'

'I'm not.'

'You're lying,' screamed Ruthie. 'Listen, I'm warning you – if you don't pack it in, I'll tell the police you weren't with me on the night Tory Delaney died. Then you'll be in the shit.'

Max grabbed her shoulders. His eyes were icy as they glared into hers. 'A wife can't testify against her husband, you silly bitch,' he hissed. 'But go on. Tell them whatever the fuck you want to. Because I didn't kill Tory Delaney.'

Jessie Keane

'Oh, sure you didn't. You were off somewhere that night. Eddie said he hid a gun for you.'

Max stiffened. 'Eddie shouldn't have said that.'

'And what are you going to do about that, "discipline" him? Send the boys round? You'll have a hard job. The poor boy's dead, isn't he?'

'You've been drinking,' said Max with disgust. His eyes had narrowed to slits. His mouth was grim. He leaned in very close and Ruthie started to feel frightened. 'Listen. You don't go to the police. You don't start any trouble. You keep your mouth shut and you do as you're told, or I get very annoyed. You got that?'

Ruthie nodded dumbly.

'I didn't kill Tory Delaney,' said Max with soft venom. 'But I'd like to shake the hand of whoever did. Serious. I'd like to buy that fucker a drink and pat him on the back. I wish I'd done it myself, but I didn't.'

'Then who the hell did?' asked Ruthie more quietly. She knew she was in danger of going too far. She could see it in his eyes. Time to tone it down.

'We'd all like to know the answer to that,' said Max, letting her go. 'But it's done. And, really, who gives a shit? The bastard's dead. End of story. Now is there anything to eat?'

Ruthie settled down after that. Went and cooked him some bacon and eggs while Max sat on the couch and listened to his favourite Mozart concerto. He thought of the haul from the department store, all used notes and stored away nice and safe for the time being. God bless the January sales. That safe had been *stuffed*. He thought of the situation he was in, keeping face by remaining married to a woman he detested. He thought of Annie, up in Upper Brook Street. He thought of her dark green, laughing eyes and her thick dark hair spilling over the pillow as she slept.

Fuck it, he thought.

No one ever said life was going to be perfect.

54

Sometimes you had to do things for a person's own good. Billy knew this to be true. When he was little and he had used swear words, his mum had washed his mouth out with carbolic soap and water.

'It's for your own good, Billy,' she had told him while he gagged and struggled. 'You don't want to grow up using words like that, now do you?'

And he didn't. Oh, Max and the boys used bad words all the time, but he wouldn't do it. His mum had taught him that standards were important, and he knew she was right.

That was why he was standing in the police station now. The desk sergeant was looking at him as if he'd just landed from Mars.

'I want to report someone running a . . .' He paused to get his words straight . . . 'a disorderly house.'

'Really?' The sergeant looked at him. Clearly a nutter. Rigged out like Sherlock Holmes, for God's sake. With a sigh the sergeant pulled out a sheet of paper and started taking down the details.

'Where?' he asked.

'Upper Brook Street.'

The copper's eyebrows raised. 'That's a nice area, son,' he said. 'Not much disorder around there, I shouldn't think.'

'Oh, there is. Posh people, too, going in and out.'

'Who's running this disorderly establishment then, son?' asked the sergeant.

This would give the boys in the back room a laugh, at least. Poor simple sod, probably a figment of his imagination. He looked shot away with his long face and his vacant eyes, his deerstalker pulled down low.

'Miss Annie Bailey,' said Billy with a tremble in his voice.

He hated to do this. He'd wrestled long and hard with his conscience about it, but it was for her own good. He reminded himself of that. She couldn't go on like this, doing bad things with all these men. She really couldn't.

'And do you have any evidence to substantiate these claims?' asked the sergeant with a sigh.

'I've got it all written down,' said Billy, rummaging in his briefcase. 'In my book.'

He placed the book on the counter. The sergeant opened it. There was nothing but illegible scrawl in there. Page after page of it.

'I've been keeping watch outside and noting down times and things,' said Billy. He looked down at the open book and at the sergeant's face. 'No, no. Not at the front. At the back.'

The sergeant turned to the back of the book. There, in neat handwriting, were clear legible details of people entering the building, people leaving, times, dates, everything. The sergeant's mouth dropped open. He was looking at the names of cabinet ministers, bankers, lawyers – even peers of the bloody realm.

'You see?' said Billy in triumph.

The desk sergeant took a breath. 'Have a seat over there, son,' he said at last. He picked up the book and the sheet of details. 'I'm just going through to have a word with my superior. Hold on. I'll be back in a jiff.'

Billy sat down, knees together, his briefcase hugged tight against his chest. This was hard, one of the hardest things Billy had ever done. But you had to protect the ones you loved. His mum had taught him that. Even if what you did seemed harsh, even if they had to suffer for it, their best interests were what counted in the end.

He loved Annie Bailey. He always had. He was doing this for *her*.

55

It was April and Annie was trying to put her cares behind her by throwing a special party. Her birthday fell on a Friday that she had scheduled for one of her regular parties, so she decided that she would make it extra-special for all the gents in attendance. There would be six additional girls, friends of Jen and Mira, to entertain the revellers. There would be birthday cake and champagne, and a reduction on the door. Fifty pounds would get you in for an afternoon of bliss.

She was going for a pink theme. She had pinned up pink balloons and streamers, there were pink tablecloths on the bar section and on the buffet. The cake itself was a masterly confection of pinks and white. There were pink flowers in profusion. Even the bloody *champagne* was pink. Perhaps she had overdone it?

'No, it looks gorgeous,' Mira assured her when

they were ready for the off. 'And so do you. Happy birthday, Annie darling.'

Mira air-kissed either side of Annie's immaculately made-up face and slipped a small carefully wrapped package into her hand. Annie looked at it in surprise.

'From Jen and Thelma and me,' said Mira. 'We hope you like it.'

'Oh – well, that's so nice of you,' said Annie, touched.

She still couldn't get used to receiving gifts. Max had been lavish with them, and the Limehouse tarts had surprised her once or twice with very small presents, but she was so used to getting the shitty end of the stick when she was growing up that she wondered if she would ever be blasé about such things. As a child, Annie got the knocks – Ruthie got the presents. Funny how she still half-expected it to be that way.

She unwrapped the long slender package and found a ladies' gold Rolex watch inside. She looked up at Mira.

'That's bloody lovely,' she said. 'Thanks, Mira.' She looked over at Jen and Thelma, seated on the Chesterfield, watching with beaming smiles. 'Thanks, Jen, Thelma. It's gorgeous.'

'It's engraved,' said Mira. 'Have a look.'

Annie took out the beautiful thing and turned over the dial.

From the girls to Annie with love.

'Some of the old boys call you the Mayfair Madam,' said Jen. 'We thought about having that put on it, but "Annie" seemed better.'

'Help me put it on,' said Annie, delighted, and Mira did so.

'Okay girls – let's get ready now,' said Annie, moving over to the door where Joshua was ready with pink champagne for the drinkers or pink grapefruit juice for the teetotallers.

The bell rang.

The party was on.

'Any movement?' asked the sergeant as he joined his young constable outside in the rainy street. Talk about April showers. What a fucking job! He envied the toffs inside having a bloody good time. A fucking sight better than standing out here with the rain dripping off your arse.

'Fifteen gents gone in there so far,' said the constable. 'Look, there goes another one. Looks busier than normal.'

For weeks they had been keeping Annie's apartment block under surveillance – ever since that weird bloke had come into the station and told them about what was really going on in there. Sergeant McKellan and his three constables had taken it in shifts to watch and record every arrival and departure. They'd noted what time the mail was delivered, when the

Jessie Keane

rubbish was emptied and when the milkman came. They'd noted – with some surprise – that there were people going into the block who seemed of good standing in the community.

As the weeks went past, a pattern had emerged. There was a major shindig once a month, and individual visits during weekdays. Over seven weeks, he and his men had clocked over a hundred men and a regular selection of between three and ten high-class trollops coming and going.

They'd checked the rubbish over and found an awful lot of empty bottles. Malt whisky, champagne, fine wines, exquisite brandies, had all been consumed on the premises. Annie Bailey was running a well-stocked bar up there.

Selling liquor without a licence, thought Sergeant McKellan, shivering in the chilly downpour. Bloody good liquor too. These people were supposing to be setting a good example, not having a fucking good time at a high-class knocking shop.

Jesus, they'd even seen a Cabinet Minister going in there, but they'd have to keep quiet about *that*. The sergeant curled his lip in disgust. These people were supposed to be his *betters*. And they behaved like this.

Monitoring the rubbish had turned up a surprising quantity of used condoms and tissues, too. Sergeant McKellan thought that there was no limit to the depravity of the upper classes. He felt badly let down by them.

As the wet, dismal weeks went by, his grievance against the toffs became more intense. He already had a warrant to search the premises because of the illegal liquor sales, but he wanted more than that. He wanted to stop this operation in its tracks, and that meant waiting and watching out in the cold and the wet. They'd gone inside once or twice and questioned Annie Bailey's neighbours. There had been music and voices, that was all they'd say. Nothing to complain about, really, although one regal old Dame in the apartment underneath Annie Bailey's select knocking shop had clutched her Pekinese dog to her scrawny chest and said in plummy tones that she suspected something was 'going on' up there. Something *nasty*.

'There goes another one,' said the constable as a distinguished silver-haired gentleman entered the block.

A taxi swerved into the kerb and decanted a blonde woman, a big black woman, a small dark-haired woman, and an obvious queer.

'Fuck, this is turning into a bloody orgy,' said Sergeant McKellan.

'Yeah,' said the constable wistfully.

The constable sneezed and fished out his hand-kerchief. Loitering around this corner, they were constantly frozen to the marrow. His trousers were wet six inches up the leg. He felt he'd never again get warm. Inside, there would be drinks, food, lovely women . . . heaven on fucking earth, he thought. He fumbled out his Vicks inhaler and took a snort up each sore, red nostril. His sergeant watched him.

'You want to put some Vaseline on that nose, Constable,' he said.

'Yes Sarge,' said the constable gloomily. He nodded across the road. 'Look. Two more.'

Sure enough, two more gents entered. Looked decent types, too. One was swaggering along, his expression arrogant, looked like a barrister. The other one . . .

'Fucking *hell*,' said Sergeant McKellan. 'That bugger's wearing a dog collar. He's a man of the sodding cloth!'

What was the world coming to? A regular orgy of depravity, thought Sergeant McKellan with pious disgust. He'd soon sort out this little lot. Oh yes. A Black Maria pulled into the kerb beside them and three more officers piled out from the back of it. Time to get on with it, he thought with relish.

'Come on, lads,' he said, and led the way across the road.

Annie opened the door with a smile on her face and found Sergeant McKellan standing there. Her smile dropped. She slammed the door shut.

A heavy hand thumped upon it.

'Open up! Police!'

Fucking hell, thought Annie.

Behind her, there was a scene of pandemonium as lords and tarts scattered in all directions. Dolly, to her credit, stepped up and said: 'What the fuck's going on?'

Annie had gone pale. Joshua dropped his tray of glasses and pink champagne spread in a sticky ooze over the costly Aubusson rug. He legged it over to his bar and started cramming bottles into boxes.

Dolly went to the door. 'What do you want?' she shouted.

'I am an officer of the law,' said Sergeant McKellan. 'I have a warrant to enter these premises.'

'We're going to have to let them in,' said Dolly to a stricken Annie, 'or they're going to break the bloody door down.'

Annie straightened herself up and nodded. The game was up. She put her bag aside – crammed full of notes from all the punters – and opened the door.

'Thank you, miss,' said the sergeant, and showed her the warrant. 'Are you Miss Annie Bailey?'

Annie nodded. She felt pole-axed with the shock of it.

'Miss Bailey, we have reason to believe that you are selling liquor without a licence on private premises, and that you are running a disorderly house here too.'

'This is a private party,' said Dolly in Annie's defence. 'It's Miss Bailey's birthday.'

'We'll see,' said the sergeant, and the constables elbowed past the two women to get a better look at what was going on.

'Who are you, sir?' one asked an elderly gentleman sitting quietly in a club chair talking to Ellie.

'Mickey Mouse,' said the old gent staunchly.

The constable got out his notebook and licked his pencil with a sigh. Rain was dripping off the poor soul. Annie almost felt inclined to offer the lad a drink.

'Mickey Mouse is it, sir?' the constable looked pained. 'And your address, sir?'

'Disneyland, Constable,' said the old gent. 'Where else?'

Another of the constables went off into one of the bedrooms and came back out with screams ringing in his ears. He looked shaken.

'Think you ought to see this, Sarge,' he said.

Leaving a constable guarding the main door into the apartment, in case anyone thought they might make good their escape that way, Sergeant McKellan went into one of the bedrooms and found on the bed, a middle-aged, naked man, all hairy legs and huge belly, hastily covering up his private parts. A glamorous blonde was zipping herself back into her dress. On the bedside table Sergeant McKellan found packets of the new contraceptive pills, boxes of tissues, bottles of baby oil and tins of Crowe's Cremine.

'What's this?' he asked, picking up a tin and sniffing it, suspecting illegal substances.

Mira tossed her blonde hair back out of her eyes. 'It's make-up remover,' she said.

Annie stood shattered in the doorway but she gave Mira an approving glance. They all knew that the cream was the best sexual lubricant going.

The police proceeded to the next bedroom and found Jen in her red, cutaway undies, scrabbling off a bed where a man, naked except for his socks, reclined. He had an erection you could have balanced a plate on. It wilted when its owner saw the police looming in the doorway.

'What the fuck's the meaning of this?' he said with all the authority of old money.

'May I ask you, sir, to stop whatever it is you are doing and get dressed,' said Sergeant McKellan formally.

'This is a bloody poor show,' huffed the man, but he got off the bed and started to dress.

The sergeant had seen enough. He went back into the drawing room and confronted Annie.

'May I ask if I might see your handbag, miss?'

he asked, indicating the Hermès bag that Annie had dropped on to one of the club chairs.

Annie numbly picked up the bag and handed it to him. She knew she was in deep shit now, and there was nothing to do but go along with it. Sergeant McKellan opened it and found it bulging with money.

He refastened the clasp and said, 'Annie Bailey, I am arresting you for running a disorderly house and for selling liquor without a licence . . .'

And that was it. I'm sunk, thought Annie through a fog of terrified gloom. Sunk without a fucking trace. Who the hell did this? Who would hate me enough to do it to me, on my bloody birthday too?

Billy stood in the rain and watched as they started to empty Annie's party guests out of her flat and into the Black Maria. Lots of them. Then the girls. And finally, Annie herself. Looking beautiful, as always. His lovely Annie. Oh, how he adored her. He was sad he'd had to do this, but she had to learn. It was for her own good. He turned away, feeling sad but justified in his actions. She would be better for it, he thought. In time.

56

At the police station they allowed her just one phone call. Annie thought long and hard about it, and called her cousin Kath. She didn't even think of calling Redmond Delaney, her business partner. You didn't involve the gangland boys in police business. As far as the Upper Brook Street business was concerned, she was sole owner and would take sole responsibility when the shit hit the fan. Which it had.

'Oh, it's you,' said Kath, sounding put out. 'What do you want?'

'I'm in the shit, Kath,' said Annie as an impassive female officer looked on in the interview room.

'What's that to me?' asked Kath coldly.

Annie gripped the receiver more tightly. She hadn't expected a warm greeting from Kath, but this was an even cooler reception than she had anticipated. Kath had chosen sides, and she had chosen

Ruthie. Being married to Jimmy Bond, one of Max's boys, who else would she choose? Mrs Max Carter, or that cheating whore Annie Bailey?

No contest.

Still, Annie had instinctively turned to family. *Big* mistake. She ought to have known better, really. But she was in a panic. She'd never been nicked before. It was bloody frightening. You'd think, at a time like this, that you could turn to those who should be closest to you.

'Look, Kath, I know you haven't got much time for me,' said Annie.

'Ha! You can say that again.'

'But I'm in a jam. I've been arrested, and I need a brief. Can you get me one?'

'Why me?'

Annie lost it. 'For fuck's sake, Kath! How long will it take you to call a solicitor and get him to come down here?'

'There's no need to take that tone with me,' said Kath.

'Sorry.' Annie clutched at her head. Out of the corner of her eye she could see the female officer smirking. 'Sorry, Kath. But do this one thing for me, will you?'

Kath reluctantly agreed that she would. As Annie put the phone down she felt that she had never been more alone. She put her head in her hands. They had taken all her belongings from her. Even

Mira's Rolex, her rings, a gold heart-shaped locket on a chain that Max had bought her and which she never took off. All taken. They'd even told her to take off her bra and her stilettos.

'You'd be amazed the number of girls we get hanging themselves by their bra straps in the cells,' the female officer had told her cheerfully, standing by while Annie self-consciously removed her bra and shoes and jewellery. 'And we had one in last week tried to dig through the cell wall with the heel of her shoe. Nutty as a fucking fruit cake, she was.'

Much longer in this place and Annie felt that she would be nutty too. Everyone else who'd been at the party seemed to have gone long before they let her out, but one of the kind souls had at least stumped up for her bail. Thank God, she thought. She didn't like the idea of being in this hell-hole an instant longer than necessary.

She gave her statement and Kath – God bless her – sent the brief down. He looked about ten years old, but he seemed to know his stuff. He left, and then she was locked up.

'Don't worry,' her brief had said. 'Bail will be posted, you'll soon be out.'

But it was many hours later when the cell door opened and she was told she could go home.

'Someone likes you,' said the female officer, not unkindly. 'Bail's in place. You can go. Don't leave

458

the bloody country though, and you'll be required to check in to your local police station once a week until your case comes to court.'

'All right,' said Annie. Her head ached. She felt shattered and sick at heart. Some birthday.

But somehow, she felt she deserved this. She had done wrong, and she was going to be punished. Annie knew that she had done more wrong than could ever be put right. She had sat in that barren cell and thought about her mother, who had never loved her. Annie had given her a lot of trouble over the years. Hitting back in the only way she could, being a brat to punish Connie for her lack of affection.

And Ruthie. Ruthie, the favoured one. She'd punished Ruthie for that, too. Punished her by ruining her marriage, ruining her life. The poor cow.

And now Annie knew that she had been caught out, and that she would be punished. Which was good. Then maybe . . . maybe she could start to wipe the slate clean.

It was all over now, her and Max Carter.

She knew it was all over with Ruthie too. All those pitiful attempts at reconciliation. Who was she kidding? Would she have forgiven Ruthie, had the boot been on the other foot? Not in a million years. And Ruthie was not going to forgive her, not ever. She had lost her sister. It was done. Time to move on.

She walked out of the police station with her little bag of jewellery in her hand. She walked smack into Kieron Delaney.

'How did you know I was here?' Annie asked him coldly. She was looking up and down the busy road for a cab. She didn't want to talk to anyone right now, and especially not to him.

'Redmond told me,' said Kieron. 'Are you all right?'

'I'm fine.' Bloody taxis, never one around when you wanted one. She was wearing a thin shift dress and it was fucking freezing out here.

'Come back to the flat with me,' said Kieron.

'No.'

Didn't I already tell him several times to fuck off? wondered Annie.

'Oh come on. Where the hell else are you going to go?'

'That's my business,' said Annie sharply. At last she spotted a cab approaching.

She hailed the cab and got in without another word to Kieron.

She wondered where to go. The Upper Brook Street apartment was off-limits. It was probably still crawling with police, probably cordoned off as a crime scene.

There was only one place in the world that would forever be home.

*   *   *

It was just like old times, thought Annie. Darren and Aretha and Ellie and Dolly and her, all around the kitchen table in the Limehouse parlour, drinking tea and keeping Ellie from eating too many biscuits. Chris out there in the hall, in his seat by the door.

'How bad is it?' asked Dolly, getting straight down to brass tacks.

Annie sipped her tea and sighed. 'Pretty bad,' she admitted. 'The brief reckons I could be looking at a two-year stretch. I was caught red-handed running a disorderly house. No argument. He reckons it's best to plead guilty, get the two years, then appeal.'

'What if you threatened to drop a couple of names to the Bill?' suggested Aretha. 'You know, girl, all those lords and stuff. They wouldn't want to be put in the frame, now would they? They got clout, those people. They got reputations to protect. Couldn't they get you offa this?'

'I couldn't do that,' said Annie. 'Look, I ran the place. I accept responsibility.'

Dolly nodded. 'Aretha, Darren, Ellie and me were lucky to get out of the nick in one bit. The pigs didn't have nothing on us, we were just there for your birthday party after all. But it was touch and go for a minute there as to whether they'd swallow it or not. Look, Annie, what about Redmond?'

'What about him?'

'Well, wouldn't he pull some strings?'

'I won't ask him,' said Annie. 'You know how it is, Doll. They take care of you but you never implicate them.'

'And is he going to do that? Take care of you . . . when you're . . . ?' Dolly couldn't say it.

When you're inside, added Annie to herself with a shiver.

Christ, going to prison. She knew it was going to happen. She knew she'd done the crime and she would have to do the time. But the thought of it was putting the fear of God up her. Her bowels felt liquid. She felt sick as a dog.

'Well, we've got to hope so, haven't we,' said Annie, dunking another biscuit. She had to eat, at least, had to keep body and soul together.

'You're being very brave about it,' said Darren. 'I'd be in bits.'

But Annie had always toughed it out. It was in her nature to stand alone and stick two fingers up to the world. Suddenly she felt tired. She'd been nicked on her twenty-second birthday. Two years had gone by since she'd first done the dirty on her sister by sleeping with Max Carter. Two long, fucking years.

And what did she have to show for it? A dodgy ex-lover, a family who didn't want to know her, and a pending prison sentence. Nothing to be proud of, now was it?

And the papers were lapping it all up. The

Mayfair Madam was fast becoming a national figure to be poked fun at by the populace. Neighbours at the Upper Brook Street apartment had tattled to reporters and the story had been seized upon with delight. Echoes of Profumo, yelled the dailies. Pillars of the community caught with their trousers down. Red-faced peers and clerics and high-flying businessmen cavorting with classy West End prostitutes. The scandal!

A picture of Annie walking along a London street wearing a fur coat and sunglasses had been found from somewhere and splashed on to front pages. 'Jackie Kennedy lookalike Annie Bailey', they called her. Beautiful, high-class prostitute, Annie Bailey.

But I'm not a fucking brass, thought Annie in dismay. *I never have been.*

There'd been photos of Mira, too. Impossibly glamorous Mira, striding along with her blonde locks glowing in the sun. She looked expensive, pampered. There were stories about Cliveden, William had been named and he had lost his parliamentary seat as a consequence, although his wife was standing by him. Either that, or Lady Fenella would lose the country estate and the title, thought Annie sourly, and she wouldn't relish that at all. Fuck it, thought Annie. What a mess it all was. But at least they didn't know that she was here in Limehouse.

'What will you do, Annie love?' asked Dolly.

'Sit tight and wait for the case to come up,' shrugged Annie. 'What the hell else can I do?'

'Your sister been in touch yet?'

'You're having a laugh.'

'Well, your room's free.'

'Thanks, Doll.'

Not a nice prospect – sleeping in the room where they'd done for Pat Delaney. But better than nothing. Better than finding a hotel, running from the press, all that shit.

Dolly gave a sudden snort of laughter. 'Fucking hell,' she burst out. 'That copper's face when he looked in the bedrooms! It was bloody priceless.'

'Gave him a fucking inferiority complex, I bet,' said Aretha.

'Get the brandy out, Ellie love,' ordered Dolly, wiping her eyes. 'Let's top this tea up with something a bit more lively.'

Trust Dolly to laugh in the face of adversity. Annie loved her for it. She almost raised a smile.

57

It was the same old routine, Kieron noticed. Orla went into the church, her flame-red hair covered with a black veil, and lit a penny candle for the soul of Tory Delaney. Never went near the confessional, he noted. Straight out to the grave and then placing the usual twelve blood-red roses into the urn. She was like a robot, his sister Orla. Precise, ordered, void of emotion. Cool as fucking ice. Petey was standing by the car at the gate, watching the surroundings. Watching not the subject but those who might wish to do her harm.

Too fucking late, of course.

Kieron looked at the headstone.

Tory Michael Delaney
Beloved Son, Beloved Brother
Rest in Peace

'I'm thinking of going away,' said Kieron.

'Oh?' She looked up. 'Where?'

'I was thinking of Spain. The light's good there.'

She nodded and went back to her task.

She wouldn't miss him, he thought. Try taking Redmond from her side and there would be a riot. But him, her baby brother? Dispensable. Out of sight, out of mind.

'It didn't work out with Annie Bailey, did it?' she said.

Kieron snorted. 'No. I wish it had, but there you go. She has troubles enough now, anyway.'

'So I hear.' Orla looked up, her green eyes locking with his. 'That unfortunate business with the police.'

'Well, you play with fire, you get burnt. I told her she shouldn't have been in that line of work. But would she listen? She would not.'

'Redmond tells me the court case is due next month.'

'Redmond knows everything.'

'Yes,' said Orla. 'He does. I thought you were a friend of hers though, Kieron. She needs all the friends she can get right now.'

'She's made it plain she doesn't want *me*,' said Kieron moodily. 'That fucking Carter's got such a hold on her.'

'Maybe she'll change her mind.'

'You think?'

'She's coming to us for dinner on Saturday. The least we can do, I think. It'll be a quiet evening, just us three. Perhaps you'd like to join us?'

Kieron kicked at a tussock of unmown grass. Annie kept rejecting him, pushing him away from her, even though he knew she wanted him really. She'd be his, if only Max Carter wasn't in the bloody way.

'Ah, I don't know. I might even be gone by then. Orla, the woman's going down.'

'Well.' Orla turned back to the flowers. 'The offer's there. And it's true she'll probably do time, but there's hope of an appeal.'

'I'm surprised you're having her in the place,' said Kieron. 'You don't want any mud sticking to the pair of you.'

'She's a friend we know through you, that's the story,' said Orla smoothly.

'Ah, sure. That's the story.'

'Yes. It is.'

Orla turned back to the flowers and started in with the murmuring under the breath again. Kieron drew a bit closer.

'Bastard, you bastard, you're dead and I'm alive . . .'

Kieron drew a breath. 'Orla,' he said.

She stopped. She put the last flower in place and stood up and faced him. 'Yes, Kieron?'

'You hated him, didn't you?' said Kieron.

'Who, Tory?' Her eyes were shuttered now. 'He was our brother.'

'He was a bastard, the worst kind.'

Orla lifted her chin. 'He was the head of the family,' she said.

'Sure.'

'And to be accorded respect.'

Kieron stared at her. 'Orla. Tory and Pat were bastards together. They were bad to the core.'

'Were? You're talking as if Pat's dead, too.'

'Don't you think he is?'

Orla paused for a beat. 'I know he is.'

'*What?*'

'Redmond and I believe he died at the Limehouse parlour. Annie Bailey complained of him before to Redmond, said Pat was taking drugs and getting out of hand. Not that it was a surprise. We knew, anyway. And he was there the day he vanished, then he was gone during the doorman's break and there was word of the Carter mob coming in and doing a clean-up that night. They carried something out of there. Annie Bailey had hurt her leg somehow, and Dolly Farrell had a tooth missing. The story was there'd been a catfight over territory, but it stank to high heaven. They were all jumpy with us after that. Guilty as hell. Oh, Pat's dead all right.'

'You don't sound very sorry,' said Kieron.

'Why would I be?' Orla's smile was chilling. 'As you say – he was a bastard.'

Kieron looked at her. 'So . . . you're glad Pat's dead.'

'Honestly? He's no great loss.'

'And so I guess you're glad Tory's dead too,' said Kieron.

Orla stared at him. 'He was my brother.'

'You can't bring yourself to say it.'

'The head of the family.'

'*Orla.*' Kieron grabbed her shoulders and stared into her face. 'We all know what Tory was. He was vicious and he was a thug and he hurt you and Redmond.'

'Kieron, stop it,' said Orla.

'No, it's got to be said,' said Kieron passionately. 'I remember it all, just as if it were yesterday. Tory was seventeen, I was eight, Pat seven. You and Red were just ten years old. I heard it all happening. I'll never forget it. I heard Tory in your room, and I *saw* . . . once I crept out and I saw what he was doing to the pair of you and I felt sick and I ran off, I was afraid that he would do it to me too if I made a sound. I saw Pat in there too, laughing and watching. Seven years old and he was already a sick little bastard, I saw him.'

Orla started to tremble. 'Please, stop this,' she said in a small voice.

'It's all right, it's all right,' said Kieron soothingly, rubbing her shoulders now, his hands gentle. 'They're gone, they're both gone, thank God. Never to return. I wanted you to know, that's all. I wanted you to know that I did it for you, for you and Redmond. I set you free of him, once and for all.'

'What do you mean?' asked Orla.

'I think you know,' said Kieron.

'No. I don't. Tell me what you mean.'

'I didn't come back from Africa just before the funeral. I was here, in England, a month before Tory was killed. When Redmond phoned long-distance to say that Tory had been shot, a friend took the message and phoned me. I was painting in Hayle. Huge beaches, vast skies. The light's good there, too. Vivid.'

'*Kieron.*' Orla nearly screamed it.

'It was easy to do. I was in the country nearly a month before. It had been eating away at me for years, what he did to you and Redmond when you were just children. And I thought, why not? No one even knows I'm about the place. Everyone has guns out in South Africa, you know. It's a dangerous country. I had a gun, I had bullets. I brought it back with me and I painted and I thought about what had been done and that it had never been avenged.'

'Go on.' Orla's face was bloodless. She looked like she might faint.

'I came up here and I watched. I was careful that no one knew I was about – not even you. I watched Tory's movements. I knew he went out to the Tudor Club at Stoke Newington every Friday night. So I went there too, and I waited outside . . . and then I shot him. No one ever suspected. Everyone thought Max Carter had done it.'

Orla stared at him. Kieron was half-smiling, knowing she would be pleased.

Then she slapped his face so hard that he reeled backwards. Then she fell on him like a fury, grabbed his hair, yanked back his head and yelled into his face: 'What the hell have you done, you bloody fool?'

Kieron blinked in shock. She was supposed to be pleased. He was *sure* she would be pleased. 'But you hated him. You had good reason to hate him.'

'Yes! I hated him!'

'Well then.'

'Well then nothing, you fucking little idiot. Yes, I hated him and I hate him still. I come here and light candles and lay flowers for Mum, not for me. And I curse his rotten soul every time I come here. I hope he's frying in hell. I detest the memory of him. If I was unattended here, you know what I'd do?'

'No. I don't.' Kieron's voice shook. His face burned where she had struck him. He was amazed at the change in her. This wasn't the Orla he knew.

'I'd dance, Kieron. Right on this fucking grave. I'd *dance* on top of him.'

'Well . . .' Kieron felt afraid. He had never seen her in such a tear.

'But Dad *doted* on him. Tory was his first-born, his favourite. Do you have any idea what it did to him, losing Tory? It drove him *mad*, Kieron. It drove him mad with grief! Our dad's an empty shell, he's nothing now. An old man with a wandering mind. And you stand there smiling like someone waiting to get a prize? Shame on you!'

'But you hated him . . .' repeated Kieron blankly. He couldn't understand her reaction, he couldn't take any of this in. She was supposed to be *pleased*.

'Of course I did.' Orla was hissing into his face, spittle flying with every word she uttered. 'What do you think I am, a fool? I know what he did to us. I know he ruined us both. I can't look at men. I can't contemplate marriage, or sex, or babies. It gives me the heaves every time it crosses my mind. Because of what my own brother did to me. How do you think that feels, Kieron?'

'And that's why I did it,' said Kieron desperately. 'Because I knew, and because I couldn't let him get away with it.'

Orla took a quivering breath and regained a measure of calm. She stared at him as if at a stranger.

'You killed him,' she said.

She'd thought of just about everyone, but never

Kieron. She had suspected the Mafia – the Americans, particularly the Barolli family, were strong in the West End and Tory had been openly resentful about their presence here and about their business links with the Carters. And the Carters. Of course the Carters. Hot-headed Jonjo or cool, controlled Max. Either one. Someone had set out to kill Queenie Carter, and that had been a step too far. No one would have blamed them for wreaking revenge.

'I did it for you,' said Kieron urgently. 'For you and Redmond. You must have wanted to do it yourselves. You *must* have.'

'Of course we did,' spat Orla.

Every day of her life she remembered it, every night she dreamed of it; a flare of faint light from the landing. The bedroom door opening, then closing softly. Someone moving inside the dark room, inside her and Redmond's room. Someone was coming to her bed.

Even now she felt the familiar hopeless terror, the awful tightness in her chest. Someone was sitting down on the edge of her bed, but she mustn't scream or tell, she mustn't cry out because she would never be believed, Tory had always told them that. Her tears were silent, like her fear. And then the covers moved, and the nightmare became unspeakable.

'Of course we wanted to kill him,' she said,

dragging in a breath to steady herself. 'But we never would. He meant too much to Dad. When Dad was gone, then we would have made our move. Not before.'

'He was a bastard and he deserved what he got,' insisted Kieron, determined to justify himself. 'He was cruel and sadistic. Messing with his own brother and sister. And he called me a pansy because I painted. Both Tory and Pat despised me because I was an artist, not a proper part of the firm like they were. Well I showed him. I'm not a fucking pansy, I'm not as soft as you all think I am.'

Orla was still giving him that odd look, as if she had never seen him before. 'You didn't have any part in the killing of Pat too, did you?' she asked.

'No. But you know what?'

'What?'

'I wish I had.'

Orla stared at him. Her sensitive, artistic little brother. The misfit in a family of gangsters. Maybe not so much a misfit after all. The thought troubled her. Blood ran deep, she thought. Deeper than she had ever thought possible.

'You did it for us,' she said at last. 'You meant to do good.'

'Of course I did,' said Kieron.

He's like a puppy, she thought. Bringing you

your shoe although he's chewed it beyond redemption. Trying to please. Creating havoc but only for the best of reasons. God help him.

God help them all.

58

Annie went to dinner on Saturday at Redmond's and Orla's house and got a nasty shock when she found Kieron there too. There was a brooding atmosphere between the brothers and sister. There'd definitely been a family row. Annie was a connoisseur of family rows.

'What did you think of the cheese soufflé?' asked Orla, making polite conversation while Kieron and Redmond looked daggers at each other.

'It was great,' said Annie, although with the court case looming she was a bit off her food. With Kieron making cow-eyes at her from across the table, she felt even less inclined to eat.

'And the lamb?'

'Superb.'

There was a silent middle-aged woman serving them, and Annie guessed she was probably their housekeeper and had been elected chef for the night. Now she was bringing in small pots of chocolate mousse. Redmond waited until the woman had left the room before he said, 'You're looking thin, Miss Bailey.'

'Am I?' Annie was startled. Redmond didn't usually get personal.

'Yes, I thought that,' chipped in Kieron. 'You are looking thin, Annie.'

For fuck's sake. Talk about Little Sir Echo. Annie felt a pang of utter loathing. She had tried so hard to get shot of Kieron, yet here they were again, him taking an interest in the state of her, her wishing he'd back off.

She couldn't forget how repulsive it had felt when he kissed her and she didn't want him thinking he could try anything like that again. When was the stupid bastard going to take no for an answer? When Max finally snapped and killed him stone-dead?

Probably Redmond and Orla had engineered this evening with the best of intentions, but she wished they'd let her know Kieron was going to be here. Because then she wouldn't have been.

Weeks had gone by since the police raid, and Annie had stayed at the Limehouse parlour with her friends. A sort of fatalism had settled over her. All right, she was going down. Fair enough. It had given her a certain clarity of mind. She now strongly felt that there were people in her life who shouldn't be there, and people who *weren't* in her life whose company she would appreciate.

She knew it was finished with Ruthie. There'd been no word from her, although Kath must have told her what had gone on. Even if Kath hadn't told her, it was splashed all over the bloody papers. Difficult to miss. So Ruthie clearly didn't give a toss what happened to her sister. Fair play to her – Annie didn't blame her. It was almost a relief to have all that over with, she thought. Now she'd get the court case done with, do the time, and then start again. Preferably somewhere else. Somewhere *new*.

She thought of Max. No good doing that. Give poor bloody Ruthie a chance now. Do the right thing for once in your life.

'Well, this is a nice meal,' she said brightly for Orla's sake, spooning up the mousse although her appetite was gone. 'The condemned woman ate heartily,' she quipped.

'Ah, don't say that,' said Kieron. 'You'll get off, never fear.'

'I don't think anything is to be gained by giving Miss Bailey false hope,' said Redmond. 'A sentence seems inevitable.'

'You're famous, Annie,' said Orla, trying to make light of it all. 'In the papers and all.'

'More like notorious,' said Annie.

'Surely it won't be a long stretch,' said Orla.

'Maybe two years.'

The thought made her blood freeze. Sure, everyone was rallying round, trying to cheer her up, but the prospect of prison was daunting. Aretha, who had done time in her youth for some unnamed crime, had told her to be careful.

'You watch out for they bull dykes in there, girl,' she'd said. 'You find yourself a nice friend and keep close. No wanderin' off alone, an' keep out of Ambush Alley.'

'Ambush Alley?' Annie had echoed.

'The *showers*, silly. They hang about in there, lookin' for fresh young flesh.'

'Do you think you'll get time off for good behaviour?' said Redmond.

Annie nodded. 'And I'll appeal.'

'Eat up that mousse now,' said Kieron like a mother hen, curse him. 'There's hardly a pick on you.'

'Thanks for the meal,' said Annie when they finished eating and were on coffee and brandy.

'It was the least we could do,' said Redmond.

'Yes it was,' said Kieron. 'After all, you were involved too, weren't you Red? And you've got off scot-free whereas Annie's going to carry the entire can.'

Redmond gave his younger brother a freezing glance. 'That's the way it works, Kieron. You know that.'

'It's all right,' said Annie, wondering what the hell had got into Kieron to talk to his brother like that. The row must have been a bad one. 'I know that. I took full responsibility. That was always the deal.'

Dirty Game

'All the responsibility and half the profits.' Kieron threw back his brandy in one hit. 'That doesn't seem such a good deal to me.'

'Well no one is asking you,' said Orla.

'Oh pardon *me*.'

'Shut up, Kieron. If you can't be civil, at least be quiet.' Orla looked at Annie. 'I apologize for him, Annie.'

'Don't apologize on my behalf,' snapped Kieron. 'I'm just stating the facts, that's all.'

'Well – don't,' said Redmond with a smile that didn't reach his eyes.

Kieron's eyes locked with Redmond's for a few beats; then his gaze dropped away. He ran a hand through his hair. 'Ah, feck it. I'm not good company tonight.' He looked at Orla. 'We've had a few upsets over the last few days, haven't we Orla?'

Orla nodded guardedly.

'It's all knocked me off-centre,' said Kieron. He turned to Annie. 'Look, let's the two of us go on to a club and leave these two homebodies to it.'

Orla shook her head. 'I don't think that's a good idea.'

'Orla's right,' said Redmond, pushing back his chair and standing up.

'I'm a bit tired,' said Annie.

She didn't fancy trying to fend Kieron off yet again. He was nice enough, but she saw him

480

clearly now for what he was – a spoiled little prick who had a talent but who threw his toys out of his pram when he couldn't get exactly what he wanted.

'Nonsense, I'll soon liven you up, girl,' he said, and bounced off to fetch their coats.

Jesus, get me out of here, she thought.

'Now where shall we go?' he said, coming back and helping her into her coat. He flashed a grin at a frowning Orla while Annie stood there silent, wondering how she was going to get out of this without making a scene in front of them all.

'Can't go to the Liberty or the Galway, now can we?' he said. 'Someone went and burned the fecking things to the ground. *I* know. We'll go to the Palermo Lounge. I've heard they get some really good acts there on a Saturday night.'

'For God's sake, Kieron,' said Orla, really worried now.

The Palermo was the jewel in the crown of the Carter clubs – and Max's favourite.

Orla was looking anxious. As well she might. Annie didn't know what had got into Kieron, but she was liking all this less and less and she was getting seriously pissed off with him. What was he thinking of, wanting to take her to a Carter club? Maybe he had a death wish or something.

'Ah, don't be looking at me like that,' laughed

Kieron, steering Annie towards the door. 'I'll be good as gold. On my best behaviour. You see if I'm not.'

Kieron drove and Annie sat silent in the car. She was feeling tense and worried. He seemed twitchy, she thought. Tapping his fingers on the steering wheel, whistling, sending her little smiles. He seemed very keyed-up.

'Actually I'd rather just go home,' she said at last.

Cheerily Kieron patted her knee. Annie pulled away, irritated.

'Ah, come on. A night out's what you need to cheer you up,' he told her.

'No it isn't.'

'Yes it *is*. The Palermo's a good club, you'll love it. Have you been there before?'

About a lifetime ago, thought Annie. She didn't particularly want to go there again, cover all that old ground. Especially not with a Delaney. She could almost smell the stench of trouble on Kieron tonight.

'Ah, but I was forgetting,' said Kieron, slapping his forehead. 'Of course you've been there. And in the Shalimar, I suppose. And the other one, what's it called . . . ?'

'The Blue Parrot.'

'That's the feller. Of course you've been in his clubs, you were in his bed often enough after all.'

482

'Just take me home, Kieron,' said Annie coldly.

'No, the evening's just beginning,' said Kieron, sending her another dementedly cheery little smile.

Fuck it, thought Annie.

Max was in his office upstairs in the Palermo. Through the floor he could hear Donald Peers warbling away at a song to wring at the hardest heart. But Max wasn't moved. Nothing much seemed to move him any more. He added up last night's takings, sipped his whisky, and thought about the bigger stash of money from the department store job, all safely tucked away.

He was doing plenty of lucrative work with Constantine Barolli's properties up West now, and he was thinking maybe of going legit. The Old Bill were getting a bit keen lately, and he was sensing a change in the air. But meanwhile there was the money from the heist. He thought of that again, and of where it could take him. Anywhere in the world he wanted.

But where did he want to go? He'd been thinking about it; every time he drew a blank. Where would *Ruthie* like to go?

Now that really did ruin the illusion of paradise. Fucking Ruthie with her drinking and her shrill accusations. What a treat! He'd rather fucking-well stop here than take Ruthie anywhere, the mouthy cow.

Annie drifted into his mind. Jesus, she was in the shit and no mistake. Running a brothel – oh sorry, judge, a 'disorderly house' – and selling liquor without a licence. The Delaneys, of course, had drifted out of the frame and left her to it. So she was going down for a stretch, no doubt about that.

He thought about Annie, inside. He didn't like it one little bit. The rough tarts in there would eat her alive.

There was a knock on the door.

'Come in.'

'Boss?' One of the boys poked his head in.

'Hm?'

'Thought you ought to know, Boss. Annie Bailey's just come in with Kieron Delaney.'

Max sat up straight. He had thought of her and now here she was. With Kieron fucking Delaney.

'Keep an eye on them,' said Max. 'I'll come down.'

And do what? he wondered as the door closed and he was alone again. Why go down at all? Let them have a drink and a dance, then leave. Why torture himself?

No good getting older if you didn't get smarter with it. She was with Delaney, why not leave it at that now? She'd made her choice, he thought bitterly. And it wasn't him. He took another sip of whisky and went back to looking at the books.

*   *   *

It was over an hour later when Jimmy Bond knocked and entered.

'That Delaney ponce is causing trouble,' he said.

Max sat back and looked at him. 'Is Jonjo in?'

'Yeah, with a girl. Kieron Delaney's been cutting in, and Jonjo's about to blow.' Jimmy cleared his throat. 'Annie Bailey's down there with Delaney.'

'I know.' He didn't want Jonjo going off on one in the middle of the club when it was packed with good regular punters.

'Ask Mr Delaney to step into the office, will you, Jimmy? Bring Annie up too.'

'There's more,' said Jimmy.

'Go on.'

'Redmond and Orla Delaney have just arrived. They're asking to see you.'

'Looks like we've got us a party,' said Max.

'You carrying, Max?'

'Is it looking as bad as that?'

'I'm not sure. I'm getting a bad feeling.'

Max nodded. Jimmy's 'feelings' were not to be ignored. His parents were settled Cockneys but his grandparents had been travellers. Jimmy had gipsy roots. Max didn't ever discount Jimmy's 'bad feelings'. On the night of the robbery, Jimmy had been keeping watch and had 'felt' that someone was about. He'd gone to what he believed to be the main door, the one all the staff entered through. The manager had come through the back, surprising them all. But Jimmy's instinct had been proved sound.

'I'm okay,' he said. 'You?'

'Packing, yeah. I'll bring a couple of the boys up too.'

'No. Just you.'

With Jimmy gone, Max opened his top left-hand desk drawer and looked at the gun and the box of bullets. He took both out, and loaded the weapon in readiness.

Max's office was small so it was a bit of a crush with five of them in it. Kieron was flushed and irritable. Max wondered how much booze he'd knocked back tonight. Annie looked tired, almost frail, not like herself. Orla and Redmond, in dark coats that set off their red hair, looked like cool alabaster bookends. Unflappable, possibly dangerous. Jimmy had bundled Kieron up the stairs and Kieron hadn't liked it at all.

'Take your fucking hands off me,' he snapped.

Max nodded. Jimmy released him.

'Wait outside, will you? Jimmy?'

Jimmy gave Max an 'are-you-kidding?' look, but he reluctantly concurred.

'Annie, Miss Delaney, take a seat,' said Max when the door closed behind Jimmy. Donald Peers was still singing away downstairs, waves of applause following each song.

'You mobsters are so polite,' sneered Kieron.

'Thanks,' said Annie to Max. 'But I'm not stopping.'

'Can I order you a taxi?' He didn't want her to stop here, either. If anything kicked off now, Annie would be in the way and he didn't like that. He wished she'd keep her arty fucking boyfriend on a tighter leash, though.

'No, you fucking can't,' said Kieron. 'She came with me and she's going home with me. I've had enough of you pushing in, Carter.'

Redmond gave Kieron a cold look.

'And you too,' said Kieron hotly. 'Come on Red, don't be looking at me like that. I know what I'm doing. There's no need to be coming along after me like I'm some sort of moron.'

'Isn't there?' said Redmond. 'Then why are you behaving like one?'

'I'm sorry about this,' said Orla to Annie. 'We thought that when you left Kieron was rather upset. So we thought we'd better come after you, make sure you were all right.' She looked pointedly at Kieron. 'I don't know what's got into him lately.'

Annie slumped into a chair. She felt exhausted and she didn't want to be here. She was very aware of Max sitting across the desk from her, watching all this interaction and wondering what was going on. She wanted to be in her bed, asleep. This was a fucking nightmare.

'It was kind of you to come,' said Annie to Orla.

'Not kind at all. We have a lot of respect for you. We admire you as a businesswoman, and we have a great deal to thank you for.'

'You have nothing to thank me for,' said Annie wearily.

'But we have.' Orla's face was blank but her voice was sincere. 'For instance, we have you to thank for solving a major problem for us.'

Annie frowned. 'What major problem?'

Orla smiled gently. 'Why Pat, of course. He was getting to be a terrible problem, and you got rid of him for us. You and Mr Carter here. Isn't that the case?'

There was silence in the room. Annie was aware that Max was tensing as Orla spoke. He was ready to move. But Orla was still coolly sitting there beside her, as if this were a bloody afternoon tea party and not an unexpected meeting that was turning out to be very scary indeed.

'I don't know what you mean,' she said finally.

'Yes you do,' said Orla. 'We know most of what happened to Pat. Nearly all of it, really.'

They're guessing, thought Annie. They're hoping I'll admit something and then their bait will have worked. I'm not falling for it.

'I don't know what you mean,' she repeated.

Redmond tutted under his breath and looked at his sister.

'Ellie is a Delaney girl to her bones,' said Orla. 'She needed to unburden herself. She wanted to go to the police but she didn't, and that's something else we have to thank you for. She confessed to us that you were all in on the killing except her. She tried to stop it, but you dealt the final blow.'

Annie's mouth dropped open. That fucking little liar. Out to save her own skin again, the miserable little grass. And to say that Annie had dealt the final blow! Jesus, it was Ellie herself who had jumped on Pat's back and slit his throat wide open.

'That isn't true,' said Annie. 'It was Ellie who slit Pat's throat.'

'Be that as it may,' said Redmond. 'We're grateful.'

'Grateful?'

'He used to abuse them when they were children,' said Kieron suddenly. 'Him and Tory.'

'Kieron,' said Orla, her face a mask of horror and shame as her secret was laid bare for everyone to hear.

Redmond's look should have dissolved Kieron on the spot.

Annie looked at Redmond. Then at Orla.

'Jesus,' she said helplessly. 'I don't know what to say.'

'Don't say anything,' said Orla, sending Kieron a furious glance. 'My brother Kieron has a very big mouth and he ought to learn to keep it shut. This is family business.'

'Oh, why hide it away? They were bastards, the pair of them,' Kieron blundered on. 'Tory was the instigator, but Pat was happy to participate, the fucking filthy nonce.'

Annie was trying to take it all in. God, all the times she had quivered with fear at the thought of Redmond finding out that she had been instrumental in the death of his brother Pat. How she and Dolly and Aretha and Darren had schemed and struggled to cover their tracks. And all for nothing. Ellie had told Orla and Redmond a warped version of events, and they had been pleased to hear that their nasty, incestuous, junkie brother had finally left the earth. *Pleased.*

'Pat was becoming a liability, in any case,' said Orla. 'Something would have had to be done about him soon.'

It was as if she was discussing something totally disconnected from her, Annie realized. This was the key to Orla and Redmond Delaney. Finally Annie understood what she was dealing with. The childhood abuse had made them like this. So cold, so detached, so unable to participate in the normal everyday things of life. Both so beautiful and both so ruined, she thought in pity. No marriage, no children, no feelings for anything except each other. And what about Kieron? What about their parents?

She couldn't ask. She looked at Orla and felt only horror and sympathy.

'If you were relieved about Pat, then . . . you must have been relieved about Tory too?' she asked.

Orla shot Kieron a disgusted glance. Then she looked at Annie. 'Of course we were. But our parents were devastated by it.'

Kieron was looking fidgety again.

'When our parents went back to Ireland, I burned down the Galway and the Liberty Lounge and we pocketed the insurance,' said Orla matter-of-factly. She smiled at Max. 'Like you, Mr Carter, we have plenty of other good things going. We didn't need them. They were Tory's invention, Tory's pride and joy. Every time I so much as thought about them I was reminded of him. I hated them because of that, and they didn't even pay well. So I got rid.'

Annie looked over at Max. Orla seemed very hot on 'getting rid'. Of people, of places. Whatever displeased her, in fact. Anything and everyone. It struck her that Orla was a very dangerous woman indeed. Christ, and Annie had been walking around these past weeks believing the Delaneys to be in ignorance of Pat's death. *Fucking* Ellie. Annie could easily have woken up dead one morning, yet Ellie had been behaving as if everything was fine. Which – for her at least, the treacherous cow – it was.

Max sat back in his chair and looked at Orla. 'I have to ask – did you kill Tory?'

'No,' she said. 'And I never would. Not until our parents had passed over, anyway.'

'Then . . . you don't know who did? You don't believe the rumours that *I* did it?' asked Max. He glanced at Kieron. 'You accused me of doing Tory at your exhibition, didn't you.'

Kieron gave a snort of laughter. 'Yeah. But only so Red and Orla would believe it and get you out of my life for good, you bastard. I'm sick up to here of you treading on my toes. I thought that when they heard that, they might do the deed at last.' He gave his brother and sister a sneering look. 'But they didn't. Oh, for fuck's sake!' He flung his arms wide in exasperation. 'Don't you get it yet? It was *me*. I did it. I shot the bastard.'

Once again shocked silence filled the room. Downstairs, the crowd roared. Donald had performed his finale. The band were taking their bows. The compère was talking loudly into the microphone, but the words were just garbled noise to the people grouped in the small room upstairs.

'I'm not ashamed of it,' said Kieron.

'Well you should be,' said Orla, her eyes suddenly bright with tears. 'You know what it did to Dad.'

'It needed doing. I can't be like you, laying flowers and lighting candles for the bastard who caused you both such grief. I had to do something about it.'

So Max hadn't killed Tory Delaney. Annie's eyes met his and she read the question there.

'So if this is the time for confessions, what about

Max's family?' she asked, turning her gaze to Redmond and Orla. 'What about Queenie? What about poor Eddie? Jesus, Max had reason enough to hate you all, don't you think, when he believed you were behind their deaths?'

'Jesus, trust you to come galloping to his defence,' said Kieron angrily.

'I'm not defending anyone. I just want to hear the truth, that's all.'

Why didn't the fool just shut up? Annie didn't even glance at Kieron's face, she was sick of his mouthing off. She'd spent all this time sitting on the fence that divided the boundaries of the Carter and Delaney manors. It hadn't been a comfortable experience. Now there was a chance of finishing their feud once and for all, and Kieron was still putting his oar in.

'It was Pat,' said Redmond to Max. 'Pat set a couple of local boys up to do Queenie at your home in Surrey. Make it like an armed robbery, shoot her . . . but her heart gave out before they could do it. I'm sorry. He bragged about it to me. Laughed about how he went down there and wore a fake moustache and a bowler hat in a pub one night and paid two locals to do it.'

Max nodded, his eyes icy. 'I traced them. The Bowes boys.'

Redmond nodded too. He didn't have to ask what had happened to the Bowes boys.

'That was always Pat's style, targeting the weak. Tory's too. And then there was this business with your young brother.'

A muscle in Max's jaw was flexing. His eyes were slits. Christ, he was going to hurt someone over this. Annie knew it.

'Pat was a bigot,' said Orla. 'Of the nastiest kind. He hated blacks and he hated Protestants and he hated homosexuals. He had a great capacity for hate and very little for love, our Padraig. He knew your brother was attracted only to boys, and he loathed him for that and for the fact that he was a Carter. He killed him. He told us. On Delaney turf, in a parlour that paid protection to our family too. It's a sort of justice, I feel, that Pat himself died in the place where Eddie was attacked. Pat had no sense. He was a creature of impulse, and some of those impulses were murderous.'

'Max, we can stop all this now,' said Annie. 'Call a halt to it before anyone else gets hurt.'

Max's fist came crashing down on the desk. Annie jumped.

'Annie, go downstairs and wait for me there,' he said.

Before Annie could open her mouth Kieron surged forward and planted both hands on the desk and leaned across to glare into Max's face.

'She isn't yours to order about like a piece of dirt,' he shouted.

'Get out of my fucking face,' said Max flatly.

'Didn't you hear me?' Kieron roared.

Annie looked up at Kieron as if he'd gone mad. Christ, he *looked* mad. Max had been thinking of her safety, she knew that. If it had sounded like an order, it was because he was used to giving orders. He meant no harm by it.

'All this acting like she's your own personal property, I'm sick of it!' Kieron gabbled on. 'Gatecrashing *my* exhibition, to which she had come as *my* guest, and whisking her off God knew where. Now how the fuck do you suppose that made me look, eh? You don't know? Well I'll tell you! You made me look like a fucking idiot, and I don't like it!'

'Kieron, calm down,' said Orla.

Annie had never seen him so steamed up. *This* was the real Kieron, she knew that now. Not a gentle artist at all, but the spoiled son of a mad family, determined that everything should go his way. It had made him a killer of his own kin. It had made him dangerous in the extreme.

Kieron turned from the desk. Redmond grabbed at his arm, but he spun away, shrugging himself free. Feeling a sudden frisson of fear, Annie got to her feet. Orla rose too. The small room was packed with bodies, it was too warm in here, too tightly enclosed. And then, without warning, there was a gun in Kieron's hand and he was pointing it at Max's chest.

* * *

Annie suddenly saw what a fool she had been in the past. She had been fearful for Kieron's safety because of Max. Now she knew she'd got it wrong.

'Well, we've all had our confession time, haven't we?' Kieron sneered. 'All the little secrets have come out and we all feel better for it, don't we? And now there's only one piece of rubbish still in need of clearing away.'

He took aim. Max stood frozen. Orla screamed Kieron's name, but he was deaf, triumphant at last to be destroying his enemy, his rival for Annie.

How deep blood runs, Annie thought in horror. Ruthie and Mum, drinking themselves steadily to death. Kieron and his violent family. He'd grown up mired in shady deals and strong-arm stuff, with intimidation and incest and a mob of boys willing to do anything the Delaneys told them to. He was no gentle artist. A predilection for mayhem had seeped into him, like arsenic into a victim's skin.

Kieron cocked the gun, ready to fire.

The audience downstairs roared as the compère announced the next act. Redmond lunged towards Kieron. Not fast enough. Max was standing there.

Christ, why doesn't he move? thought Annie, frantic and terrified.

She saw Kieron's finger tighten on the trigger as if in slow motion. Without a thought in her head she flung herself around the desk. Orla's screams rang in her ears. Annie threw herself at Max, thrusting him aside.

The bullet smashed into her, knocking her into the chair which fell beneath her as she crashed into the wall. Such an impact. A loud explosion, deafening. Then smoke and the stench of cordite and a fierce, all-encompassing pain.

She couldn't breathe. She fell, seeing smears of blood – *her blood* – spattering over the wall behind Max's desk.

The world began to float around her. She lay on her back, something digging into her hip, Max's face leaning over her. His mouth was moving, but she couldn't hear. Everything was peaceful and warm and the pain was slipping away from her, going to another place.

I love you, she tried to tell him. *I've loved you for ever.*

But she couldn't speak and now it was strange but everything looked blurry, too. The world was going.

Dig deep and stand alone, she thought vaguely.

She was alone again.

But that was fine.

Peaceful.

She was gone.

59

Uncle Ted answered the door in a dirty vest and red braces that evening to find a uniformed copper standing on the doorstep. Beside him was a smaller man in a plain beige mac. He was middle-aged and had the narrow eyes and thuggish demeanour of a small-time crook.

Ted drew back a little, fearing the worst. All right, he'd bought a few cartons of fags off a docker mate and had sold them around the East End, but so what? Hardly a nicking offence, was it? Everyone was at it. Why pick on him?

'Is William Black in?' asked the plainclothes copper, ignoring Ted's aroma of stale sweat. The man looked as if he hadn't shaved or washed for days.

Ted looked truculent. 'Billy? Who wants him?'

'Detective Chief Inspector Fielding.' He flashed his warrant card. 'This is Constable Lightworthy.'

Fucking hell, thought Ted. *What had the simple sod been up to now?* But he was relieved. At least they were after the loon, and not him. He always thought of Billy as the loon.

'Who is it, Teddy?' roared a female voice over the din coming from the telly.

'Police, Hild,' said Ted, opening the door wider. 'Well, you'd better come in I suppose.'

The two coppers were escorted into a shabby fug-filled front room where a fat, grey-haired woman and a vacant-looking, hump-backed man were watching a black and white television. The woman watched them with malevolent eyes.

'What d'you want with Billy?' she demanded. Then she turned to her son and cuffed him hard around the ear. Billy cowered back. 'You been up to no good again, you little shit?'

'No need for that, Mrs Black,' said the detective in distaste. 'Billy's been helping us with our enquiries. We just want to ask him a few more questions, that's all.'

'Oh.' The jowls quivered, the mean mouth set in a line. 'Well you'd better get on with it then.'

'Is there another room we can use, Mrs Black?'

'No, there ain't. Anything you got to say to Billy you can say in front of me.'

Ted sank down into his armchair and resumed his telly-watching. Billy rubbed his ear and looked up at the policemen warily. Every surface was covered with dust and bags, the coppers noted. Gingerly they picked their way through the mess to get to where Billy was sitting. They couldn't sit down, there was no room. The constable took out his pencil and notebook. Over the din of the television and under the hate-filled eyes of his mum, they talked to Billy.

'You helped us out grandly with the Bailey case,' said the detective.

Billy looked uncomfortable. He didn't like to think about what he'd done to Annie, but he'd had no choice in the matter. He'd done what was *right*. He nodded warily.

'And we were wondering what you know about Max Carter,' said the detective.

Billy's mum looked at him.

Billy shrugged. 'I know him. Everyone around here knows Max Carter. But I don't know anything about him,' said Billy.

'Is that the truth, Billy?' The detective knew it was a lie. He knew that Billy did the milk run around the parlours and halls for the Carter mob, slipping easily around the harder areas of the streets because everyone knew he was harmless and under Max's protection. The detective knew that Billy was always hanging around on the periphery of Max's other business dealings; he must have seen things, heard things, that could be useful.

'He just said he didn't know nothing, didn't he?' snapped Hilda.

'So he did, Mrs Black. Perhaps it would be better if we continued this conversation down the station.'

'Don't you go starting that!' stormed Hilda, slapping her pudgy hand on the arm of her threadbare chair. Dust plumed up. The constable thought of his mum's house, neat as a new pin. You could eat off the floor. Fuck it, if you ate off the table in this pesthole you'd be asking for the squits.

'Then please don't interrupt, Mrs Black,' snapped the detective. 'I'm here to talk to Billy, not to you.'

She huffed and turned her attention back to the telly. Billy was looking at the floor, one arm wrapped around his upper body as if to shield it from a blow.

'Billy,' said the detective. 'Tell us what you know about Max Carter.'

'I don't know nothing about Max Carter,' said Billy, looking up to watch the constable writing that down in his notebook.

Billy had lots of notebooks. He liked keeping notes. It was one of his little compulsions, he couldn't help it. He thought of them all, years' worth of notes, all hidden away up in his room in an old brown suitcase of his dad's. Lots of things about Max and the boys in there. But things that would never be told to a soul. He was daft, but he wasn't as daft as all that. He knew you didn't rat on the Carter boys. You did that, there'd be trouble. Max would be *upset*.

Fielding looked at Constable Lightworthy. They'd had a long day. They were still looking into the department store robbery, trying to pin it on one of the big firms. Everyone knew the Carters and the Delaneys hated each other, and this had happened on Delaney turf. So the Carters were favourite. But try proving it.

Billy had given them some hope. He had been prepared to rat on Annie Bailey, who was known to have been Max Carter's sister-in-law and his mistress too. The next step was to get him to spill the beans on Carter himself.

He was digging away at it all, patiently. The department store's manager had been badly traumatized by the event, but he had said he had seen one of the men's faces. They had pieced together an Identikit of the man they wanted to question. He didn't bear any resemblance to Max or Jonjo Carter, or to any of their henchmen. It was frustrating, but still he kept with it, digging further.

The store job had been nicely done, you had to admit that. None of the missing cash had been found as yet. Personally, it looked like such a professional job that Fielding doubted the cash would ever come to light. Neat as anything. He'd been over it time and time again, the way the alarm had been disabled and finally he had thought to himself, *wait a fucking minute.*

Whoever did the job disabled the alarm by getting into the frame room and accessing the phone lines. He'd had a chat with some Post Office boys and they thought that only a skilled GPO engineer would understand the workings of a frame room. So maybe the man whose face had been spotted was a telephone engineer?

Maybe he'd even done work in the store before and was familiar with the line layout. Detective Chief Inspector Fielding had chatted it over with his superior, who had nodded and smiled.

'Yes. All well and good, but how many thousand GPO engineers are there in England? Five? Six? That's the ones that are working. What about those who are retired?'

It was a bugger. But Fielding was like a terrier. He didn't ever let go. He was quietly confident of a result. There was also the question of whether or not an insider had been involved. He had his chaps checking that even now. Who'd moved on unexpectedly, who was suddenly flashing a lot of cash about, whose bank accounts had received an unexpected boost.

All in all, Fielding was satisfied with progress. Big strides were being made, but not big enough. The long reign of the powerful career criminal, much feared and much admired, might soon be over. Slipper of the Yard was getting quite a name for himself, and Fielding was feeling jealous. He was within two years of retirement, and he wanted to leave on a good note.

He wanted to go for the hat-trick.

He wanted to send down two big East End crime clans.

He wanted to nick the Carters, and the Delaneys.

'Come on, Billy lad,' he said. 'Let's get down the station and have a proper chat.'

Billy shuffled off to get his coat. Hilda glowered at the two men but stayed silent. She was a bully, and easily cowed if you called her bluff. They'd met plenty like her. Ted carried on watching the telly. It wasn't his arse on the line, so what did he care?

It was only when they got down the station with Billy in tow that they heard about the shooting at the Palermo.

60

Ruthie was in the drawing room at the Surrey house with a glass of vodka and orange halfway to her lips when Dave barged in looking keyed up.

'Can't you knock?' she snapped, embarrassed at the way he looked at her, the way his eyes lingered on the glass in her hand.

Her eyes followed his and then flicked back to his face. She felt her cheeks get hot.

'Just having a nightcap,' she said. 'To help me sleep.'

'Max just phoned through,' said Dave, politely ignoring her feeble explanations.

Ruthie thought that it was typical of Max to phone the hired help, not her.

'I'm sorry, Mrs Carter. He said your sister's been shot.'

Ruthie froze in shock. 'What?'

'I can take you up there, Mrs Carter. Right now.'

Ruthie gulped. Looked at the drink in her hand,

then at Dave's face. She nodded stiffly, feeling a sense of acute unreality.

'Yes, I'd better . . .' she started, then her face crumpled and she put a hand to her mouth. 'Is she going to be all right?' she managed to say.

'They don't know yet,' said Dave, his eyes slipping away from hers.

Oh Jesus, it's bad, thought Ruthie.

'Where did it happen?' she whispered, trying not to cry.

'In the Palermo, Mr Carter says.' He swallowed, looked awkward. 'We ought to get going, Mrs Carter.'

Ruthie nodded, put the glass down, and went to get her coat. And that's when the annoyance set in. No, it was more than annoyance, it was anger. She shrugged into her coat and then got into the car and felt suddenly furious with Annie, because this was bad news, the very worst, and getting it made her feel she might throw up at any minute.

As the car zipped through the night she sat in the back seat thinking of all the treacherous things her sister had done to her and knew that, despite everything, she still loved Annie very much. And she was boiling with rage because she didn't want to love Annie at all, she wanted to hate her.

'Tell me what happened,' she said when she found Max in the hospital waiting room, blood all over his shirt and his face grey with strain.

'Tell me' was something she never, ever said to Max.

'Kieron Delaney shot her,' said Max.

'Is she . . . ? I mean . . .' stammered Ruthie, her mind in a spin.

'I don't know. She was bleeding a lot. A *lot*.'

'Do they think she's going to be all right?' Ruthie forced herself to ask.

'They can't say yet. The bullet clipped an artery in her chest. Missed her heart by an inch. It happened in the Palermo. He was aiming for me. He got Annie.' Max looked straight at his wife. 'She jumped in front of me.'

Tears spilled over then and slid down Ruthie's cheeks. *Trust Annie to go for the grand gesture*, she thought in irritation. Again the anger rose. Stupid little bint, arsing around with all sorts. Now look where she'd ended up.

'Did they get him?' she managed to say.

Max shook his head. 'He ran off. The Delaney twins were there too, I told them they'd better go. We had to have the ambulance. It was life or death, she's in emergency surgery right now.'

Ruthie started to cry harder. Max did what he hadn't done for a very long time; he put his arms around his wife, held her close and tried to give her comfort.

* * *

For the rest of the night Max and Ruthie sat in the bare, scruffy waiting room. People came and went down endless corridors as they waited to hear what was happening to Annie.

She's going to die, thought Max.

He didn't think he would ever forget the horror of the moment when she'd collapsed against him, blood spilling from her mouth and her chest. The aghast expression on Kieron Delaney's face as he saw what he had done. Orla screaming and rushing forward, Max holding Annie on the floor as her eyes looked up at him, bewildered, weakening . . .

'Stay with me,' he had said to her. 'Annie, *hold on*. Hold on, lovey.'

Redmond icily controlled as always. Picking up the phone, dialling 999, saying 'ambulance please', giving crisp directions, then slapping the phone back down.

Annie starting to shiver with shock. Redmond taking off his coat and draping it over her. Blood everywhere. Orla's screams turning to quiet sobs of distress. Jimmy bursting into the room, his face a mask of dismay as he took in a scene of carnage. Kieron shoving past him, running away down the stairs. The audience roaring and stamping down there, oblivious to the drama being played out above their heads.

'The bloody little idiot,' Orla muttered brokenly.

Annie's eyes glazing, closing . . .

'No! Annie, come on. Stay with me,' Max urged her.

But it was no good.

She was going.

'Where the *fuck* is that ambulance?' shouted Max.

'Mr Carter?'

Max and Ruthie looked up. The surgeon was there, his dark green gown stained brown at the front. *Annie's blood*, thought Ruthie, feeling sick. He looked young in his cap, his mask pushed down around his neck. Too young to be trusted with Annie's life, surely?

'How is she?' asked Max.

The surgeon took a breath, looked at Ruthie.

'This is Miss Bailey's sister – my wife,' Max told him.

The surgeon nodded, looked at Max again. 'We've patched her up, Mr Carter. But she's lost a lot of blood. She's not out of the woods yet.'

'Thank you.' Max put his arm around Ruthie's shoulders as she broke down again and wept. 'When can we see her?'

'Maybe tomorrow. Go home now and try to get some rest. Phone tomorrow and we'll see how she's doing. The police will want to talk to you about this, I should imagine.'

61

When Annie awoke, Max was sitting beside her bed.

Hospital? she thought. *That smell.*

She tried to remember how she'd got here. She'd been in the club, she remembered that. Then she'd been in an ambulance. After that . . . nothing.

'Hello,' he said.

Annie felt him take hold of her hand, squeeze her fingers.

'Hmm,' she said. She'd meant to say hello. She swallowed and tried again. 'Hello.'

Jesus, could that be her voice? It sounded raw and hoarse with disuse. Her whole body ached. *Christ, such pain.* She winced.

'You gave us a right fright there,' said Max.

He looked dishevelled, she thought, not like himself. A dark stubble on his chin. His hair disordered as if he'd been running his fingers through it, his white shirt unbuttoned at the neck.

God, but she was tired. It was annoying how tired she felt.

She closed her eyes and was back in oblivion again, so peaceful, so dark.

She'd come up out of unconsciousness several times before, but this time was different. Before, her body had been a sea of pain. Before, she had felt weighted down, inert. She had no strength to move. There had been bright lights, fuzzy faces . . . and Max, there by her bed and saying hello. Had she dreamed that? She wasn't sure.

But this time she opened her eyes and clearly saw the room around her. Wood panelling. She was in Upper Brook Street. No, she wasn't. The bed was facing the wrong way, the light was fainter.

She saw an open window, thin white curtains moving in a breeze. She could smell not disinfectant but new-mown grass. She could hear birds singing.

I'm in heaven, she thought. *I died and now I'm in heaven.*

There was no pain now, but her body still felt heavy. She tried to raise an arm but it felt like a ton weight and she let it fall back on to the bed. Something stirred over by the window. A woman in a chair there. A woman in a white cap. She looked over at Annie and put down her knitting and came over to the bed.

An angel.

'You're with us at last then?' she asked.

Annie nodded. But she was tired. She closed her eyes and was gone again.

62

Ruthie was still furious. After three days of anxiety
and police questions and waiting and hoping,
Annie finally came back to full consciousness at
last. Her surgeon was confident that she should
make a full recovery from the wound caused by
the bullet that had passed straight through her
body and embedded itself in the wall behind Max's
desk. In its passage it nicked her aorta and one
lung, but missed her heart and her spine. She was
lucky.

After two weeks of being hospitalized, Annie
was pronounced fit enough to go home, providing
she had nursing care. Without debate, Max had
her moved to the Surrey house and hired the best
private nurses to attend her round the clock. And
he stayed at the house. He'd never stayed there
for Ruthie, but he stayed for Annie.

Which only added to Ruthie's rage. In fact she

513

was royally pissed off with the whole thing. Max dropping everything for Annie but never for her was a bitter pill to swallow. But then – she'd learned to live with that a long time ago.

She kept away from Annie's room for some time. Max would be there, or the nurses, and she was full of resentment that Annie got the five-star treatment while she was disregarded totally. When she finally went up to the wood-panelled guest room at the front of the house – yes, he'd put her in one of the best rooms, with the French windows and the balcony and the views out over the garden – she didn't enter. She just stood at the door and looked in.

The nurse was changing Annie's dressings. Annie was sitting up half-naked against the pillows and she was wincing in pain as the bandages were pulled away from the pus-covered dressings on her chest.

Does that stupid woman have to be so rough about it? wondered Ruthie in irritation. Ruthie didn't know which peeved her most. Annie for getting herself into this state, or the nurse for handling her with such apparent lack of care. Annie cried out as the nurse tried to pull the dirty dressing away from the wound.

Ruthie found herself rushing in and over to the bed.

'Don't pull her ruddy skin off,' she said, pushing

the woman back, away from her sister. Annie was sweating with pain, she saw. That enraged Ruthie even more.

'The dressing has to come off, Mrs Carter,' said the nurse, colouring up with annoyance.

'Why not use a bloody crowbar and have done with it? Go on, get out, I'll do it.'

And so Ruthie found herself nursing her sister back to health. Part of her wanted to let Annie rot, but she couldn't do it. Despite everything that Annie had done, she didn't want to lose her. And now she had something that demanded all of her attention, the booze didn't seem quite so necessary as it had before.

Ruthie carefully dabbed the dressing free of the healing wound with warm water. Annie lay back weakly on her pillows and watched her sister's face as she worked with gentle hands. Much gentler than the nurse's, feeling Annie's pain and not wanting to add to it.

'You shouldn't be doing this,' said Annie as Ruthie put on fresh dressings and then helped her lean forward a little so that she could look at Annie's back and attend to the exit wound.

Ruthie repeated the procedure she had performed at the front.

'I'm your sister,' she said roughly. 'Who else should do it?'

After that, Ruthie had a word with Max and

they disposed of the day nurse's services but kept the night nurse.

'Are you sure?' he asked her, more than just a little surprised.

'That woman was far too rough,' said Ruthie. 'It's better I take over.'

So Ruthie took over during the days, changing Annie's dressings, feeding her, bathing her, bringing her bedpan and finally helping her to the bathroom. Inch by inch, Annie was mending. Max came up to see her. Ruthie's excellent care of her sister was working small miracles every day, he could see it. The colour was coming back into her cheeks. She was gaining a little weight. Ruthie fussed around her constantly.

'I don't deserve this,' said Annie sometimes, her eyes sad as she watched her sister hustle efficiently around the sickroom.

'Rubbish,' said Ruthie, folding towels and pouring barley water and straightening the bedspread.

Annie caught her hand. 'I don't deserve it,' she said, holding Ruthie's eyes with her own.

'You're my sister,' said Ruthie firmly. 'I want to do it, it gives me the higher ground for a change, Annie Bailey. Just be a good patient and shut up and let me get on with it.'

Annie had to smile. 'Now you're even talking like a nurse.'

'Well, listen to me and you'll hear a lot of sense,'

said Ruthie, but she almost smiled back. 'You can go out in the garden this afternoon. It's warm. The fresh air will do you good.'

'Yes, Matron,' said Annie.

'You're doing fine now,' said Ruthie. 'That wound's as good as healed.'

'Thanks to you.'

'Nonsense. You're as strong as a horse, that's all. Take more than a bullet to stop *you* in your tracks.' Ruthie tidied the sheets and told her to lean forward, then plumped up the pillows.

'I'm off up to London this afternoon,' said Ruthie while she worked. 'Going to stay at Queenie's place up there for a bit.'

'Oh.' Annie frowned. It had been so nice having Ruthie around her. But she understood. Annie was well enough now to manage on her own, and this situation must be slowly killing her. Max coming up and sitting on Annie's bed and the pair of them talking quietly and holding hands. She'd walked in on them once or twice and quietly excused herself. She never stayed in the room if they were together.

Now, Annie was stronger. They would be together even more. Max seemed hardly capable of keeping away. She thought that Ruthie accepted that, but of course the poor mare didn't want to stop here and see it with her own eyes.

Annie caught her sister's hand as she came and

sat on the bed for a moment. 'You've been wonderful,' she said.

'That's me. Wonderful Ruthie.'

Annie laughed. 'Mum always said you were.'

'Dad always said *you* were.' Ruthie looked at Annie and felt that whole mix of emotions again, the anger, the annoyance, the jealousy and – yes – the love. She wanted to forgive her, but she couldn't bring herself to say the words.

'I can't ever begin to thank you enough, Ruthie.'

'We're family. We don't have to thank each other.' Ruthie freed her hand and stood up and looked down at her little sister. 'Now you keep well, okay? No more getting shot. No messing about.'

Annie nodded, feeling desolate. This felt like goodbye. Hell, this *was* goodbye. She knew it. Ruthie wouldn't be coming back here again, not while she was here.

'Goodbye now,' said Ruthie, and dropped a quick kiss on to Annie's cheek. Then she hurriedly left the room.

It was only when Ruthie had closed the bedroom door behind her that she broke down and cried her heart out.

63

'Ruthie's gone up to stay in Mum's place in London,' said Max as he brought their drinks out into the garden.

Annie was sitting under the shade of the big willow tree in the Surrey garden. Summer was at its height, the lawn was bleached yellow and the air was hazy. Birds sang. Bees hummed. Max put the drinks on the table and sat down with her.

'I know,' she said, thinking that he would always call the house in London 'Mum's place'. Queenie had reigned supreme there, and in the annexe here. In a way, she still did. 'She told me.'

'Are you two all right now?' Max was watching her acutely.

Annie shrugged. 'As all right as we're going to be.'

'I was worried,' said Max. 'When she started looking after you.'

Annie laughed. 'What, you thought she was going to do me in?'

'It crossed my mind.'

Annie shook her head. 'That's not Ruthie. You must know her by now. She's been spitting mad about all this, but she's good right through to the bone. She couldn't squash a fly, much less hurt me.'

'She had every right to be spitting mad,' said Max.

'I know.'

'I was mad at you myself when you did it, told her about us. It was only ever meant to be sex between us. I thought you understood that. But now I see you were too young to understand anything except getting back at your sister.' He sat back and sighed. 'Truth is, I felt bad about it. Really bad. I was the one who should have known better.'

'But Max – I chased you.'

'Yeah.' He smiled. 'You did.'

Annie looked away, down the garden.

'I think you know it wasn't ever "just sex" for me.'

'I've come to know it. Slowly.'

'I've always been in love with you,' said Annie.

'I know.'

Annie looked round at him. 'Fuck it, Max. You're not supposed to say that. You're supposed to say "I love you too".'

'It goes without saying,' teased Max.

'Men,' sniffed Annie. 'It doesn't ever go without saying. Women need to hear it.'

'Okay then.' Max looked her dead in the eye. 'I love you, Annie Bailey. Even if you are a fucking lunatic. You stopped a bullet for me, and I'd stop one for you.'

Annie stared at him. 'I'm going to jail, Max,' she said. 'You know they postponed the trial because of me being hospitalized; well now they've re-scheduled.'

His face clouded. God, how she loved his face. So strong, almost brutal, but saved by a masculine beauty that she would never tire of.

'Maybe it won't be for long,' he said. 'I'm looking into things.'

Annie shook her head, ignoring his platitudes. 'The date's set for the trial. Six weeks' time. Taking a bullet's not going to stop them sending me down.'

'Then we'll make the most of those six weeks,' said Max, and he took her hand and kissed it.

64

Max sorted her out with a proper, hotshot brief for the trial. Mr Jerry Peters, her defending counsel, was an expensively-suited tall man with a florid complexion and too much fluffy ginger hair. He told her that she was almost certainly going down, but there were mitigating circumstances and they were going to make full use of them to lessen the sentence.

'Aren't you supposed to promise me you'll get me off?' Annie asked as she and Max sat in Jerry's plush office in the Law Courts.

'I don't deal in lies with my clients, Miss Bailey,' said Jerry smoothly.

'And what are these "mitigating circum-stances"?' she asked.

'A disturbed childhood. Your father left when you were nine . . .'

'Eleven.'

'Eleven.' He made a note. 'Your mother drank. You and your sister had to fend for yourselves. Little wonder that you ended up out of your depth.'

Which wasn't exactly how it had happened, but she supposed he did have a point. She'd always had to make her own way in the world, with no support. Her entrepreneurial spirit had always been there, lying dormant. If she hadn't seduced her sister's bridegroom on the night before the wedding, she wouldn't have been flung out of Connie's house and been forced to retreat to her Aunt Celia's. Once there, it had only been a matter of time before her business skills kicked in and she landed herself up to her neck in the shit.

'And?'

'*And* none of the neighbours complained. Not one.'

'And?'

'And you were doing a service to these poor unfortunate women. Without your protection, they would have been walking the streets, at the mercy of men who would exploit them.'

Annie had to suppress a smile. Hard to imagine Mira or Jenny or Thelma on the streets. In luxury apartments being kept by wealthy admirers, perhaps. On the streets? Never in a month of Sundays.

'Well, you've convinced me,' said Annie as Max sat silent beside her. 'Anything else?'

'There's been a lot of Press interest in this. They'll dig around and try to find more juicy morsels to titillate the readers. Is there anything else I should know, bearing that in mind? We don't want any nasty surprises.'

'I ran a parlour in Limehouse when my aunt took off unexpectedly. I carried on, kept it going for her.'

Jerry stared at her face, then nodded and made more notes.

'How many girls?'

'Three. And one boy.'

'But your aunt told you it was a massage parlour, not anything else? Not, for instance, a brothel?'

'I was never under any illusion about what went on there.'

'You must have been, surely?' He prompted her with his eyes.

Annie took the hint. 'When my mother kicked me out due to a family disagreement, I went to stay with Celia. At first, I didn't fully realize what went on there . . . but after a while, I did. And when Celia vanished, I took over the running of the place.'

'So it was an established business. You carried on running it as a favour to your aunt. You were almost running a public service, isn't that true?'

'I suppose so. Celia had lots of older clients. She gave them discounts. She was very sympathetic to their needs.'

'*Definitely* a public service,' beamed Jerry. 'Now, have I warned you fully about the Press?'

Jerry had warned her about the Press but he hadn't warned her enough. Outside the court when the trial began it was a madhouse. Flashes went off in her face, questions were shouted. Max was there with her, though, and a line of Max's boys established a way through for her up the courthouse steps and into the building, elbowing the rabid reporters out of the way.

'Jesus,' she said as she sat in the lobby and Jerry Peters came to greet her dressed in his working clothes of black gown and grey wig. 'I didn't expect so much Press interest.'

'It's a titillating subject,' said Jerry. 'The Press will lap it up.'

Bastards, thought Annie. Talk about a three-ring circus. They wouldn't be so bloody keen to dish the dirt if it was their backsides on the line here.

When she at last stood in the dock and heard the dreaded words 'All rise' and the judge came in all po-faced and looked at her like she was shit to be scraped off his shoe, she knew she was in trouble.

'Let's hope we don't get that Bartington-Smythe asshole,' Jerry had said in chambers. 'He's a Puritan to his boots.'

Judge Bartington-Smythe glowered down at her. *Oh fuck*, thought Annie.

Well, she'd done all she could do. Her dress was dark and demure, covering her from neck to wrist to ankle. Even her friends, sitting across the court from her, had toned it down to show their conservative support. Aretha and Dolly and Darren looked positively respectable sitting there watching the proceedings. No Ellie. After all her backstabbing, Dolly had made it clear she wasn't welcome to accompany them to the trial. No Ruthie or cousin Kath, but then she hadn't expected them to show up. But Max was there across the court. He winked at her. She felt like she was going to throw up with fear, but his being there gave her comfort.

'Do you plead guilty or not guilty to the charge of exercising control over three prostitutes and keeping a disorderly house?' asked the judge.

'Guilty,' said Annie, as Jerry had instructed her. *So lock me up*, she thought. *Get on with it.*

But first it all had to come out. Annie closed her eyes and ears to it as much as she could. She looked at the judge sitting up there looking down at her and thought, *hypocrite*. His posh mates had been among her clients. She was faintly surprised to realize that he hadn't been one himself. Several judges and barristers were among her regulars.

It was tiring. She was well now, the bullet scar

was still there but it would fade within the year, the doctors told her. But she had been left weak and easily tired by the shooting. She could have done without all this shit so soon after the event.

It'll pass, she told herself. She shut out the shouts of laughter from the Press gallery, the judge's admonitions to them, Jerry's impassioned pleadings in her defence, the cruel jibes of the prosecuting counsel, the endless summings-up and evaluations of all her many and various sins.

Finally, it was done. She stood in the dock and Judge Bartington-Smythe glared at her. She looked at Dolly's face, taut with worry. *Good old Dolly.* Darren was chewing his nails and Aretha was so tense she looked like she was carved from ebony.

Good luck, girl, she mouthed at Annie.

She was standing alone again. She took full responsibility. All the pillars of the community who had flocked to see her girls were unnamed, home free. Her girls were out of the frame too. She alone stood accused, and in the judge's summing-up was such venom that she knew she was sunk.

'I do not accept that you are ignorant of the law, Miss Bailey,' he said in a voice that chilled her to the marrow. 'I therefore fine you one thousand pounds and order you to pay costs of one thousand five hundred pounds for keeping a disorderly house and exercising control over prostitutes. I also sentence you to eighteen months' imprisonment,' he said.

Annie clutched the front of the dock for support. Eighteen months! For fuck's sake, she would die shut away in some hell-hole for that long. She felt dizzy suddenly, her ears buzzing. She looked over at Dolly, who had tears streaming down her face. Darren was talking to her, putting his arm round her shoulders. Aretha was patting Dolly's back. Annie looked straight at Max, whose face revealed not a flicker of emotion.

Rotten, cold-hearted sod, she thought in fury.

Then the judge cleared his throat and went on. 'But as this is your first offence it will be unconditionally suspended for one year, during which you will be required to conduct yourself as a model citizen . . .'

The old boy droned on and on, while Annie stood there with her mouth hanging open.

Suspended.

She was not going down.

Annie looked over at Dolly, Aretha and Darren. A slow grin spread itself over her face. Dolly suddenly let out a delighted shriek. Aretha jumped up and punched the air. Darren grinned and blew Annie a kiss. The Press gallery went crazy. Judge Bartington-Smythe gave them all a look of sour disfavour.

Annie looked at Max.

He winked.

Jesus Christ, he'd bought the judge. She couldn't

believe it but it was true. He'd bought the fucking judge!

The court was in uproar. In a daze Annie found herself shaking Jerry by the hand, found herself being hustled outside, fetched up at the door of the court with Max by her side. His boys formed a cordon around them as they left the court building.

'You bought the fucking judge,' Annie hissed at Max as they emerged into bright daylight and the Press went crazy, bulbs flashing, crowding around, asking if there was any comment. 'Didn't you?'

'I did tell you I was looking into things,' said Max, slipping his arm around her shoulders.

'Any comment, Miss Bailey?' asked someone, shoving a microphone in her face.

'No comment,' she said, and Max's boys got them down the steps and away.

65

Ruthie was down in the country, wandering around
Max's big imposing house alone. She'd spent some
time in London while Max and Annie had been
here together. She'd gone shopping, caught up with
Kath and Maureen, had some fun for once. Hadn't
touched a drop, either.

She'd been following Annie's trial in the papers
and on the telly. She hadn't been able to bear the
thought of going to court and watching Annie
squirm up there. Poor little cow. The Press were
calling her 'the Mayfair Madam' and making a
big joke out of the whole thing. Not mocking the
well-to-do men who'd shagged the girls there, oh
no. It was always the women who paid and the
men who got the gravy.

The phone was ringing. She went into the
drawing room and picked up.

'She got off,' said Kath's voice in outrage. 'Jimmy

just came home from the court and told me. Talk about the devil looking after his own.'

Ruthie sagged with relief.

'Ruthie? You there?'

'Yeah, I'm here.'

'She got off, can you believe that?'

'Yeah. Thanks for letting me know, Kath.'

Quietly Ruthie replaced the receiver. Kath was still babbling away, full of bile towards Annie and all that she had done. But Ruthie felt calm now. She thought of Annie, and of Max, the cunning bastard.

I knew you'd come to the rescue, Max Carter, she thought with the ghost of a smile. *You never could resist being the hero could you?*

She went to the window and looked out at the bright clear day. Gordon was out in the garden, cutting back the plants and tidying up. Autumn was coming in fast, and the beeches were beginning to turn red. She watched him from the drawing-room window. Big Dave was in his flat over the garage, no doubt eyeing up his posters and reading his smutty magazines.

She was alone.

She looked over at the drinks tray, but it didn't have any appeal. Funny how Annie had been her downfall and also her saviour. She had started drinking when Annie had betrayed her; she had stopped drinking when Annie needed her. *Maybe*

I'm just weak, thought Ruthie. *Weak like Mum was*.

She shivered when she thought that she could so easily have gone the same way as Connie, down that slippery slope to death by drinking. She went over to the tray on the sideboard and picked up the bottle of vodka. Deliberately she carried it through to the kitchen and tipped the contents down the sink. She put the bottle in the rubbish bin then gave a dismissive brush of the hands.

Picking up her bag, she took the keys down from their hook and went out of the back door and over to Queenie's annexe. She let herself inside, then went along the quiet hallway to the cosy little sitting room. It was still kept immaculately clean, dusted, cared-for. She looked up at the portrait over the fireplace, at the gimlet-eyed Queenie glaring down at her.

'Well, you old bag,' said Ruthie. 'I'm going. You never wanted me here in the first place, did you?'

Ruthie smiled. Queenie couldn't answer her. The mean thin line of the lips and the imperious stare said it all. This wasn't a woman who would welcome a rival for any of her sons' affections.

'Do you know what I thought I'd do?' Ruthie asked the dead woman in the portrait.

Ruthie rummaged in her bag and came up with

a cheap cigarette lighter. It had been Connie's, and she had kept it out of sentimentality. It reminded her of her mum, who had been a disgusting old lush but who had nevertheless given life to her. She flicked it with her thumb and a flame ignited. Ruthie stared at it, then at Queenie, up there like royalty. Named as a Queen and regarded as one by all the boys and by everyone on Max and Jonjo Carter's manor. Ruthie thought of Annie – a worthy successor if ever there was one. The thought tickled her and she smiled. Annie would be more than a match for Queenie, dead or alive. Annie and Max. Maybe some things were just meant to be.

'I thought I'd do this place,' said Ruthie. 'Then the main house. Then your London house. Burn the whole lot to the ground.'

Only silence answered her.

Ruthie smiled at the portrait's glassy blue eyes for a moment longer, then flicked the lighter shut.

'But you know what?' she asked. 'It isn't worth it. What would I be proving? That I care enough to bother? Strangely enough, I don't. Not any more.'

Ruthie tucked the lighter back in her bag. 'I'm free as a bird,' she told Queenie.

She had freedom from a loveless marriage, freedom from a drunken mother, freedom from all care. She had it within her grasp now.

'I can go anywhere and do anything I like. And you know what, Queenie Carter? I think I will.'

With that she turned and left the room, walked along the hallway, left the annexe.

Rest in peace, thought Ruthie as she relocked the outside door. *You old bag.*

66

Max had taken a suite in a posh but discreet hotel up West to keep Annie out of the way of the Press after the trial. No way was Max going to doss down overnight in the Limehouse brothel – on Delaney territory – and the Press would have a field day if he did, they both knew that. He thought the Palermo's little flat might contain too many bad memories for Annie. They could have gone to his mum's old place, but it was cheerless, less a home than a meeting-place these days.

So, instead of slopping out as she had expected, Annie found herself on the morning after the trial bathing in luxury, then breakfasting not on horrible prison food but on delicious kedgeree and vintage champagne. Max went out to do some business at lunchtime, and Annie made some calls, thanked her lucky stars and then had a surprise visitor.

'Redmond told me you were here, so I thought

I'd stop by. You know, you're a lucky woman. I seriously thought you were dead that night at the Palermo,' said Orla, breezing into the suite and settling herself on a small, ornate sofa.

'So did I.' Annie wasn't surprised Redmond had known where she was. She knew that the mobs kept careful tabs on each other. For sure Max knew where Redmond was, too, at any given moment.

'And I seriously thought you were going down yesterday.'

'Me too.'

Orla smiled. 'So what are your plans?'

'I'm going straight,' said Annie, frowning. All right, she'd been lucky this time – thanks to Max. But she was not going to push her luck and risk ending up in the dock again if she could help it. 'Got to keep my nose clean. I've had enough of being a Madam anyway. I got into it by accident, but I'm getting out of it by design.'

'Shame,' said Orla. 'You're a good business-woman.'

'Well, if that's true,' reasoned Annie, 'then I can make a go of something else, can't I. Something legit.'

'I came to say sorry,' said Orla, her smile fading fast. 'About Kieron. I never thought he had it in him. First he shoots Tory dead, then he tries to shoot Max Carter.'

'And how is Kieron?' asked Annie coldly. Not

that she gave a fuck. But if Orla could make an effort to be civil, then so could she.

'It's big of you to ask that, since he damn near killed you. He's abroad, I think. Painting, probably.'

Kieron had spoken to Annie weeks ago about the Spanish light. He would be there, she thought. Lying low. But he would be back. She felt sure of that.

'I don't think he's right in the head,' said Annie. Even the thought of Kieron Delaney gave her the jitters now.

Orla smiled. It was the most chilling smile Annie had ever seen.

'We're all disturbed. My father's senile, my mother lives in a fantasy world where her "boys and her girl" can do no wrong. We're career criminals, for the love of God. But she's always seen only the good in us. Refuses to see the bad.'

'Pat was bad,' said Annie, seeing in her mind's eye that horrible night when he'd died.

'So he was. And not much missed.'

'And Tory too.' Annie shook her head in wonder at all that Orla had suffered, and at the hands of her own family too. 'You've really had the shit kicked out of you. But you're not disturbed. Damaged, perhaps.'

'Damaged,' considered Orla. 'Now that's probably the right word for it, I'd say. Do you know,

I was wetting the bed until I was eighteen. Terrified of the night, I was. When I reached puberty and couldn't share a room with Redmond any more, the terror got worse. I had to have a light on all night. But I was still scared. I peed myself nightly, I was so scared. Even though by then there was a bolt on my door because I couldn't sleep in a room alone without one.'

Annie looked at Orla and felt her heart might break.

Damaged, she thought. *Yeah, that's the right word.*

'Kieron saw things happening,' said Annie. 'Maybe that excuses what he did, to some extent. To see that must have affected him too.'

'Still, he had no right to treat you like some sort of star prize,' said Orla. 'What gets into men, that they think they own a woman, have rights over her?'

'Well, no one has rights over you,' pointed out Annie.

'No,' said Orla. 'And I'm glad of that.'

Annie paused.

'No boyfriends then?' she asked. 'No husband? No children?'

Orla shook her head. 'No,' she sighed. 'I can't see that happening for me. I'll concern myself with business, I think. I want nothing of all that.'

'I never had a brother,' said Annie, her mind still on children, because she was late. And she was *never* late. She felt sort of different too. Her tits were sore and swollen. Her stomach too. There could be no doubt about it, no doubt at all.

'None of mine were worth having,' sniffed Orla. 'Except Redmond. He sends you his regards.'

'He must be a comfort to you.'

Orla shrugged. 'All we have is each other.'

'I'm sorry,' said Annie.

'Ah, don't be,' said Orla. 'It's enough. We make the best of it.'

God, what a life. Annie looked at Orla and thought how brave she was. Had such horrors happened to her, would she be so strong? She doubted it.

Orla moved quickly off the subject of her family after that; it was obvious to Annie that it hurt her even to mention it. Instead she talked of lighter things – how Elizabeth Lane was becoming the country's first female High Court judge and how David Bailey, the famous fashion photographer, had just got married with Mick Jagger as his best man.

Max came back in, greeted Orla with cool civility and then retired to the bedroom. Orla took the hint and got up to go, and Annie thanked her warmly for coming.

'A pleasure,' said Orla, and left – a cold, quiet woman with a damaged past and no future.

'What's up, lovey? You look sad,' said Max, coming in and leaning over the back of the sofa to kiss her neck.

'It's just Orla,' said Annie. 'I feel sorry for her.'

'Well don't,' advised Max. 'The Delaney twins are a pair of vipers, not to be trusted – or pitied.'

Annie frowned. So for all that had happened, Max still hadn't changed his mind about the Delaneys. She didn't suppose he ever would. She stood up and went into his open arms. He kissed her, and she relaxed into his embrace.

'I've got something to tell you,' she said against his lips.

'And I've got something to tell you,' said Max. 'I thought we'd take a holiday. Now you're clear of the courts.'

Annie stared at his face, dark and brooding and intensely sexual. He loved her, she knew that now. He'd done things for her that had proved it to her, once and for all.

'That sounds good. So what did you have on Judge Bartington-Smythe?' she asked, smiling.

Max's blue eyes were suddenly wide-open, the picture of innocence.

'Come on, Max, give. Was he shagging his housekeeper, or entertaining rent boys?'

'So you think I'd try to pervert the course of justice, is that what you think?' Max pulled her closer into him, smiling.

'I *know* you would, Max Carter.' Annie looked at him and felt luckier than she had any right to be. 'Where shall we go?'

'Anywhere you want. The sky's the limit. Now what do you have to tell me?' asked Max.

Annie told him. Max gave a shout of laughter and kissed her again for a very long time. No further words seemed necessary.

67

After leaving the hotel, Orla's driver took her to the florist. She bought one dozen blood-red roses. Then Petey drove her to the cemetery and pulled up outside the gate.

'Go for a walk, Petey,' said Orla as she got out of the car. 'I want to be on my own.'

He looked unhappy, but it wasn't his place to question what a Delaney told him to do. He strolled off. Orla went into the church and lit candles for Tory and Pat, so that she could phone her mum in Ireland tonight and tell her that she'd done it. Then she walked out through the deserted grave-yard until she came to Tory's grave. No resting place here for Pat, she thought. By all accounts he was feeding the fishes. Carefully she bent and removed the dead blooms and replaced them with the bright new blooms.

As she did so, she spoke to the dead brother who had abused her and ruined her young life.

'So here we are again, you and me, Tory Delaney. Me alive and you dead as a plank of wood. Bet you wish those positions were reversed, now don't you?'

The priest, Father Michael, was going into the church and he paused when he saw Orla Delaney away in the distance tending her brother's grave. A devout girl, that Orla – and generous in her donations to the church fund. God knew what her family got up to, but it was not his job to judge them, only to minister to their needs. Not that they ever made much call upon his services. Certainly Orla never set foot inside the confessional, which grieved him; but it was her decision.

He watched Orla finishing her weekly task of refreshing the blooms on her brother's grave. Ah, she was a good girl. And then his jaw dropped as he saw Orla, right there on her brother Tory's grave, lift her hands to the heavens and dance.

68

At the same time as Orla Delaney was amazing
Father Michael, Ruthie Carter was boarding a train
at Waterloo. She opened the door to the first-class
carriage and just before she stepped inside she took
off her engagement and her wedding rings. The
elderly porter put her luggage in the compartment
and waited for his tip. She put the two rings in
his outstretched hand.

'What the . . .' He looked at them, then at her
face.

'Keep them or sell them, I don't care which,'
said Ruthie. 'Either that or I'll throw them in the
rubbish bin, it's up to you.'

The porter looked at the rings. They looked
expensive. There were diamonds, and gold, and a
large cabochon-cut emerald that caught the light
like green fire. He shrugged and slipped them into

his pocket. Ruthie boarded the train, and the porter shut the door after her.

She was going to have an adventure.

She'd never had one before.

Now the world was opening up to her at last.

69

'Notes,' said Detective Inspector Fielding.

Constable Lightworthy had almost been nodding off behind the wheel. He didn't know why they were here today, watching Billy Black again, who was loitering on his usual corner outside The Grapes public house.

They'd been watching Billy for months, looking for something, anything, with which to nail Max Carter, to tie him in to the Tory Delaney killing or the department store job – or anything else they could stick him with.

Lightworthy was sick of all this. The DCI was gnawing away at it like a dog with an effing bone. Even the Super was running out of patience with him.

'Notes, sir?' he asked, straightening up.

'He's always scribbling in notebooks,' said Fielding, straightening up suddenly in the passenger seat. 'Rubbish at the front, facts at the back.'

'Yes, sir.' *So the poor bastard's not quite right in the head. Everyone knows that. So what?*

'So where does he keep them? Start the bloody car,' said Fielding. 'I've got to get a warrant.'

Billy had lots of notebooks. For years they had all been packed away safely in his bedroom in an old suitcase. They told all about the Carters and their boys and Annie and parlours and money-laundering through the clubs and billiard halls – and of getting rid of Mad Pat Delaney's dead body in a covert clean-up operation.

When the doorbell rang a couple of days later, Billy was in the wasteland they called their back garden, sitting on the bench in the sun. Uncle Ted let the four coppers in, and Mum looked surly as she ushered them through to see Billy.

'Hello again Billy lad,' said the head copper.

'Hello,' said Billy. He'd been expecting them. They'd been watching him for a long time, he knew that. Things had started to get a bit hairy, Max had warned him to be careful. That was why he'd done what he'd done – and not a minute too soon, by the look of it.

'They've got a warrant to search the house,' said Mum, all a-quiver with moral outrage. 'What you been up to, you little runt?'

'Nothing, Mum,' said Billy.

'We'll start upstairs. If you will show us to Billy's

room, Mrs Black, we'll get this over with as soon as possible.'

Billy sat there peacefully and listened through the open back door as the coppers went thundering up the stairs to his room. He let out a sigh and sat back in the low autumn sun, his deerstalker shielding his eyes from its glare as he gazed off down the garden towards the little metal incinerator Uncle Ted used to burn the garden rubbish in. A faint curl of smoke rose from its chimney, but the fire was out now. He had already checked that all his notebooks were burned to nothing. All that time and effort, gone into dust and ashes.

He thought of Max and Annie, together. They were going away, leaving Jonjo in charge. He wouldn't work for Jonjo.

As the coppers thumped about upstairs in his room, he felt a new peace seep over him. Life would go on for now, without them. He would manage. And one day – who knew? – perhaps one day he might see his beautiful Annie again.

Epilogue

When Annie walked into the Limehouse parlour one sunny morning it was just like she'd never been away. Chris let her in with a smile, she strode along the hall and there in the kitchen, seated around the table, were Dolly, Darren and Aretha. It was cosy in here, and Dolly was pouring tea. No Ellie raiding the biscuit tin for once.

Aretha stood up and gave Annie a brisk high-five. 'How you doin', girlfriend?'

'I'm good, Aretha.' Annie looked at Ellie's empty seat.

'I had to get rid of that treacherous little tart, she was doing my head in,' sniffed Dolly. 'How the hell are you, Annie love?'

'Blooming,' said Annie with a grin, taking off her coat and sitting down. 'How's tricks?'

'Busy,' said Dolly with satisfaction.

'Glad to hear it. Hey, I've got some news for you.'

'Come on then,' said Darren, scooting his chair closer to hers, his eyes alight with interest. 'Out with it then.'

'I'm up the duff,' said Annie.

A whoop went up around the table.

'For God's sake!' smiled Dolly.

'You pleased?' asked Aretha.

'Who's the daddy then?' demanded Darren.

'Who do you think?' asked Annie, giving his arm a thump.

'Is it all working out then, you and him?' asked Dolly, pushing a full mug towards her.

Annie picked it up, absorbing its warmth, smelling the fragrant tea. She cupped her hands around it and took a moment to consider. She looked around at her three very best friends in all the world.

'Yeah,' she said at last. 'It's taken a while, but I think we're getting there.'

'Girl, it sounds like you are doin' just *fine*,' said Aretha with a broad grin.

Yeah, Aretha was right. Everything in Annie's world was very fine indeed. She was in love with Max Carter and that love was returned. She was carrying his child. She felt peaceful now about what had happened with her and Ruthie. All that was gone. And she was going straight.

Whatever came next, Annie knew that she could face it head-on, no worries.

None at all.

Also by Jessie Keane:

BLACK WIDOW

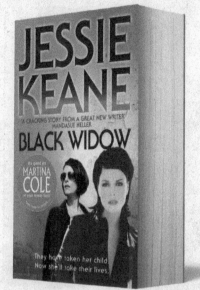

In Dirty Game, Annie Bailey was an East End Madam.
In Black Widow, she's trying to save her daughter's life...

Annie Bailey had done it all: Madam, mistress and gangster's moll.
Now she's Annie Carter, and she's taking over the East End.

But Annie knows that it can't last. Everything is going so well:
she's living in Majorca, with Max Carter by her side and her
beautiful daughter, Layla. If life has taught her one thing,
it is that everything can change in the blink of an eye.

One minute she's lying by the pool, the next she's out cold.
When she comes round Max and Layla are gone.
It's not long before she gets the demands. They want money
or she'll be getting her little girl back in pieces.

There's only one thing Annie can do – she heads back to the East End
of London and gathers the Carters together.

Now there's a score to settle, and it's being settled Annie Carter style...

Also by Jessie Keane:

SCARLET WOMEN

She was a madam in a brothel, then a gangster's moll.
Now Annie Carter owns the East End of London,
and God help anybody who crosses her...

It's 1970 and there's a killer on the loose in London.

When gang boss Annie Carter gets a call, suddenly it's personal.
A close friend of hers is the latest victim, and another friend
is in the frame for the murder.

With the hated Delaney gang still causing trouble, and the NY mob family,
the Barollis, making no secret of the fact that they hate her,
she senses trouble brewing.

To save her old mate, Annie has to find out who's been
targeting her friends. Before long she's diving head-first into
the seedy underbelly of the streets.

How long before the killer strikes again?
And who will their next victim be?